Trapped

Samantha heard Connor's footsteps behind her, growing closer, and her despair gave her added speed. Then she felt his arms catching her as her legs collapsed under her and he turned her around to face him.

"What the hell?" Connor cursed under his breath as he felt the slim, womanly body under the rough clothes.

Her eyes met his, and he flinched at the unhappiness in them. He couldn't tear himself away from the glistening dark blue whirlpools swirling with such naked emotion.

A girl for God's sake. A slip of a girl. And she had fooled them all. He didn't understand the surge of warmth or protectiveness that flooded him.

Suddenly she was in his arms and he was stroking her hair. He tipped her face up to his, and she reached, almost desperately, for his lips. Connor could feel her trembling, and it spawned a hunger and desire he hadn't expected. As he pressed his lips to hers, there was a sweetness and longing that did more to arouse him than any experienced passion. His arms tightened around her, and reason left them both. There was only need....

Dear Reader:

You are about to become part of an exciting new venture from Harlequin—*historical romances*.

Each month you'll find two new historical romances written by bestselling authors as well as some talented and award-winning newcomers.

Whether you're looking for an adventure, suspense, intrigue or simply the fulfilling passions of day-to-day living, you'll find it in these compelling, sensual love stories. From the American West to the courts of kings, Harlequin's historical romances make the past come alive.

We hope you enjoy our books, and we need your input to assure that they're the best they can possibly be. Please send your comments and suggestions to me at the address below.

Karen Solem
Editorial Director
Harlequin Historical Romances
P.O. Box 7372
Grand Central Station
New York, N.Y. 10017

Swampfire

Patricia Potter

Harlequin Books

TORONTO • NEW YORK • LONDON
AMSTERDAM • PARIS • SYDNEY • HAMBURG
STOCKHOLM • ATHENS • TOKYO • MILAN

To my mother and father for their unwavering faith,
encouragement and love. And to Dena Rosenberg
and Marge Gargosh whose encouragement,
suggestions and advice were so valuable to
Swampfire.

Harlequin Historical first edition September 1988

ISBN 0-373-28606-6

PATRICIA POTTER

is a former award-winning journalist with a passion
for history and books. As a reporter with the *Atlanta
Journal*, she met and reported on three presidents and
covered Southern news stories as varied as the space
launches and the civil rights movement.

This resident of Atlanta, Georgia, has her own public
relations and advertising agency. Her interests in animals and travel are not especially compatible, but she
does manage to fit them both into her busy schedule.
Her reading runs the gamut from biographies to es-
pionage, and she is currently the president of the
Georgia Romance Writers of America.

Prologue

The sound of hoofs beating against the summer-baked ground woke Samantha from an uneasy sleep. Apprehension, fear and joy had all battled for her attention throughout the long dark night.

She brushed aside the ominous rumblings, and every fiber of her being sprang hopefully alive as she reminded herself happily that this would be her wedding day.

She was out of bed in seconds, throwing open the light green draperies. Everything was so important today... the weather, her father's whereabouts, the servants....

The window was open, and she reveled for a moment in the sweet air, fragrant with yellow jasmine, sweet bay and the heavy scent of magnolias. How she loved that enticing mixture. It seemed to celebrate life, so lush and abundant in this northeast corner of South Carolina.

A carriage was disappearing down the dusty ribbon of road and she wondered what errand could be taking her father out so early. The first glimmers of light were just now signaling the coming of dawn, spreading pale shades of pink and gold and lavender across a cloud-spattered sky. Dawn, she thought, the dawn of the first day of my life with Brendan. Never had a day been so welcome.

She breathed deeply again of the scented air, enjoying the cool breeze. It would turn blistering hot later in the day, but that didn't matter. Nothing mattered except her escape with Bren.

A twinge of fear returned but was quickly suppressed by happiness, blocking any thought of the consequences that were bound to result from this day's events. Her father would be angry, very angry, but he would have to accept the marriage. He would have no choice. And maybe it would mean the end of the bitter feud between the two families.

Her characteristic optimism asserted itself. She would meet Bren at their usual place and they would travel to Charleston, where a friend would marry them. Another friend had offered them the use of his house in the city for a month. What happened after that depended upon their families. Both Bren and Samantha were prepared to make their way alone, if need be.

Posh on politics anyway, she thought. A pox on all their houses, Tories and Whigs. They had split the parish apart and had deepened the hatred between her father and the O'Neills.

Samantha pushed the unsettling thoughts aside. She and Brendan could overcome anything. They had loved each other for years, and nothing would stand in their way. She went to the mirror and stared at her reflection. By nightfall she would be Mrs. Brendan O'Neill.

She regarded herself critically in the glass. Her face was much too small, her lips too full, her eyes too large for her taste. Bren always called her his merry little wood sprite when she would much rather he called her beautiful. Her dark blue eyes danced with lively curiosity and glowed with a passion for life but only her long dark hair met with her approval. It blazed with a sheen like the rich mahogany that decorated every corner of Chatham Oaks.

Enough daydreaming. Samantha hurriedly slipped on a blue day gown and tied her hair back with a matching blue ribbon. She ran down the stairs, eager to know where her father had gone and when he might return. With luck he would be at Monck's Corner until evening. The war had made the Williamsburg district a dangerous place for Tories and Whigs alike, and he now traveled with guards. That would account for the many hoofbeats she had heard.

She headed for the kitchen, her favorite place in the morning. The old cook, Maudie, had practically raised her and was her principal source of both comfort and information.

But as she neared the door, she was stopped by the distress she heard in the older woman's voice.

"Wha' we goin' tell the chile?"

Maudie's daughter, Angel, sounded equally hopeless. "Marse Chatham, he say he whip us if we say anythin' to her."

"Mr. Bren, he mean everythin' to that girl. She has a right to know."

"Well, I ain't going to be the one to tell her."

Samantha couldn't wait another minute. She threw open the door.

"What should I know?" she demanded of the two.

The silence was deafening. "Maudie," Samantha begged, "what should I know?"

The old woman's face dissolved into tears. She took one of Samantha's hands. "Your pa knows about you and Mr. Brendan." She swallowed, trying to conquer her own fear. "They's fightin' a duel this mornin'."

An involuntary cry like the sound of an animal in pain was wrenched from Samantha's throat. "No! No! Father will kill him. Bren is no match for him."

Before either of the slaves could say another word, Samantha was out the door, racing for the barn. She quickly haltered her mare and used the fence to mount. Sundance, sensing her mistress's fear, needed no urging to stretch into a fast gallop.

Samantha knew the dueling spot well. It was a lovely clearing shaded by giant cypresses and laurels, five miles from her father's plantation. She had often thought it obscene that such a beautiful, natural wood had become a killing ground. She could never pass it without shuddering.

It was this clearing that drew her now. She leaned low on Sundance's neck and urged her to run faster. She had to stop her father. Never had she imagined that the joy she and Brendan shared could come to this.

Samantha was heedless of the branches that cut her bare legs, the torn dress, pushed up to her thighs, and the hair that escaped its ribbon and flew wildly behind her. "Faster," she urged the horse. "You must run faster."

She saw the clearing up ahead. I'm going to make it ... I'm in time, she thought, her spirits suddenly soaring.

The sound of pistol shots split the early-morning quiet. As Samantha pulled her horse to a stop, she became aware of the complete silence. As if in another time, she realized that the birds had stopped their singing, the squirrels their chattering.

Almost in a dream, she threw herself down from the horse and ran to the still figure on the ground.

Brendan's gold hair sparkled in the early-morning sun. His eyes, as blue as her own, were open and staring blankly at the sky. His white linen shirt was stained a bright red by the growing circle of his blood.

Samantha cushioned his head in her arms. "Bren," she whispered. "Bren. Don't go away. Don't leave me alone. I love you. I love you so much. Don't go away."

She was unaware of the tears that flowed down her face, or of the silent threatening figure of her father. She was unaware of everything, even the horseman who had arrived just seconds behind her.

Springing from his horse, the man roughly took her arm and pulled her up, pushing her away.

Kneeling beside Brendan, he gently closed his brother's eyes. He looked up at Samantha with fury and grief in his dark gray eyes. "This is your doing," he said cruelly. "You killed him...it is by your hand as well as your father's."

He gently picked up the still form on the ground and carried him to the horse, placing Brendan's body across the saddle that would carry him for the last time. Connor O'Neill then mounted behind him and slowly disappeared among the trees.

Samantha knelt beside the pool of blood on the ground, her mouth making tiny choking noises of unbearable grief.

Chapter One

The trees are weeping this afternoon, Samantha thought desolately as she sat, motionless, in front of the window of her locked room. Silver-gray moss dripped from the great live oaks like the tears of an imprisoned fairy princess. How could she ever have thought them merrily enchanted or magical. They were like everything else these days . . . sad, painful, decaying.

The dark gray visage of the sky brought back memories of Connor O'Neill's eyes and the cruel accusation he had thrown at her that terrible morning twelve months ago. His eyes had been a cold slate gray flashing with the darker storm clouds of fury. She would never forget them; they taunted her nightly. "Oh, Bren," she whispered in the loneliness that surrounded her like a cloak. "I need you."

She leaned against the window and sighed. Her beauty was still there, but now it had a hollow look. She was thin, the soft curves of her body now angular, more like a young boy than a nineteen-year-old woman. Her hair hung listlessly around her pale face. The sparkle in her eyes had been replaced by a haunting, hunted look.

There had been another terrible fight with her father, climaxing once more with her being made a prisoner in her own home. The fights had become successively worse since the morning of the duel when he had bodily dragged her away from the scene of Bren's death.

When they had reached the house, she had turned on him, her hands and dress stained with blood. She was near shock and

her body was shivering with reaction, but her voice was clear
and calm.

"I hate you, Papa. I'll hate you 'till the day I die for this."

Her father's face turned red with fury, and his hand reached
out. The sound of the impact against her face echoed across the
room and she went down on the floor, but her eyes never left
his. They were cold, accusing, and Robert Chatham turned
away, unable to meet them.

"I warned you," he said, self-justification making his voice
harsh. It was the first time he had struck his daughter, and he
was both ashamed and startled by his action. "I warned you,"
he repeated, "to stay away from that Irish rebel trash. Now
you've destroyed your reputation and any chance for a decent
marriage. It's your doing. Not mine."

How could it be her fault? She and Bren had loved so innocently, so completely. They had wanted only to be together. She
sunk back on the floor, her face in her hands, her life in pieces.

Robert Chatham's anger faded slightly at the sight of the
shattered girl in front of him. She had ruined his dreams of a
fine marriage. It would take a long time to repair the damage
done to his daughter's reputation on this day.

"Go to your room," he said roughly. "You will stay there
until you learn respect for your father . . . and obedience."

"Respect!" she spit out. "Never." She stood up shakily, her
hand on her stinging cheek. She turned, her eyes filled with
sparks of fruitless rage, and left the drawing room.

Her defiance kept her going until she reached her own room.
Then she surrendered to the grief and fell sobbing on the large
feather mattress where the night before she had shivered with
joyful anticipation.

She had remained in her room for three weeks, the first week
subsisting on bread and water ordered by her father until she
apologized and agreed to obey him. Maudie had sneaked her
tempting morsels, but Samantha would have none of them. She
was doing her own penance, and food no longer held any at-
traction for her. She even thought of refusing food altogether,
but some instinct within her failed to cooperate. Absently

crumbling the bread with restless fingers and slowly eating the tiny bits became an exercise to pass the time without thinking.

The punishment ended when her father saw how thin and listless she was growing. He was frightened by the silent, accusing wraith that had replaced his lovely daughter. He ordered her downstairs, to his table, and she obeyed. The meals were terrible, silent, bitter affairs. Samantha had decided to live, but she was exacting her own revenge by her accusing silence.

Over the next few months, a truce of sorts was called. She was polite and answered when spoken to, but no more. She was courteous to her father's guests but never friendly. Most were put off by her quiet distance and haunted eyes, despite a beauty that had become almost ethereal.

The house was increasingly full of British officers and Robert Chatham's Tory friends. Charleston had fallen, and the British swarmed over all of Williamsburg, committing depredations among all who would not join them. She quietly despised them while keeping her face blankly polite.

Samantha's coldness had kept all prospective suitors at bay until Colonel William Foxworth.

Samantha was passing a door when she heard the haughty British voice talking with her father. She was about to pass when she heard the O'Neill family mentioned.

"You will be amply rewarded for this information," the accented British voice promised.

"I want them dead—both of them," her father said.

"They will be sent to the prison ships" came the reply. "Many of them die quickly. If they don't agree to join us, of course."

"The O'Neills?" Her father's voice was deadly. "Never. They're a stubborn lot. Like all Irish. They have no loyalty to their king or to any authority. Troublemakers."

"You're still entitled to any property we seize," the British officer said.

There was a silence. "Their plantation?"

"It's yours. We want South Carolina in the hands of loyal Englishmen like yourself."

Samantha could contain herself no longer. She flung open the door and faced her father.

"Do you have no honor left at all?" she accused him, ignoring the tall figure in red. "It wasn't enough to kill Brendan."

Robert Chatham's face went white as he looked from her furious face to the shocked expression of his guest.

"You will leave this room," he said in a tight, pinched voice. "I will see to you later."

Samantha looked at him helplessly. "Don't, Father. Please don't. Haven't you done enough?"

"Do you forget? They killed your mother," her father said furiously. "Now leave us before I have the servants take you out."

Samantha knew he would do just that. She turned on her heel, resentment and anger stiffening her body, and left the room, slamming the door behind her.

Chatham was turning to the British officer with an apology when he saw the interest in his guest's eyes.

"That is a very lovely young lady. She's quite outspoken."

"And not very obedient," Chatham said ruefully. "She is young and feels passionately about everything."

"Not a bad trait if properly directed," the officer said, his interest growing. "Is she bespoken?"

Chatham cocked his eyebrow. Could Foxworth possibly be interested in his daughter? He was certainly presentable and well connected.

"No," Chatham said. "There's no young man."

"I would like to call on her . . . if that's agreeable with you. And her."

Chatham felt a sudden surge of hope. Perhaps this would be the answer. "Of course," he said. "I would be honored."

"And your daughter? She seems to be sympathetic toward the rebels."

"Samantha is nonpolitical. She had a childhood fancy on a rebel."

"And where is he now?"

"Dead." The reply cut off any additional inquiry.

Foxworth looked curiously at him but asked no more questions. He wanted to see the girl again, to see if that anger could be channeled in a different direction. My God, but she was a lovely creature.

"I'll be on duty for the next several days," he said. "If it meets your approval, I'll call on Miss Samantha on my return."

"Yes, yes, of course," Chatham replied. "And the O'Neills?"

"They will be arrested this afternoon. Both of them."

"Good," Chatham said. "Once they're gone, perhaps we will have some order." The officer gave Chatham a brief salute and left.

Chatham went up to his daughter's room. She was reading and didn't bother to look up when he came in. Her silence angered him again and he took the book.

"Despite your unforgivable conduct," he said, "Colonel Foxworth wishes to call on you."

"No," she said flatly. "I will not receive him. I will receive no plundering, murdering invader."

"You will," he said. "You will or . . ."

"Or what?" she asked. "You've done everything you could to me."

"Not quite," he said thoughtfully.

Fear erupted throughout her body. She suddenly felt her father capable of almost anything.

"You will receive Colonel Foxworth. And you will be pleasant to him. Do you understand?"

Samantha bit her lip. "Yes," she said finally.

"And you will remain in this room for three days because of that outburst in the study." He took the book she had been reading. "Without any diversion. I want you to think on your attitude and how it had better improve."

That had been two days ago. She had one more to go before she was released. Before she could ride again like the wind, ride fast enough to escape all her torments.

Samantha fidgeted nervously while Colonel Foxworth pressed his invitation to the officers' ball next Saturday.

She had grown to despise the haughty self-assured arrogance of the man and his persistence in pursuing a courtship he knew repelled her. Did he really think she would come to look kindly upon a murderer and an arsonist?

She watched him now with unfriendly eyes. He was a handsome man, in a cold, calculating way, she thought, and was probably used to getting his way with women. His scarlet uniform was precisely tailored and hugged a well-formed body. His eyes were pale blue and cold, and she couldn't help but contrast them with the dancing sea-blue eyes of Brendan. His hair was neatly trimmed and powdered and held back with a satin ribbon.

She knew other girls would probably find him attractive but she couldn't. He reminded her more of a snake, coiled and dangerous and quite ready to strike at enemies and innocents alike.

"Your father quite approves," he was now saying. "He believes you should be getting out more."

She stared at him, recognizing the veiled threat in his words. He had become increasingly confident in the past several months, an attitude encouraged by her father.

She wished she could suppress the revulsion that swept over her. He knew she did not welcome his attentions; she had made it quite clear. She saw him only because of her father's threats.

In a cold, distant voice, she heard herself balking. "I have not felt well this week, colonel. I really don't believe I would be much company for you."

"You are always good company, Miss Chatham," he said. "Your beauty alone is always stimulating." There was only a slight trace of sarcasm in his voice.

He reached over and touched a ringlet of her hair. "It is so lovely."

Samantha jerked her head back. "Colonel Foxworth, you take too much for granted. And I think I must refuse your generous offer. I'm sure I will be much too ill to attend your party."

His smile was tight, his eyes angry. "We'll see, Samantha. Perhaps you will feel better tomorrow. I'll send the regimental surgeon to see if he can assist."

"That will not be necessary," she replied coldly. "I should be fine by Monday."

He stood, rage clouding his eyes. He had enjoyed a challenge but this rebuff, by God, was going too far. He wondered for a moment whether she was worth it, but then he thought again of the vast plantation and wealth of her father. She was an only child, and her husband would inherit. He was the third son of an English lord and had little but a useless name. It was important that he marry well.

Curbing his anger, he leaned over her hand and kissed it. "I will look in on you tomorrow. Perhaps you will feel better."

"I doubt it," she said coldly. "Henry will see you to the door." She rang the servant's bell and without another word left the room, leaving him fuming.

Shivering from the encounter, she went to her room and changed to a light cotton dress. She would go for a ride and forget her unwanted suitor, forget about a life that had grown increasingly intolerable.

She waited until she saw Foxworth's horse leave the plantation. She didn't want another confrontation with him nor questions about her unusually quick recovery from her illness.

Samantha hurried to the stables and watched as Hector, the groom, placed the sidesaddle on Sundance. How she wished she could ride the way she had as a child, wild and free with her knees pressed against the horse. Her father had forbidden such unseemly conduct and threatened Hector with a whipping if he acceded to his daughter's strange whims.

As the horse was saddled, Samantha stroked her and fed her an apple. Sundance's coat was a rare pale gold that seemed to ripple and dance in the sun.

Her dam had been one of the last gifts from Samantha's mother. It had been her first full-size horse, and she had loved her dearly, mourning for days when she died foaling Sundance. But then she had been caught up by Sundance's need. The filly had barely survived its first few days. It seemed that Sundance was the only thing left of Elizabeth Chatham's love for her, and Samantha adored the young horse as only a lonely little girl can.

Even as a tiny filly, Sundance would follow Samantha wherever she went and would wait impatiently at the gate for her to appear each morning. The two seemed to form a special bond that precluded anyone else. A bond that had only grown firmer when Bren died. Samantha spent more and more time with the horse, brushing the golden coat and talking to her softly. It was her only refuge.

Once the horse was saddled, Samantha mounted and guided Sundance toward the river. It was time to visit the cave, the place where she and Bren had met so many times and where they had planned to meet the last day. She had avoided it during the past year, not wanting the pain of remembering. Now she would welcome it. She needed to feel the presence of Bren, to remember the warmth of his smile.

The cave was on the boundary of Chatham Oaks, downriver from Glen Woods, the O'Neill plantation. The plantations were separated by two others, and the swamplike forest that held the Pee Dee within its banks had provided privacy for the two young friends and, later, sweethearts. Samantha and Bren had been introduced to the cave by Bren's older brother, Connor. It had been Connor's favorite place as a boy, and after exacting a vow of secrecy, he had shown it to the two youngsters.

How she had worshiped Connor then. He had been so much older, so much the young gentleman, so sure of himself, yet he had taken time to entertain two ten-year-olds. He had treated them as adults, never speaking down to them but showing them the ways of the forest, sharing his own love and fascination for its creatures, instilling in them respect for all life that dwelled in it. He had taught them how to shoot, laughing when she outshot Bren, who, instead of getting angry, had admired her skill. It was then, she thought, that she had realized how very special Bren was. She had always, she realized now, been in love with Bren.

Then came tragedy. She never quite knew everything that had happened, but she knew Bren's mother died, followed by her own mother's death. Her father had blamed the O'Neills for her mother's death, and there were threats and gunshots. She was forbidden ever to see Bren again, as was Bren to see her.

But the adult quarrel was not theirs, and they both had developed a fine skill for stealth and lies. They continued to meet through the years, almost always at the cave. They would then explore the woods or just sit quietly and talk.

Bren had told her that his brother was just as adamant as his father about them not meeting, and she did not see Connor again except for brief glimpses when they passed on the road or in Georgetown. In later years he was gone much of the time, traveling to England until the war started, and later to the north. He had purposely kept his distance from Chatham Oaks and the Chatham family. The duel was the first time in years she had seen him up close. She thought of him now, buried alive on a prison ship. She had heard of their horrors and prayed that he was still alive. Despite his words *that* day, she still remembered his kindness and patience to her as a child.

The cave was overgrown and, despite her familiarity, difficult even for her to find. She pushed aside the overgrowth that covered the entrance and adjusted her eyes to the dim light.

The sun pushed sparingly through the laurel at the entrance, its rays mellow and subdued. Samantha sat and stared at the varying patterns across the cave floor, wondering at the quiet peace of the place. Tears gathered at the corners of her eyes as she thought of the hours she and Bren had spent here, talking, laughing, planning a future. She was unaware of the smudge they made down her cheek as she buried her head in her hands and wept for Bren and Connor and herself.

The light was growing dim, and she knew she must return before search parties were sent out for her. She wiped the dried tears from her face and searched the cave. There was an old bracelet Bren had made her from seeds. They had dulled with time, but to Samantha they still shone like priceless gems. She fondled it, thinking to take it home, then thought better of it. Her father had taken to entering her room without announcement. She even suspected he had searched it. She would leave the bracelet here, where it would be safe.

There were two packets of clothes they had accumulated in preparation for their escape. They were damp and smelled slightly of mold but were still in good repair. There were the homespun trousers and shirt she had stolen from the store-house at the plantation. She and Bren had thought she might have to travel at least some of the way in disguise. He had also brought rough clothes; his own elegant and well-tailored garments might attract unwanted attention.

She fingered both packages now, lingeringly, as if to stop was to lose Bren again.

Samantha finally tore herself away and slowly, forlornly, took leave of the beloved cave. She found Sundance happily munching the high grass and easily mounted her. Without looking back, she gently pressed Sundance into a canter.

When she reached the gates of Chatham Oaks, she dismounted and walked Sundance to the stable, wanting to cool her down gently. It had been a hot day, and she had ridden the horse hard on their return. Hector was talking to a peddler and didn't notice her approach. She took Sundance in the back way, not wanting to bother Hector and knowing he would insist on caring for the horse if he saw her. She unsaddled Sundance and brushed the mare to a bright sheen.

As she left, she was surprised to see Hector still in heavy conversation. She ducked behind the door when she heard the name "Marion."

"That's what Maudie heard," Hector was saying. "That Colonel Foxworth told the master that Tarleton was setting a trap for Colonel Marion. At the Coursey plantation."

"It will be more a trap for Tarleton, thanks to you," the peddler replied. "Be careful, Hector. I'll be back next week."

Hector turned around toward the stable door and saw Samantha. His face went stiff with fear. "Miss Samantha. I didn't hear you."

She saw his fear and wanted to quiet it. "Don't worry, Hector," she said. "I won't tell anyone."

His face relaxed slightly. He was her own age, and they had, in a way, grown up together. When they were children, she had taught him to read despite the ban against it. His English was as good as her own, although he usually, for his own protection, adopted the speech of most slaves.

"You're helping the Swamp Fox," she stated.

Fear flooded back into his face. "No, miss." The lie was written all over his face.

"Don't worry, Hector. I have no love for the British. I'll keep your secret." She started to walk away, then turned back. "Hector, I want to help."

"You, Miss Samantha? It's dangerous."

"Less so for me than for you. Who would suspect the daughter of one of the strongest Tories in South Carolina?" Her voice was bitter. "I want to do it . . . I need to do it . . . for Bren, for the O'Neills."

Hector stared at her with indecision. She could be invaluable, and he knew her courage and determination. "It will have to be just between you and me," he said finally. "No one else. You tell me, and I'll get word to Colonel Marion."

"Why are you doing this, Hector?"

He looked at the ground, then up. "I'm just a slave, Miss Samantha, but I think if the colonies get free of England, perhaps some of us will have a new chance for freedom."

The longing in his eyes startled her. Slaves were part of her world, had always been so. It had never occurred to her that they might want something else.

She placed her hand on his shoulder. "If I can ever make that happen, I will. And I will let you know everything I hear."

Her father was angry at dinner. "Colonel Foxworth said you declined his invitation to the dance."

Her smile surprised him. "I've changed my mind," she said. "You can tell him tomorrow. I'm sure," she said meanly, "you will see him. There are probably a few more homes you want to burn."

"Damn it, Samantha, I don't want to hear that tone from you." His voice gentled. "I'm glad you've agreed to the dance. He's a fine man, has a fine name. He would make a good husband."

"No," she said flatly. "I'll go to the dance with him, but I'll never marry him. Never."

"Think about it," her father pleaded. "He's already indicated he will ask for your hand if you give him the least encouragement."

It suited her purpose at the moment to placate him, but she vowed silently that she would die before marrying William Foxworth.

Chapter Two

Connor knew that as long as he lived he would never get the stench of the prison ship out of his system. It was something that would stay with him forever. The smell dominated everything.

The O'Neills had been taken two weeks earlier and forced to watch their home burn when they refused to join a Tory regiment and give fealty to the Crown. Their wrists had been tied and they were bundled into a wagon with other Whig sympathizers. Just before they left, one of the O'Neill servants had slipped a knife into Connor's belt. It proved a poor boon. Connor had no sooner sawed through his bonds and those of his father when he was discovered by an observant British officer. The man had him rebound and, on arrival in Charleston, reported him as a troublemaker.

The two men were lodged in the Exchange overnight, and the next morning were singled out for attention because of the knife. An iron band was bolted to the right ankle of both men, and a chain, padlocked to a ring on the band, connected them to the other prisoners deemed recalcitrant.

Lying in the lower hold of the prison ship, Connor could still hear the ominous ring of the hammer as it closed the iron on his ankle. He was never without pain from the festering sores caused by the constant chafing of the cold iron against his skin. But even that was minor compared to the smell.

The hulks were ships of death. The pent-up air was pregnant with putrid fever, foul with deadly contagion, tainted with sweat and rotten food and body waste. The heat was stifling and it was nearly impossible to breathe. But Connor and his father had somehow managed to survive this far.

It was always dark, too dark to even see each other's features. Twenty of them were chained and marked for particularly harsh treatment. They were allowed topside only two hours a day, barely long enough to accustom their eyes to the light and to try, futilely, to wash. But they had only seawater and no soap, and they mostly just rearranged the filth.

The food was wretched. Wormy bread...spoiled pork... suet...peas. They received less than two-thirds of the ration of a British seaman, and hunger was constant.

Connor watched his father weaken. The older O'Neill's spirit had floundered fifteen months earlier at Bren's death; the endless misery of the prison hulks was taking what little remained.

Connor sometimes wondered why he tried to stay alive in such a place. Many others did not. There were deaths daily...and not all from fever or disease. Many just gave up the struggle to stay alive.

But Connor had scores to settle. He knew from other prisoners that it had been Robert Chatham who had informed on his father and himself. He had also learned that Chatham had been granted Glen Woods, their confiscated estate. Chatham was going to pay...he would pay for every moment Connor and his father spent in this hell. And he would pay dearly.

Connor counted the days and held them firm in his mind. To let go of time was to let go of sanity. It had been nearly four months now...four months since he was taken aboard the prison ship. As the endless days stretched out, Connor retreated to the one activity that kept his mind alive. He would remember, page by page, word by word, books he had read. He had always had an unusually retentive memory; now he honed it to an art. He could remember complete books and often shared them with his father and the other prisoners on his chain. It helped keep them alive, maintained some spirit in souls battered and bruised by brutality and deprivation.

And then smallpox invaded the ship.

The stench was worse than ever as the sickly sweet smell of disease and death permeated everything. There were cries for doctors, but none were allowed aboard. The only way to quit the ship was to die. Many succumbed rapidly to the disease; only the strongest survived.

Connor had been inoculated early in the war during an outbreak in the militia; Gerald O'Neill had not, and he had neither the strength nor the desire to fight the horrible ravages of the disease.

The older O'Neill died slowly, his groans lost amid the curses poured out by the exhausted and the dying. His last movements caused barely a ripple in the endless restlessness.

His last cry was for Brendan, and it struck Connor with the old anguish. Although the oldest by far, Connor had long recognized that his brother was the favored one. His father had tried to disguise his feelings, but no one could miss the light and sparkle that came to his eyes every time he looked at his light-hearted, golden-haired son.

Nor could Connor resent the fact, for he, too, had loved Bren in a special way. Bren was born to laughter and joy just as their mother and father had been. He had been full of puckish humor and the source of unending pranks. But none came from maliciousness, just an irrepressible zest for life.

Connor, on the other hand, had been born serious and responsible. He once even questioned whether he was a changeling, because his nature was so unlike that of the rest of his family. From the time he was a young lad he had regarded the world with solemnity and had assumed an affectionate guardianship of his brother, who was twelve years younger. That voluntary guardianship later extended to his father and the plantation when, after Connor's mother died, Gerald O'Neill had turned to drink for comfort. For the past ten years, Connor had, for all practical purposes been master of Glen Woods, one of the richest indigo plantations along the Pee Dee River. Now, at thirty-two, he was the master of little. The plantation house had been burned, the lands confiscated, and his brother and father were dead.

Perhaps his father was lucky, Connor thought, as he held his lifeless body in his arms. He smoothed back the hair on his father's head and felt the vermin that infested it. How his father had hated the dirt and tiny creatures that made him their home.

Connor tried to shift his burden, but the chain that linked him and the others to the walls of the ship prevented all but the slightest movement.

Connor had not yet told the guards of his father's death. He knew from experience on the hulks that the dead were granted little dignity. They were tossed like unwanted sticks into long-boats and barely covered by a few feet of sandy ground on-shore. Storms invariably unearthed them, and it wasn't uncommon to see the bodies washed back out to sea. Connor meant to plead for a dignified burial despite the cost to his pride. He might prevail with a British officer on deck; down in the hold he had little chance. The guards below were Tory ruffians who gloried in inflicting every humiliation they could.

Hate overcame his sorrow. Another O'Neill death due to the Chathams! He had never thought hate could be so obsessive, could be the sole reason for survival in an existence not worth surviving. He would stay alive, if for no other reason than to destroy the Chatham family. And he would exact an equivalent amount of agony from them in doing so.

When the hatch was finally unlocked and the guards descended into the pit, Connor waited patiently until the chain was released from the wall. He picked up his father, a task made possible only by the fact that his father had lost even more weight than he himself had.

The guards did not question him. It was seldom that one of the chained prisoners was not sick or needed assistance from the others. Three had died in the past week.

Once on deck, Connor slowly adjusted his eyes to the light, glad of the cloudy day, which reduced the intense pain. He cursed an existence where sunlight was to be dreaded. When his eyes could tolerate full exposure, he searched the deck for a British officer.

He found one staring his way, the man's eyes on the burden Connor held. The officer started toward him.

"This man is dead," the officer said, his voice full of anger toward the Tory guards. "Why wasn't he taken out earlier? Why is he still chained to these men?"

One of the guards cringed at the officer's disgust. "No one tol' us, sir."

"Do it now," the officer ordered, glancing with something like pity at Connor.

He started to turn away, but Connor stopped him with a plea. "Sir..."

The officer turned around. "Yes?" he said impatiently.

"He's my father. May I have permission to bury him? On shore."

The Englishman studied the prisoner carefully. The man's clothes were in rags, his face bearded and filthy, but there was a quiet dignity about him.

His intelligent eyes held a supplication that the officer sensed was sincere. God, he hated duty on these prison ships. He had been assigned here three months ago when his own ship was sunk and there had been no other sea posts available. He prayed nightly for a new ship.

He turned to the guards. "Unchain both of them," he said. He turned to Connor.

"Your name?"

"O'Neill."

"I'm going to allow you ashore with the next work party. You can bury him there and mark it."

"Thank you."

"Thanks are not necessary," the British officer said. "I would hope you would do the same for me."

Connor watched the shore as the chain was removed from his manacle. It was the first time in four months he had not been attached to a chain, and he felt a sudden surge of hope. Perhaps, just perhaps, he would also have a chance to escape.

Connor buried his father on a slight hill, under a great oak tree. He borrowed an ax from one of the woodcutting prisoners and fashioned a crude cross. The effort exhausted him, and he sat beside the grave while the others moved down the beach, cutting and gathering wood for the cooking fires. The guards moved with them, sympathetically leaving Connor with some privacy. All thought him too weak to run.

Connor rested for several minutes, then began to edge toward the woods. He was well within them when a guard checked back and found him missing.

When Connor heard the alarm, he gave up any idea of stealth and started to run. His determination for revenge increased his endurance, and he managed to stay ahead of his pursuers for some time before his legs gave out and folded beneath him. He dragged himself deep into the brush and covered himself with leaves. Footsteps rushed past him and then returned slowly. A musket rustled the surrounding bushes as one of the guards searched for him methodically.

Connor decided he would not go back to the ship. He would rather die. When the musket inevitably prodded him, he turned suddenly, pushing it away, but not before it exploded, sending a red-hot ball of iron through his side. The abrupt movement threw his pursuer off balance, and Connor grabbed his tormentor's musket with renewed strength. Using it as a club, he bludgeoned the man until he lay still. Connor slung the man's powder horn over his shoulder and tucked the stock of the gun under his arm. Holding the weapon as a crutch he disappeared into the dense forest.

Racked by hunger and exhaustion, and tortured by the fiery pain in his side, Connor staggered from tree to tree until his determination could no longer sustain him. He had captured a few crabs the night before, risking exposure on a clear beach to find them, but his stomach, weak from the months of spoiled and inadequate food, had refused the sweet meat.

Hunger had become a fierce enemy, grinding away at him, sapping his strength, diverting his mind from the need to run and run and run.

It competed with the pain in his side, which had grown stronger through the night and following day. He knew the wound was not fatal in itself, but he feared the bloodletting and infection. He needed help and he needed it soon.

This part of the Carolinas, he knew, harbored both patriots and Tories. He had to be careful lest he run into the wrong people. He would not survive a return to the prison ship. Nor did he want to.

There was little left in him. He had used every last fiber of his strength. Each step had become like crossing a mountain. No longer able to stand, he slumped against a fallen log and mercifully fell into unconsciousness.

The voice came as though from a distance, like an echo that kept ringing in a valley. Barely able to distinguish the words, Connor stirred sufficiently to reach for his gun. It wasn't there.

"Ma...Ma," the voice was saying. "Ma. There's a stranger, hurt."

He tried to shake the cloudiness from his eyes, to focus on the sounds. The pain came back in waves, and he flinched as a hard callused hand touched his face. He couldn't prevent a groan as the coals in his side flared anew.

"It's all right, mister," he heard a woman's voice say. "Rest easy... I'll help you."

As he struggled to regain full consciousness, he heard the woman address someone else.

"'Tis likely the one they've been scouring the woods for...dang lobsterbacks...well, they'll not find him if I have anything to do with it. Johnny, go get some blankets and bandages and some a yer pa's whiskey. And, mind ya, keep a sharp eye."

Connor felt rather than saw her presence. He tried to sit, but her hand urged him to stay still.

"Where...where am I?"

"The Santee," she answered, "and I sure don't see how ya made it this far...not as bad as ya look."

"I stole a boat," he said slowly, understanding finally that he had found a friend.

"Where be it?"

"It wasn't a very good boat," he said in a painful whisper but with a trace of wry humor that didn't escape her. "It sunk."

"I'll see if we can't find ya a better one," the woman said. "Ya can't stay here long...they been searching all up the coast. They want ya mighty bad."

The boy arrived back with blankets, bandages and a jug and watched with avid curiosity as his mother gingerly removed the rag that had once been a shirt. She touched the puffed, jagged skin around the bullet wound, causing Connor to utter an involuntary curse.

"It ain't good," she said finally, "but could be worse. I'm goin' wash it out with this whiskey. Ya best take a drink first."

Connor needed no second urging. The pain was coming in waves and he knew the agony involved in subjecting the raw wound to alcohol. He took a long pull from the jug and placed the piece of wood that Johnny offered between his teeth. The pain was worse than he'd imagined, worse than any he'd ever experienced. It was as if his entire side had exploded into flames and he bit hard on the wood to keep from crying out.

"There," the woman said. "It's over. That'll cleanse it."

He looked up, trying to concentrate on her face instead of the waves of pain that assaulted him. Through a haze, he saw a tall rawboned woman with a face made old by hardship.

She straightened. "I'll get ya something to eat...stay as well hid as ya can. Johnny will keep watch."

"I'm beholden to you. I wouldn't want any trouble to come to you because of me."

"Trouble's already been here," she said bitterly. "Those lobsterbacks took my John a year ago. Haven't heard a thing since. Don't know if he's alive or dead. They say some were taken by ship to fight English battles in other lands." She spit on the ground. "Never had much, jest a few acres, but he were a good man and worked hard. Any trouble I can cause 'em, I will. And so will Johnny. I be back directly with some stew."

Whether or not it was Connor's hunger that made it so, the stew tasted delicious, and Connor ate his fill. He felt his strength returning and managed a smile. "I wish I could pay you something."

She drew herself up, her proud stance making her suddenly beautiful. "Ya'd be paying me by getting away...." She looked down. "Ya best be getting some sleep now. I wish I could take ya to the cabin but we already had Tory visitors and I 'spect they'll be back."

When Connor woke again, the sky was darkening. He could see the first twinkling stars playing hide-and-seek among the heavy clouds. A loaf of bread and a jug of water had been placed beside him while he slept. His side still hurt badly, but the food had eased the pain in his stomach and he felt considerably better than he had a few hours ago.

He heard a rippling in the water just beyond his resting place and tensed, relaxing only when he heard the young boy's voice. "Mister?"

"Johnny," he replied. "I'm here."

The boy appeared in a small dugout. "The lobsters are all over the place...Ma says ya'd better go." The boy grinned as he saw Connor search the ground anxiously.

"If it's yer gun yer looking for, it's in that bush behind ya. I hid it before I knew ya were a patriot."

Connor looked at the boy's wistful face. "I wish I could leave it for you but I might have a greater need for it." He thought a moment. "I promise you'll get a rifle. I'll get it to you someway. What's your name...and your mother's?"

"I'm Johnny Brown, my ma's Ellie. It stands for Ellen. Ain't that a pretty name?" The last was spoken with shy pride.

"It is, and she's a pretty woman. You tell her I said so. And tell her I'll be forever grateful to you both."

Johnny stepped onto the shore and turned to help Connor into the dugout. Laying his musket and powder next to the bagful of food that Johnny had provided, Connor picked up the paddle.

"Good luck, mister" came the whisper from shore.

Connor was grateful the night was black, the moon hidden by dark clouds. He was still weak, having lost, he guessed, nearly four stone during his imprisonment. The ache in his side persisted, but his optimism had returned. He had a full stomach, a fair boat, a river that would take him all the way home. And he had his freedom.

For the next two days he traveled at night and hid during the day. There were frequent patrols, but he was painstaking in covering the small dugout and himself. During the day, as he lay silent, he carefully planned his next steps. He would join Francis Marion. He had heard that Marion was still at Snow Island, which lay at the confluence of Lynch's Creek and the Pee Dee. Fran had been his commanding officer at Sullivan's Island, and they had established a firm friendship. He had gone on several of Fran's initial raids against the Tories. From Marion's camp, he could exact his revenge.

Revenge was now his driving force. It minimized his pain, exhaustion and loss. It had become his sole reason for living.

He had been on the river three days, and he was growing impatient with his pace. But he felt the need to progress slowly, particularly on the winding waterway, which could easily steer him into British patrols. His food supply was gone and his side was feeling better. The combination dulled his caution. Knowing he was near his old plantation, he lost himself in thought and missed the sight of a flickering fire just ahead.

"Halt! Who goes there?"

The sharp summons broke through his reverie and Connor cursed his carelessness. He didn't know if he had been seen or whether the sentry was responding to the sound of his paddle against the water.

He steered the boat over to the bank and reached for his gun before climbing out and melting into the underbrush. He felt like a hunted animal, as he had several days earlier. But this time he had a musket and could strike back.

Connor had hunted along the banks of the Pee Dee all his life. Once he was in the woods, every tree was familiar. He knew he was less than a mile from Glen Woods.

He heard footsteps crashing through the underbrush. The searchers were making no effort at stealth. All the better. Connor waited patiently behind an ancient cypress as one set of footsteps approached. He caught a glimpse of the red coat and smiled to himself. He was in luck. The Tories in the area knew the woods as well as he did, but these British soldiers were babes in *his* woods and would pay for their ignorance.

His musket came crashing down on the unwary soldier, who fell silently, blood rushing from a wound to the head. Connor waited for the other sentry, having concluded from the sounds that there were only the two of them.

A noise came from behind him, and he swung around, his musket at ready. The second soldier saw him at the same time, but the man's musket was pointed away. Connor fired and watched as the man slowly fell, his face contorted by surprise and sudden terror.

Just then, Connor's ankle was jerked from under him, and his musket jammed into his wounded side. He could feel the sudden surge of blood as the wound reopened.

He threw out his hand as he fell, and it hit the now rolling body of the first soldier. Out of the corner of his eye, he caught the flash of a knife in the man's hand and twisted just in time to avoid it. Connor had no chance to wonder how the man had recovered so quickly; he was fighting for his life.

His left hand grabbed for the knife, and it went spinning into the woods as the British soldier lost his hold.

Both men were hurt, but both were fighting for survival, and their desperation gave them strength. They rolled beneath the trees, each trying to get a hold on the other. Connor felt his strength ebbing from the loss of blood and knew he had to end the battle quickly. With one hand, he pinned the soldier to the ground, while the other searched for a weapon. His hand touched a nearby rock and his fingers closed around its sharp edges. His arm came up, then down, and he flinched at the ugly sound as the rock made contact with the side of his enemy's head. The man's struggle suddenly ceased, and Connor wearily sat up. His shirt was soaked with blood. He knew he was bleeding but he couldn't stay where he was.

He checked the soldier, this time making sure that he was dead. Damn, he was getting careless.

Connor considered his options. He didn't know when the two sentries were due for relief, but it probably wouldn't be long. He also knew he couldn't go far with his wound. It hurt like hell, and movement would only increase the bleeding. Yet these woods were alive with Tories and the British.

The cave. He hadn't been there in years, not since he had shown it to Brendan and the young Chatham girl. Once he had revealed the secret to them, he had felt it belonged to them alone and had never returned. Concealed by an odd twist of terrain, it was impossible for someone who did not know its exact whereabouts to find. He had discovered it only by accident when one of his dogs had chased a rabbit inside.

He could wait there until he regained some of his strength. Then he would find his way to Marion's stronghold.

Chapter Three

Samantha played along with Sundance but her heart wasn't in the game. She hid the apple behind her back and allowed the large golden mare to search for it, nuzzling her hair, her neck and finally, with a satisfied wheeze, discovering the treat.

Samantha watched the apple disappear into the horse's moist mouth with a crunch. If only an apple could bring her such delight.

She was sunk in the lowest depths of gloom. She had been eavesdropping again, an activity for which she found she had an unsuspected talent.

Placing her head next to Sundance's, she rubbed against the silky mane and soft skin. The horse, in turn, nuzzled her again, this time curiously. Sensing that all was not right with her mistress, the mare whinnied with concern.

What to do now? Samantha had played her new role much too well. She hadn't realized that the new sparkle in her eyes and blush in her cheeks would be so misunderstood. They had been caused by the fever of the excitement of doing something for the rebel cause and striking back at her father and Foxworth.

The ball had gone very smoothly. She merely had to smile, and the British officers were tripping over one another to talk to her. They talked about their exploits, their upcoming "dangerous missions," and wouldn't she give them "a little token" to keep them safe? They talked openly of Colonel Tarleton's plans to catch the "damned Swamp Fox" and asked if they might call on her, while all the time she memorized dates and places and units and blushed becomingly. Too becomingly. Toward the end of the evening, she couldn't miss the glare sent her way by Colonel Foxworth, nor the surprised glower of her father.

And then, today, almost a week later, she had heard the two of them plotting again, and this time she was the principal subject.

"I want an answer," Foxworth was saying as she pressed her ear against the library door. She could hear the anger in his voice.

"I want this marriage as much as you do," her father had said. "I give my consent. I swear to you she will give hers. There are ways."

"I'm sure you will find them, my dear Robert," Foxworth said smoothly. "And I don't think she'll find it too distasteful. I do see a certain interest in her eye. I think she just enjoys the game." He laughed softly.

"What about O'Neill?" Her father's voice was suddenly harsh.

"Oh, I don't think he'll get far. They found a lot of blood, and he couldn't have been very strong after four months in the hulks. We'll probably find him dead somewhere."

Her father snorted in disgust. "How in the hell did he get away, anyway? You said there was no way they could escape."

Samantha could almost see the Englishman's shrug. "His father died. A tenderhearted navy lieutenant allowed O'Neill ashore to bury him. The man will pay for his act of mercy, by God."

Shivering at what she had heard, Samantha sensed steps moving toward the door, as if the two men were parting. She had scampered into the kitchen with the excuse of finding an apple.

Connor alive! Gerald O'Neill dead! She thought of the older O'Neill as he had been many years ago. Kind, like Connor, with bushy red hair and a gift for story telling. How he had loved to tell stories of the little people and their mischievous doings. A tear slipped down her cheek, although she had thought all her tears gone. "Please let Connor be safe," she begged her private God. She had given Him little attention lately and feared He might ignore her entreaty. But perhaps . . . this time . . .

Her own plight suddenly overwhelmed her. "I can't marry him, I won't," she whispered to Sundance, but even as she said the words, she knew her father meant his. She didn't want to think of his "ways," but she suspected they would involve people and things she loved. There was no longer any choice. She had to leave before he could threaten her. For once he had, he might well feel obligated to fulfill his threats if she then disappeared.

Samantha felt a coldness creeping over her. She had no place to go, no friends. Her father had seen to that, she thought bitterly. When he had publicly forced Brendan into the duel, he had sullied her own reputation by accusing her and Brendan of being lovers. This she had all heard later.

Samantha had been shunned, by Brendan's friends, who felt his death was her fault, and by her own, who feared her reputation might tarnish their own. Not that it had mattered to her. Her loss had been too shattering for her to care about erstwhile friends. The British officers' ball had been her first public outing since Bren's death.

Her loneliness settled around her like a smothering cloak. "You," she whispered to Sundance, "are the only one left."

A woman alone, with no money. It seemed hopeless. And she wouldn't leave Sundance, no matter what. A moist nose nudged her cheek, as if in sympathy.

If only she were a man, Samantha thought suddenly. She would go into the swamps with Colonel Marion. She would live free with no one to tell her what to do or who to marry. They called him the Swamp Fox. It had been meant as no compliment when Colonel Banastre Tarleton had pinned the name on him after Marion had disappeared into a swamp after a particularly long chase. "As for the Swamp Fox," Tarleton had said, "the devil himself could not catch him."

Marion's men, instead of taking the term as an insult, had adopted it with pride. Patriots throughout the area loved to embellish the exploits of the elusive Swamp Fox, to the discomfort of British and Tories alike.

"If it weren't for this hair," Samantha thought out loud, fingering a long black curl that fell from the knot at the back of her head.

She knew there were several boys who rode with Marion. One was Marion's nephew, and another, the son of one of his lieutenants. Both had been seen in the midst of battle.

Would it be possible . . . ?

Samantha knew she could ride as well as any man, and she had found, as a child, that she had a natural talent for marksmanship. But could she really fool anyone for a long period of time?

Her mind charged ahead. She had information of value to Colonel Marion. Hector had not yet had a chance to deliver all the information she had gathered at the ball. Growing up on an indigo plantation, she had learned enough about dyes to know that a little would take the sheen from her hair and roughen the softness of her skin. She could bind her breasts. The rest of her body was still angular; she had never regained the round softness she had had prior to Bren's death. Food was no longer a pleasure; in fact, little was a pleasure.

Her mind was suddenly made up. She would disappear tonight. First to the cave, where she would change into boys' clothing, and then to Snow Island, the lair of the Swamp Fox. Somehow she would find her way in . . . she must.

Samantha took up the scissors and hesitated, regarding herself solemnly in the mirror.

Why did her hair seem extraordinarily striking tonight? Perhaps things always seemed dearest when one was about to lose them. The long tresses seemed particularly bright and alive in the candlelight, and she remembered how Brendan had loved them. How he had run his fingers through the long curls, saying he could see flames leaping from them. She had thought the image nonsensical but had loved it all the same.

"Brendan," she whispered, "I wish you were here." Whatever she did, she couldn't seem to dull the constant ache inside her. She leaned against the table below the mirror, her hand with the scissors rising to her head.

Once she committed her intended act, there would be no turning back. Was she ready for that?

She thought of Foxworth and the possessive way he had touched her hair tonight. She had wanted to scream but had merely moved away, keeping her face a smiling mask.

Thinking of his unwanted admiration for the hair Brendan had loved gave her the strength to complete her task. She grasped a handful and, without hesitation, started cutting.

She cropped it close to her head, shorter than the current male fashion, which dictated shoulder-length hair tied neatly at the nape, but who knew when she might have a chance to trim it again? She would, after all, be a boy and unconcerned with fashion.

The remaining hair swirled in fine waves around her head, giving her a pixie look, still much too feminine to suit her. She took the dye mixed earlier and rubbed the dull brown mixture into her hair. Immediately the shining black turned a dull heavy brown. She combed it back and looked once more at her reflection, marveling at the change. The face was still too delicate for her new role, but an application of the dye would change that. She quickly fingered it on her cheeks, kneading it into her skin until a stranger looked back at her from the mirror.

There was no longer any trace of the young woman who had stood there minutes earlier. Samantha studied the reflection of an unkempt country lad with a sly smile on his weathered face.

Only the clothes were out of character. Her day dress was, at the very least, incongruous with her new role, but it would have to do until she reached the cave.

Samantha swept the hair up from the floor. She wanted no clues that might point to what had happened this night. She packed it in a carrying bag and sat at her desk.

Taking out pen and paper, she dipped the quill into a bottle of ink and wrote hurriedly, heedless of the blots that splashed across the paper.

Papa...I cannot marry Colonel Foxworth. I am going north and plan to make my own way as a governess. Do not try to find me.

Samantha

The others in the house had retired hours earlier. Samantha pulled on her cloak, carefully placing the hood over her shorn head. She took one last look at the room where she had lived her entire life until now. Her gaze fell on a miniature of her mother. She thought momentarily about taking it but discarded the idea. If found, it would surely give her away. A tear slipped down her newly browned face but left no trace. The dye was very strong and resistant to water.

Samantha scolded herself. This was no time for remembrances. She wrapped herself in the cloak and opened the door quietly.

She had no trouble quitting the house. Familiarity made each step a given and she made her way easily, stepping over those spots that creaked. The door closed behind her and she crept over to the barn.

A bright full moon now lighted her way, holding court for the thousands of twinkling stars that paid homage. Ordinarily Samantha would have stopped to admire the beauty of the sky, but now she only wished the nighttime wasn't so bright.

She quietly opened the barn door and made her way to Sundance's stall. She flinched at the horse's welcoming whinny. "Shh...." she whispered, fondling the inquisitive muzzle. "No," she added quietly, "no apple now."

She started to lead the horse from the stall. It was dangerous to take her, Samantha knew that. Everyone knew Chatham's prize gold mare. But she couldn't leave her. She would have to concoct some story.

"Where are you going with that horse?" The voice, so familiar yet so unexpected, startled her into stillness. It was unusual for any of the stable help to remain there overnight. One of the horses must be ill.

"Who's there? Who's that?"

A lantern shone in Samantha's face and a rough hand grabbed her.

"Hector!" Samantha cried. "It's me, Samantha."

The light came closer, searching. A hand pulled the hood from her cloak. A gasp of surprise came from the young slave.

"Miss Samantha?" His voice was puzzled. He recognized the voice, the cloak, the stance. But the face....

The light from the candle, cloaked in its glass cage, danced across Hector's bewildered face.

Samantha smiled. If she could fool Hector, she could fool anyone. She blew out the lantern and took his arm as she led Sundance to the door.

"It *is* me, Hector. Really it is. But I'm leaving. I can't stay here any longer. Not with the man who killed Brendan and wants me to marry someone I despise."

"But where you going?"

"It would be better if you didn't know," Samantha said softly. "My father doesn't know you are here tonight, does he?" she said, suddenly anxious for him.

"No," he said. "Damen was a little restless. I jest thought I'd stay awhile." Samantha knew there was a special bond between Hector and the midnight-black horse called Damen.

She squeezed Hector's shoulder. "I've got to go... I'll remember you and Maudie... tell her I love her."

Afraid to say anything else lest her resolve falter, she led Sundance out the door and walked silently beyond the trees. She bridled the horse and threw a blanket over her back. Samantha hunted for a mounting platform and finally found a fallen tree. She had to make a small leap and was grateful when she landed precisely where she'd intended on Sundance's back. She could explain stealing a horse, but it might raise questions if she had also taken the time to steal a saddle.

Whispering quietly to Sundance, she guided her toward Brendan's cave.

Samantha guessed it was about three hours before dawn when she reached the cave. She would stay only long enough to retrieve the clothes she had hidden a year ago and take her bracelet of seeds.

She swung her leg over Sundance and slid carefully to the ground, reassuring the horse as she did so. Samantha knew Sundance would not wander, and she tied the reins loosely to allow the mare freedom to graze.

Discarding her heavy cloak, she took the carrying bag, which contained the hair, matches, candles and food, and entered the dark cave. The moonlight was not strong enough to penetrate the overgrowth at the entrance and the cave was pitch-black. Just inside, she paused, trying to adjust her eyes to the darkness, but it was like being blind. She stumbled, and the bag flew from her hands. Frantically she stooped down, her hands running over the floor of the cave. She needed to be gone before sunrise.

Her hand hit something unexpected, and she recoiled, frightened. If only she could see! The object she had felt remained still, and she moved toward it once more, her body trembling slightly. Her hands reached out and felt a foot. It didn't move, but it was warm, though clammy. Whoever it might be was alive.

She renewed her search for her bag and finally located it. She fumbled as she groped inside it for a candle and matches. Once she found them, she quickly scratched a match against the wall of the cave and gave life to the candle.

The glow from the candle grew stronger, and she cautiously approached the figure outlined on the floor. As she leaned over, the light caught a dirty bearded face. She couldn't stifle the gasp that rose in her throat at the sight of Connor O'Neill.

She knelt beside him. "Connor," she whispered. "What have they done to you?"

Her candle ran the long length of him. He was so thin, and his clothes were in rags that barely covered him. His shirt was crusted with blood, and when she touched his side, the ugly red stain was wet and warm. He was still bleeding. As the candlelight hit his legs, she flinched at the heavy iron shackle bolted to his ankle.

He moaned and her left hand traveled to his cheek. "Connor?" Her soft question was met with silence, and she realized he was unconscious. His face felt cold and clammy despite the unseasonably warm temperature. It was late October, but the days had continued hot and humid.

"Oh, Connor, what should I do?"

She tried to remember her medical books. Like most mistresses of a plantation, she was often called upon to attend ailing slaves, but she had only a superficial knowledge—herbs for a fever, poultices for cuts. They had always called a doctor for more serious wounds or illnesses. She knew from experience that clammy cold skin followed the loss of a great deal of blood. She also knew it often preceded death.

Warmth. That's what he needed now. Spilling some wax onto the floor, she set the candle firmly in its makeshift holder. She then hurried outside, took the blanket from Sundance's back and gathered as much dry wood as she could handle.

Once back inside, she built a small fire and covered Connor with the blanket. She found the two bundles of clothes she and Brendan had left and hurriedly changed into those meant for her.

She had to return to Chatham Oaks and talk to Hector. He could get Maudie's store of medicines and then try to reach one of Colonel Marion's men. Perhaps the Swamp Fox could find a doctor and get Connor safely away. She had heard that Connor O'Neill had once ridden with the colonel and that the rebel leader was known for his loyalty.

Samantha wrapped the blanket tightly around Connor and snuffed the candle.

She reached Chatham Oaks just before sunrise. She had only minutes before the plantation would awaken. Tying Sundance well out of sight, she slipped through the trees to the slave cabins and knocked lightly at Hector's door. It opened almost immediately.

For the second time in a matter of hours, he stared at her.

"Miss Samantha, what are you doing back here?" In his consternation, he forgot his protective slur.

Samantha slipped past the door and looked at him. "You've got to help me…I found Connor O'Neill. He's badly hurt…in the cave. You've got to get me some medicine and somehow get word to Francis Marion."

Her words ran together and her expression was drawn and anxious. She suddenly collapsed on the floor and buried her face in her hands. "He'll die, Hector, and I can't stand it. I just can't, not again."

He put his hands on her shoulder and guided her back to her feet. "Don't you worry, Miss Samantha. I'll get your medicine from Maudie . . . you stay here."

Hector was out the door and back again within minutes with a small package. "I didn't tell her you were here," he said. "I just told her someone was sick. . . ."

"You best go now. When your father wakes up, he'll send us all searching for you. I'll be able to get to Colonel Marion. Don't you worry. I'll have someone at the cave tonight."

She looked at his face, alert and caring, and knew she could trust him. She smiled suddenly, an echo of the old Samantha shining through her new exterior.

"Oh," she said. "And I need a pail . . . and some soap. A lot of soap."

He didn't question but took his own water pail, stuffing it with lye soap and the package of medicine he had coaxed from Maudie. "Thank you," she said. "I'll never forget you."

He opened the door and watched her slip back through the trees.

Light was filtering slowly into the cave by the time Samantha returned. There would be numerous searches today for both Connor and herself, so she led Sundance inside, thankful that the cave was large enough for all three of them. It was tight going through the narrow entrance, but the space went back into a hill and was deep and wide at the far end.

The fire had burned to small embers, and Connor lay exactly where she had left him.

She felt his face again and it seemed a bit drier, but she questioned whether there really was a difference or whether it was simply hope on her part.

Samantha let the fire die down, mindful that the smoke would be visible in the daylight. Taking the bucket down to the river, she filled it and quickly returned to the cave. She heated a cupful of water in a container on the dying coals and added a portion of gum from the white poplar tree. Making a poultice from her discarded dress, she gently applied it to Connor's side.

Connor jerked as his unconscious body felt the new pain, and a small cry escaped his tightly clenched lips. Then his body relaxed as the poultice's soothing components took effect.

Now that the cave was lighted, Samantha took careful inventory of her patient. She had never seen anyone so dirty. Well, that she could fix. It was the rest of him that bothered her. She remembered his face as bronze from the sun, a striking contrast to his light hair and sea-gray eyes. Now it was white and pasty-looking, the skin tightly drawn. His once compact form had wasted away to bare bones and his body was a mass of open sores and infected bites. The iron cuff around his ankle had rubbed the flesh raw. He would always carry its scars.

Pity and compassion filled her. How could anyone do this to his fellow man? How could anyone survive this kind of treatment?

She took another piece of dress and the soap and water and sat next to him. Gently she started washing him, his face first, then the area around his wound. She was afraid to scrub; she didn't want to bring back the pain. But some of the layers of dirt came off, and she knew he would feel better once he did waken.

Then what? What would she tell him? How could she explain her presence in the cave? She remembered his words the day of the duel. Now his father was dead, and he had gone through torments she couldn't even imagine. All because of her father. He must not find out who she was.

After she had cleaned him as well as possible, she leaned back against the wall of the cave. She had not slept at all the night before, and she was exhausted. Maybe a few minutes' sleep.

Samantha woke to the sound of Connor's voice. He was raging and thrashing around under the blanket. His eyes were open, but they were blank, and she suddenly realized he was delirious. She felt his face, and it was cold, too cold.

"Chatham...I'm going to kill him...destroy him...destroy all the Chathams...Brendan...Father...Chatham...I'll make him pay."

A cold wave swept over Samantha. She froze at the sound of the hatred in his voice. Then she caught herself. He was obviously much sicker; she had to do something.

Connor was shivering despite the warmth of the day and the blanket. There was nothing else to warm him. Perhaps she could share the warmth of her own body.

She lay next to him, disregarding the stench that still hovered around him despite her efforts. She wrapped her arms around him, and her hands stroked him, soothing and comforting. She could feel his body gradually relax and the shivering quiet. She finally felt his slow, easy breathing of sleep, and she too gave way to it.

When she woke, he had somehow turned around without waking her and was holding her tightly in his arms. She looked at his peaceful face and doubted he was aware of his actions. She felt a confusing sensation from his closeness. Slowly and patiently she untangled herself. Her shirt had opened and her breasts seemed larger than normal. Her breasts. How could she have forgotten them. He might wake up anytime and her disguise would be discovered.

She found a piece of underclothing she had discarded with the dress and bound the anatomy that could so easily betray her. She looked down at herself and saw nothing but a boy's slim build under the brown homespun shirt. She then took the dress, her feminine underclothing and the long strands of hair outside the cave. Listening and watching carefully, she quickly buried the lot.

There was nothing left of Samantha Chatham.

Chapter Four

Connor O'Neill woke later in the afternoon. Samantha felt, rather than heard, his listless movement. When she turned around, she saw his gray eyes flicker open and slowly survey the cave.

They finally rested on the young boy who watched him anxiously. He tried to move and had to clench his teeth to keep from crying out at the pain. His side was in agony. When the pain receded, he looked again at the boy.

"Who are you . . . how did you find this cave?"

"Me 'orse found it," Samantha improvised. "Good thin', too. 'Eard ya cry out. Found ya mostly dead."

"You . . . you've been taking care of me? I thought . . ." Connor shook his head as if to clear it. "It must have been a dream."

"Whada ya mean?"

"Nothing . . . my thanks for your help."

"'Twern't nothin'. Should be someone to 'elp ya. Word's been gotten to the Swamp Fox."

"Then I owe you thanks again," he said, falling back on the floor. "I don't think I could make it alone."

Connor saw from the lad's dubious expression that he didn't think so, either.

He smiled, and Samantha, with a sudden rush of warmth, realized how like Bren's his smile was. Like Bren's, yet different. It had a quiet charm all of its own . . . even through the beard and dirt.

She resisted a sudden impulse to go to him, to touch him. "Ya need a bath bad, mister," she said finally. "I tried to wash ya but were afeered of 'urting ya."

Connor smiled again. "You're right. I do need a bath. Is that water over there?"

She nodded and carried it to him, along with soap. "I found some clothes 'ere, too, mister. . . ." She pulled out the package that Brendan had packed and offered it to Connor.

A shadow crossed Connor's face as he recognized Bren's clothes. But then he caught the expectant look on the boy's face and twisted his expression into a wry smile. "There seems to be no end to your miracles," he said gently. "What's your name?"

"Sam . . . Sam Taylor," Samantha stumbled.

"Your family?"

The small face turned hard. "Dead. Redcoats. 'Tis off to join Marion, I am."

Connor looked at the solemn young face. "You are very young."

"Kin shoot as well as any man . . . ride, too. Stole the 'orse I 'ave from some fat Tory. I heerd there's others my age with Marion and men younger 'n me fightin' with Washington."

Despite his pain, Connor had to restrain a smile. Men younger than me, indeed.

Well, one thing was for sure. The boy obviously could take care of himself . . . and he had taken very good care of Connor. He knew he had been very sick. He must have been. Delirious, in fact, to have dreamed of a woman next to him. There were just fleeting impressions of warmth, but they seemed so real.

Connor took the bucket of water and soap and gingerly started washing himself. He took off what was left of his shirt and painfully tried to remove his trousers. His side, however, wouldn't allow him to bend.

"Sam," he said to the boy, who had turned away.

The boy's head moved just slightly in his direction.

"Can you help me take off these trousers . . . ?"

There was a small silence. "Me?" the boy asked.

Connor's smile returned. "I don't see anyone else."

Samantha reluctantly approached him and knelt beside him. She tugged at the buttons, grateful that her rising blush was hidden by the dye on her face. She finished unbuttoning them and, averting her eyes as Connor raised himself slightly, she pulled the offending rags from his body. She had to pull and tug to get them over the iron band.

"And the under trousers," Connor added mercilessly. "I don't want anything left."

Samantha knew her face was in flames now; surely even the dye couldn't hide it. "Ya'll get cold," she said hopefully.

"You yourself said I needed a bath. How can I get clean without getting these rags off first," Connor answered reasonably. He handed her the knife he had retrieved from the fight the night before. "Just cut them off."

Samantha closed her eyes. I'll just think of something else, she thought, as she cautiously started cutting the cloth. It was impossible. There was no way she could avoid the protrusion between Connor's legs.

But it was not to end there. Connor then asked her to help him wash. Her embarrassment and desire to end the ordeal as soon as possible made her diligent, and rougher than she intended. Connor yelped several times as she rubbed unmercifully at his tender skin.

Each moment was an agony of embarrassment. Despite the weight loss, Connor's body reflected the discipline of thirty years of hard work. Under her hands, hard muscles rippled where the last months had stripped him down to whipcord. Her hands faltered as she neared his manhood. She did have rudimentary knowledge of such things. She had, after all, grown up around animals, but she had never seen a naked man before. Bren and she had decided to wait until marriage to embark on what both expected to be a splendid adventure. It was a decision that Samantha had lived to regret.

At last it was over and she helped Connor into Bren's clothes. Ordinarily they would have been much too small, but now they hung from him and he needed a rope to keep the pants up.

Cautiously, Samantha made her way to the river and fetched another bucket of water. On her return, she washed Connor's hair. Patiently, she washed and rewashed, painstakingly removing the lice. Intent on her task, she missed the inquisitive looks cast her way.

With a final grunt of satisfaction, she declared Connor fit for human companionship and he sighed with pleasure at being reasonably clean for the first time in months. He scratched his beard but, after considering Sam's rough washing, decided he'd not ask any more favors. Despite the wound, he now felt better than anytime since he had been taken four months ago. The weakness would disappear. And he was free, free to avenge his family.

Connor didn't realize that his expression had changed and a muscle throbbed in his cheek, but Samantha did, and she sensed why. Getting up, she found the bread and meat she had packed the night before. She offered Connor the larger share, knowing that he needed far more than she.

Connor resisted, demanding that they share equally. "You need to fill out yourself if you're going to ride with Marion," he teased. "He doesn't take tadpoles."

Sensing he wouldn't eat at all if she didn't take her full share, she finally consented. Despite the fact she had eaten nothing all day, she wasn't hungry. She had one more hurdle to go. Would Marion take this particular tadpole?

Samantha looked down at Connor. His thick, slightly curling hair was now close to the ash-blond color she remembered, and he had tied it back with a tiny piece of cloth. He was sleeping peacefully, exhausted from the last five days of running.

Sliding down against the cave wall, she studied her own situation. She had few doubts that someone from Marion's camp would be here tonight. Hector was reliable and he knew of the cave; it had been here that she had taught the young slave to read.

She leaned her head back. Colonel Marion had to accept her. There was no turning back now. But how long could she continue the masquerade? There were so many coincidences already. The disappearance of Samantha Chatham...the appearance of Sam in a cave Samantha knew about.... She wished she had thought of another name, but Sam had popped out, and it was too late now to change it. And then, of course, there was Sundance...."

With luck, no one would associate the well-educated Tory daughter with a barely literate rebel boy. She would have to keep a distance from Connor; he would be the only one who had really known her before. But as she looked at him now and recollected the slow easy smile and the quiet gratitude he had shown her, she knew it would be difficult. He had stirred something inside her, something she thought dead forever, and, she knew suddenly, it had nothing to do with his being Brendan's brother.

The light withdrew slowly from the cave, inch by inch. Samantha watched the filtered rays retreat, knowing they were trailing a setting sun. It shouldn't be long before they had company.

She heard Connor move and went to him, offering a cup of water. He sat up slowly, obviously stiff and still in pain. His face was hidden by the growing shadows.

"How long have I been sleeping?"

"Afternoon long," Samantha told him. "Ya be better?"

"Yes, thanks to you," Connor replied, his features slightly contorted by the effort it took to sit. He was anxious now, anxious to move and get on with the business of war and retribution. "Are you certain Marion's coming?"

"Not certin of ennythin'. Jest know word's been got to 'im."

Connor shook his head and smiled. "You don't have much to say, do you?"

"Ain't much to say."

"What about that horse you said you stole. Where is it?"

Samantha shrugged her shoulders toward the back of the cave. "Back there. Redcoats won't find 'er."

Connor's curiosity took over. "May I see her?"

"Iffen ya want. She's jest a 'orse."

Samantha lighted the candle and went toward the back. In seconds she reappeared, leading Sundance. It was, she knew, a precarious moment, but better now than later in front of others.

She watched Connor stiffen in recognition. The horse had been well-known in the parish. "Where did you get that horse?" he said tightly.

"Pasture . . . not far from 'ere. I found a bit and reins in a barn. I couldn't find no saddle but doan need one ennyway." Just then Sundance decided to play and bumped her backside with a cold nose.

"Seems pretty familiar for a stolen horse," Connor said. There was a bit of a question in his voice but no suspicion she could detect.

"'Ave a way with animals, I do," she replied. "Always 'ave. Pa said he never seen the like."

Connor relaxed, a wide grin spreading across his face. "Do you know that's the prize mare of the biggest Tory in the Carolinas?" The grin grew into a chuckle. "You know horse-flesh, Sam, I'll grant you that."

Samantha decided she had pushed her luck far enough. "I best wait outside."

Connor nodded and emitted a low whistle to the horse, who cocked two perfectly formed ears but stayed exactly where Samantha had left her. Connor shook his head and only Sundance heard the low whispered, "I'll be damned."

Their movements were so quiet Samantha didn't realize she was no longer alone until two men appeared directly in front of her. Hector stood well to the side of them.

"Tha's the boy tha' tol' me 'bout Mr. O'Neill," Hector said, giving no other sign of recognition. Samantha silently blessed him.

The two men were dressed in homespun britches and leather jerkins, and each wore a leather cap with a cockade of white paper.

While Samantha regarded them, they, in turn, inspected her suspiciously. They had considered the possibility of a trap, but both were friends of Connor O'Neill and neither had wanted to pass up a chance to help him.

The taller of the two furrowed his brow. "O'Neill?"

She nodded her way toward the laurel covering the cave. "Tha' way."

"You first," the man replied, still wary of the situation.

Samantha slid through the opening, and the two men followed silently, one lighting a match against the darkness. He held it up, and his eyes followed its faint glow around the cave.

Samantha quickly found a candle and held it to the match. The spreading light settled on Connor who, on hearing the footsteps, struggled to sit up.

The man who had spoken earlier grinned and reached his friend in two large steps, placing his hands on Connor's shoulders.

"Connor. By God, we thought you dead. You don't know how glad it is we are to see you. You know how dour Francis is. Even he smiled at the news. We'd heard you'd died on that damned prison ship. We thought this might be a trap."

Connor's welcoming smile faded. "My father died. I might have, if not for the help of Sam over there. I'm glad to see you, Peter."

Peter Horry took the candle from Samantha and held it over Connor. He studied the pallor in Connor's thin face and his obvious pain as he tried to straighten. "The damned British," he said tightly.

"And Robert Chatham," Connor said bitterly. "I hope he's quaking now, he should well be."

Horry's expression changed. He had known Connor since they had fought together early in the war and respected his steadiness and unfailing good nature. This was another Connor, one he would not like to have as an enemy. "You'd better not let Fran hear you say that. He doesn't like personal grudges."

Connor's face tightened and a muscle pulled at his cheek. "He has taken everything I held dear," he said. "No one will stop me."

Horry knew when to retreat. "Davey's with me," he said, "and we have a doctor outside. I wanted to make sure everything was all right before getting him involved."

Connor nodded as the second man approached him, a smile breaking through his grim countenance. He said nothing but his long firm handclasp expressed his support.

Horry disappeared and returned with a man dressed somberly in black broadcloth.

"Here he is, doctor. See if he can ride."

Connor reluctantly submitted to the doctor's quick examination. He flinched as the man examined his side, probing around the wound.

"He's a damned sight better than he should be for a man who's been in those death ships," the doctor pronounced. "That gunshot wound's going to be mighty painful for a while, but if he's careful I think he can ride. Probably be safer than staying here. What's that on the wound?"

Connor grinned and nodded toward his watchful companion. "Ask Sam. He made it. He did a lot more... cleaned me up, fed me... kept me warm when I was cold last night."

"How did you know about keeping him warm?" the doctor asked.

"Seen it b'fore," Samantha said simply.

The doctor turned back to Connor. "He probably saved your life. After a heavy loss of blood, patients sometimes have a severe drop in body temperature. If not attended to, they can die. You were lucky someone was here."

"I know," Connor said.

The doctor bound the wound in clean linen, warning Connor about jarring it, and gave him a draught to quicken the healing.

Peter Horry and Davey helped Connor to his feet. Connor groaned slightly at the pain but he shook his head when the two looked at him questioningly.

"What about him?" Horry said, nodding his head toward Samantha.

"'Tis aimin' to go wi' ya, I im," she said, fighting to keep the tremor from her voice.

Horry shook his head. "I'm sorry, lad. You're much too young. Besides, Marion would have our heads if we brought in a stranger."

Connor looked at the boy's face in the candlelight. It was full of despair. Sam had helped him; now he must return the favor.

"He goes with me," he said simply, and the tone allowed no debate. "Besides," he added wryly, "he's one hell of a horse thief. He seems to have stolen Chatham's favorite mare. It's a talent we can always use.''

Horry revised his estimate of the boy, particularly when the light caught Sundance standing easily in the shadows.

"He'll have to be blindfolded," he said dubiously.

Connor nodded. "Did you bring an extra horse?"

"Aye . . . we weren't going to make you walk."

"Sam can ride behind me," Connor said. "We'll lead his horse." He looked over at the boy, "Is that all right with you?"

Samantha nodded, her face beaming.

"There's redcoats all over," Peter warned. "We have to be particularly careful. No talking." The last was directed at the boy.

The sides of Connor's mouth quirked upward in a dry smile. "You don't have to worry about him . . . he talks less than Davey."

Once outside the cave, Hector appeared with three horses, and the two strangers helped Connor mount. Samantha stood patiently as a blindfold was placed over her eyes. Then Connor took her hand and she swung up easily behind him. Placing her arms trustingly around him, she was careful not to touch his wounded side. As the four horsemen quietly disappeared among the ancient cypresses, Hector silently slipped back to Chatham Oaks.

Despite the little voice inside that told her to keep her distance, Samantha enjoyed riding behind Connor, her legs touching his, her arms wrapped around his chest. She could feel little flickers of flames playing with her senses. He made her feel warm and safe and . . . something more.

It was an unsettling experience, riding blindfolded, and it did peculiar things to her thinking. She had the feeling that she and Connor were the only two people in the world. She savored his nearness, knowing that she could never experience it again.

Her father's hatred for the O'Neills had made sure of that. Connor O'Neill despised everything her family represented.

She wished she could hate her father. But despite herself, she could not. She was, after all, part of him. She had tried so hard to please him, but she couldn't remember him ever giving her a kiss or a touch or even a word of praise.

She wondered what he would do now. Undoubtedly, the search for her would be private. His pride would never allow him to make her defection public. He would not wish to alienate Colonel Foxworth and ruin the possibility of a future marriage, but Samantha knew she would have to be careful. Very, very careful.

She had already made several mistakes, starting with the name. Then there was the accent. She had begun it, thinking to place the boy as far as possible from Samantha Chatham. But it would be difficult to maintain.

Her hands fell and rested on Connor's hips. She couldn't bear to think anymore about her situation. She had had little sleep in the past two days and fatigue was beginning to take its toll. She was trying to stay upright in the saddle but her mind and body were reluctant to do her bidding. Giving up the effort, she rested her head against Connor's back and fell into a half sleep.

Connor was having an equally difficult time. He was still very weak and in pain, but every step took him further from his existence as a prisoner. Never had the moon been more beautiful as it rode high in the sky, slightly veiled by lacelike clouds. The stars seemed to welcome him back and he relished the breeze as it whispered quietly through the giant cypresses. He was back in the place he loved most.

He felt Sam's hands fall to his hips and the light burden of his head as it rested against his shoulder. Bless him, Connor thought. He was a strange lad, so solemn and taciturn, so determined to be a soldier. Yet Connor had felt an underlying gentleness under the rough exterior and sensed a sadness that transcended even his own.

He owed the boy his life and the chance to revenge himself. Connor made an oath to take Sam under his protection and provide for him.

Relieved by his decision, he settled down to concentrate on surviving the long ride.

Chapter Five

Samantha was startled fully awake by a loud piercing whistle that shattered the early-morning calm. Connor, who had slumped down in the saddle, also straightened.

She felt the horse slow and tried to detect what time it was, but the blindfold kept her world black, and she was suddenly frightened by the void. She clutched tighter to Connor and took comfort in his low whisper, "It's morning, Sam, and we're almost there."

Her hands tightened even more, and Connor felt a jab of sympathy for the young boy. No matter how brave he pretended to be, the lad must have some fear, being led blindfolded into an armed camp, not knowing what to expect.

Connor smiled slightly. Sam, he knew, would not appreciate the implication. The smile quickly turned into a grimace as the pain in his side struck. He was eager for this long nightmare of a ride to be over.

He had been in Marion's camp before. The base on Snow Island was amply protected by a network of pickets. There were two circles of them, one mounted on the peripheral and the second, on foot, nearer the heart of the camp. They were surrounded by swamp. Marion knew a hundred ways in and out, but to most, the terrain was impenetrable. The British were constantly frustrated in their attempts to find the camp.

Connor followed his companions into the deep recesses of the island, realizing that hidden eyes followed his every movement.

They finally reached a small clearing dotted by dimly burning fires. Connor turned around and untied Sam's blindfold, watching as the boy scanned the strange scene before him.

It was just dawn, and what light there was barely penetrated the gigantic cypresses and stately evergreen laurel overhead. The trees seemed bound together in a centuries-old embrace, like the vaults of the Gothic cathedrals Samantha had seen in books. Faint white smoke from the fires caught in the long gray moss that hung from the trees like the beards of ancient patriarchs.

Rifles and muskets were stacked against the tree trunks and sabers hung from the boughs above them.

The scene seemed unreal to her as she slipped from the horse. She watched as Connor carefully dismounted, almost falling as his feet touched the ground. Her quick hand reached his elbow and steadied him, and he nodded his thanks.

A group of men approached, swelling in numbers with each step. They were led by a man dressed in a close-fitting crimson jacket of coarse material. A black leather cap graced his head with a silver crescent on its crown inscribed with the words, Liberty or Death.

His air of authority told Samantha immediately that this was Colonel Marion, the Swamp Fox, and she looked at him with amazement.

He was no taller than herself and weighed little more. His body was thin but gave the appearance of tempered steel. His skin was swarthy and his nose aquiline above his projecting chin.

But what drew her attention were his eyes. They were black and piercing. They radiated power, and Samantha instantly understood why men would follow him anywhere.

Marion's eyes traveled from her to Connor, and a slight smile touched his lips. He clutched Connor's shoulders with both hands. "Welcome, Connor." He studied his friend for a moment, his mouth tightening as he noticed the iron ring.

"We'll have that gone soon enough," he said. "And we'll have to fatten you up." His smile was unexpectedly gentle.

"And what do we have here?" Marion continued, as he turned his attention back to Samantha.

Connor grinned. "A good horse thief," he said. "He 'found' one of Robert Chatham's horses and then found me. If it wasn't for him, I might not be alive."

"Then I owe you my thanks," Marion said to her. "Connor and I have been friends many years. I would hate to lose him."

He turned back to Connor. "But why did you bring him here?" There was a slight rebuke in his voice.

"Sam's father was killed by the British," Connor explained. "He was on his way to find you when he found me instead. He apparently has no place to go and longs to be one of Marion's men."

"He's very young," Marion said dubiously.

"You already have several others not more than fourteen," Connor answered. "And I can vouch for his way with horses. I'll take responsibility for him."

Marion regarded her once more. "Can you shoot, boy?"

"Yessir," she answered.

Marion turned to a man next to him. "Get the boy a rifle."

Samantha took the rifle, and Marion pointed to a branch some fifty yards away.

She quickly inspected the rifle, ensuring it was correctly loaded. Balancing it in her hands to get the feel of it, she remembered her childhood lessons. Aiming carefully, she slowly pulled the lever. The clearing exploded with sound, and Samantha watched proudly as the branch floated to the ground.

Marion clasped her shoulder. "Fair enough, boy. But if you come with me, you'll have to follow orders, and follow them exactly. No going off on your own. Agreed?"

"Agreed," she replied.

Marion looked at her closely. "Shooting a man is not like shooting a rabbit for food. It's something you never get used to, something that will follow you all your life. Never use a gun carelessly or without strong need to protect yourself or your comrades."

Samantha nodded.

"You're welcome, then." Marion turned back to Connor. "Both of you look like you need sleep. I'll send for a blacksmith later to take care of that shackle. There's some roasted sweet potatoes and salted beef prepared. You better get some . . . it won't last long.''

Connor found his endurance at an end. He was barely able to stand long enough to greet old friends before stumbling toward a tree, where he slid to the ground.

Samantha watched him anxiously. When another man started to approach him, she stopped him. "Needs 'is sleep, 'e does," she said, the concern in her voice warning him away. She fetched some potatoes and meat and took them to Connor, insisting that he eat, then sleep. She begged a blanket for his head and sat sentinel over him until he was buried in a deep sleep. Only then did she find her own blanket and tree and, within minutes, was also asleep.

Marion watched the new arrivals with fascination. "It would appear Connor's been adopted," he said to Peter Horry. "Do you know anything about the lad?"

"Nothing more than Connor told you. He didn't say a word all the way here."

"There's something about him . . . something that doesn't fit," Marion said. "Keep an eye on him for me, will you. And ask young Billy James to do the same. They're of an age."

"Aye, Fran. I didn't want to bring him, but Connor insisted and he was in no mood to argue with. If we hadn't brought him, I don't think Connor would have come with us."

Marion sighed. "He's had a bad time of it, but he's always had a sure instinct about people. I would trust his judgment above any other."

Horry turned to Marion. "I don't think the boy is the problem."

"What do you mean?"

"It's Connor . . . he's bent on killing Chatham. I don't know if you can keep him under control."

Marion's face hardened and his black eyes brightened. "There will be none of that if he wishes to stay here . . . we will not become involved in personal battles. Not even for Connor."

Samantha woke sometime in the afternoon and took stock of her surroundings. She felt freer than ever before. It was glorious to be rid of the corsets and stays and petticoats that had plagued her for nineteen years.

As she rose, she noted the sleeping figures scattered about on the ground. She searched for another fully conscious human being but could find none. Francis Marion traveled and fought by night and slept by day. It was a backward world, she thought, one of which she was now a part.

She made her way quietly to the rough corral. Sundance separated herself from the other horses with a soft welcoming whinny and approached, nuzzling her mistress in search of an apple.

Samantha stroked her gently, whispering apologies. She opened the gate and let Sundance out of the corral.

The horse followed behind her to the edge of the clearing and through the deep forest to a pool. The black glassy water was filled with water hyacinths and lilies. Occasionally an errant sunbeam managed to filter through the dense growth above and strike the surface.

Samantha had attained her goal, but she didn't know what to do next. Colonel Marion's words had struck her like a fist. "Shooting a man is not like shooting a rabbit." She had never even done that. Her targets had always been inanimate . . . a stump, a mark on a tree, an old bottle.

When she was making her plans, she had thought only of fleeing her father and an unwanted suitor, never of taking a life. She had thought of living in the open, of riding free, of adventure. She had never thought of death.

Nor had she thought she might meet Connor O'Neill, or feel what she was feeling toward him. She had soundly believed her heart dead forever, and now it was springing to life again, and it must not. Connor would turn from her swiftly and surely if he ever discovered that she was Samantha Chatham.

But just thinking of him made her tremble. How could it happen so fast?

"That's a fine horse."

Samantha started. She had not heard the soft footsteps approach. She looked toward the sudden intruder.

"'E's well enuf," she replied shortly.

Her companion was a boy, probably not more than fourteen. He was neatly clad in leather breeches, cotton shirt and high boots. He stuck out his hand. "I'm Billy James. I saw you leave and was afraid you might get lost. It's easy to do out here."

She stared at his hand before reluctantly putting out her own. Friends were a luxury she couldn't afford. It was too easy to make a mistake. She turned back to the pool, dismissal in her gesture.

Billy ignored the message and sat down. "It's real pretty out here, isn't it. I come myself sometimes."

"'Tis a place for bein' alone," Samantha said rudely.

Billy flinched at the blatant invitation to leave but remained seated and regarded the newcomer curiously. Colonel Marion had asked him to befriend the lad and, in doing so, keep an eye on him. It was going to be more difficult than he'd thought.

"I've never seen a horse follow someone before...like a dog," he said to break the silence.

Samantha sniffed loudly, as if Billy's observation was of no worth at all.

Billy tried again. "I would like to be your friend," he said hopefully.

"Doan need no friends," she said abruptly. "Jest to be lef' alone." It was difficult to rebuff the boy's good-natured attempt at friendship. She experienced a sharp emptiness inside. She needed a friend more than she had realized.

She glanced at the boy, and the loneliness suddenly shone in her eyes. It was gone instantly, but Billy James saw it and wondered.

"We take care of each other, us younger ones," he said carefully, not wanting to spoil that brief moment of communication.

Samantha was instantly wary. She had given away a piece of herself. "'Tis used to being alone, I am," she said. "'Tis wha' I like."

Billy nodded, unwilling to push any further. "If you need anything, I'll be around."

She nodded her head, but her eyes were once again shuttered.

She watched as he disappeared through the forest, then sighed. What had she gotten herself into?

Connor was finally awakened midafternoon by one of the men. The blacksmith had arrived.

The bolt in the shackle had rusted, and it took the blacksmith more than an hour of chiseling and hammering to break the lock. Every blow was agony as the iron jolted the already torn flesh. But when the metal finally parted, Connor knew it was well worth the pain. He was finally free of Britain's bond.

While his side still hurt, he was able to move much easier than yesterday, and he sat for several minutes, savoring his new freedom. He knew he would never again take it for granted.

He bandaged his ankle and gently pulled on some boots provided from recently captured British supplies. Now all he needed was a shave. Then he would feel quite human again.

As he looked into a small mirror, he wondered at the scarecrow that stared back at him. The beard was substantial, and of the same blond color as his hair. His cheeks were sunken, and new lines framed his eyes. Only his eyes seemed familiar, yet they, too, were different. There was a new hardness to them, a glint of steel.

With a borrowed razor he quickly stripped the beard from his face and looked closely again.

The face was thin and pale, but there was a new strength in it. It would take some time to accustom himself to it.

Such musing was wasteful. His life would never be the same and it was time to get on with the future.

He was just finishing washing when Marion approached him.

"An improvement, Connor."

Connor smiled slightly. "I never thought shaving could be such a pleasure.... I just deprived a million small creatures of their home."

Marion laughed. "It's going to be good to have you back with us...I've missed you." He turned suddenly serious. "About that boy...Sam?"

Connor was instantly wary. "Yes?"

"What do you know about him?"

Connor thought about it for a moment. What *did* he know? He suddenly realized he knew almost nothing. Sam Taylor had revealed little of himself in the cave.

"Not much," he admitted wryly. "I do know that if he had not come by, I might be dead now. I know he gave me food meant for himself, and that he spent hours trying to wash me." The smile came back. "A little too enthusiastically, I'm afraid. I was rubbed raw."

He looked at Marion's unsmiling face. "Why? Do you think he might be a British spy? If he is, why didn't he turn me in? There's a hefty price on my head."

"No," Marion said, his face puzzled. "It's not that. I would just like to know more about him."

"He is closemouthed," Connor replied. "But I'll try to find out what I can."

Marion paused, as if considering his next words very carefully.

"There is one thing more to discuss between us," he said. "I suggest we move to a more private spot." Marion turned without further explanation and led the way toward the woods.

Samantha stayed on the bank near the pool for hours, allowing Sundance to graze to her heart's content. The longer she stayed away, the longer she could avoid difficult questions. In her mind she started to weave a totally new background for herself.

The nice thing about it was that she could invent people that she liked, a father who cared about her, a way of life that she had always longed for.

Sam's story developed slowly, piece by piece. A father who had come over from England to make his fortune and who had shared everything with his son, until the redcoats came. As she elaborated the story in her mind, it became more real than the life she had left behind.

Finally satisfied, she left her private place and started back to camp. She put Sundance back in the corral and went to find something to eat.

She stopped suddenly as she recognized the voices of Connor and Francis Marion nearby.

"I'll not have you going after Chatham," Colonel Marion was saying. "We have other more important things to do. If every man were here to satisfy a personal grudge, that's all we would be doing. One day we will all have to live together again. If you fight a man fairly—in battle—you can do that. If you burn the roof over his children, he will never forget, and he will never stop hating."

"You think," Connor said, his voice taut with anger, "that I could ever live in peace with Chatham, or he with me, for that matter."

"That is something you will have to decide," Marion said. "Our orders are to disrupt supply routes and communications, to keep the British well occupied here and unable to move north. We have less than one hundred men to do that. We cannot afford to lose even one." His voice turned pleading. "Bide your time, Connor. I need you."

There was silence, then Connor's reluctant consent. "I'll wait...for a while. But I will pray every time we go out that he will be there. Then, by God, nothing will save him."

"Fair enough," Marion said.

"Fran..." Samantha heard Connor hesitate, then continue. "Chatham's daughter. What have you heard of her?"

Fran Marion's voice was suddenly harsh. "Why? Thinking of taking revenge on her?"

"I just want to know," Connor insisted, his voice once again full of anger.

"I understand she's gone north...to nurse a sick relative. Hector, the boy who sent word to me about you, is a slave on the Chatham plantation. He says she's gone."

"Has she married?"

"No," Marion said reluctantly. "It was rumored she was to marry one of Tarleton's officers."

"She didn't mourn long for my brother, did she?" Connor's voice was a combination of rage and disgust.

Marion, ignorant of the fact that Samantha was one of Hector's principal sources of information, did not reply.

Feeling sick, Samantha melted back into the woods, and, there, alone, she doubled over and sank to the ground in anguish.

Samantha hid in the shadows until dusk fell and hunger overcame the hurt. She had eaten little in the past two days, and she could no longer deny the growing ache in her stomach.

Fires had been lighted, and she could smell sweet potatoes roasting over the coals. She thought suddenly of the tables at Chatham Oaks . . . groaning under mounds of fresh ham, buttered vegetables, freshly baked breads and rich pecan pies. She instantly dismissed the traitorous thoughts. Those things, as wondrous as they seemed now, went hand in hand with Colonel Foxworth and her father's unbridled hatred. She was well rid of them.

As she shyly approached one of the fires and took some potatoes, the sound of a fiddle was heard and the rough voice of one of the soldiers.

The forest was suddenly alive with accompanying guffaws and shouting, and even Samantha in her dark mood had to smile. She went and sat alone against a tree, nibbling at her food to make it last longer.

The fiddle turned to dancing music, and several of the men danced together. Their feet went in all directions, provoking ribald insults from the onlookers. Amid the laughter and fellowship, Samantha had never felt lonelier.

As Connor approached Sam through the crowd he was surprised at the hostility on the boy's face. He had felt a closeness between them during the previous day and the long night. Even now he recalled the earnestness of the boy's piquant expression as he had so diligently removed him from the ranks of the unwashed.

While he had decried Connor's unwashed condition, Sam was none too clean himself today. His face was smudged and looked weathered, adding a hardness to the fine features underneath. Despite the facade of independence and roughness, Sam had shown him unusual generosity and care yesterday. There had even been a couple of minutes of rare charm when the boy had dropped his guard.

But as he looked at him now, Connor saw nothing of the boy who had so trustingly leaned his head against his back during the long ride. There was, instead, suspicion and wariness.

Connor disregarded it. He was, by nature, happiest when he could offer security and love to those he cared about. Hate had been a stranger to him until the death of his brother. Even in war, there had not been anger, only a strong sense of duty and sadness that violence was necessary. Though very capable, he had been a most reluctant warrior.

This was a trait he shared with Francis Marion, and it had forged a bond between them. More than anything, Marion longed to return to the quiet peaceful life of a planter. Although a master at war, he despised the death and hatred it spawned and prayed for its end.

Sam was a casualty of war, Connor thought as he looked at the boy, one of many, some as young as eleven and twelve, who had taken up arms. Some were running toward something; others away. Connor wondered briefly which was the case with his young friend.

"Can you use a pistol?" Connor said as he got close enough, seeking to break the ice in an impersonal way. Instinctively he knew that was the only way to reach the boy.

"Nev'r 'ad one" came the reply.

Surprised that Sam admitted an inadequacy, Connor had to restrain a smile. "All right," he said, "tomorrow I'll teach you."

Samantha nodded, still not condescending to smile. "Ya look some better," she said finally, her attitude still distant.

"Thanks to you, my friend."

"I ain't yer friend," she retorted.

Connor could no longer contain his smile. The voice was so belligerent, yet it did not match the expression of the eyes that regarded him so solemnly.

"You are *mine*," Connor said firmly, "even though you may not admit to me being yours. I'll see you in the morning," he said, before the boy could protest.

Chapter Six

The sun was completing its downward trail through the sky, sending up an array of colors. Hues of gold and pink and the brightest orange melded into one another and surrendered into one bright steady glow before sinking completely beyond the heavily laden trees.

The camp was all business. The fires had been doused and ghostlike figures moved about checking their rifles, buckling on their swords and filling their powder horns. Samantha's new companions moved quietly and efficiently, a hint of anticipation in their low voices.

She sat against a tree, her fascinated eyes scanning everything, absorbing the scene. The tales of Robin Hood came to her mind, and she could scarcely believe she was a part of it.

"Sam...Sam Taylor." The voice broke the spell, and she looked to see Marion above her. The small man looked like a giant, and a twinge of fear flickered through her at the distinct aura of controlled danger that seemed to surround him. He was like a tiger ready to spring, tense and wary, and she knew, suddenly, she would never want to be his enemy.

The image was shattered as he smiled and she suddenly realized that he understood how lost she felt. Alone...away from family...in unfamiliar woods...with armed strangers.

A small wry smile on her face admitted to all those feelings, and something else. Determination. Marion felt reassured.

"Stay here and take care of Connor for us," he said finally. "Billy James will help if you need anything."

Samantha wanted to object. She needed to stay away from Connor and discourage any additional familiarity. But Marion's black eyes were mesmerizing and she nodded her head in obedience.

"We'll be back at sunrise," Marion promised softly.

He was gone as suddenly as he had appeared, as were the other shadowy figures. The noise of man was replaced by the expanding chorus of crickets and the deep hungry croak of bullfrogs. The wind whispered menacingly through the heavy growth, and the moss sent weblike shadows dancing over the ground.

The forest sounds seemed magnified. Samantha jumped at the hoot of a nearby owl and shivered at the rustling of unknown night creatures. Suddenly, Marion's order did not seem such a bad idea.

She found Connor's resting place. He was sleeping again, peacefully, his face free of the pain that had haunted it earlier. She gently felt his forehead. It was cool to the touch, but her hand felt as if it were on fire. She stared at him as the moonlight played over his face.

She studied his features. He was uncommonly handsome now that the ragged beard was gone. Each feature was strongly defined: a fine straight nose over a wide mouth and a determined chin. There was strength in his face, but it was tempered by humor and a quiet warmth. It was a good face, and it seemed no place for the hate he was harboring.

Despite her best intentions, she didn't want to leave his closeness. She gathered her own blanket and settled several yards away, near enough to hear if he needed anything, yet far enough away to escape the lightning that seemed to strike her every time she ventured too close.

Closing her eyes, she joined Connor in a world that precluded worry and pain.

Connor woke early the next morning as Marion's brigade returned successfully to camp. He was surprised to see the boy a few feet away, despite his hostility the night before. A slight smile played over his face as he deduced it was the night sounds that had brought Sam so close. The boy's smudged face looked peaceful and innocent, and Connor felt a surge of protectiveness.

True to his word, Connor spent the morning teaching Sam the difference between a musket and a pistol.

Marion's raid during the night had netted his camp a number of new weapons from a British supply train, as well as badly needed powder. They would keep the powder and trade some of the muskets to the rebel Colonel Thomas Sumter for blankets.

Connor showed Samantha how to measure the powder charge correctly and shake it into the pistol, and he watched carefully as she tried on her own. She listened and observed intently, understanding instantly and quickly repeating the technique perfectly, winning a smile from Connor.

Connor pointed at a target, and Samantha aimed carefully, pulling the trigger slowly as instructed. A flicker of disappointment and shame crossed her face as the bullet went far off its mark.

"Remember," Connor said, "a pistol is not a rifle. It doesn't have the accuracy. You have to allow for that. Always make sure your target is close enough to hit, because you only have that one shot. Try again." Connor's patience lasted the morning, and he secretly applauded the young boy's growing skill with the cumbersome weapon. The boy now knew the range in which he could realistically expect to kill or cripple a target, and Connor felt he could adequately protect himself.

"Well done," he said finally. "I would be proud to travel the river with you."

Samantha knew that was high praise indeed and could not restrain her wide grin of pride. Connor was suddenly aware of her blue eyes, and they struck him like a sword. They reminded him of Brendan. His face clouded and his mouth tightened. It would not do to get too close to the boy; he didn't know if he could survive another loss. And yet there was something about him that demanded his attention and care. Gratitude, perhaps, but there was something more. Caring about someone made him feel alive again.

Neither of them had time to think much about each other in the next few weeks. Marion had ordered the camp moved. It was a technique he used to keep the British confused. He constantly moved his men from one site to another and prepared traps in the previous locations. If the traps were sprung, the location would be abandoned and not reused at a later date.

Connor had held the rank of major in the militia, and Marion now restored it, making him one of his top aides. Samantha, with her way with "'orses," was assigned to care for the animals. She was happy with her duties. It kept her busy and useful and, more important, away from Connor. Any doubts that Marion or others had about the young newcomer disappeared with her careful tending of the animals.

Sometimes several days would pass before Samantha would do more than catch a glimpse of Connor. She kept to herself, avoiding friendly overtures and disappearing with the golden mare for hours at a time. No one wondered or worried about her any longer. It was her own business as long as she carried her own weight, and they all agreed she did.

October disappeared into November, and Samantha was forced to share a tent with Billy James when the rains came. She was carefully polite with him, never inviting confidences but feeling more and more comfortable with Billy's acceptance of her reticence. Billy never pried and it was a quality she appreciated.

The routine was almost always the same. When there was a raid, Marion and his men would leave after sunset and return at dawn, bringing with them British supplies and sometimes American prisoners rescued from British hands. Some would stay on while others made their way back home. When there were no raids at night, there was music and dancing, tall tales and card games.

It was a world in which Samantha became increasingly comfortable. But when Connor approached her, she would always find an excuse to disappear on an errand. Her studied avoidance puzzled him, but he himself was busy. Marion had made him his contact with General Greene's army in North Carolina and he was often gone from camp.

His absences were hard on Samantha. Despite the cautious inner voice that helped her to keep her distance, she was drawn to him by some inexplicable need.

Early in September, posters had appeared on the main streets of every occupied city and town, offering a reward of one thousand guineas for information that would lead to the capture of "one Francis Marion, who styles himself a brigadier general of the rebel militia." Less than a week later, the towns woke up to discover the posters had been replaced by similar handbills, so recently printed that on some the ink was not yet dry. The new ones offered one thousand continental dollars for information leading to the apprehension of "one Charles Cornwallis, who styles himself a major general of foreign troops that have dared to invade the sacred soil of South Carolina." They were signed by Francis Marion, brigadier general, militia of South Carolina.

Angered by the impudent gesture, Cornwallis agreed to a personal bodyguard and additional rewards for the rebels who were known to serve under Marion.

The reward offered for Connor was seven hundred guineas in gold, and Samantha lived in constant fear that someone would try to claim it, especially when he was off by himself.

Samantha's face lighted up with joy as she watched Connor ride into camp on the first day of December. He had been gone nearly two weeks. She saw his eyes search the camp and fasten on her with a slow smile. Instantly she replaced her own smile with the mask she had perfected.

Connor's smile didn't falter, and he rode directly to her, dismounting lazily, his searching eyes taking in her disheveled appearance. "I have a small present for you."

Samantha shuffled her feet before responding. "Thought ya might be lost," she said finally.

Connor's smile reached his eyes. "You missed me then," he said, his gray eyes twinkling at the unwilling admission.

"Didna say that. Jest thought ya might be lost."

"Here." Connor thrust a package at her. "We'll look at them later... I have to see Francis."

Samantha looked suspiciously at the package, her blue eyes veiled. "Doan need ennythin'." All the same, Connor couldn't miss the way she clutched the small bundle.

"I know you don't," he said gently at the show of pride. "But I just happened to find these and thought we could work on them together."

Connor put his hand on her shoulder, but she squirmed out of his reach. "I'll see you later," he promised, and strode over to meet the approaching Marion. The two exchanged greetings, then disappeared into the woods, their heads together, their voices lowered.

Samantha stared at the package in her hands. Disappearing into a small thicket where she could hide from ever-watchful eyes, she unwrapped the package and found two reading primers. She couldn't help giggling to herself. Connor had apparently decided to teach her to read . . . she, who had haunted her father's library, one of the largest in the colonies. No book, magazine or newspaper had been safe from her thirsty mind.

Her giggles grew quiet as she wondered how she would handle this latest problem. How could she stumble through something she knew so well without appearing either too stupid or too smart. "Damn."

Her expression surprised her. She was even beginning to think like her companions. Never, in her past life, would she have thought of cursing. The idiocy of the whole upside-down world struck her. A full-throated laugh escaped her, signaling her whereabouts to the man who had come in search of her.

She felt his presence before she saw him, and the laughter came to a quick end.

Connor stood in front of her, a puzzled look on his face. He had never heard the youngster laugh before, and he liked the sound of it. He tipped his head to one side, ready to hear the reason for it.

Samantha returned his stare, her face solemn, and Connor wondered if he'd imagined the sound.

"Doan need these," she said, casting a suspicious eye at the books beside her. "Know all I need to."

Connor's voice grew impatient. "I know...you know 'orses and how to shoot, and you know the woods. But you need more. After the war, this country will be hungry for educated men. You can do anything you want to do."

"I'm doin' wha' I want," she replied stubbornly. "You ain't my pa."

Connor's eyes flickered dangerously. He had decided to help this boy and, by God, that was what he was going to do. With or without Sam's cooperation.

"What he should have done," Connor said quietly, his patience coming to an end, "was taught you some manners."

Samantha saw the determined glint in Connor's eyes and made ready for flight. Unfortunately, Connor saw her intent just as quickly. His hand fastened on hers like a steel band. She stopped struggling and stared up at him with the look of a trapped animal.

Connor instantly dropped his arm. "It's for you, Sam," he said, not completely comprehending her sudden defenselessness.

But she was gone. Connor sighed, frustrated, and picked up the books. There would be another time.

Connor slept several hours and woke just before sunset. There was to be a raid tonight. Fran had received information about the transfer of a badly needed load of salt. He welcomed the prospect of activity; it would keep his mind away from thoughts of his family and of the elusive Sam.

They rode out as dusk settled around the forest. Samantha and Billy James were left to see to the remaining stock. Samantha had not yet gone on an expedition and was not eager to do so. Uncertain as to whether she would actually be able to shoot someone, even a redcoat, even Foxworth, she was not anxious to test herself.

The night was bright, the moon full in a cloudless sky. Billy was teaching her some of the finer points of card playing when a series of whistles announced a visitor. From the signals, both knew it was someone to be trusted though not a member of the band. They stood ready, rifles within reach.

Samantha almost shouted as Hector rode in, smiling as he recognized his former mistress. His smile, however, came and went quickly, and he addressed Billy James directly.

"Colonel Marion's riding into a trap," he said. "I heard them talking in the corral. Colonel Tarleton planted the information. You've got to stop them."

Samantha's admiration for Billy soared. The boy quickly absorbed the information and melted into the woods to speak to the sentries. Several were recruited to accompany them, others ordered to stay at their posts.

"Come on, Sam," Billy ordered. "Your horse is the fastest," he added, knowing that the gold mare would let no one else ride her. "I'll lead you out of the swamp, and you race for Marion from there. He's at the Garrison place."

She needed no urging. Connor was in danger. So was Marion, whom she had come to admire greatly. She stuck a pistol in her belt and quickly saddled Sundance.

She and the others were ready at the same time, and Billy handed her a rifle, which she slid into a holster in front of her. She chafed at the slow pace out of the swamp, but she realized the necessity; there were patches of quicksand and false trails everywhere.

It seemed hours before they reached solid ground. Billy had given her directions and she urged Sundance to a gallop immediately. Only too clearly did she remember that last time they had raced to prevent a disaster. It couldn't be too late this time.

It couldn't be.

Chapter Seven

Francis Marion, Connor O'Neill and Peter Horry rode at the front of the column. Francis always led; no one knew the terrain as he did, and he could pass through the swamps as quickly and confidently as others followed defined roads on hard ground.

There was anticipation this trip. Their quarry was salt, a commodity now more important than gold. The British had captured all the sources, and salt was as vital to life as water. The patriot sympathizers were suffering as much from its lack as Marion's men, and the capture of several wagonloads would lift the spirits of the entire countryside. It would also teach the British a much-needed lesson about hoarding.

One of Marion's spies had heard in Georgetown of a shipment of salt destined for the Garrison Plantation, a Tory stronghold. It was to have a fairly small guard since the Garrison farm was some distance from Snow Island and believed to be relatively safe.

Marion's brigade was now accustomed to all-night rides, and their reach was growing longer each week. The salt was well worth the extra effort.

Dawn was just breaking over the hills when they sighted the Garrison place. Connor rode back to the others, warning them to stay in the trees until the three of them could scout out the farm.

As promised, wagons were lined up in front of the rambling home, but it was quiet...too quiet.

Marion watched carefully from the trees, his eyes searching for the tiniest movement.

Something was very wrong. It was dawn, yet there was no crowing of roosters, none of the movement expected of an awakening farm, no smoke from a fireplace being readied for a morning meal.

He saw a quick movement behind a barn and caught a glimpse of green. Just then, Connor returned from a quick survey of the surrounding area.

"It's alive with Tarleton's Tories," he said.

"It's a trap," Horry agreed, arriving back with a similar report.

Marion looked at the two men. "We'll let them believe we've sprung it," he said softly.

"Connor, you take thirty men back into the woods. Peter, you take another fifty and establish an ambush down the road. I'll take the rest and ride in. Just before we get to the clearing, I want Connor to fire a rifle. Let them think one of their men was too eager. My group will make a run for it, and hopefully most of Tarleton's men will come after me. Then you move in, Connor, and take the wagons. We'll keep them busy down the road."

Marion waited twenty minutes to give Horry's men time to ready the ambush. He then innocently led the remaining force toward the farmhouse.

A low whistle alerted the Tories in the farmhouse and barn, and they were preparing to lift and sight their muskets when a shot rang out.

Tarleton, dressed in green and covering the front upstairs window, swore under his breath. He watched as Marion quickly turned his horse and dashed back into the woods. He could hear the drumbeat of the retreating horses.

He turned to William Foxworth. "I'm going after him. You stay here with ten men and guard the wagons. And find out who fired that shot. I want him court-martialed." He was wild with anger and frustration and didn't wait for Foxworth's acknowledgement.

His dragoons were already mounting the saddled horses that had been secreted in the barn. Three minutes after Marion turned tail, Tarleton and his dragoons were in pursuit.

Connor watched from his vantage point. He had reloaded his rifle and every instinct was now ready for action. He could feel the restlessness of the men behind him, but it was vital that Tarleton be caught in Marion's trap before he sprung his own. He observed the movement behind the windows of the farmhouse and knew that Tarleton had left a small guard of indeterminate size. He wished he knew exactly how many. His men would be excellent targets for those hiding in the farmhouse. Abruptly he made a decision. Signalling to three other men to dismount, he slid from his horse. The four men talked for several minutes before filtering through the trees toward the farmhouse.

Connor and his three companions carefully approached the back of the house, running from tree to tree. Finally, crouching close to the ground, they reached the back door without raising the alarm. Connor tried the latch while the others covered him. There was no response and they quickly entered a back hall. Connor put his finger to his lips, then spread his fingers, indicating they would all count to ten before striking.

Connor and one of his men took the stairs. At the count of six, they reached the top and looked through an open door. A British officer, dressed in the green of Tarleton's dragoons, was facing the window, three Tories beside him.

Eight...nine...ten. Connor and his companion quietly entered the door and, as they heard a crash from downstairs, cocked their pistols. The sounds were ominous in the small room, and the four at the window straightened, one turning his gun on Connor.

At the sight of two men, both with pistols pointing in their direction, the Tory who had raised his gun dropped it.

"You gentlemen will do the same," Connor said softly, his eyes steely. "Now!" The last was directed at the British officer. Connor watched them as they dropped their pistols and unbuckled their swords, all four struggling against the anger of being taken so easily. Connor went to the door and yelled down, "Daniel...Mick..."

"All's well down here," both said.

Connor looked at his captives. "How many more are there?"

"Enough to keep you here," Foxworth sneered.

"Perhaps," Connor said easily. "We'll see." He ordered his companion to tie the four men while he kept them covered. Three of them were hog-tied, hands and feet, but when they reached Foxworth, Connor stopped them. "Just tie his hands behind his back. I have use for him."

Foxworth's eyes glared with hate across the room. "I'll not help you, you damned rebel."

"You don't have a choice," Connor said softly, "Colonel . . . ?"

"Foxworth . . . William Foxworth. Remember it, because I'll see you hang if it's the last thing I do."

"It might just be that, colonel," Connor replied. "Especially if you don't do as you are told."

"May I know who you are?"

Connor laughed. "Does it make any difference?"

"I like to know my enemy."

"O'Neill," Connor said. "Connor O'Neill, major, South Carolina militia." He didn't expect the shock that registered on the officer's face, but it was gone as quickly as it came, and there was no time to wonder about it.

Taking one of Foxworth's arms, he propelled him toward the door. "You and I," Connor said, "are going to check the rest of the farm together."

Foxworth struggled, but his hands were bound tightly behind him, and O'Neill's grip was like steel. He had no choice but to walk alongside the man, cursing him every step of the way. So this was O'Neill . . . the man Robert Chatham hated so viciously.

Once the captured Tories downstairs were also bound and gagged, Connor pushed Foxworth out into the yard and toward the barn, signaling the remaining riders in the woods to approach. As they came close, Connor told them to take the salt-laden wagons. He and his three would locate any British stragglers. He watched as his men hitched four horses to each of the wagons and disappeared down the back road.

He then led the struggling Foxworth to the barn as one of Marion's men followed behind them. The other two stationed themselves at the back and front of the main house.

Connor was nearly to the barn door when he heard a voice drawl, "That's far enough...."

Connor heard a shot and saw Mick, the man behind him, fall. Taking advantage of Connor's surprise, Foxworth twisted out of his grip and, falling, rolled away from him, leaving Connor a prime target.

Samantha reached the Garrison farm just as Connor was leading Foxworth toward the barn. From her position, she could see what Connor could not ... a musket extending from the loft of the barn. She heard a voice and saw Mick drop. The man in the loft dropped his spent weapon and reached for another. Without hesitation, she drew her rifle and spurred Sundance into range. Gone was her fear of firing. Gone was everything but the need to protect Connor. The attention of the Tory in the barn was concentrated on the man below him. He never saw the rider, or the rifle, or the bullet that entered between his shoulders.

Connor turned and stared at the slight figure on the gold horse. He couldn't stop the smile that spread over his face, despite his concern. "Damn good shot," he said as she approached him. "My thanks once more."

Samantha didn't answer. Her attention was suddenly focused on the British officer on the ground. The man's eyes were glittering with hatred and for one instant she thought she saw in them a flicker of confused recognition.

She wheeled the horse and without a word disappeared back into the woods, leaving Connor puzzled. He forced Foxworth up and into the barn, this time using every ounce of caution. Finding it empty except for six horses and the dead body in the loft, he tied Foxworth securely to a post and gagged him for good measure. He took the horses, leading them over to Mick, who was now standing, clutching his shoulder, which bled profusely.

"Let's get out of here," Connor said. Whistling to the sentries by the house, he helped Mick onto a horse. When the two

others appeared, Connor was already astride. Each grabbed a
horse and swung themselves on, and leading the rest of the
British horses, they galloped down the road after the salt wagons.

The various groups of Marion's brigade straggled back late
that evening. The ambush had been successful. Tarleton, in his
eagerness to capture Marion, rode straight into its midst, and
Tory losses were heavy, though Tarleton himself escaped. But
the arrogant Englishman had been unable to follow his neme-
sis and was left cursing his tired wounded troops and swearing
revenge.

Samantha and Billy were among the first in. She had never,
she thought, been so long in the saddle, and every muscle in her
body ached. As she dismounted, she slipped awkwardly and fell
in a small heap at Sundance's feet. Embarrassed, she couldn't
restrain a small nervous giggle, more from tension than any real
desire to laugh. Then the giggles exploded into laughter as she
thought of herself lying in the dust in the middle of the woods
after killing a person. Billy recognized her reaction for what it
was, the residue of a hard bitter day, and instinctively knew it
was his companion's first blooding. He had felt much the same
the first time he had killed a man. He reached out his hand,
grasping hers, and pulled her up, wondering at her lightness.

Billy's regard for his reclusive tent mate had magnified a
hundredfold during the night. Being fifty yards behind her, he
had not seen the rifle pointed at Connor and had not realized
what was happening until he heard the shot and saw a man
crumple in the loft of the barn. It was a spectacular shot for
anyone, and it said much for Sam's quick reflexes and steady
nerve. Billy had also been impressed with Sam's riding ability
during the day, and uncomplaining nature. All his earlier
doubts were gone and he wanted, more than he realized, for
them to be real friends.

Samantha, for her part, was completely drained. She wasn't
sure, but there was a possibility that Foxworth had recognized
her. If so, it could mean nothing but trouble. She was surprised she felt no regret at killing another person, and her lack
of feeling shocked her. She remembered Marion's words and

felt that something might be wrong with her. Her aim had not been killing the Tory but protecting Connor. As she struggled to justify her action, she was grateful for Billy's silent but sympathetic company.

She soon discovered exhaustion was not hers alone. They were all too tired to do more than munch on the inevitable potatoes and kernels of dry corn. Tomorrow there would be hunting parties because they now had salt with which to preserve the meat. Despite their weariness, none slept. They were filled with exhilaration at their prize and with the tension from the violence, and the combination was too potent for sleep to come easily. Instead, they huddled in small groups, recounting the day's events, while Angus McIntyre played wistful airs on his fiddle.

Samantha had seen little of Connor since he rode in with Marion. She had watched as he first saw to Mick's care, then to protecting the precious salt from the threatening rain. He later huddled with Marion and Horry, planning for distribution of the salt. She was glad for the respite; she didn't want to have to answer questions about her abrupt departure from the Garrison place. Most of all, she didn't want his gratitude. Whatever she did, she owed it, and more. She would never be able to pay for her family's injustice to him.

By the time Connor had finally completed all his work and gone to look for her, Samantha had climbed into the small tent she shared with Billy. She pretended to sleep when she heard his whisper and was grateful to Billy, who shooed him away. Somehow, she would face him tomorrow.

She left the tent early the next morning . . . just as dawn was breaking. A slight mist gave everything a soft blurred look, and she breathed deeply of the air bathed with the fragrant smoky scent of late fall. She found Sundance and fed her some of the precious grain she had been hoarding. Without saddling the horse, she took the mare from the corral and mounted her from the rough fence. She used her knees and her hands on Sundance's mane to direct the mare down to the river and along the bank. Although it seemed she was alone in the world, she knew that Marion's pickets were probably aware of her progress. She dismounted at a particularly lovely spot. A willow tree, still green despite the lateness of the year, sparkled with tiny slivers of water. In the quiet of the morning she could hear the flutter of birds as they hunted their breakfast. The untouched peace of the spot contrasted with the violence and death of yesterday, and salted tears mingled with the soft mist that washed her face.

She felt the hand on her chin before she saw him; his steps had been so quiet even Sundance hadn't warned her.

She looked up slightly, her eyes meeting Francis Marion's.

"Tears?" he asked gently.

She could only meet his stare headlong without denial.

Marion placed his jacket on a fallen tree to protect them from the dampness. Urging her to sit, he then took the place next to her.

"You did very well yesterday," he said softly. "As well as any of my men. You saw a danger, and you met it. There is no need for sadness or regret."

He looked into her blue eyes, and Samantha thought suddenly that he could read her very mind. There was nothing she could hide from him . . . but she must. She ducked her head.

"Is it killing that Tory?"

"No," Sam replied honestly. "He was going to kill O'Neill."

Marion sighed. No one could miss the attachment the boy had for O'Neill. But why couldn't Sam Taylor just accept Connor's friendship? Was he afraid of rejection? Certainly Connor had not given him any reason to believe that; in fact, his friend was frustrated at his failure to reach the boy.

"Can you tell me about what's troubling you?" he asked quietly. "We've come to value you highly, you know. All of us."

Samantha's tears increased. She was glad the mist had turned into a soft rain, but she knew even the rain couldn't disguise the misery in her face.

"'Tis nothing . . ." she said finally, grateful for his concern but unable to confide in him. "I thank ya for yer bother."

Marion was more puzzled than ever. Despite the seeming delicacy of the lad, he had been untiring, uncomplaining and efficient. Yesterday he had proved his mettle. Connor had told him the boy had real worth, but he had never expected the quality he was finding, nor the sensitivity. It worried him more than a little. And he didn't know why.

"I don't know about you," Marion said finally, "but I'm hungry. I've sent some men to check traps and if we have fresh meat, you will share it with me."

Samantha looked up gratefully, a small smile on her face. "I would like that," she said in a low voice.

Again, something rang a bell in Marion's head. The voice, usually rough and simple, seemed cultured. He dismissed the thought. Almost every one of his small band had something to hide; this lad probably had less than most.

As they walked back, Marion could not keep his eyes from the gold mare that walked so docilely behind the boy.

"I wish you could help me train my horses that well," he remarked, shaking his head.

"Jest takes time...'n 'fection," she answered.

"I don't think it's quite that easy," Marion said. "Like Connor said, you seem to have a knack for horses." He turned serious. "You can do whatever you want, stay here and take care of the horses or ride with us. Anytime."

Samantha looked at him solemnly. She knew the words meant total acceptance, and she felt shame at her deception. She just nodded.

The smell of roasting meat met them. The traps had indeed yielded some prizes. There were a number of rabbits and a score of possum. A wild boar had also been found in one and was now being butchered for a feast tonight.

Marion waited as Samantha put Sundance back in the corral and they walked together into the clearing. Marion saw Connor start their way but shook his head, warning him away. He suspected the boy wasn't ready for Connor.

The pair served themselves some rabbit and hominy. For a reason neither could explain, they felt comfortable together. Although their meeting had yielded no answers, there was a quiet understanding between them.

Samantha was the hero of the day. Everyone had heard of her timely appearance and extraordinary shot, and those who had been put off by her reticence gathered around to offer their congratulations. She accepted them awkwardly...shy-ly...and gained more friends by her modesty. To rid herself of the unwanted notice, she finally crept back into the tent and slept away the rest of the day.

Chapter Eight

Fury filled the room as the two men faced each other in the dark mahogany study at Chatham Oaks.

"I want to know where she is!" Foxworth didn't even try to temper his tone. It had risen steadily during the past ten minutes as he sought answers he wasn't getting.

"I've told you all that I am going to," Chatham said. "You have no right to demand anything." He was growing increasingly angry with Foxworth's arrogance and persistence. He had no idea where his headstrong daughter had gone, none at all. He had contacted everyone he knew, without success. She had disappeared into thin air and his ignorance did not improve his temper.

"She wanted to get away and think," Chatham added. "She asked that I not tell anyone her whereabouts."

"Not even her betrothed?" Foxworth said scathingly. "I don't believe you."

"I think," Chatham said, his voice now just as haughty as Foxworth's, "that you are the reason she wanted time to consider the engagement. And now I am beginning to see why!" His eyes burned through his companion's. He was not used to being questioned in this rude manner.

Foxworth returned the angry glare. "I don't think you know where she is . . . in fact, I might know more than you." He did not miss Chatham's quick startled response.

Could it be true? Foxworth thought. Could Chatham really not know his daughter's whereabouts? Perhaps that momentary thought yesterday . . . but no . . . it could not be. No girl could shoot like that. But Samantha *could* ride. He had watched her several times and noticed the oneness between the girl and her horse. That's what had placed the nagging thought in his mind yesterday. The horse. There could not be another like it, not in this parish.

He abruptly changed the subject. "That horse Samantha liked so much, what has happened to it?"

Chatham stared at his visitor in surprise. Foxworth had never before declared any interest in horses. It had been the one thing, in fact, he disliked about the man. He seemed to abuse horses, and Chatham, if nothing else, appreciated good horseflesh.

He answered slowly, suspecting a motive behind the question. "She was stolen not long after Samantha left on her trip."

"I think I might know where your horse is," he said slyly.

"Where?" Chatham demanded. The disappearance of the mare had vexed him as thoroughly as that of Samantha.

"With Marion," Foxworth said. "I saw it at Garrison's place when Marion raided it. A young boy was riding him," he added, his eyes never leaving Chatham's. "There was someone else there."

Chatham refused to humor him. He shrugged as if it were a matter of great indifference.

"O'Neill," Foxworth said. "Connor O'Neill. He is a major with that rabble."

The British colonel watched with malicious pleasure as Chatham's face blanched. "You are sure?"

"He introduced himself...tall, blond, cold gray eyes. I must say he didn't look as if prison affected him overmuch."

"You let him get away?"

"My dear Robert, I couldn't very well do anything else. He had a gun on me." Foxworth's lips tightened as he remembered his humiliation. "They don't fight like gentlemen. But don't worry, I'll get him, and Marion, as well." He watched Chatham under his slightly lowered lashes. "And we'll get that boy who's riding with them and with him your horse."

Chatham's interest in the horse had dissipated. His only concern now was O'Neill. The man must know of his role in his imprisonment and the confiscation of Glen Woods. He must double his guard. Suddenly he wanted his guest gone; he hated the supercilious look and haughty attitude that conveyed, more directly than words, the man's disdain for South Carolinians, whether loyal to the king or not. Maybe he *had* been wrong in pursuing his daughter's marriage with this man.

In any event, he had no more patience with the officer. There were more important things to consider now with O'Neill free. He never once wondered at the identity of the boy on Sundance...the thought that it could be Samantha didn't enter his mind.

"After your experience of yesterday, you must want rest," he said to Foxworth. There was sly maliciousness in his voice, but he was too distracted by the news of O'Neill to enjoy Foxworth's discomfort at this moment. "I'll see you out."

Frustrated at his inability to pierce Chatham's silence and learn more of Samantha's whereabouts, Foxworth nodded curtly. "If you hear anything from your daughter..."

"When she decides to see you, I'll let you know," Chatham said, wondering at that moment if he himself would ever see his daughter again.

After Foxworth had taken his leave, Chatham wandered about the empty house. Despite the past bitter year, he missed his daughter's presence. The realization stunned him.

When his wife had died eight years earlier, he had sworn he would never love again. He knew he could never survive another heartbreak as complete as he had suffered then.

Robert Chatham had never thought himself capable of love after his strict and joyless childhood. A younger son, he had been barely tolerated in a house dominated by dissension. His parents' marriage had been one of convenience and their dislike for each other grew with time. His mother had had numerous affairs, his father mistresses, and in between they had exchanged accusations and blows. They were too busy for their children, too busy even to carefully select their governesses and tutors, and Chatham's earliest memories were of abuse. He had eventually escaped to the colonies, where his drive and intelligence were finally appreciated. But the scars remained, and he guarded his privacy and freedom jealously. Until he met Elizabeth Matthews.

They met at a party, and he had been fascinated with the lively young beauty who had her choice of young men. He knew he was dour and humorless and was startled when she showed interest in him. He never knew it was the challenge that he presented that had interested her. And then her curiosity turned into love, and Elizabeth Matthews, against all advice and counsel, married the cool Englishman.

Chatham, for his part, felt like a moth attracted to the flame. Nothing else existed in his world but the warm, laughing Elizabeth. When a daughter appeared, he resented the intrusion and begrudged every moment the child took of Elizabeth's time. His jealousy increased, as did his obsession with Elizabeth, and he did what he could to limit her friendships and contact with others.

Because of her love, Elizabeth acceded to his wishes, with the exception of Margaret O'Neill, who had been her schoolmate and lifelong friend. She loved Margaret like a sister and had watched fondly as her daughter, Samantha, and Margaret's son, Brendan, became inseparable. The two of them giggled over a marriage between the two, a fond dream that had made them even closer. Because of her husband's prejudice against the O'Neills' Irish roots and his opposition to any real friendship Elizabeth might have, she often kept their visits secret.

Fever broke out throughout the parish and nearly every household was affected. Elizabeth learned that Margaret was very ill and, without a moment's hesitation, ordered a carriage. She found her friend nearly dead with the fever and the usually laughter-filled house dark and somber.

She barely recognized Margaret, who was struggling for every breath. Her green eyes were huge in her white and pain-etched face. Her smile was a grimace.

Maggie O'Neill died later that day. Elizabeth Chatham, desolate and alone, arrived home to a furious husband. He refused to listen to her explanation and ordered her confined to her bedroom while he slept elsewhere. His anger was so complete that he missed the flush in her face and the feverish brightness in her eyes. When a maid brought her breakfast the next morning, she found her mistress unconscious. Elizabeth followed her friend into death by only two days.

Robert Chatham sat alone in their room for several days after his wife's death, nursing one bottle of brandy after another. At first he blamed himself; if he had noticed the signs, perhaps a doctor could have saved his wife. But that thought was too painful, too unbearable, and in his guilt he sought someone to blame. The O'Neills. They had brought the fever into his house.

On the third day, he took his pistol and rode to Glen Woods. The house was shuttered, and a black wreath sadly decorated the front door. Bolstered by the brandy, Chatham didn't stop to knock but threw open the front door.

"O'Neill," he roared.

The sound roused Gerald O'Neill from his stupor. He, like Chatham, had been drowning his sorrow in a bottle. Connor, working in the barn, also heard the shout and came running.

O'Neill stumbled from his second-floor bedroom to the top of the stairs and stood there confused, staring at Chatham. "You!" he exclaimed with surprise. Then his face crumbled. "Elizabeth ... I heard ... I'm sorry, Chatham."

"You killed her," Chatham said distinctly, venom in every word. "And now I'm going to kill you." He carefully leveled his gun, aiming at O'Neill's heart, just as Connor came flying through the front door. Immediately comprehending the situation, Connor dived for Chatham's arm, just as the gun discharged. The impact spoiled Chatham's aim, and the bullet went into Gerald O'Neill's arm.

Connor wrestled the older man to the ground, hitting him several times before Chatham stopped struggling. Connor rose slowly, clutching his neighbor's arm tightly and forcing him out the door. He pushed Chatham down the steps and followed him to his horse.

"I should kill you, Chatham," he said quietly, watching the older man mount. "It is only because of your wife that I don't. But I warn you ... if you ever step foot on Glen Woods again, I won't let that stop me."

Chatham's face twisted in helpless rage. "You Irish bastards ... you killed Elizabeth and I'll see you rot in hell for it."

Connor looked at him coolly, his gray eyes like flint. "I have no doubt you'll be there, too, after the way you treated your wife. At least now she will be free of you, but I feel sorry for your daughter."

At that, Chatham tried to run Connor down with his horse, but Connor was prepared and quickly sidestepped.

"You stay away from Samantha...all of you stay away from her or I'll finish what I started," Chatham yelled, and then he dug his heels into the horse's side and galloped down the drive.

After that day, Chatham had stopped living in every way except breathing. His daughter grew up, much as he had, under the tutelage of strangers. He resented her presence and never missed her when she stole away to spend time with Brendan, or Hector, or to ride her horse.

And then she was seventeen, and he had found a use for her. He needed an heir. And that meant a marriage for Samantha, to the right kind of husband, one English-born with English values and loyalties.

When a servant told him of Samantha's meetings with Brendan, he had become so enraged that he disregarded the consequences to his daughter's reputation. He sought out Brendan O'Neill and accused him publicly of seducing his daughter, making it impossible for the proud young man to avoid a duel. The result had filled him with vengeful joy.

That joy had faded somewhat when he set himself to the task of finding a suitable husband for Samantha. He discovered that by destroying her reputation he had made a "good" marriage highly unlikely. No one wanted soiled goods, particularly when it was known throughout the parish. Foxworth's interest had seemed the perfect solution.

So why, he wondered as he paced the house, was he having second thoughts about Foxworth? And why, after all these years, was he feeling the ache of loneliness?

Chapter Nine

Connor rubbed his side. It had been nearly two months since the wound but it still caused him pain, and a long ride increased the discomfort.

He eased from the saddle, his long lean form reflecting the deep weariness he felt. He had been thirty hours in the saddle and both he and his horse were nearly numb from exhaustion.

Even Marion, who never seemed to tire, was stumbling as he walked from the corral. The others were dismounting as slowly as Connor, each concentrating on every move.

Suddenly Samantha was there, her small intense face hidden in the predawn darkness. She took Connor's horse. "I'll rub 'im down fer ya," she offered.

Connor merely nodded, too tired to argue. He reached Marion, and their eyes met.

"We pricked them well this time," Marion said. "There's not a place they'll feel safe now."

"But we paid a price."

"We always do," Marion said. "But there are now five hundred Americans free that were not yesterday. They will be joining Greene or Washington...and now every American prisoner will have hope."

"I wish we could have enlisted some. We need more men."

"They never would have made it back, they weren't horsemen." Marion gave Connor rare praise. "Not like you...."

Connor nodded his appreciation for the compliment. "I'll be getting some sleep. You, too, I hope."

"I'll just check the pickets. We'll move camp again tomorrow. The British will be active after last night. We did more than sting their pride."

The two men separated and Connor made his way to his tent. Early winter weather was often uncertain and wet, and they were all using the tents stolen from the English. He crawled into the small space, disregarding the rumbling of his stomach. Nothing was more important at the moment than sleep and rest for his sore muscles. As he started to turn, his hand hit a plate and cup. He searched it and found food and wine. Mindless of where it came from, he gratefully swallowed a draught of the wine and quickly consumed the bread and jam, feeling the ache in his stomach disappearing.

Just before he fell asleep, he wondered momentarily about the good samaritan. It had to be Sam. Damn the boy, anyway. He was so giving, yet he would never let Connor help him in return. Tomorrow he would have a talk with the stubborn, elusive Sam Taylor.

Once again, it was not to be. When Connor finally rolled from his tent, the camp was already moving. Samantha and Billy James had gone ahead with the extra horses, and Connor was ordered to stay behind to see to the setting of the traps: deep pits covered by brush, nets set to envelop the curious, rope snares that would sling an unwary stranger up by a foot. The men were all expert at setting them by now and needed little supervision. Connor insured there was nothing left behind, not a bullet or scrap of clothing or even a bone. Finally, he swung up onto his horse and led the others to Marion's new camp on the bank of a tributary of the Pee Dee.

Like the others, the new spot was well off the path of traveled waterways yet adjacent to fresh water and good hunting. When Connor arrived, work parties were digging latrines and putting up tents. The sound of rifles told Connor hunting parties had been sent out. There was little worry that their shots would alert the enemy of their location. The swamps muffled and distorted sound, and anyone who tried to follow the pattern of rifle or musket shots would find himself hopelessly lost in the dangerous swamplands.

The swamps *were* dangerous for those who didn't know them. The lowlands were home to every type of snake known to the colonies. The reptiles were so numerous that hunters often heard them dropping into the water at night, and an unwary trespasser was in constant danger. There were also wild boar, who had little fear of man and would attack without provocation. Panther, bears, wolves... all were more at home here than the intrusive two-legged animals who had disrupted their domain. And then there was the quicksand.

It took a particular kind of person to live here, Connor thought. It was a lonely, dangerous, barren life in a hostile, though often lovely, environment. Fever was so prevalent that Francis Marion drank vinegar daily, swearing it warded off infection. Indeed, it seemed to work for him, for he, unlike most of the others, was never felled by illness. But though he often urged the others to follow his suit, no one could seem to force the wretched liquid down their gullets on a regular basis.

Thoughts filtered through Connor's mind as he entered the new camp. He had been surprised at how easily Sam Taylor had adapted, and without complaint, despite an often inadequate diet and uncomfortable shelter. In fact, his calm acceptance had separated him from the majority of the men, who grumbled long and hard about everything from the food to the nightly rides.

The boy had long since been wholly accepted. He worked hard with the horses, always willing to take on a new chore and often volunteering for the most menial of tasks. His performance at the Garrison place had further consolidated his support, and Connor had been both surprised and rather pleased as Marion took a special interest in him. He could have no better mentor.

But Connor was still puzzled at the way the boy continued to reject any attempt at friendship or offer of help from him. And yet the boy was always there to help when he needed him, almost a guardian angel. The thought of the rough-spoken ragamuffin as an angel gave him pause and a smile spread across his serious face.

The boy obviously had a need for privacy. He didn't use the latrine Marion insisted upon at each site, and he never bathed

with the others. He had been teased initially, but as he continued to prove his mettle, everyone had learned to respect his ec-
centric behavior and his disappearances. Not even Marion
could leave the swamp unnoticed by the pickets, but there were
many little pockets of privacy within Marion's perimeter, and
Sam had a talent for ferreting out each of them.

Amusement lurked in Connor's eyes as he remembered the
gifts in his tent last night. None could have been of greater value
at the time, and it made him all the more determined to see Sam
and thank him. He still had not thanked the boy for his intervention at the Garrison place...Sam seemed to flee every time
he came near, and Fran had warned him against pressing the
lad. That was something else again. Fran and the boy seemed
to have a special understanding, and it irked Connor that Fran
succeeded where he did not.

Connor put his horse in the newly constructed corral and
made his way to the cooking fires. There were hunks of venison roasting over the hot coals, and he cut a piece from a flank.
Thank God for fresh meat again. He ate rapidly, accepting a
cup of sour wine, before going in search of the evasive Sam,
who seemed, once again, to have made himself scarce at his
arrival.

Samantha was careful to avoid a chance meeting with Connor. He haunted her every waking moment and even those
when she tried to lose herself in sleep. She tried to tell herself
that it was only guilt she was feeling, but she had come to realize it was more than that. She melted when he smiled at her,
his gray eyes crinkling in warmth and his mouth softening from
the hard tight line it had become. It was difficult to keep from
responding in kind. So she kept her distance, though she knew
it was increasing his curiosity. Colonel Marion understood. He
never pressed her for answers, but he knew she was afraid of
something, and his quiet empathy gave her strength.

Marion had been true to his word that day in the woods and
left her to make her own decisions. She chose to stay with the
horses, where she knew she was valuable, and no one had
questioned her preference.

Time had little meaning in the swamp other than the frequent absences of the raiding parties and the endless waiting for their safe return. This last raid had been torture for her, knowing that her companions were attacking a large detachment of British troops taking prisoners from Kingstree to Georgetown. She had been elated at their safe return and glad she had thought to put the food Hector had brought earlier in Connor's tent.

Samantha wrinkled her nose as the smell of her own clothes hit her nostrils. She was still wearing the same homespun garments meant for her elopement, supplemented by an ill-fitting British jacket. There were no extra clothes to go around, particularly any that would fit her slender frame, and she feared taking them off to wash and revealing herself to someone who might chance upon her. It was much too cold to bathe in the creek with them on, so she suffered through, knowing she was not alone in her newfound slovenliness. She was among woodsmen who believed one bath a year sufficient for cleanliness and that any more invited disease. Only Marion and Connor, Majors Horry and James and young Billy seemed to make much effort toward that particular virtue.

A mischievous grin lighted her fine features. Her maid, Angel, had complained about her frequent baths and costume changes, constantly reminding her young mistress that she was inviting her death by so much unhealthy washing. According to those standards, she should certainly be healthy at the moment. Besides, she thought with certain satisfaction, the smell would definitely keep Connor at a distance.

Samantha knew she couldn't avoid Connor forever. Whenever he was in camp, she could feel his eyes following her every move, and it became a game to slip from his grasp just when he thought he might catch up with her. It was a dangerous one, because it only made him more determined.

She saw that determination as he approached her and Billy the first evening in the new camp.

"I would like a word with you, Sam," he said, his grim look permitting no argument. Billy quickly made to rise, stopping only at his friend's restraining hand. The young James looked at Connor's determined expression. Major O'Neill was his commanding officer and there was no way around the fact.

"I'll see you later, Sam," he said as he squirmed from her hold, leaving her uncomfortably defenseless.

"Ya had no right," she said finally, her eyes avoiding O'Neill's.

Connor dropped to the ground with an easy looseness and grace. Realizing how much he seemed to upset the boy, he kept his voice soft.

"How old are you, Sam?"

"Old enough," she replied noncommittally.

"Do you ever answer a question directly?" Connor said.

The urchin shrugged.

Samantha could feel Connor tense and could sense him trying to hold back his frustration.

"Someone put some food in my tent last night?" Connor attempted another tack by making it a question. It went unacknowledged.

The major attacked directly. "Was it you?"

He was surprised when he finally received an answer.

"Yes," she said simply, knowing that by the simple process of elimination Connor would discover his benefactor eventually.

"Where did it come from?"

Samantha finally looked up at him, her sea-blue eyes shrouded. "A boy seekin' the colonel . . . he brung it."

"But why me?" Connor persisted.

"Ya needed it most," she said, her eyes cast downward now. "Yer still too thin."

Amusement crept into Connor's wry smile. No one was thinner than Sam, and the boy's lean frame had become, if anything, more wiry in the past weeks.

"I'll have no more of that, Sam," he said with stern kindness. "I told you once Marion didn't take tadpoles. He might throw you back if you don't eat more."

Samantha stiffened. "He wouldn't. He and me . . . we're friends."

Connor put his hand on the boy's thin shoulder. There was a certain amount of hurt in his voice when he answered. "I wish you considered yourself my friend."

The youngster looked up at him and Connor was struck by the directness in her eyes. They were as blue as Brendan's had been, and the realization burned him like a hot poker.

The sudden pain was only too obvious to Samantha, and her face softened in understanding. She and Brendan had often teased each other about their matching eyes.

Her hand went, almost involuntarily, to Connor's arm in comfort and mutual hurt. It was gone so quickly that Connor thought he must have imagined it. But he felt a sudden empathy between them, and the weight of his emptiness lightened. He was afraid to spoil this first beginning of friendship. More than anything, he wanted to adopt this boy whose independent spirit and generosity knew few limits. After the war he would reclaim his estate and offer Sam a real home. But he knew better than to mention this now. One step at a time.

"There's a boy down on the Santee," he said finally. "John, his name is. He and his mother helped me escape. I promised him a rifle. Fran isn't planning anything for a few days, and I thought I might go down that way. I was hoping you would keep me company." He grinned. "I can't think of a better protector."

Samantha knew it was a fool's move to agree, but the sudden thought of several days with Connor made her reckless. She nodded, her blue eyes now veiled.

Connor rose, his mission accomplished. "We'll leave at dawn," he commanded.

Dourly, Samantha watched him leave, knowing that she was tempting the gods, and that the gods were seldom kind to those who mocked them.

Chapter Ten

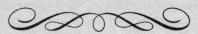

She was mad, utterly mad, Samantha berated herself the next morning as she saddled a nondescript chestnut gelding.

She tried to ignore the anxious nickering from Sundance, who hovered at her shoulder. After being shoved several times, she took a few moments to reassure the horse that she would, indeed, be back. Sundance was much too beautiful to go on *this* trip, for she would surely draw attention.

As Connor approached the corral he saw Sam talking to the golden horse. He had always been a superb rider, but never had he experienced the silent understanding Sam seemed to have with horses. They would hold still for the boy during shoeing or doctoring when they wouldn't for anyone else. The camp blacksmith thought Sam walked on water when he wasn't bewitching horses. Perhaps it was the patient care and constant affection that no one else seemed to have time for. Whatever it was, it intrigued him.

Samantha turned and her blue eyes widened with wonder at the sight of the stranger before her. Even she had trouble recognizing the Connor O'Neill she knew. A dirty blond stubble distorted his strong features and a black patch covered his left eye. It appeared she wasn't the only one who knew dye. Connor's blond hair was now an unappealing brown, and his face the blustery color of a drinking man. As she stared, he limped toward her, a twinkle in his one gray eye.

"Are you ready to help a poor cripple, wounded in the service of His Majesty?" The slow, amused, cultured voice belied the disguise and Samantha couldn't help but smile in return.

"Ya better be mute, as well," she warned, an answering tease in her voice.

Connor's voice changed to a sullen whine. "Aim to git me due...from them what owes me. 'Twas promised a rebel farm, I was, for my services...."

Samantha stifled her silent laughter but she couldn't resist an insolent observation. "'Tis sure I am that the British would love to gi' ya yer due for yer services...but I 'ardly think it be a rebel farm."

Connor laughed, delighted at her rejoinder. He gave her a playful swat.

Try as she might, Samantha couldn't still the insane exhilaration that filled her as they left the camp.

It was the most beautiful time of the day, this first glimpse of morn. For her, each dawn was a fresh beginning, and the soft pastel shades on the horizon only added a gentle sweetness. The forest celebrated life as scores of birds started their winsome songs and squirrels jumped from tree to tree with unrestrained playfulness.

Samantha shivered with the joy of being part of the primeval rhythm of the forest and the life within it. It was ever changing, ever beautiful, and this morning she felt she truly belonged.

Connor noticed the lift in her shoulders and the eagerness with which she greeted the sights surrounding her. Few saw the swamp's compelling loveliness and mystery, and he was quietly pleased that Sam was among them.

They moved almost silently through the morning, following the route of the Pee Dee at a distance. The British used the river as a supply route despite Marion's constant obstructions, so they were cautious to keep out of view of the water.

Little was said during the morning. Connor concentrated on the trail, keeping alert to dangers. Occasionally he would point out a shrub or tree and remark on its unique qualities and its role in the cycle of the forest. He was always encouraged by the interest in Samantha's eyes.

At midday they stopped beside a pool and shared a sparse meal of dried venison. Despite their easy comradery during the morning, Samantha kept her face turned toward the ground and her comments to monosyllables. She had enjoyed the morning tremendously, reveling in Connor's companionship, but her sense of impending doom had grown from a small whisper to a nagging shout.

Connor broke the silence.

"I have some business in Georgetown," he revealed, searching her face. "I'll want you to stay in the forest."

"No," she insisted. "Ya brung me ... I'll stay wi' ya."

"All right," Connor answered, a pleased expression on his face at getting the response he had hoped for. "But we'll stay apart in case anyone recognizes me."

"They won't," Samantha said with conviction. "Even me knowin' better barely knew ya."

"Just the same," Connor replied, satisfaction obvious in his voice, "you will keep a distance. That's an order."

"Yessir, sir." The tone was impertinent, the head tilted mischievously.

Connor couldn't keep the laughter from exploding. The boy had absolutely no manners, no sense of authority. "You," he said sternly, "are going to meet your match someday." Rising, he reached down and clasped Samantha's hand, pulling her up, amazed at her lightness. "Come on, we'll reach Georgetown midafternoon. I have some friends there."

As they approached Georgetown, Connor frowned at the wooded fort constructed on the main road leading into the gracious town. Georgetown had always been a favorite of his and the fort and the red-clad soldiers made a mockery of its dignity.

He went through the guards first, whining and complaining and demanding to see "someone in 'uthority."

Samantha stayed back, waiting several minutes after seeing Connor cleared. Finally, she made her own way to the guards, her heart beating so loudly she was afraid they would hear it and suspect her.

"Your business, boy?"

"My pa sent me to git some pretection from them rebels." She held out a note for inspection, but the guards just waved her on. Samantha awkwardly kicked the horse, almost falling from the saddle, and heard the derisive laughter of the guards behind her. Following Connor's directions, she came to an imposing brick home with a white picket fence and a gaslight. She took a moment to wonder at the people who lived there; she knew the gaslight was a great luxury.

Samantha Chatham had been to Georgetown many times. She had been to the shopping areas and to many of the fine homes lining the river and the main road, but never to this neatly maintained, quiet street. It puzzled her that she hadn't. Perhaps these were well-known patriots, but then wouldn't they have been dispossessed by the British?

It didn't really matter. Connor wouldn't have asked her to meet him there if it weren't safe. With renewed confidence, she slipped deftly from the saddle and handed the reins to a servant dressed in livery. Quickly running up the steps, she knocked at the door, surprised when it was opened by a woman, and even more surprised by the woman's attire. Nearly the whole of her was visible. Samantha had never seen a woman wear less. At least not in public.

The woman was beautiful; there was no question about it. Bright titian hair tumbled down her back and framed a classically lovely face. Eyes like emeralds laughed at Samantha's wide-eyed stare. She was wearing nothing but a revealing nightdress, and the overall impact drew one's attention from the tiny lines around her eyes and mouth.

"You must be Sam," she said, her voice both warm and amused. "Connor is waiting for you...anxiously, I might add."

Suddenly aware of her visitor's startled and bashful eyes, the woman gentled her voice. "Connor woke me just a few minutes ago. I haven't had time to dress...but come in. You can't stay out there gaping all day...the British might wonder."

In a daze, Samantha entered an elaborately decorated foyer. The interior was a strange combination of taste and outrageousness, dominated by a profusion of mirrors and settees. Who was this woman? And what did she have to do with Connor? It was the last question that plagued her and caused a hesitancy in her normally buoyant walk.

She followed the woman wordlessly into a large kitchen.
Connor was sitting at a table, wolfing down a plate of ham and
eggs. At the sound of approaching footsteps, he looked up, a
wide smile on his face. "Sam . . . you had no trouble?"

Her eyes narrowed suspiciously as she looked at Connor...then the woman...and finally the well-equipped kitchen.
Even the aromatic smell of cooking couldn't quell her growing
rebellion or the sick feeling in her stomach. Connor's smile
faded as he saw her confusion.

"This is Annabelle," he said. "She has been a friend for a
long time."

He didn't hear Samantha's muttered oath, but he couldn't
miss the sudden dislike in her expressive eyes.

Annabelle also saw it and tried to pacify Connor's young
friend. "We've all been working for General Greene and Marion," she said softly, putting a hand on Samantha's shoulder.
"You have no cause to worry."

The depth of the youth's growing antagonism startled her. If
it had been a woman, she would understand . . . she had always
raised the ire of other women. But a strange boy who had no
reason to dislike her? It made no sense.

She sighed and summoned a servant. "I have matters to see
to," she said abruptly, but not before her eyes caught Connor's and her mouth curved into an intimate smile.

"Who's she?" Samantha demanded rudely, as Annabelle
swept from the kitchen.

Connor regarded his young charge quizzically. During his
seventeen-year acquaintance with the woman, he had never
seen another male remain immune to her charms. Annabelle
made no pretensions about what she was . . . the madam of the
finest bordello in Georgetown. But Connor had also found her
a warm, witty and courageous friend whom he liked very much.
His father had brought him here when he was fifteen "to be
taught the art of love by an expert."

"If you want to learn carpentry," his father had said with a
twinkle, "you apprentice to a carpenter. If you want to learn
horses, you study under a horseman. Love is no less a skill."
With those words, he had left Connor in the tender hands of
Annabelle, who was then twenty and the undisputed main at-

traction of Mrs. Apple's Salon for Gentlemen. When the esteemed proprietress had retired to marry a customer, she sold the establishment to Annabelle, who quickly changed the name and added both sophistication and a quiet discreet elegance to what was now known simply as Number Two, Cherry Street.

Connor had never forgotten that night when Annabelle, kind and understanding and gentle, had initiated him into the rites of lovemaking. He had been a very apt pupil and had returned frequently over the next few years. Gradually they had become friends as well as lovers, and it was Connor who had loaned her the money to buy Number Two. The loan had been quickly repaid, but it had inexplicably changed the relationship. By mutual unspoken consent, they were no longer lovers, but their friendship had grown stronger. Connor would trust Annabelle with his life and, indeed, had done so several times. She had offered, along with her girls, to gather information of use to the rebels. Since they often entertained British officers, much of what they learned was invaluable.

But none of this could he explain to Sam, who sat puzzled by his strange surroundings. Suddenly Connor doubted the wisdom of bringing the boy with him. But they were here now and he had to make the best of it. Perhaps he could give Sam what his father had given him seventeen years earlier... the first lesson in a most enjoyable endeavor. Connor smiled to himself, wondering how best to go about it. Sam was very stubborn about accepting anything from him, even his thanks.

After mulling over the problem while Sam sullenly picked at a plate of food, Connor finally decided to talk to Annabelle; undoubtedly she would have a solution.

Samantha's limited concentration on the food was further distracted as the kitchen was invaded by a horde of young women, all shockingly dressed in wrappers or disgracefully low-cut flimsy gowns. Even more disconcerting was their unabashedly affectionate greeting of Connor. Several of them even leaned over and planted wet kisses on his face. She felt a great urge to smack them all, particularly Connor, who sat there with a grin on his face and a personal word for each of them. He certainly didn't seem to object to their clothing, or lack of it.

Her mouth drooped dangerously toward her chin as she pushed away the nearly full plate. Annabelle was obviously a loose woman. No one else would entertain a gentleman in such clothes, although she was beginning to wonder whether Connor was a gentleman after all.

Samantha was widely read but little experienced, and it had never even entered her mind until this very minute that Connor had brought her to a . . . a "house of joy." Suddenly she understood, and her face grew hot and fiery red under the dye. Her eyes searched for a place to hide, but there was none. Then the hilarity of the situation struck her, and she had to stifle the waves of laughter that threatened to unmask her.

Connor, whose attention had been distracted by the friendly greetings, glanced over at his young charge and furrowed his brow. Sam looked as if he had swallowed a whale. His face was suffused with . . . could it be laughter? Sam?

Samantha saw Connor's attention focus on her face and doubled the effort to contain the waves of laughter building inside her. With a sudden inspiration, she started choking and immediately felt Connor pounding on her back. Slowly she regained control.

When she could finally speak again, her words came in spurts. "Ain't used to so much vittles," she claimed in apologetic tones, still trying to restrain the choking sounds, which sounded suspiciously like laughter. Fortunately Connor in his concern overlooked the similarity.

"I think you need some rest," he said, and Samantha nodded gratefully, eager to leave all the eyes, which were now staring directly at her.

Following him out of the room and up a circular staircase, Samantha couldn't help but notice Connor's familiarity with the house. He led the way down a long hall lined with rooms to another staircase leading to a third floor. At the top there were only two rooms. Connor opened the one on the left.

It was a masculine room, and unlike the lavish colorful interior of the rest of the house, it was tastefully simple, decorated with beige and dark brown and lined with books. There was one large bed with a matching carved desk and armoire. It looked like a place where Connor would be at home, and she was struck with jealousy.

"Ya seem mighty at 'ome," she remarked surlily.

The corners of Connor's mouth turned slightly upward in obvious amusement at the observation. "Annabelle and I have business interests together...and I stay here sometimes. It's quite safe."

"With all 'em knowin'?" she questioned with a slight sneer. "I 'spect they 'ave redcoat vis'tors."

She hated the look of satisfaction that entered Connor's eyes. "Indeed, they do," he admitted, his grin growing wider. "And the more there are, the better for Fran."

Samantha turned away, her face set in disapproval.

Connor saw the expression and laughed. Sam would, soon enough, have new appreciation for Annabelle.

He turned toward the door. "You stay here," he said. "No matter what, don't leave. The house will soon be filled with Annabelle's 'clients' and there will be British and Tory among them. I want your promise you will stay put."

Samantha kept her face turned away. "Wha' 'bout ya? 'Tis more risky fer ya than me."

"I have business," Connor said sharply. "And I am very careful. Do I have your promise?"

She knew there was no choice and nodded slightly.

"Say it," Connor's voice demanded. He knew how determined his young charge could be.

"I gi' me word," she answered slowly.

Connor nodded. "And don't open the door for anyone but Annabelle," he commanded. With quick sure steps he disappeared out the door, leaving Samantha looking forlornly after him.

Connor settled his rangy frame into a comfortable leather chair in Annabelle's study and gave her his lazy smile.

She answered it with a warm one of her own. "You finally got away from my girls," she observed with amusement. "They always have wagers on which one will get you into bed first."

Connor laughed at her remark. She liked the sound of his laughter. It was full and hearty and without maliciousness or undertones. Annabelle felt the usual stab of regret that they were no longer lovers, but his friendship was even more important. He was the only man who had ever treated her with respect, who had admired her brain as well as her body and certain admitted skills. Since that first loan many years ago, they had joined in other business ventures, and when the British had invaded South Carolina, Connor had given her a large sum of money to protect and invest in her name. He had known, even then, that he would likely be a prime target of the British since he fought against them in 1776 at Sullivans Island.

She looked at him now. He was still dressed in ragged homespun, and his face, as it was, wouldn't turn any heads, but his one eye sparkled with warmth and humor, and it was all she could do to keep her distance. "You'd better stay well out of sight. No one would believe you could pay my prices, or that I would even let you enter."

"You wound me, ma'am," he answered with false hurt. "Tiffany and the others didn't seem to find any fault with my appearance."

Annabelle laughed, and the sound was like tiny chimes. "They," she said with emphasis, "have no discernment.

"Now," she added, "speaking of discernment, tell me about that young waif you brought here. He seemed oddly put out about me."

"Sam," Connor said with a wry smile, "seems to be put out by everything. I don't think he trusts anyone...except perhaps Marion."

"But why here? You know how dangerous it is...for you...for me...for the other girls."

Connor sat forward, his face now serious. "Annabelle, you know I wouldn't do anything to endanger any of you. Sam has saved my life twice...first when he found me after I escaped from the hulks. I would have died without his intervention and care. He gave me his own food when he was hungry. He saved me a second time on a raid, shot one of Tarleton's men just as the man was ready to shoot me. He is unruly and rude and stubborn, but he's also brave and generous to a fault. My family is gone, and I would like to do something for him, if he will let me, perhaps even adopt him. But I have to win his trust first, and that has been nearly impossible. I thought maybe this trip would accomplish that.''

Annabelle looked at him, a tender smile on her lips. "Still rescuing strays and outcasts. Very well. What can I do?"

There was a glint in Connor's eye. "Remember my first visit here?"

Annabelle laughed. "How could I forget. I've never had such an enthusiastic student." Then her look grew wary. "You don't mean . . ."

"Exactly," Connor said with some satisfaction.

"Who?"

"I'll let you decide that."

"Let me think about it," she said slowly. "Maybe Tiffany . . . she's young but she has a good heart. She would be gentle."

Annabelle looked up at Connor. "Your young friend didn't like me, not at all," she remarked. "Maybe he's not ready."

Connor looked at his business partner with a grin. "I have the utmost confidence in your establishment," he said, closing that particular subject. "Now," he said, "what do you have for Fran?"

Annabelle went to her safe and took out several sheets of paper. "We've written down everything we think important. You can commit them to that fascinating memory of yours."

"And, Annabelle," he added, "Sam and I need some new clothes."

Annabelle answered him, the twinkle back in her eyes. "Now that's something we can both agree on."

Connor laughed softly. She knew his fondness for tailored clothes only too well. "Can you send someone out for them . . . nothing fancy, just something sturdy that won't attract attention."

"It is done," she said.

"And I need a rifle . . . for a gift."

Annabelle nodded. "I'll have them both in the morning. And where are you going now?"

"There are a few other people I have to see in Georgetown."

Annabelle knew better than to ask any more questions. The less she knew, the better for everyone concerned.

"I'll see that your young friend is well taken care of," she assured him.

Annabelle walked Connor to the door, admiring his lithe catlike movements. He had spoiled every other man for her. But then perhaps that had been done even before Connor, when at fourteen, alone and penniless, she had sought refuge at Mrs. Apple's. The name still made her smile. Mrs. Apple was, in truth, Miss Sarah Wentworth, who didn't think her real name would attract many customers. With a sort of fiendish humor, Miss Sarah had bought the house on Cherry Street and re-named herself Mrs. Apple. There was no question about her wisdom in doing so. Mrs. Apple's Salon became widely known up and down the coast.

Annabelle had never regretted her choice of an occupation, except for the few times she let herself think that things might have been different with Connor. She was wealthy and inde-pendent and even had a certain notorious stature that amused her. She no longer was available to customers, except when she so chose, and she selected her girls carefully and treated them well. Her customers knew that if they mishandled one of her girls, they would forever be barred from Cherry Street. It was a threat that kept them in line. There was no disgrace worse among the men in town than that of being exiled by Anna-belle.

Annabelle shook such thoughts from her head and went to the parlor to greet the first customers of the evening. Seeing that they were well received, she then turned the duties over to Mary Jo, her usual hostess.

She told one of the servants to prepare water for a bath, and another to take a bathtub to Connor's room. Walking up the two flights of stairs, she knocked at Connor's door. She heard a muffled "Who's 'ere?" in reply.

"Annabelle." There was a long silence, then the door opened, and she saw the boy looking up apprehensively. This time she studied him at great length, wondering how this wisp of a lad could possibly have rescued Connor not only once but twice. Nothing about him seemed unusual or different from the scores of homeless boys that drifted around the major towns. Except for the eyes. How could she have missed them before.

They were huge and the brightest blue she had ever seen. She caught a glimpse of lively intelligence in them that was quickly replaced by a blank stare. Just what was he trying to hide?

"I'm tol' 'tis rude ta stare," the boy said with insolence.

Annabelle coughed, trying to cover a laugh. What an odd creature.

"Connor thought you might like a bath," she said quietly, moving aside for the two servants with the bathtub to enter. They were followed shortly by two others, each carrying large pails of steaming water.

Samantha watched carefully, thinking that nothing had ever looked quite so wonderful. Connor might be back and catch her in the bath but she was almost willing to risk it.

"Connor won't be back for some time," Annabelle quietly assured her. "You will have privacy."

Samantha looked at the beautiful redheaded woman standing in front of her, her eyes strangely compassionate. Did Connor love her? The thought was extremely painful.

The proximity of a hot bath suddenly overcame any objections. "Thank you," she said slowly, momentarily forgetting her rough speech.

She didn't catch Annabelle's raised eyebrows or the stiffening of her smile as the older woman realized that not all was as it appeared. Could it be that Connor was being betrayed after all?

Annabelle left, closing the door behind her, and Samantha hurriedly discarded the distasteful clothes along with the cloth that so tightly and painfully bound her breasts. Within seconds she was deep in the lovely hot water, reveling in its clean warmth. The joy was so intense that she closed her eyes and drifted happily into another world.

Chapter Eleven

Samantha rested so contentedly in the warm bath that she didn't even hear the door open.

"I've brought you some towels," Annabelle announced as she marched into the room and stopped with a gasp.

Splashing upright, her blue eyes full of fear, the young girl reached for some cover but there was none. She could do nothing but stare up at Annabelle with a sinking heart.

"Connor doesn't usually make these kinds of mistakes," the woman said unexpectedly, her body shaking with laughter. She had been afraid young Sam might be a traitor, but apparently he had just been hiding the fact that he wasn't a boy.

And a boy, Annabelle thought with continued amusement, he certainly was not.

Giving the girl a chance to regain some composure, Annabelle turned around and locked the door. She had intended to lock Sam in until she had some answers. Now she didn't want anyone else to disturb her.

Samantha had sunk deeper into the tub, her arms over her breasts, her face a mixture of mortification and anxiety.

Annabelle's laughter suddenly stopped and her twinkling eyes filled with warm interest. "It's all right...I won't hurt you. I just want to know you won't betray Connor."

"Betray Connor?" There was such bewilderment in the voice that Annabelle knew that was an unwarranted fear.

Her eyes studied her surprising guest with rapt attention. If there was one thing she might know better than men, it was women. She could always spot the beauties, even when they were at their worst, and many were when they came to her. Now, looking over young Sam, or whoever she was, she wondered why she hadn't spotted it immediately and, even more, why Connor hadn't. Sam had all the signs of being a beauty.

"Stand up," Annabelle commanded, and Samantha obeyed. Despite her anxiety and shame, she stood proudly. Bravo, Annabelle thought to herself. The girl had more than a little spirit. Connor was right about her courage. There were no tears at being caught, no lame excuses.

Although much too thin, she would have a lovely figure if filled out. Her breasts were perfect mounds and the hips were slightly rounded. No wonder she had chosen the heavy rough homespun clothes; only they could adequately disguise her distinctly feminine body. Her skin was odd, partly cream, partly spotted with dark patches. Annabelle's eyes went back to her dark face. She raised her eyebrows in question. "Dye?"

The girl nodded, a momentary flash of humor in her eyes. "I had enough to touch up my face, but not the rest of me. I didn't think anyone would see it . . . or, if they did, would think I had a fatal disease and run away."

Annabelle chuckled. Sam had a sense of humor despite her awkward predicament. Her estimation of the girl was rising with every minute. Annabelle's expert eyes scanned the rest of her. Her hair was a dull unattractive brown, but it didn't go with her coloring. It was cropped short but curled slightly around the gamine face. Annabelle handed her a towel and watched the graceful moves as Samantha quickly wrapped it around herself and faced her interrogator again.

"And your hair? That's dyed, too?"

Samantha giggled, partly from nervousness, partly from thinking how ridiculous this whole conversation was. Here she was, the once very proper Samantha Chatham, standing naked in a bordello, being questioned by a madam. Her sense of doom had apparently been most perceptive.

When she looked back at Annabelle, she saw a studied fascination. She nodded. "It's usually very dark."

"Will you tell me why this masquerade?"

"I had no place to go," she said truthfully. "I could ride and shoot, and I wanted to join Colonel Marion. I knew they wouldn't want a woman."

Annabelle's suspicion turned into admiration. The girl had spunk. Then she suddenly realized that Sam's speech was cultured and soft, completely unlike the first words she had spoken.

"Who are you?" There was no softness in the voice now.

"My name really is Sam..." the young girl answered slowly.

Annabelle led her to the bed and saw her seated before taking a chair directly in front of her. "You are going to tell me everything," she said. "Everything."

Samantha searched Annabelle's face. At this point, she had little to lose. If she didn't tell everything, Annabelle would expose her to Connor. She was Connor's friend, probably his mistress. Samantha's desperation was reflected in her face, and Annabelle's expression softened.

"You love him, don't you," Annabelle said unexpectedly, remembering the girl's hostility and the way her eyes had seldom left Connor.

Samantha nodded miserably, tears forming in her large eyes.

Annabelle felt a deep sadness. She knew this girl was meant for Connor. There was a corresponding strength and courage and, she suspected, gentleness between the two of them.

"Then why are you so afraid to tell him who you are... or—" her amusement returned "—what you are?"

Annabelle could hardly hear the low voice.

"Because my father's a Tory... because he would send me away and I don't think I could bear that."

Annabelle felt a quick surge of relief, or was it fear? "That won't matter to Connor...."

The girl's look was desperate and so filled with unhappiness that Annabelle's heart, which she thought well guarded, was pierced by the agony she saw there. She put a comforting hand on the younger woman's shoulder and reached up to touch a strand of her hair.

The gesture was so sympathetic that Samantha blurted out the truth. It had become too large a burden to carry.

"My father," she repeated, her voice now strong and clear, "is Robert Chatham."

Annabelle dropped her hand, and her face went white with shock. "Oh my God," she said.

She couldn't help but stare at the vulnerable young girl in front of her. Connor had made no secret of his hatred for the Chathams, and she had listened more than once to his threats. But with Connor, they were not mere threats, they were promises. She had heard him curse the name of Robert Chatham and his daughter, Samantha. Sam.

The shock in Annabelle's face told Samantha that she knew everything, and that fact pierced her to the core. She didn't know why she had confided in a woman who must be Connor's mistress.

Annabelle, too, was wondering why she had assumed this role in what now appeared to be a tragedy. She loved Connor, but it was a love she knew would never be returned. She had known for a long time Connor was one of those rare men who would love only once, and she had felt this girl might be the one. But now...

"Will you tell him?" Samantha's voice was small, pleading.

"He will find out you are not all you seem rather soon," Annabelle replied. "Connor is not stupid. He generally knows the difference between a male and a female. And then what?"

"Maybe I'll have proven my value," she said in a low voice.

"From what he told me," Annabelle said with a smile, "you have already done that. But what happens when he finds out who you really are?"

Samantha looked directly at Annabelle. "I've tried to stay away from him, truly I have. But I can't. Perhaps ... it is possible that I can make him love me so much it won't matter."

Annabelle kept the doubt out of her face. Connor was as single-minded and stubborn as any man she had ever known. He was gentle and tolerant and usually good-natured, but heaven help those who betrayed him or those he loved.

She wanted to know more about Samantha Chatham. From everything Connor had told her, she was the selfish spoiled daughter of his arch enemy and had led his much-loved brother to his death. That description didn't match Connor's comments about young Sam, the boy who had twice saved his life and who was "brave and generous to a fault."

"Tell me everything," she asked Samantha. "Tell me about Brendan...and how you found Connor and what you've been doing with Marion."

Samantha started slowly. "I loved Brendan from the time I was ten years old," she said. "I loved him with all my heart and soul. He was my only friend and I was his, and after our mothers died, our families hated each other." Her tears ran unheeded down her cheeks, her small face reflecting all the pain she had felt on what she thought would be her wedding day. Annabelle flinched as she listened to Connor's bitter words that day.

She talked for nearly an hour, words and emotions flooding from her mouth. She described everything that happened to her in the past few months and her confusion when she realized she was falling in love with Connor, though she knew it could never be.

When she finished, there was silence. Annabelle had no words; for the first time in her life, she was completely stunned. Finally she leaned over and took Samantha into her arms. "If I had a daughter," she said softly, "I think I would like her to be just like you."

Samantha's tearstained face was tight with disbelief. She had been so sure Annabelle would tell Connor everything. "You won't tell him, then?"

"No, I won't tell him, but understand, he will find out, and the way he finds out will mean whether there is a future for the two of you."

"If it's not with him," Samantha said softly, "there won't be one at all."

Annabelle looked at the determined girl. Was she, Annabelle, betraying Connor by not telling him the identity of his young friend? She believed now, with every instinct she had, that if Connor could only forget the past, Samantha would make him very happy, much happier than the proper belles he was known to visit. It was worth risking his wrath.

"Why are you doing this?" Samantha's blue eyes were direct yet clouded by doubt.

Annabelle's own eyes now filled for the first time in years. "Because I love him, too, and you saved his life. Not once, but twice. Because I think you might be able to give him something I can't, that I never could. He is my friend, and I want to see him happy."

Samantha reached out her hand and placed it gently on Annabelle's. "He is very lucky to have someone like you."

The two women looked at each other, both knowing instinctively that they had, despite all their differences, entered a strange friendship that would prove to be both long and true.

"Come on," Annabelle said suddenly. "You must get dressed, and we have to get you out of here before Connor returns. I don't think it particularly wise that you sleep in the same bed, as I had planned. We have," she added wryly, "somewhat of a shortage of available beds." Despite herself, she smiled, and was delighted to see that Samantha did, too. No bluestocking, this one. She was indeed rare.

"Where, then," Samantha asked, "do you suggest I sleep?"

Annabelle laughed, a full-throated deep sound that was extremely pleasant. "Connor wanted one of my girls to introduce you to the wonders of the opposite sex. I'll just tell him you've accepted and you can stay in my room tonight. I'll be busy downstairs."

"But what do I tell him in the morning?" she questioned, partly amused by Connor's suggestion and partly annoyed that he had taken such a liberty.

"Somehow, Samantha, I believe you will think of something," Annabelle answered, a small chuckle still in her voice.

The two exchanged small smiles of perfect understanding.

Samantha snuggled in the huge feather bed, enjoying the intoxicating feel of the satin sheets and the huge rose-colored comforter that made her little more than a tiny bump in its folds.

It had been a most unusual day. The morning had been wonderful, more precious than any time she had spent since Brendan's death. She recalled Connor's lazy drawl and slow smile as he talked to her about the swamp, never talking down to her but simply sharing a love and interest with someone he considered an intelligent companion. It had endeared him to her even more, and she now shivered with inexplicable yearning as she thought of him across the hall. Annabelle had been wise to separate them.

Samantha smiled to herself as she thought about Annabelle. Never in her wildest imagination had she ever dreamed she would not only like and admire a woman of her occupation but be so happily ensconced in her bed.

When Annabelle had led her into her room she hadn't been able to resist a gasp of delight. The room was the epitome of good taste and beauty. Decorated in gray blues and soft rose colors, it was a tranquil haven.

Annabelle had smiled at her reaction. "This is my own private place," she said. "You needn't worry about anyone coming in. No one, not even Connor, will enter without an invitation." There was a hint of sadness in her voice, but it was quickly gone.

"Consider anything in this room yours," she had finally said, her voice soft. "You will not be disturbed until morning."

"Thank you," Samantha had replied in a small voice.

Annabelle had merely nodded and left.

Number Two was now noisy and filled to overflowing. One room was devoted to gambling, another was a large room where gentlemen were served drink and delicacies while they talked and chose a companion for the evening. Despite Annabelle's earlier teasing observations about Connor's appearance she had few worries. Her place was probably the most neutral ground in Georgetown. No questions were ever asked for fear that questions might be levied in return. Annabelle barred any talk of politics in the public rooms, and failure to abide by the rule meant instant removal. There were no exceptions.

The British officers and Tories who patronized Number Two were extremely careful not to offend Annabelle. It was the one place in Georgetown they could relax away from the mounting hostilities and the growing rancor of Georgetown's population.

Annabelle, therefore, did not worry about her unusual guests as she quietly greeted old customers and inspected new ones. She had a quip for most of them and laughingly fended off their amorous proposals, suggesting, instead, one of the girls she thought would best meet their taste. It was a fairly quiet night and it gave her time to think about Connor and Samantha Chatham.

She wished she knew why she had chosen not to tell Connor. It could easily destroy the friendship she valued so highly.

She knew one reason was Samantha herself. The girl was an arresting mixture of vulnerability and toughness, of spirit and gentleness. She had Annabelle's own instinct for survival but had gone about it in an entirely different though equally unconventional manner. Annabelle didn't know if she herself would have been brave enough to make a life in a swamp among the hard woodsmen that comprised most of Marion's small brigade. If only Connor could be made to see the girl for what she was instead of the vastly inaccurate portrait he had painted in his mind.

Lost in her scheming, Annabelle missed the flurry in the front hall as a tall commanding figure in green entered.

Mary Jo scurried over to her. "Colonel Tarleton is here, Annabelle. He wants to see you."

Annabelle brought herself back to the present. Tarleton had visited Number Two several times, each time requesting her favors. She had always refused and sent him to Darlene, the prettiest and brightest of her girls. Each time, Darlene had emerged with valuable information.

But this was the worst possible time. "Bloody Tarleton" was a British cavalryman whose main responsibility was to quash Marion. He had earned the name after his men had bayoneted one hundred and thirteen Americans to death and wounded nearly two hundred more, after they called for quarter and showed a flag of truce. He was probably the most feared and hated of all the British.

Colonel Banastre Tarleton strode into the room, his green uniform immaculate on his tall well-formed body and his red hair neatly combed and without powder.

He bowed to Annabelle, who tried to keep the distaste from her eyes. The colonel was well-known for his fondness for the ladies. It was probably his only weakness, with the exception of his obsession with Marion.

"Annabelle," he said in greeting. "As lovely as ever. And as distant," he added wryly, seeing the brief cloud in her eyes.

"I'm just a little tired tonight, colonel," Annabelle said lightly. "And what brings you to Georgetown? I thought you were encamped near Monck's Corners."

He smiled, a most charming smile if Annabelle had not known of his exploits. "It looks like Marion has retreated back into the swamp for a while . . . and I needed a bit of rest from hunting that damn fox."

"He still eludes you, Colonel Tarleton? I'm surprised." Annabelle had to fight to keep a tone of malicious satisfaction from her voice.

Tarleton's face grew taut and his eyes flickered dangerously. "Oh, we will get him," he said, "and I will take great pleasure in seeing him hang, along with Peter Horry and Connor O'Neill."

"O'Neill?" Annabelle said with interest. "I thought he was in prison."

"He was," Tarleton said shortly, angry at the picture of his helplessness against the rebels but stirred by her unusual interest. "He escaped several months ago and is now one of Marion's officers. There is a substantial reward for his capture, but I doubt he will venture out alone. When we take them, we will take them together."

"And you think that might be soon?"

"Sooner than anyone thinks . . . we have a few tricks of our own," he added.

"I imagine you do," she said lightly, using her ability as an actress to summon up a show of admiration. "And who may I get for you tonight?" she asked, wondering what he would think if he knew Connor was, at this minute, two stories over his head.

Tarleton leaned over and touched Annabelle's lightly rouged face. "The fairest of all," he said, smiling his admiration.

Annabelle smiled through her dislike. "I'm sorry," she said. "I am feeling unwell tonight, and you know I no longer allow myself that pleasure." She called over Mary Jo. "Is Darlene available?"

Mary Jo nodded. "She's just now free."

Annabelle looked at Tarleton, waiting for his assent. He looked at her longingly and then grinned. "If I can't have the diamond, then I'll take the pearl."

Annabelle could not restrain a smile in answer to the extravagant compliment. Just for a moment she wished he weren't the ruthless man she knew him to be.

"How long do you plan to stay with us?"

"I am heading north at dawn," he said regretfully, "so it shall not be long."

"Come visit us again, colonel," Annabelle said. "You are always welcome."

She watched Tarleton follow Mary Jo up the staircase, allowing herself a secret smile....

In the room upstairs, Samantha was having great difficulty sleeping. Her body felt as though she were reclining on a cloud, but her mind refused to accept such comfort after so many nights on the hard ground. After several hours of trying to sleep, she still lay wide-awake worrying about the coming day. She would be with Connor all day and he would inquire about the night's experience. She had to be alert. Moaning softly, she left the soft bed and curled up on the hard floor with only a thin cover. Within minutes, she was sound asleep.

Annabelle wandered the house restlessly. Earlier in the evening she had sent one of the servants out after the clothes and the rifle Connor had requested. It would not be the first time a certain storekeeper had been awakened for one of Annabelle's odd requests, and he had ceased to question them. He was always well paid for his trouble, and his rare visits to Annabelle's were free.

She knew that Connor had returned long before Tarleton had entered the premises, and she suspected that, as usual, he would be up and wanting to leave early.

Carrying the set of clothes meant for Connor, she climbed the two sets of stairs and listened for sounds before knocking lightly on his door. It opened almost immediately, and Connor stood in the candlelight, awake and wary.

Annabelle slipped into the room and closed the door. "Tarleton's downstairs."

Connor almost choked. "You keep the damnedest company, Annabelle."

She returned his direct gaze. "Yes, I do, don't I," she replied, a hint of laughter in her voice.

Connor turned and strode over to a chair, settling in it gracefully. "Good Lord, I would love to take him," he said thoughtfully.

"Oh, no you don't," Annabelle answered quickly. "It would be the end of all of us. I just wanted to warn you. Delay your departure till well after he's gone."

"Sam?"

"He's safe . . . he's with Tiffany. Neither of you are to leave your rooms until I say so."

"Yes, ma'am," Connor replied with unaccustomed obedience. He knew how much Annabelle risked; he would not ask any more.

Annabelle looked at him with unabashed affection. He was wearing only breeches, and she thought she had never seen so perfect a man. In the three months since his escape, his skin had recaptured the glow of the sun and his lean hard frame had gained enough weight to strengthen the corded muscles in his chest and arms. She could still see the bright scar from the musket wound but it seemed only to accentuate his powerful maleness.

"You look well, Connor. The British obviously didn't do too much damage."

His face suddenly tightened, his mouth clenching in a taut line, and his eyes frosted over in a way she had never seen before. "They left their mark, Annabelle." A muscle twitched in his jaw. "It was as much a hell as there can be on earth."

"Oh, Connor," she said, wishing she had never made such a lighthearted comment. "I'm sorry."

With concerted effort he made himself smile again, but it was only a shadow as he struggled to erase the memories. "One day..." He stopped.

"One day, what?"

Connor tried to relax but he was like a coiled spring. "Perhaps," he faltered, "when I repay some debts... when I kill Chatham... I'll be able to let it go."

Annabelle looked at him with something akin to pity. "This compulsion for revenge does not become you, Connor."

He gave her a crooked grin. "Maybe not, but I think it might be very satisfying."

"What about Sam?"

"Sam? What does he have to do with it?"

"He needs you right now," Annabelle said softly. "He's had his own losses, and they've been every bit as hard as your own."

Connor's brow furrowed. "What do you know about Sam? He's said very little about himself."

Knowing she had said too much, Annabelle retreated. "I can see it in his eyes, and you could, too, if you weren't so absorbed in your desire to avenge yourself."

Connor was quiet, wondering if her words were true. He had tried repeatedly to reach Sam, but he had done it all on his own terms.

He smiled wryly. "You, too?"

"What do you mean?"

"He seems to make friends with everyone but me. Fran, Billy and now you."

"Have you ever thought there might be a reason?" she replied enigmatically.

Connor raised his eyebrows in question.

"Perhaps he senses the anger in you... perhaps he doesn't quite trust it and, therefore, trust you."

"Damn you, Annabelle," he said fondly. "Do you always have to be so irritatingly rational about everything?"

She laughed. "And do you have to pose all your questions in such an unflattering way?"

Connor laughed, his dangerous mood now gone.

Annabelle left minutes later and went to her own room. She was immediately frightened at the sight of the empty bed.

Frantically her eyes scanned the room until they rested on the small form huddled in the far corner.

A smile lighted her face as she studied Samantha, realizing why the girl had left the bed. Long black lashes covered her memorable blue eyes and her short hair only emphasized her delicate facial bones. Annabelle decided to let Samantha sleep a bit longer while she had breakfast prepared. Perhaps by then Tarleton would be long gone....

Samantha quickly pulled on the fresh clothes, looking thankfully at her new friend. They were perfect. Bulky and ill-fitting. They would hide a figure much more voluptuous than her own. And they were clean. Marvelously, wonderfully clean.

Annabelle smiled at her delight. She could hardly believe such enthusiasm coming from a plantation owner's daughter. Not over these clothes.

"Eat," she commanded, now entirely caught up in her role of mother hen.

"Connor?"

"He's eating in his own room. I told him you were still sleeping."

Samantha needed no additional urging. She was ravenously hungry, having eaten little yesterday, and Annabelle had provided a heaping plate of eggs, ham, hot bread with butter and honey.

As she ate, Annabelle talked. "I told Connor you were with Tiffany last night. And I told Tiffany that you were too shy but didn't want Connor to know. She will not give anything away. The last thing she wants is for Connor to doubt her charms. I also advised Connor not to say anything... that it's your business."

Samantha laughed. "You're very thorough."

Annabelle did not return the smile. When she spoke again, her tone was unexpectedly severe.

"Know what you are doing, Sam," she said. "Because if you don't, you will ruin more than one life. Connor doesn't like lies. He won't abide them. Tell him as soon as possible. Don't let him find out on his own."

"But you didn't tell him."

"No, I didn't, and I might well regret it," Annabelle said softly. "I want you to have your chance because I think it might be good for both of you . . . but God help both of us if Connor finds out and doesn't understand." Her voice was suddenly all business. "He's waiting for you. By the way, I had a visitor last night . . . Colonel Tarleton."

Samantha's face whitened. "Tarleton?"

"Don't worry. He left several hours ago, but be extra careful. I think he's left the city, but he's in the vicinity, planning something nasty."

Samantha reached up and kissed Annabelle's smooth cheek. "Thank you for everything. . . ."

"I just hope I've done the right thing" came Annabelle's worried farewell.

Chapter Twelve

It was one of those rare December days that seem to favor the South. The sun shone brilliantly in a sapphire sky, nurturing the earth. It was warm for the week before Christmas; the cool breeze gave the only indication of the lurking winter.

Samantha unbuttoned her new coat, enjoying the caressing touch of the sun and the teasing play of the slight wind.

She and Connor had replayed yesterday's caution, Connor leaving first and meeting her in the woods. They had been traveling more than an hour in silence and she was the first to break it.

"Annabelle is very beautiful," she said in a voice so low that Connor almost missed it.

He looked back in surprise. They were the first words to come from Sam all morning. It was difficult, but he was trying to follow Annabelle's advice and move at Sam's pace. The boy had been extremely discreet about last night and Connor's only hint of what had transpired had been Tiffany's saucy wink.

He turned and looked directly at Sam, who was several feet behind him.

"Yes, she is," he agreed amiably.

"Nice, too," Samantha added, wanting dreadfully for Connor to expand on her own words.

"Yes," Connor said unhelpfully.

Samantha bit her lip in frustration. She wanted to know more about Connor and Annabelle's strange relationship but didn't know how to approach the subject. Connor was offering no assistance at all.

She tried again. "'Ave you know 'er long?"

"Long enough," Connor replied noncommittally, a twitch of amusement on his lips. He knew Sam was curious but he was damned if he was going to let the boy get away with his usual terse conversation.

They rode in silence for another few minutes, Samantha unwilling to show any more interest but bursting with the need to know.

"I bet lots of men like 'er."

This time Connor couldn't stop the smile. This was an entirely new Sam. Perhaps last night had been a good idea after all.

"I thought you didn't approve of her."

"Didn' say that," she snapped back. "Jest said she was pretty."

"And nice," Connor goaded, and heard a murmured oath in response.

Samantha surrendered momentarily, feeling completely thwarted. She suspected Connor enjoyed baiting her, and she wondered how she could turn the tables.

Connor chuckled at the fierce curiosity behind the questions. The exchange had served to relieve some of the tension he had been feeling, knowing that Tarleton had been under the same roof last night and was probably not far at this moment. Whatever else he was, Tarleton was no fool. Last night had been a little too close for comfort.

They rode in silence until noon, when Connor stopped at a small clearing off the trail. They both dismounted and fed the horses before unpacking their noonday meal.

Unlike yesterday's spare repast, today's offerings were a feast. Annabelle had packed cold chicken, fresh bread, butter and cheese and a bottle of expensive French wine. She had given the bundle to Samantha to carry, in the event Connor was searched, but neither of them expected the riches cleverly contained in the old blanket.

They ate with pleasure, saying little. Connor then stretched out against a tree, his long frame looking extraordinarily attractive even in rough farmer's garb. Samantha longed to lean over and touch him. The yearning she had felt last night grew in intensity; every nerve end was inflamed, every thought imagined the feel of his mouth against hers and his body pressed against her own.

"Sam . . . ?" Connor's quiet voice jerked her back from the impossible daydream.

With every bit of control she could summon, she looked at him expressionlessly, her fingers drawing deep gulches in the dirt.

He started slowly. "If you ever need anything, if anything happens to me, go to Annabelle. She will help you."

"Why would she?" Sam asked, probing.

"There are many who call themselves friends, Sam. But few who really are. Friends are those who would die for you or you for them, those who can be trusted completely, regardless of the cost. Once in a great while, you are lucky enough to find one. I have been luckier than most. I have two, Annabelle and Francis. Annabelle will help you because she will be helping me. Besides," he added, "she was well taken with you."

Samantha felt a sick lurch in her stomach as she considered Connor's carefully chosen words. Friendship and honor and honesty were so obviously essential parts of him. Annabelle was taking a very big risk for her, and she still did not understand exactly why.

"Do you love 'er?"

Connor's face furrowed. "In a way," he said slowly, carefully. "Probably not the way you mean it, but there are many different kinds of love. I trust her, and I can't say that about many people. . . ."

"Do you bed 'er?" Samantha could not contain the question any longer and shocked herself when it spewed out so indelicately.

She was unprepared for Connor's roar of laughter. "That, Sam, is one question a gentleman does not ask another."

"I ain't no gentlemen."

Connor covered the laughter that shook his body with a cough. Sam was too earnest and he did not want to break this fragile beginning.

He finally got himself under control, and his voice was gentle.

"I expect you learned something last night about love...at least the physical part of it. Another thing you should learn. Don't ever mix it with business or friendship. It is a deadly combination."

"You mean ya can't be friends and bed, too?" she asked, truly trying to understand this strange position of Connor's. She and Bren had been the best of friends and this had lessened none of their desire for each other.

Connor was uncomfortable now. "Let's just say it is rare."

"But Annabelle..."

"Enough about Annabelle," Connor said as he contemplated Sam attentively. "Just know that she will help you if you ever need it."

Connor was surprised to see the sudden desolation in the boy's eyes. Samantha was, in fact, thinking of Annabelle's last warning. "Connor doesn't like lies...he won't abide them." Was she destroying that friendship between Annabelle and Connor? The lies were becoming worse and worse, one leading to still another. She was drowning in them.

Her obvious distress struck Connor, and he wondered what he had said to provoke it. He searched around for something to say.

"You must miss your father," he said, coming to the wrong conclusion altogether. "I know how you feel. I lost my father, and my brother. You remind me of him...."

Samantha was up on her feet and running before he could stop her, seeking sanctuary somewhere...anywhere. What had started as a great adventure was quickly turning into a nightmare. Every word had become a betrayal.

She heard the footsteps behind her, and she ran faster, her need carrying her like a frightened fawn through the forest.

Connor's voice called to her and his footsteps grew closer. Her despair gave her added speed. Then she felt his arms catching her, keeping her from falling as her legs collapsed under her. Connor turned her around to face him. "What the hell?"

To his complete astonishment, young Sam was crying as if his heart were breaking. And the sound was not that of a boy.

Connor's grip loosened as he eased Sam to the ground, feeling the slim womanly body under the rough clothes. He cursed under his breath.

Samantha knew she had given herself away, and the knowledge caused a new tide of tears. She hated herself for showing weakness, but nothing could stop the anguished sounds that tore from her throat.

Connor watched her helplessly. Emotions flickered across his face...confusion, interest, pity, anger. All were quickly lost in compassion. He had never seen such grief in so small a bundle.

His hand stretched out to her, offering comfort, seeking to stem the pain, trying to understand what had just transpired.

Connor took her chin in his hand and turned it up toward his face. "Hush, little one," he crooned. "Nothing can be that bad."

Her eyes met his, and he flinched at the unhappiness in them. He couldn't tear his gaze away from the glistening dark blue whirlpools swirling with such naked emotion.

"Is it what I said about your father?" he asked, still searching for a reason for her sudden flight. He saw her fight for control, saw her chin lift, almost defiantly, and felt a sudden admiration.

A girl, for God's sake. A slip of a girl. And she had fooled them all. He studied her closely now and saw, as Annabelle had, the finely etched features. A confusing surge of protectiveness flooded him. Her tears only seemed to emphasize her strength in the past months as he recalled her stubborn, uncomplaining behavior.

His lips curved in a small smile. "What is bothering you so cruelly?" His voice was kind, sympathetic, and it started a new rush of tears. Suddenly she was in his arms, and he was stroking her hair, whispering what were meant to be comforting words. She buried her face in his chest, aching for his nearness and fearing it at the same time.

He tipped her face up to look at it, and she reached, almost desperately, for his lips. When they met, Connor could feel the trembling and it birthed a hunger and desire he hadn't expected. As he pressed his lips to hers, there was a sweetness and longing that did more to arouse him than any experienced passion ever had. His arms tightened around her and reason left both of them. There was only need.

His lips left Samantha's and traveled lightly over her short hair, kissing the crown and moving down to her eyes, where he tasted the salty tears that still ran softly down her cheeks. His hands gently explored her body, finding the hidden curves and feeling the cruel binding around her. His hands made their way inside the shirt and quickly unleashed her breasts, and he looked with wonder as they stretched against the rough cotton garment.

An internal voice kept telling him to stop. Every instinct told him she was inexperienced, a virgin. But he sensed her need was as great as his own, and her hands and eyes pleaded with him until he was aflame with the want of her.

"Please," she said softly, and the one word made any further denial impossible.

Neither noticed the slight chill of the December day as he undressed her slowly, fascinated by the perfect breasts, which grew taut under his soft touch. Her whole body arched toward him in an instinctive response as old as life itself. He spread his coat on the ground and tenderly shifted her onto it, his eyes never leaving her. He waited for some sign of hesitation or reluctance, but there was none. Instead, her hands reached for his fastenings and with intent freed him from the last barrier between them.

Her fingers wrapped themselves in the wisps of golden hair on his chest while he in turn stroked her cheek and moved on to her breasts, awakening senses she had never known she had. His hands wandered further down, to the dark patch between her legs, and he felt her shiver with desire. He could feel his manhood stretching toward her... but still he waited, touching her until she was almost maddened... then gently lowering himself into her.

There was a momentary blockage and a soft cry, but as he hesitated, Samantha pushed her body up and toward his in an agony of need as she felt his steel like hardness penetrate the warm welcoming world inside her. Little explosions of ecstasy followed each other like growing waves on a stormy sea, each stronger and wilder and reaching further than the last. His strong rhythmic moves became drumbeats inside her, igniting tingling fires throughout her body. She thought she could bear it no longer, so deep was the pleasure.

Samantha felt she was rising and falling in some enchanted world she had never imagined, a place of incomprehensible sensation. "Connor," she cried as the final explosion came, leaving shuddering aftershocks, and she heard the echoing sound of her name on his lips.

In the gentle aftermath, he lay contentedly within her, quivering slightly from the intensity of the union, feeling a euphoric sense of well-being. His hand touched her cheek in acknowledgement of the gift, and his lips drew into a slightly bewildered smile. He felt her tremble under him, and he slowly, caressingly withdrew and moved next to her, his face a study in contrasting emotions.

His eyes had seldom left her face during the joining, fascinated as he was with the ever-changing expressions of discovery, delight and rapture. He had never suspected a virgin of so little fear, so much passion, such complete giving. Now the happy fulfillment in her eyes held him captive.

"Connor," she said again, and he loved the sound of his name on her lips. Her soft voice made it music.

A deer, which had wandered close to the clearing, started at the human voice, and its frantic retreat broke the silence…and the spell. Connor's expression changed as he stared at Samantha in sudden dismay. My God, what in the hell was he doing? Never had he lost control like this. He tore his eyes from her and buried his face in his hands. The softness that had been there moments before was gone, replaced by the self-hatred that was swelling inside him.

"Connor?" Her voice was low, troubled by the sudden changes in his face.

When he looked up at her, his face was ravaged, his mouth compressed in a tight line. "I'm sorry, my God, I'm sorry."

"No," she cried, "Don't be . . . I wanted you. . . ."

He looked at her as if she were a stranger, as if he hated her. This time his eyes saw the discoloration of her body, the darkness of the face against the creamy white of her shoulders. He had questions, but they were stifled under his growing disgust with himself.

"You were under my protection," he said slowly, painfully. "I betrayed that." He looked at her steadily now, his gray eyes bleak. "Get dressed, Sam," he said. "Or," he added wryly, "is it Sam?"

She nodded miserably.

"So that much is true?"

She felt his anger like a physical blow, never realizing that its aim was inward and she was only receiving the echoes.

She reached slowly for her clothes, watching Connor as he jerked his on, tearing a fastening in his haste. She heard the long bitter oath that followed the mishap and realized how deep his rage.

As she completed her last button she saw him stare at his jacket on the ground, her virginal blood a bright red stain across its brown color. He kicked it violently out of sight, knowing he could never wear it again, not with its brand of his dishonor. He looked at her once more, his expression gentling as he saw her hurt and confusion. "It's not you, Sam...it's my fault. It should never have happened."

He took her hand and, none too gently, hurried her to the horses, wordlessly packing the blanket on which they had dined. He helped Sam mount, then mounted himself in continued silence and pressed his chestnut into a fast walk.

Samantha followed well behind him, afraid of his glowering presence, convinced that he hated her for her trickery. But those few moments in the woods were worth it, she told herself. She would not regret them.

Connor was thinking only of how he had betrayed her. She was just a child. A child who had trusted him, and he had taken from her what should have been saved for a husband.

He had no idea how old she was...only that she was obviously much older than the fourteen he had assumed. But to him, she was still too young to know enough to be on her guard against what had just happened. She had been a virgin. He had known that even before piercing the fragile gate, but he had gone ahead anyway. Damn his soul! Whatever had possessed him? He had never before felt such guilt, such complete misery at his own actions.

What to do now? She obviously couldn't stay with Marion...not this child-woman, he thought, forgetting the past three months. She said she had no family. Connor had no one he could trust with her...except Annabelle, and that was obviously out of the question. Something knocked at his senses. Annabelle. Tiffany. Did they know? And what about last night? His face grew bleaker as he considered the various possibilities, and he didn't like any of them.

Perhaps he could offer her marriage, but at the moment he had a questionable future and no home. He also had something he had to do first. Kill Chatham. That remained his first priority, and he could not marry while that vow dominated his every thought. What did he know of her? Nothing. Less now, in fact, than three hours ago. His thoughts tumbled in his head. One fact was undeniable, he had badly wronged her...and that simple truth made him hate both of them.

They traveled in silence for several hours before reaching the Santee. The joy Samantha had felt yesterday and this morning had become a leaden ball in her stomach. She tried to summon back the warmth of their lovemaking, but Connor's unyielding hostility and the unasked questions hovering around her like birds of prey made it impossible. She had thoroughly destroyed those things most precious to her through one impulsive act.

She could now smell the sea and guessed they were near their destination. Connor had told her earlier that the Brown farm was on the coast. She dreaded the arrival, afraid she would be forced to answer the questions she knew were plaguing Connor. She knew he wasn't ready to learn her true identity and that meant more lies. She closed her eyes at the devil's web that snared her so thoroughly. She knew she loved Connor as she would no other, and she ached for an understanding that she knew was not in him.

They approached the small farm with caution. The fences were in disrepair and the field overgrown save one small, neatly tended patch. At the sound of horses, the door opened, and

Samantha watched as a middle-aged woman emerged, an ancient musket set firmly in her hands.

She looked at Connor without recognizing the bearded wounded man of four months ago.

He dismounted and walked to her. "Mrs. Brown," he said softly. "You don't remember me."

The woman shook her head, trying to recall the gently spoken man who regarded her so kindly.

"Four months ago," Connor said, "you risked your life for an escaped prisoner."

Ellie Brown focused on him, recognition dawning on her face. The man bore little resemblance to the ailing scarecrow she'd remembered except for his soft courtesy and the gratitude in his voice.

"Ya made it then," she said. "I 'ad 'oped so, but . . ."

"Johnny. Is he well?"

"Aye," she said. "'E's out trappin'." Her worn face creased in a smile. "'E never 'ad any doubts. 'E ain't never stopped talkin' of you."

She looked up at the lad who was still mounted. Connor's eyes followed her glance and clouded. "This is Sam," he said simply, letting the woman draw her own conclusion.

Her face spread into a wide smile. "Come in . . . both of ya. Johnny will be mighty grieved if 'e don't see ya."

Samantha looked askance at Connor, who merely nodded his assent. Her heart broke at his curiously indifferent expression. She dismounted slowly, standing alone as she watched Connor unpack several bundles and take the new rifle from its place on the saddle.

She saw his expression gentle as he handed the woman the packages. "Some salt," he said, "and quinine." Both, he knew, were invaluable. "And for Johnny," he continued, handing her the rifle.

"'E said you wouldna forget," she responded shyly, a wide smile making her almost pretty.

Once inside the poor but scrupulously clean cabin, they were offered some cider. "We don't dare stay long," Connor said. "There are redcoats all over the place."

Ellie Brown nodded. "They stop by 'ere often, knowin' 'ow I feel 'bout 'em."

Connor's expression grew anxious. "They didn't know about me?"

"Nay," she said. "They kept ahuntin' but never found nothin'." Her attention turned to Sam. "Is 'e your boy?"

Samantha hated the blank look Connor threw her way. "No," he said levelly. "He's just accompanying me on *this* trip." His voice emphasized the fact there would be no more.

Just then the door banged open and a young boy hurled himself into the room. He had seen the horses and didn't know if his mother needed protection. He studied the tall stranger closely before his face relaxed, and he grinned. "Mister," he said. "I knew ya'd be back."

"Aye," Connor replied with a smile. "I had something to deliver," he explained, indicating the rifle on the table.

Johnny rushed over and picked up the firearm wonderingly. His mother owned the one old musket, but it was of little good except at point-blank range.

Connor carefully explained the rifle to him, promising it was the same type of weapon that won the day for the patriots at Kings Mountain earlier in the year. The Tory Patrick Ferguson had invented the breech-loading rifle but the British Army had stubbornly retained the Brown Bess musket. Ironically, Ferguson himself died at Kings Mountain, the victim of one of his own muzzle-loaded rifles. He was buried at the battleground, where a thousand Tories were killed, wounded or captured and the rebels lost but twenty-eight men.

Johnny's eyes were large with adoration, and Samantha couldn't help but smile at Connor's obvious affection for the boy. His eyes caught her face and softened slightly as he saw her smile and they shared Johnny's excitement.

"We have to go," he said suddenly. "We have a long journey tonight."

The woman rose reluctantly. The strangers' presence had brought something fine into the lonely cabin. She had not seen Johnny this happy since his pa had been carried away. She nodded, thankful for the unexpected visit and presents. The salt was particularly welcome. Now Johnny could hunt for food and they would be able to preserve it. It could mean the difference between a full belly and starvation.

"Thank ya," she said gratefully.

Connor took her hand in his. "Thank *you*," he replied. "Not many would risk what you did. I wanted you to know that it was not in vain."

She blessed him again with a special smile that wiped the bitter years from her face. "God go with ya," she said, and watched as the two horsemen disappeared down the dusty ribbon of road.

Chapter Thirteen

As the afternoon turned to dusk, Connor knew he was being unfair. Still he maintained the uncomfortable silence between himself and the girl. She had tried to speak once, but he had harshly rebuffed her.

He didn't know why he was purposely punishing her, especially since it only exacerbated his own wound. If only he could stop remembering the feel of her, the softness of her body next to his, the passion in her eyes. He could not rid himself of the images, and this served only to intensify his anger and dull his customary instinct for danger.

He had not expected a British patrol on this particular road, but even so he had been a fool to use it. He had thought only of speed. There was an abandoned cabin in the swamp that he had used several times. Once there, perhaps he could get some answers from Sam Taylor, and he wanted to do so face-to-face, not on horseback, where she could avoid his eyes.

The road took a sudden fork, and a British barricade appeared in front of them, guarded by red-coated foot soldiers and the green-clad Tories of Tarleton's dragoons. Connor quickly inventoried his alternatives and found only two. Turn and risk pursuit, or bluff their way through. But these were not the casual guards at Georgetown's gates; they were experienced wary men, bloodied by years of partisan warfare.

His decision was made for him when he recognized two of the Tories, former neighbors with whom he had shared card games and occasional drinks. Eye patch or not, they would very possibly recognize him.

Connor turned to Samantha. "Pretend to lose control of your horse and turn him toward the woods. When I'm several lengths ahead, call me and I'll turn back to help you. It might give us a few extra seconds."

A tightening of her mouth was her only sign that she understood, and he silently applauded her quickness.

Her appreciation of his approval was dimmed by their danger. If caught, Connor would hang.

With an imperceptible kick to her horse, Samantha pulled cruelly at the bit, sending him into a circle. Frightened at the unexpected pain, the horse bucked and bolted toward the woods. Looking as if she could barely hold her seat, she called out "''Elp!"

The soldiers at the barricade viewed them with amusement and stood there watching until one of the Tories suddenly realized the whole scene was much too contrived. "They're Marion's men," he yelled, not quite sure but feeling the necessity to stop them. Muskets were immediately shouldered and fired at the escaping pair. Connor was almost at Samantha's side when her horse stumbled and she scampered to clear the saddle before he went down on her. She fell and rolled over once as Connor turned and reached his hand down for her. Her left arm remained still at her side, but her right grasped his and he swung her up behind him. He felt her arm go around his chest as he kicked the horse into a gallop and they disappeared into the wood.

Nearly half of the British guard raced for their horses, but it was as if the two had disappeared into thin air. The British scoured the woods for several hours before giving up the chase.

Once deep in the woods, Connor guided his horse through thickets that ordinary men would never attempt, disregarding the rough brambles that tore at his clothes and cut his face and body. He heard the pursuit growing distant, but even so he found a small stream and followed it several miles, leaving no trace of hoof tracks.

He felt Samantha's right arm around him and wondered why she didn't use the left one. He could feel her face pressed tight against his back. He had heard no word from her but knew her body must be as cut and torn as his own. Even the horse was red with nasty scratches.

Feeling comfortably away from his pursuers, he glanced around. "Are you all right?"

Her voice was small and weak. "Yes."

Connor was not reassured. He saw a small clearing ahead and guided his horse toward the space. A huge moss-covered oak provided a cave in the dense underbrush.

Connor halted the horse and turned carefully in the saddle, trying not to jar his fellow rider. He saw Samantha's white face and her lips clenched shut in pain. She winced at his movement.

Connor's eyes traveled to her left arm, which hung at an odd angle. Very gently he slid from the saddle. Reaching up, he placed his hands around her waist, careful not to touch the arm, and lifted her down. He then eased her to the ground, admiration and concern in his face. The arm must have been agony on that ride through the trees, yet she had made no sound. She looked at him, her eyes misted with pain yet her voice determined. "Are you sure it's safe to stop?"

"Yes, little one," he said softly, "it's safe." Then in a more scolding voice, "You should have told me."

A new wave of pain flickered across her face, but with great effort she smiled slightly. "There really wasn't much opportunity. A broken arm seemed preferable to a broken neck."

Connor knelt beside her, feeling for the break, his fingers sure but gentle. She couldn't stop the involuntary gasp as they probed the injured spot. He looked at her, his face a mask of concern. "We have a long way to go...I should try to set it. But it will hurt like all the furies in hell." His eyes were asking for her consent.

She nodded. There was no choice. She knew she could not travel with it as it was. Connor's smile of approval was almost worth the pain. She watched as he went to the horse and retrieved what was left of the wine they had shared so contentedly earlier in the day. She took several long swallows and nodded to him. He cut a small branch and put it in her mouth; both knew they could not afford a scream at this time. It was a measure of his respect that he didn't feel the need to tell her.

Connor didn't take any more time. He knew if he hesitated he might not be able to go through with it. He gave the arm a quick jerk to straighten it and sighed with relief as he felt the bone fall back into place. It would have to do until a doctor looked at it.

Samantha was unconscious. He took advantage of the moment to place the arm between two pieces of wood and bind it tightly using strips of blanket. Fashioning a rough sling, he stabilized the bound limb against her chest. After completing the task, he sat and thoughtfully regarded her slender still form, grateful for the oblivion that had temporarily erased her pain.

She looked so young, so vulnerable. In addition to her arm, her body was a mass of cuts and bruises, and the new clothes were torn and soiled. Connor's eyes traveled upward to the awkwardly cropped hair now tangled with twigs and brambles. Her small face was smudged with grime and long black eyelashes shuttered her remarkable eyes. He smiled slightly, thinking that he had never seen anyone quite as beautiful.

He couldn't stay the hand that wandered to gently stroke her cheek and pluck an errant leaf from her hair. He had never expected a woman to have the kind of courage he had witnessed today. He felt a consuming tenderness as he looked at her, remembering her passion, her resigned acceptance of his hostility and, finally, her silence, despite great pain, on their wild ride through the forest. She was so contradictory; one thing belied another...one day a precocious lad, the next a passionate woman. Today he had seen any number of Sams and he did not understand any of them.

He sighed, feeling the chill in the air now that the sun was descending. He was already beginning to regret his earlier abandonment of his jacket. They had only the one horse and two blankets, one of which he had partially shredded for Sam's bandages. He had not anticipated camping in the woods during this trip. The abandoned cabin was five miles upriver, but he didn't think Sam could make it now. He considered a fire, but they were much too close to British troops and the smell of smoke traveled quickly through the woods.

He had made a fine mess of things, he thought bitterly, starting this morning with the unexpected unveiling of his companion. He had handled everything very badly, particularly when he allowed his anger to cloud his caution. He owed it to Sam to take care of her.

Connor unsaddled and hobbled the horse. He took what was left of the one blanket and wrapped it securely around her, covering her with the second. Then he sat, his back against a tree, watching her rest and wondering about her.

She had spoken little today, but when she had whispered his name there had been no hint of the illiterate speech. With a jolt, he recalled her later words: "A broken arm seemed preferable to a broken neck." Unlikely words indeed from an unschooled farm lad.

But why? The question haunted him. Why the masquerade? Who and what was Sam Taylor? The only thing he couldn't question were her loyalties. She had proved herself repeatedly and never more so than today.

Connor disliked riddles and this one more than most. He had not understood this noon when he had found himself caught in a tide of emotion he never suspected lurked within him. He liked women, liked them very much indeed, and he enjoyed their favors. But he had never loved and was beginning to think he never would. Before the war, he thought to marry because his way of life demanded it of him. He had searched for a congenial companion who could run the house gracefully and bear heirs. But none excited him or gave him reason to believe he could actually enjoy their constant presence for years to come. He had delayed the decision over and over again, despite innumerable campaigns against his bachelorhood.

Sam's unrestrained, unquestioning, undemanding giving was totally new to him, not only in her lovemaking but in everything she did. He suddenly realized he liked everything about her: the proud tilt of her head, her undeniable courage, her impish humor and her almost annoying competence in practically everything she attempted.

But, damn it, who in the hell was she?

His questions stopped when he heard a quiet movement and saw her looking at him. Her eyes were huge and matched the deep blue of the darkening sky.

"You're shivering," she said, all of her concern turned in his direction. Mischief touched her eyes though pain was etched on her face. "Your temper rid you of your coat and now you'll have to get warm with me."

He shook his head. "I would hurt you."

"You will hurt me far more if you stay out there freezing," she retorted. "I promise I'll not attack you...though," she added with a strained smile, "I would be sorely tempted were it not for this damned arm."

He hesitated but was suddenly decided when she made to discard the blanket herself. Keeping the one torn blanket wrapped about her, he lay beside her, careful to avoid her left arm, and covered them both with the second. He had thought her closeness would be disturbing, but it wasn't. There was only a sense of rightness as his arms went around her and they both took delight in the warm comfort of each other's bodies.

It was sometime in the early-morning hours when Connor woke, startled for a moment as he sought to remember where he was. He felt Sam in his arms and hesitated to move, not wanting to wake her. Why did it seem so natural, as though he had been there before? Hazy memories of another night crept into his mind. The cave. When he had been so ill...the vague impression of warmth...of a woman. So it had been Sam. He smiled quietly to himself and went back to sleep.

They rose at sunrise, both of them feeling ominous rumblings in their stomachs. Neither had eaten since noon the day before and Annabelle's leftovers had been packed on Sam's horse. Her hunger was muted somewhat by the distracting throbbing in her arm, and Connor noticed her eyes weren't as bright as usual. There was nothing to do, he thought, but travel. He couldn't afford the sound of gunshot or the time to trap. Snow Island was still hours away, but perhaps they could stop at the abandoned cabin. It should be safe from British eyes and ears, and perhaps he could catch some fish.

He helped her mount, his hands uncommonly gentle. His questions were stilled this morning; he had decided during the night not to press her. There was obviously a strong reason for her actions, and she would tell him when she was ready. Until then, he would take her as she was.

Conversely, Samantha had decided during the night to confess everything. She could no longer bear the lies…or the fear that he would find out on his own and believe the worst. She had to make him understand.

Connor pulled himself up behind her and she leaned back against his chest. Both felt a curious ache of longing as, locked in their own private thoughts, they made a slow careful path through the woods.

Despite the fact that Connor rode slowly, cradling Samantha carefully in his arms, her pain was evident. Each time he felt her body tense and heard her involuntary intake of breath he winced, feeling her pain as his own. He realized they would never make Snow Island and he headed for the cabin. Fran would worry, but there was no help for it. He was not going to subject her to any more pain.

Lord, she was light. It was almost as if a feather rested against his body. Again, he thought of the several times she had given him food that should have been hers. Guilt welled up within him. He had taken, almost without thinking, everything she had offered, including her virginity, and had given damn little in return. He had treated her abominably yesterday when she had needed tenderness, and his distraction had almost killed her. Yet there had been no word of reproach or complaint. He tightened his arms around her and his lips touched the top of her ruffled hair. He could not believe the desire that flooded him or the tenderness that held him so firmly in its grip. He wanted nothing more than to have her next to him, and it frightened him to think that he wanted it to be forever.

They reached the cabin just before noon, and Connor, despite her protests, carried her inside the cabin and set her down gently on a rough cot. He pushed a wayward lock of hair from her eyes and smiled slowly at her suddenly suspicious countenance.

"You aren't angry anymore?" The question came slowly. She was still bewildered at his change of moods in the past two days.

"Not at you," he replied softly. "I was never angry at you. Just myself."

"And now . . . ?" There was still wariness in her voice.

His hand took hers. "And now I think I should still be. You are just a child."

Her chin stuck out. "I'm nineteen."

His eyes laughed at her. "Nineteen. You look no more than fourteen."

"I know," she said with a hint of satisfaction. "I planned it that way."

His face lost the smile. "Will you tell me why?"

Her eyes seemed enormous to Connor as she considered the question. He felt as if he were being drawn into the eye of a hurricane as he looked directly into them.

Connor knew she was wondering if she could trust him, and it wounded him that distrust still hovered between them. He could stand it no longer.

"It's of no matter," he said gently. "I'm going to see if I can't catch us a fish for lunch. You stay here . . . rest."

Glad the decision had been made for her yet contemptuous of her last-minute cowardice, she nodded. "Thank you," she said in a low voice.

Connor didn't answer but slammed the door on his way out. Damn her, he cursed. Damn her for thanking him when it should be the other way around. Damn her for making him so confused . . . so uncertain of himself. He felt like a schoolboy kissing his first girl, a most unlikely and unsettling sensation. Why couldn't she trust him . . . when she had given him everything else? And why was it so important to him that he have her trust?

Connor built a small fire before looking for a strong branch from which to fashion a pole. He made a hook out of a pin and easily located several choice worms in the soft ground under a willow tree. There had been some string in the cabin and, his weapon ready, he dropped it into a deep pool. Within a short time he had three large trout as trophies.

He quickly cleaned them and placed them over the hot embers, watching as the flesh turned white. The aroma made him realize how hungry he actually was and Sam must be even more so.

As they cooked, he quickly set several traps, hoping for some game tonight. He still dared not shoot. On returning, he retrieved the fish and carefully stamped out the fire. When he was sure there was little danger of unnecessary smoke, he doused the area to catch any lingering sparks.

Sam's eyes were closed when he returned, bearing his precious gift. He touched her lightly on her good shoulder, and she sniffed with appreciation, opening her eyes slowly. They widened at the sight of the three fish resting temptingly on a large piece of bark.

"Hmm," she said, a greedy hand snatching a large piece and stuffing it into her mouth. "I never thought anything could taste so good," she murmured between bites.

Despite his own hunger, Connor watched her with fascination. Her eyes sparkled as she carefully chewed in the way that people accustomed to hunger do, prolonging every bite. Instead of questioning it, he joined her in eating, taking pleasure in her quiet presence and companionship. All too soon, the fish were devoured. "You are a man of many talents," Samantha said finally. "I never suspected that under the soldier's exterior lurked a cook of such excellent quality."

"I have many talents, ma'am, of which you know little."

"I doubt that not at all," she answered teasingly. "I discover them daily." Now the imp was back. "But I think I can easily name my favorite."

"You are forward, miss," he answered with mock severity.

"And you are being presumptuous. How do you know which it is? It could well be your talent for producing one-eyed disgruntled soldiers of the king."

He leaned his head back and roared with laughter.

"If you didn't have a broken arm and look like a chimney sweep, I would show you quick enough," he said, still chuckling.

She looked down at herself, her face settling into a small frown. "I do look rather horrible, don't I? And these poor clothes...and they were new!" Her eyes lighted up with thought. "The creek where you caught those fish . . . maybe I can wash?"

Connor suddenly wished he had held his tongue. "I think you are beautiful just as you are."

It was the first compliment he had ever paid her, and she clutched it to her heart. A bright light in her eyes told him how much it meant to her.

He felt as if a knife had twisted in his stomach. He should have told her that yesterday . . . that and other things. Instead, he had stalked off like a damned fool, leaving her to think God knows what. He put his hand to her face, holding her chin between his fingers, his gray eyes probing her blue ones. "You are lovely, you know. You are lovely and brave and generous, and—" his eyes twinkled "—you can shoot better than any woman I've ever met, a fact for which I am very grateful."

Her smile was timorous, not quite sure that shooting well was a particularly admirable trait in a lady yet desperately wanting those warm gray eyes to remain looking at her so fondly. Her whole face was a question as to his intentions.

But he was damned if he knew what they were. Never had he been drawn so completely to a woman or felt such contentment at just being with her, nor a passion like the one that had haunted him constantly since yesterday morning. Every touch was like playing with fire: warming until you approached too closely and then extremely painful. He had never wanted a woman as much, nor feared one more. He wanted to say he loved her, but he couldn't, not as long as she didn't quite trust him, not as long as some mysterious secret hovered ominously between them.

Samantha completely misread his thoughts. Despite what he had said, she knew she looked terrible. Dirty. Skinny. Her hair uncombed and clothes filthy. She tried to see herself through his eyes and she was not impressed: a girl who acted more like a boy than a lady, who had adapted to cursing as a perfectly acceptable form of communication, who had, happily enough, spent a night in a brothel—never mind that Connor had taken her there—and, finally, who had wantonly surrendered her virginity on a forest floor with what she considered shameless abandon. She was no longer wifely material, Sam thought wryly. And if that wasn't sufficient to send a proper gentleman galloping in the opposite direction, her identity as a Chatham certainly would. A dark cloud settled in her eyes, and her mouth turned uncharacteristically downward. She must tell him before things became even more complicated. Perhaps after she washed...perhaps cleanliness would give her the needed dignity and courage.

She looked up at him, her eyes pleading. "I want to wash. Please."

There was nothing she could ask that he wouldn't grant...not when he saw the sadness in her eyes.

They walked together down to the creek where Connor had fished an hour earlier. The sun was back today, and he first took off her boots, then his own, before revealing his treasured piece of soap. When she raised her eyebrows in question, he grinned. "In the prison ship, I didn't have a bath for four months. Now I never go anywhere without soap." The smile left his face as he remembered those endless days and nights of feeling the filth accumulate and being helpless to do anything about it.

Samantha had been on the verge of confiding in Connor, but the sudden tension in his face stopped her. Her eyes went involuntarily to the scars on his ankle.

"You've never told me about it," she said softly.

"You saw me...that night in the cave," he said slowly, painfully, wanting to forget that wraith he had been but knowing he never could. "The worst was watching my father die. Slowly. By inches. And knowing it was intended. Planned for both of us. Only I cheated them...cheated the British and cheated Chatham."

Samantha watched the muscles in his face flex with emotion as he continued. "I had a brother...not much older than you...Chatham killed him, too. His daughter...his damned daughter...seduced him, then told her father he had ruined her. He never had a chance." Connor's voice was so bitter she scarcely recognized it. "Brendan fought for her honor...what honor there was." Something inside Samantha died a slow painful death as she recognized the hatred in his words. "Months later she was engaged to a damned British butcher."

Samantha's voice was low...so low he could barely make out the words. "Maybe she loved your brother...."

"Love. So much she killed him? That is what she did, as much as if she had aimed the gun herself. Chatham had been looking for an excuse for years to do us harm. She handed it to him on a silver platter."

Connor struggled for control. There had been no reason to tell her what he had, no reason to drag her into the dark corners of his life. But he had a strange compulsion to tell her everything...to open his life to her in exchange, perhaps, for her to do the same.

Any such hope was quickly dashed. A look of total anguish had settled over her white face and he cursed himself once more as an unfeeling idiot. He should not have burdened her with his own problems...not when she so obviously had her own.

He forced himself to relax and took the soap and a rag he had found in the cabin and started washing her...first her face, then her hands and finally her feet, talking to her about nonsensical things...all the while blaming himself for her tight pinched lips and the sorrow in her eyes.

Chapter Fourteen

During the next several days, Connor courted Sam as he had never courted a woman before. He pampered her outrageously, in every way he could devise.

He had decided to stay at the cabin while Sam rested and at least some of her bruises healed. Game and fish were plentiful and he felt no urgency to return to Snow Island. It was near Christmas, and Fran had nothing major planned.

The days were near idyllic. The sun stayed with them, though the nights turned cold. Even that, however, was a boon, since they sought warmth together. Their bodies melded comfortably and Connor felt an exquisite joy in merely holding her close.

During the day they would walk together, hand in hand, or just sit, her head buried in his lap as he would recite sonnets. He told her about his strange ability to remember, almost word for word, anything he read. He told her about the prison ship, this time more dispassionately, and how he had retreated into remembered words to survive. He talked as he had never talked before... because he wanted her to know everything there was to know about Connor O'Neill.

He knew he had fallen in love with her completely. Joy welled up inside him when he looked at her and saw the softness in her eyes. There was an unspoiled freshness about her so natural he knew it would be there forever. She would be part child when she was ninety and, God, how he wanted to be there with her. Now. Ten years from now. Fifty years from now. She had brought a warmth and delight to his solemn world and he cherished every minute of it.

Only one thing gave him pause. She never talked about herself. Never. Even when he gently gave her the chance. At even a hint of curiosity, she retreated inward and he felt himself locked out.

For now it didn't matter. He didn't care who or why or what troubles she left behind. Connor felt loved as he had never felt before . . . and he loved as much in return.

Even the slightest touch of their hands was a gentle kiss. A promise.

On the third day, they sat beside the trout stream, his pole in the water, her body leaning comfortably against his chest. He was recounting the old bishop from *Canterbury Tales*, and she giggled in anticipation.

"Something," he said wryly, "tells me you have heard . . . or read . . . this before."

There was a guilty gleam in her eyes.

"You wretch," he said. "You will never know what I went through to get those damned readers."

Her giggle turned into full laughter. "You were so serious . . . so intent on betterin' me."

"So Sam does read?"

"Some," she admitted with a half smile. She had totally given up the rough speech and had been grateful he had not questioned it. Even now there was no accusation in his voice, only quizzical amusement.

"I suspect a bit more than some," he retorted. Then he leaned down and kissed her laughing lips, feeling their sweetness and responsiveness.

He drew back as if burned. He remembered how quickly he had lost control only three days earlier. There was her arm to consider.

Connor looked at her closely. Despite her laughter, her haunted look had never quite disappeared over the past several days. He guided her head into his lap, and his fingers played with her short hair and soothingly touched her face. One hand clasped hers, and he knew he had never felt so close to another human being. It was enough, just then, to have her so near.

Samantha's feelings were swirling. She had abandoned any idea of telling Connor who she was. The bitterness in his words two days ago had told her he would never understand, never forgive. But she couldn't give him up, not now. She couldn't imagine a world without him, nor did she want to. She would take what minutes or hours or days she had left, but deep inside, an emptiness clawed at her very being as she realized the pit she was digging for herself.

She looked up at Connor's face, memorizing the half-closed lazy eyes and every line of his strongly etched features. Her right hand slid into his shirt and her fingers played with the short blond hair before moving on, caressing...stroking... teasing.

She felt Connor's body tense and sensed his struggle for control until he, too, surrendered to an urgency too strong to conquer.

He leaned down and his lips brushed hers, first with infinite gentleness and slow exploration, then becoming more insistent, more demanding as his passion grew. His tongue explored hers, and she relished the sensual intimacy as her own played dancing games with his. Her hand went to the back of his neck and tangled in his thick blond hair; her body arched up...wanting...searching...needing.

Connor was caught in the same whirlwind, unable to restrain the wild exultation he felt at her nearness, at her desire which so goaded his own. Then he slowed, remembering her arm and bruises. He forced himself back, searching her face and seeing a want as deep and endless as his own.

"Your arm..."

"Damn" she started, but stopped, an abashed look on her face. "Posh," she corrected herself. "Posh on my arm." There was a decided gleam in the blue eyes.

"Are you sure?"

"I've never been so sure of anything in my life," she said with a slow tantalizing smile that held an invitation so completely wanton he couldn't restrain a smile.

He carefully unbuttoned her shirt, letting his hands treasure the already stiffening breasts. He leaned down and his lips played sensually with the red-tipped nipples while his hands gently disengaged the fastenings on her breeches. Despite his growing fervor, he was infinitely careful to avoid hurting her. Trembling with restraint, he carefully drew her to him, his lips finding hers once more.

Samantha felt the gentleness of his lips and knew the mammoth effort required of him as concern battled desire.

"I want you," she said slowly, distinctly. "I want you a part of me...I want to feel you warm inside me." Then she said the words he had wanted to hear. "I love you, Connor. I'll always love you." Her hand touched his face, and there was such yearning, such love in the slight caress that he felt humbled...and then elated as joy coursed through him in waves.

They joined again...quietly, gently...as the sun covered them with a blanket of gold. Their passion was evident in every slow touch, each one an act of love in itself. It was a communion of giving, both yielding their own pleasure for that of the other and, in return, receiving twice the bounty. It was a voyage of endless adventure and discovery as they explored each other's bodies and tasted of each other's wonder. Carefully, very carefully, he entered her, resting on one arm so not to disturb her injured one, but reaching out, sharing, creating a cocoon in which none but the two of them existed...carrying her into spiraling worlds of sensation and enchantment. When it was over, they both knew something extraordinary had changed them forever, and they lay, touching, silent, stunned.

They watched together as the sun dipped below the trees, sending a rainbow of colors stretching across the sky, each shade more brilliant than they had ever seen.

It wasn't until the chill breeze became cold that they stirred, reluctant even then to move away from each other for even a moment and break the exquisite bond that held them.

Connor knelt, looking at her, wondering at the gloriously passionate yet gentle soul that lay within her. He reached down and kissed her softly, then took her hand and pulled her up. They walked slowly, still partially in a daze, to the cabin. He lit a candle against the growing darkness and touched her again.

"I'll go check the traps," he said gently. "I'll be back soon, love." His low voice caressed the last word. He paused at the door. "I don't want to leave you . . . not for a minute."

Her face reflected the same sentiment, and he had to force himself out the door. They needed food tonight and would need more in the morning. They would leave in the morning; Fran would already be more than a little worried.

It was dark when he returned, two rabbits in hand. He prepared a small fire outside and cooked both, preparing one for dinner and saving the other for breakfast. They said little as they ate, although their eyes and faces spoke volumes. By unspoken consent, they slipped into blankets on the old cot, Connor's arms wrapped lightly around Samantha's waist.

The sun sneaked intrusively through the cracks of the cabin. Sighing with contentment, Samantha snuggled more completely into Connor's hard curves. Her face touched his and she thought how strange that she enjoyed the stubble on his cheek. But then she delighted in almost everything about him.

Connor was also loath to move, luxuriating in the sense of possessiveness he had with Sam in his arms. He had never felt this way before, rejoicing in her nearness, terrified of losing her. He would, this day, ask her to marry him.

They finally rose, dreading the thought of the return to Snow Island, where they would no longer share a private world of their own. They ate silently, then walked hand and hand down to the creek to wash. Connor quietly helped her bathe, then sat her on the bank.

His eyes searched her face. "Is it really Sam? Your name, I mean."

Samantha felt her heart stop. It took all her strength to look back at him, her eyes quiet but her emotions churning inside. How could she lie to him? But the alternative meant watching the warmth in his face change to hatred. She looked at the ground and her voice was toneless. "Yes . . . well, nearly. My father wanted a boy." There was more than a thread of truth in that.

But he had caught the "nearly" and his eyes forced her to continue.

1. How do you rate: _____
   (Please print book TITLE)
   1.6 ☐ excellent   .4 ☐ good   .2 ☐ not so good
   .5 ☐ very good   .3 ☐ fair   .1 ☐ poor

2. How likely are you to purchase another book:
   in this *series*?   by this *author*?
   2.1 ☐ definitely would purchase   3.1 ☐ definitely would purchase
   .2 ☐ probably would purchase   .2 ☐ probably would purchase
   .3 ☐ probably would not purchase   .3 ☐ probably would not purchase
   .4 ☐ definitely would not purchase   .4 ☐ definitely would not purchase

3. How does this book compare with romance books you usually read?
   4.1 ☐ far better than others   .4 ☐ not as good
   .2 ☐ better than others   .5 ☐ definitely not as good
   .3 ☐ about the same

4. Please check the statements you feel best describe this book.
   5 ☐ Realistic conflict   18 ☐ Too many foreign/unfamiliar words
   6 ☐ Too much violence/anger   19 ☐ Couldn't put the book down
   7 ☐ Not enough drama   20 ☐ Liked the setting
   8 ☐ Especially romantic   21 ☐ Made me feel good
   9 ☐ Original plot   22 ☐ Heroine too independent
   10 ☐ Good humor in story   23 ☐ Hero too dominating
   11 ☐ Not enough humor   24 ☐ Unrealistic conflict
   12 ☐ Not enough description of setting   25 ☐ Not enough romance
   13 ☐ Didn't like the subject   26 ☐ Too much description of setting
   14 ☐ Fast paced   27 ☐ Ideal hero
   15 ☐ Too predictable   28 ☐ Slow moving
   16 ☐ Heroine too juvenile/weak/silly   29 ☐ Not enough suspense
   17 ☐ Believable characters   30 ☐ Liked the subject

5. What aspect of the story outline on the back of the cover appealed to you most?
   31 ☐ location   32 ☐ subject
   33 ☐ characters   34 ☐ element of suspense in plot
   35 ☐ description of conflict

6. Did you feel this story was:
   36.1 ☐ too sexy
   .2 ☐ just sexy enough
   .3 ☐ not too sexy

7. Please indicate how many romance paperbacks you read in a month.
   37.1 ☐ 1 to 4   .2 ☐ 5 to 10   .3 ☐ 11 to 15   .4 ☐ more than 15

8. Please indicate your sex and age group.
   38.1 ☐ Male   39.1 ☐ under 18   .3 ☐ 25-34   .5 ☐ 50-64
   .2 ☐ Female   .2 ☐ 18-24   .4 ☐ 35-49   .6 ☐ 65 or older

9. Have you any additional comments about this book?
   (40)_____
   (41)_____
   (42)_____
   (43)_____
   _____
   _____

Thank you for completing and returning this questionnaire.

NAME _____
(Please Print)

ADDRESS _____

CITY _____

ZIP CODE _____

BUSINESS REPLY MAIL

FIRST CLASS   PERMIT NO. 717   BUFFALO, NY

POSTAGE WILL BE PAID BY ADDRESSEE

NATIONAL READER SURVEYS

901 Fuhrmann Blvd.
P.O. Box 1395
Buffalo, N.Y. 14240-9961

"It's Samara," she blurted out, thinking of the first thing she could offer other than Samantha.

"Samara," he repeated, enjoying the sound of it. "It's lovely."

Her lips pursed in disagreement, and he laughed, his eyes twinkling at the expression.

"I asked," he said gently, "because I felt it only proper that I know the name of the woman I ask to marry me."

He was prepared for anything but the sudden pain and despair in her face. His hand reached out and grabbed hers, knowing instinctively that she was ready to flee.

His hand was unyielding, and she twisted for a moment before standing silent, her eyes downcast, wanting at this moment to be both in his arms and a million miles away.

"Sam...Samara..." His voice was quiet but determined, and she knew he was not going to release her.

"I love you, Sam. I want you to be my wife. I know I don't have much to offer you now...not until this damn war is over, but I love you, more than I thought it possible for anyone to love another. Tom Edwards is a minister. He can marry us at Snow Island. Fran can be my best man..." He stopped, confused by the growing misery in her eyes. A great void filled him as he read the answer in her face.

"Is there someone else?" he asked tightly, not understanding at all. She had been a virgin, and she had proclaimed her love last night. He couldn't believe she would have given herself so freely, so passionately, if there was another man.

She shook her head slowly.

"Then why?"

"You don't know anything about me, about my family, my background...."

"Only because you won't tell me," he said gently. "But I know everything I want to know. I know I don't want to lose you."

Her eyes were darker than he had ever seen them, and her mouth trembled. She lifted her chin and looked at him squarely. "You won't lose me. I'll be here as long as you want me. But I can't marry you."

"Why?" It was a confused cry, pleading, demanding an answer that he could understand.

She answered in the only way she could. "Because," she said slowly, "I *do* love you. Whatever else you believe, you must believe that."

He looked at her set face and knew defeat. Anger emerged from his confusion. Anger mixed with sorrow. She would play his mistress but not his wife. And why should she? He had not been whole for a long time; bitterness had eaten away at him, and only Chatham's death would change that. Is that what Annabelle had warned him about days ago when she said Sam may have kept her distance because of his hate? If so, it was something he couldn't change. But it was another reason to kill Chatham. He added it to the growing list.

Samantha wanted to die as she watched his face change and his warm gray eyes turn to slivers of ice. She felt tears begin to form in her own and she turned her back to him; he mustn't see them. She could hear his retreating steps and felt her heart crumble into tiny pieces.

This is the longest day in my life, Samantha thought with anguish.

Connor had helped her mount, but his hands had been merely efficient, not gentle. His mouth had been set in a rigid line, and his eyes, his beautiful gray eyes, had been as cold as any winter storm. He had become a complete stranger, possessed by an obsession held only barely in check. An obsession she had unwittingly fueled.

He rode at the front of the saddle and she immediately understood why. There was far less contact that way. She remembered how possessively he had cradled her in his arms just three days ago, and the ache inside her grew to enormous proportions.

He had said little since he left her at the stream that morning. When she had reached out a tentative hand to him, he had pretended he didn't see it and turned away.

And now, his straight unyielding back shouted at her, accused her, pushed her away.

She kept her hand on the saddle. She had instinctively put her right arm around his waist but hurriedly removed it when she felt him flinch at her touch.

The ride would never be over...they would go on forever...in this frozen silence. It suddenly made her think of Tantalus, the son of Zeus, who had offended the gods by stealing their nectar and ambrosia and giving them to mere mortals. In punishment, he had stood up to his neck in water but could not drink, and over his head hung fruit he could not reach. For all eternity. Was that her future?

She had stolen the forbidden fruit and her punishment was to ride behind Connor but not to touch him...to love every part of him but not to have him believe it...to be asked to be his wife and have to say no. She closed her eyes against the horrible irony.

Would the trip never be over, agonized Connor. The gait of the horse unavoidably threw their bodies in contact, and each time was more hurtful than the last. Every touch was a brand searing him, a knife twisting deeper inside him.

He loved her...he loved her with an intensity that shook him still. How much light she had brought into his life, not just in the past few days but in the months he had known her as Sam. Her laughter and caring, tenderness and understanding, it had been a fraud. All of it. He didn't know what she wanted, but it obviously was not him. Why, damn it. Why? If it was something in her past, why couldn't she...why wouldn't she trust him? He could have sworn she loved him...how could she have pretended so well?

He suddenly stiffened. She was an actress. A very good one. She had had them all fooled for months. Damn her. Damn all women.

What now? Sam wondered hopelessly. Would he tell Colonel Marion? Would she be ordered to leave? Leave Connor, never to see him again. That was even worse than seeing him daily but not being able to touch him.

Connor studied his alternatives. He could tell Fran...should, in fact. Women had never been allowed in Marion's secret camps for numerous reasons. He had little doubt that Sam would be banished if her sex became known. But not to see her again, he couldn't stand the thought. He decided to say nothing. Whatever else had happened this week, he still owed Sam. She had saved his life twice and he couldn't bear to think of something happening to her. He would make her promise to stay in camp, to tend to the horses and leave the raids to others. He would ask Fran for more courier duty... perhaps even request reassignment to Sumter or Greene. *I love her... damn... how can I ever stay away?* He released a long sigh, which sounded more like the moan of an animal in pain.

The sound brought tears to Samantha's eyes. She angrily wiped them away with a sweaty hand, crisscrossing her face with dark smudges.

I love him so much, how can I live without him?

I love her... damn... how can I ever let her go?

The answers eluded them both and nothing seemed real but the weary clip clop of the overburdened horse as they made their way steadily toward their destination.

Chapter Fifteen

Connor and Samantha arrived back at Snow Island silent and stiff. Connor had been wrong. Marion, always unpredictable, had left days earlier with three-quarters of his men for Nelson's Ferry, a principal supply area for the British.

Connor cursed roundly. His place was with Marion, and instead he had been playing with an empty dream, making a fool of himself to a woman who didn't want him. With little ceremony, he impatiently helped Samantha down and, without additional words, saddled a fresh horse.

"Connor..."

He turned at the sound of her voice, his face a hard mask, his eyes icy. His expression didn't change at the plea in her eyes.

"You stay here," he said harshly. "Heaven help you if I find you trailing after us or gone when I get back. Do you understand me?"

She nodded miserably. "Are you going to tell Colonel Marion?"

She flinched at his look. There was no mercy, no compassion in it. The Connor of the past four days was gone, replaced by a stranger.

"I don't know," he said, and then seeing her complete desolation, he weakened. "I'll say nothing until we talk again. And it's general now, Marion was promoted while we were gone." With a wry smile that was full of pain, he looked at her as if he were seeing straight through her soul before tightening his knees against the horse and disappearing into the dusk.

Connor rode swiftly. Though tired, he welcomed the lonely ride through the swamp. It gave him time to consider the past four days, which had played such havoc with his life and emotions. Four days. It seemed a lifetime. He had never thought two people could be so perfectly attuned to each other, had never believed he could feel such tenderness, such love. It had, for such a short time, been paradise. And then the fall. Such a long, long drop when he realized she didn't feel the same, didn't want the permanence he craved. Damn. Damn her. Damn him for letting it happen, for making himself vulnerable.

There was still a puzzle that wouldn't go away. It stayed in his mind, goading him, tormenting him. Her eyes had been so full of pain when she had refused him. But why... why... if there was a reason, why would she not confide in him? He would fight the devil himself for her; surely she should know that.

When he returned, they would talk... he would force an explanation from her, find out more about her. Perhaps that was it. Perhaps something in her past frightened her.

He kicked his horse into a gallop and concentrated completely on the task ahead.

Fran Marion and his troop of one hundred and fifty men had taken Nelson's Ferry and were having great success in capturing unsuspecting supply boats that wandered unaware into their trap. The rebels were badly in need of powder and flint and the British were generously making their raid a very lucrative one. Marion, however, missed Connor. O'Neill had proved to be his best scout and he could not shake a nagging fear about his delayed return. It wasn't like Connor to be late. Fran also fretted about young Taylor's safety. If they weren't back when he returned to Snow Island, he would dispatch some spies to learn whether they had been taken.

He had just doubled the sentries when he saw Connor's tall form riding in.

Connor came straight to him. "A British troop, better than four hundred men, are just five miles from here."

"Did they see you?"

"No, I was riding parallel to the road. They're dragoons and they'll be here within the hour."

Marion wasted no more time. He ordered his men to mount and fade back into the swamp. The British supplies had already been sent ahead and the boats burned.

As Marion started to leave the ferry, a sentry rode up and reported another British troop straddling the path to Snow Island.

He called his top officers. "Connor . . . Horry. Take the men into the swamp and position them. They've never dared yet to meet us inside."

Connor took half the men and saw them carefully perched in trees overlooking a deep creek, knowing Horry was doing the same. Marion's woodsmen blended into the woods as completely as a deer or any other natural creature. They watched as the British approached and established pickets along the creek's edge, but did nothing until evening fell.

Through the night, Connor could hear the occasional bark of a rifle and a subsequent cry. Not a single British picket, nor their replacement, survived the night. Sentry duty that night was a sentence of death.

There was a stalemate the next morning, the British not daring to enter the swamp, the rebels unable to leave it.

Connor was the first to sight the white flag, asking a temporary truce and meeting. He and Marion went to meet the British commanding officer, a Major McLeroth.

Both knew of McLeroth, a Scotsman who had few of the bloodthirsty qualities of many of the other British officers in the Carolinas. They were quietly amused at the officer's complaint.

"It is," the Scotsman argued, "contrary to all laws of civilized warfare to shoot pickets." With a look of righteous indignation on his face, he dared Marion "to come out of the woods and fight."

Marion's mouth twitched, his eyes fairly dancing at the lecture, and Connor had equal difficulty withholding a smile. Suddenly Marion's eyes went black, the amusement gone.

"And I feel it is contrary to all laws of civilized warfare to burn the houses of all who will not submit to you," he said, his eyes flashing dangerously. "That is far more indefensible than shooting pickets. As long as you persist in the one, we will persevere in the other.''

Marion turned to go, but the major stopped him. ''I have a proposal.''

Marion raised his eyebrows in question.

''I will put fifteen of my best marksmen against fifteen of yours. Let them decide this battle.''

Marion had few doubts over which group would win in such a contest. There were no better shots in the South than his woodsmen. What he couldn't understand was why McLeroth, with his advantage in numbers, would make such a suggestion.

Marion nodded curtly and the two men agreed on a time. Marion and Connor returned to the men and asked for volunteers, warning each that it could very well be a matter of suicide. No matter how good the Americans, shots at nearly point-blank range would be deadly.

There was no lack of volunteers and Marion and Connor selected carefully. No family men were taken; the others were chosen on shooting ability. Connor's offer had been quickly denied by Marion.

They watched as the two groups of men approached each other. The Americans in their torn and tattered homespun and the British in bright red uniforms. Attention was so focused on the opposing groups that Marion, who seldom missed anything, didn't notice that the British ranks were growing thinner. At the moment agreed upon, the fifteen redcoats suddenly retreated, leaving the Americans standing alone, stunned amazement on their faces at their sudden reprieve.

None were as surprised as Marion, who sent Connor and ten men after some prisoners while he retreated back across the creek in preparation for a British trick.

An hour later Connor returned with a British lieutenant in tow. The man's horse had gone lame, and he had lagged behind the main column.

It didn't take long for Marion to extract an explanation. The lieutenant, though chagrined at his capture, was nonetheless proud of his commander's successful ruse. McLeroth had not known about the second British troop and thought he himself had stumbled into a trap. Believing that Marion had far more men than he did, especially after the decimation of his sentries, he had opted for escape.

Connor, Major Horry and Marion stared at one another completely dumbfounded. Marion ordered the release of the lieutenant, and as soon as he was out of hearing range all three exploded into laughter.

With McLeroth gone, Marion's troop easily avoided the second British detachment and were well on their way to Snow Island. Connor could no longer avoid Marion's questioning glances.

Marion turned his sorrel toward Connor and rode side by side. "We were worried about you and Sam." There was no hint of censure in his voice.

"We ran into a British patrol and Sam's horse was killed. He fell and his arm was broken." Connor had caught himself just as he was about to say "she." He continued. "I knew of an abandoned cabin and thought he should rest before traveling any farther."

Marion nodded. "He's all right?" There was something in Connor's face and voice that puzzled him . . . a flash of secrecy that was uncommon.

"Yes," Connor said shortly. "But I think it would be well if you made sure he stays in camp for a while."

Marion nodded, still mystified over Connor's cautious answers. He knew that Connor had taken Sam with him to forge a friendship. Something had happened, and it obviously went beyond the boy's injury. He had hoped that an attachment to the boy would, in some way, dull the hate that festered inside Connor. He was too good a man, too honorable, too caring to be so obsessed.

Marion moved from what was obviously an uncomfortable topic. "And how is Annabelle?" he asked, a gleam in his eye. He had always found Connor's friendship with Georgetown's leading madam intriguing and he was most grateful for the information she contributed.

The question coaxed a reluctant laugh from Connor. "In bad company," he answered with a slight smile. "I shared the house with Colonel Tarleton four nights ago."

Fran couldn't restrain a grin. "That should have been interesting."

"Annabelle said he was bragging about a few surprises he had for the Swamp Fox."

Marion's grin evolved into a chuckle. "And wouldn't he have been surprised to realize with whom he was sharing shelter that night."

Connor's smile widened. "I think poor Annabelle almost fainted when he mentioned that I am now almost as wanted as you. A dubious honor, but he reassured her that I would never leave the swamp. He did leave her some rather interesting information. Cornwallis is planning a major expedition against Greene in the next few weeks."

The amusement quickly left Marion's face. "I'll send a courier as soon as we get back."

"I would like to go," Connor said quietly.

Marion quickly recognized the determination in his voice. He didn't like losing Connor again and courier duty was beneath his rank, but there was the advantage that Connor was respected and would be quickly heard and believed. And it was obviously important to him. Connor made few requests.

He nodded. "But first you get some rest. You look like hell, if you'll permit me to say so." Without waiting for a reply, he rode to the front of the column.

Connor slept through the rest of the day and night. It was his first sleep in more than forty-eight hours and his exhaustion overcame him. It did not, however, keep Sam from sneaking in and out of his jumbled dreams. When he woke with the first rays of sun, he felt drained and depressed.

He found Marion around a small fire and accepted a rare cup of tea, one of the many gifts contributed by the British in the past several days.

"Do you still want to go to General Greene?" Marion asked.

Connor nodded, his eyes searching the clearing for Sam. "I've already committed everything to memory and there would be nothing to find if the British somehow intercepted me."

"Except you, my friend, and that would be a very great loss indeed," Marion replied with a smile. "You would find no mercy from them."

"If Georgetown is any example of their competence, I'll not have any trouble," Connor said lightly, then his voice turned dead serious. "I want to go, Fran. And I would like to stay if there's a battle brewing . . . if it's all right with you."

Marion's eyes bored into him. "No," he said. "It's not all right. You know how much I need you here."

"Greene is going to need every man he can get against Cornwallis," Connor replied. "I'll come back after it's over."

Marion looked at Connor's troubled eyes. "But that's not the real reason, is it?"

Connor looked askance.

"What's bothering you, Connor?" Marion's voice was unusually sharp. He wanted to pierce the emotional armor that Connor seemed to be wearing.

Connor's eyes were bleak, the color of the sea on a dismal day. He just shook his head.

"It's not still Chatham?"

Connor looked up in surprise, his eyes clouding even more. He was startled to discover he hadn't thought of Chatham in days. Thoughts of Sam had crowded everything from his mind.

Now thoroughly exasperated, Marion tried probing further. "Sam, then? Are you worried about him?"

Connor grabbed the lifeline. "He was almost killed. I think you should consider finding another place for him."

"And where would that be?" Marion asked softly. "He seems to have no family except us. I thought you liked him."

Connor's voice was suddenly hard. "I just don't want him to get hurt," he said stubbornly.

Marion couldn't keep the confusion from his face. This was a different man than the one he thought he knew. Contradictory. Uncertain.

His hand went to Connor's shoulder. "I'll look after him. You have no need to worry. And, Connor, if you think Greene needs you, stay. But you will be sorely missed and not simply because you are my best scout."

Connor merely nodded, but Marion couldn't miss the relief and gratitude in his eyes.

Connor knew his next chore would be more difficult. He went in search of Sam. He could not miss the mixture of relief and anxiety on her face when they rode in yesterday. But she had quickly slipped away and he had been too weary to try to find her. But he would this morning, by God.

It was not nearly as hard as he expected. As if she had known he was looking for her, she was sitting in a little niche on the bank of the creek. He was painfully reminded of another similar spot.

"Sam?"

She looked up, her heart in her enormous glittering blue eyes. Quickly she looked down and clasped her hands tightly, pressing together painfully. How could he not know how much she loved him? How beautiful he was this morning with the sun hitting his unruly blond hair and steel-gray eyes. His face seemed etched in stone.

"Sam . . . please talk to me." The plea stabbed her with renewed force. He should never have to plead with anyone. Particularly not with one who loved him more than life itself. But she could say nothing.

She felt her shoulders grasped and shaken and she forced herself to look up at him. What she saw brought forth new waves of misery.

His eyes were anguished and confused, and his mouth was set in a firm bitter line.

"I am leaving, Sam," he said slowly.

"Leaving?" Her soft question spoke her bewilderment and grief. It played across her face, misting her blue eyes.

"I'm joining General Greene in North Carolina. Cornwallis plans a major offensive."

"Leaving . . . because of me?" The question agonized.

Connor's eyes softened and he lied. "No . . . I received some information from Annabelle that must be delivered as soon as possible. Already I've dallied far too long."

"Because of me," she repeated with a small cry. Tears glittered in her eyes.

He took a short curl in his hand and fondled it, wanting desperately to run his hands through the short hair and summoning all his willpower not to do so.

He straightened up. "You know if you have any trouble, I'll help you. If that's why you won't marry me, we'll solve it together."

She was suddenly in his arms, sobbing her heart out, and he crushed her to him. All their resolves disappeared, lost in their enormous emotional and physical hunger for each other.

"Don't go," she pleaded. "Don't leave me," and then she remembered those same words said eighteen months ago in a clearing, and she felt a terrible premonition of disaster.

His hands were comforting her, his lips kissing away the tears, and she felt the longing rising within her, fighting the sudden chill that was enshrouding her.

She pulled away, and Connor saw stark terror in her eyes. Her hands were cold, and her face more frightened than he had ever seen it.

"Don't go, Connor," she whispered. "Please don't go."

"Say you will marry me."

She closed her eyes. Dear God, what did it mean...this coldness running through her? Was it telling her disaster lay in North Carolina or in marriage?"

"I can't," she cried.

"You want me, I know you do," he pressed. His hands were feverish now, his mouth famished for the taste of her. He would force her to admit she loved him. As his hands sought and released her breasts from their binding, his mouth found hers with combined lust and tenderness. It was a deadly mixture and Samantha's defenses collapsed as her body traitorously pulled toward his, every nerve singing in response to his touch.

Their coupling was wild and abandoned. Disregarding her still sore arm, Samantha lifted her body to meet his and she climbed and climbed, cherishing each thrust as she urged him deeper, wanting him to touch the very essence of her soul, feeling the need to fill a lifetime with this moment. The final explosion ignited millions of star bursts and both lay back exhausted but not contented. The fear and uncertainty that had added a frantic urgency to their lovemaking still hovered like an evil presence between them.

Connor quietly drew his pants on and helped Samantha do the same. He gently replaced the binding around her breasts and pulled her homespun shirt down. Hesitant to ask questions for fear of the answers, he played with a blade of grass.

"I didn't mean for this to happen," he said finally. "I don't want a mistress, Sam. I can't take bits and pieces and be satisfied. I never thought I would find anyone like you . . . and now I can't imagine living without you. But I'm not going to do it this way. I want it to be open and happy and forever or not at all."

Samantha searched his face and knew he meant every word. Every fiber of her being called out yes. But then her mind envisioned his face going livid with hate, and she couldn't stand that . . . not ever. It would be best if they parted now, with their memories.

"I can't," she whispered.

"And you can't tell me why?"

"No."

He merely nodded, his steely eyes hooded, his back straightening with determination. "I've talked to Marion and he said he will look after you."

"He doesn't know . . . ?"

"No, I'll not tell him, but I think you should. Soon." His tone was casual and she would never know what it cost him to make it so.

"Must you go?"

There was a short bitter laugh. "Yes, Sam, I must go."

"When?"

"As soon as I can saddle a horse."

He turned and walked away, never hearing her whisper, "Please be careful . . . I love you."

It was Christmas Eve and the sound of frivolity filled the woods. The notes of homemade fiddles and flutes intermingled with laughter from the daylong tippling. Fires flickered in the growing dusk and the first star of evening had appeared. The smell of roasting meat was everywhere, venison, wild boar, quail and duck. But under it all was a current of melancholy among men too long away from family and home. It was in their raucous laughter and in the sad songs they sang. They filtered away from the main party and gathered in smaller groups, talking about sweethearts and families.

For some, it was their fourth Christmas at war, and time did nothing to ease the loneliness, particularly among these men left tonight in the woods. Those with homes nearby had filtered away during the past few days and had at least some hope of seeing loved ones, however brief a visit it might be.

Sam had been invited to join several of the small groups and she had tried hard to smile and laugh. But she soon retreated to the rough hut that was now her home. There was a deep hollow inside her, and nothing could soothe its constant ache. She had thought last Christmas unbearable, but now there were two O'Neills to mourn, and she didn't know how she could stand it. A sole tear trickled down her cheek.

Connor had left four days ago. He had gone without another word after their parting at the creek. She had tried to steel herself against the loneliness but couldn't. Every time she heard a bird it was accompanied by his soft amused drawl as he talked of its peculiar habits. No one loved the woods as he did, and he was everywhere. She missed him every minute of every hour and every hour of every day.

Marion had moved the camp again, this time to the William Goddard plantation on the other side of the island. It had been used before and there were rough huts, lean-to style, to keep out the cold and rain. There were also storage bins for food and a barn that had been strengthened and barred for prisoners. It meant Marion could now take prisoners for trade, something impossible in other locations.

But the relative comfort of the new camp meant nothing without Connor.

Locked in her own private misery, Samantha didn't hear the steps or see Marion's cool appraisal as he looked at her small sorrowful face and the telltale dirty ridge made by a wandering tear. He almost passed on, reluctant to invade thoughts so obviously private and painful. But she sensed his presence and looked up, her eyes unfathomable in the growing dark.

"I have something for you," he said quietly, and was encouraged by her trembling smile. "May I sit down?"

She nodded, afraid he would hear the tears in her voice if she spoke.

He had two items in his hands, one packaged. He handed her the unwrapped gift first. It was a small leather cap, the badge of Marion's brigade, and it sported a white cockade. This drew a tiny smile. It was obviously a sign that she had been completely accepted. The small cockade was worn by all in camp so they could immediately identify each other in battle.

Marion handed her the second gift. "This is from Connor," he said slowly. "He asked me to give it to you."

He watched as the boy clutched it for a moment, then a new tear traveled down the cheek, only to be wiped away in embarrassment. He wished, more than ever, that he knew what had transpired on Connor's mysterious trip that made Connor wish to leave the encampment and Sam so unhappy. Marion sensed that Sam wanted to open the package alone. He put his hand on her shoulder. "We're all lonely tonight, Sam. You're not alone."

She nodded but her hooded eyes never changed. "Thank you," she said. "And thank you for the cap."

"You've earned it. Several times over."

After he left, Samantha fingered the package, still not wanting to open it. It was enough that Connor had thought of her, had asked General Marion to give it to her despite his anger. She wished with all her heart that she had had something to give him.

She lay there through the night, watching the stars fill the clear sky and listening to the now soft music wafting in the wind. The revelry had evolved into homesickness or drunken oblivion and she could sense more than one lying awake this night. She gathered her blanket around her, wishing for Connor's warmth, and tried to sleep. But she lay wretchedly awake, a leather cap with a cockade tilted awkwardly over one eye and a wrapped package tucked possessively in her arms.

Chapter Sixteen

Connor arrived in western Carolina Christmas Eve. Having met with Green two days earlier, he had been sent on to meet with General Daniel Morgan, the Old Wagoner. After three days of steady riding he was excruciatingly tired and even more depressed.

General Greene's army was vastly outnumbered by Cornwallis's four thousand, which now included the famous British brigade. Only eight hundred of Greene's twenty-three hundred men were fit for duty and they were down to a three-day supply of rations. Their clothes and shoes were deplorable, and morale was low.

Connor's intelligence had forced Greene into a reluctant decision. Against all conventional wisdom, he would divide his command and try to lure Cornwallis into doing the same. Morgan, in the west, might have a fair chance of defeating a portion of Cornwallis's army while there would be little or no chance if the southern Continental and British forces met head-on. Greene needed weeks to fortify his forces. It was a calculated risk that Connor fully appreciated.

He had reached Morgan's camp at noon and made his report. As he strode from the tent, prepared to find a blanket and piece of ground, he crashed into a familiar stocky figure.

As he stepped back to see the man's features, his tired face creased into a smile.

"Denney, how good it is to see you!"

The other man had returned the smile. "And you, Connor. I heard you were with Marion. How fare you?"

"Well enough," Connor replied, "though I'm devilish tired. I would hate to count the miles I've been the past three days."

"It's been better than three years since I've seen you." Denney Demerest's hearty voice quieted. "I heard about your brother and father. I'm damned sorry, Connor."

Connor just nodded, a muscle throbbing in his jaw, his fist tightening into a ball. He had been thinking of both of them all day. Christmas had always been a festive time at Glen Woods, full of surprises and laughter, people and parties. The loss struck him anew.

Denney saw the clouds in Connor's eyes and wished he had said nothing. He grasped Connor's shoulders. "Do you have a place to stay?"

"A piece of ground," Connor answered wryly, "and right now that sounds curiously welcoming."

Denney grinned. "I think I can do a little better than that. My uncle has a plantation two miles from here. I'm staying there and there's plenty of room."

Connor smiled slowly. "My thanks, Denney, but I can't impose."

"Just think, Connor. A bed. A real bed. And a hot bath. And there's plenty of everything. They're planning a Christmas ball tonight and all of Morgan's officers are invited."

Connor's face became even more reticent. "I don't think…"

"Colonel Henry Lee is going to be there. I understand he's going to be sent east to join your Swamp Fox. It would be an excellent chance for you to meet."

"I've nothing to wear…just what I have on," Connor said, still trying to extricate himself from the invitation.

"You can borrow something of mine…I keep extra clothes there. They might be a little full for you—" this was said with an admiring glance at Connor's hard lean frame "—and a little short, but your boots will cover that."

"Denney, I'm damned tired…"

"You can get some sleep this afternoon. I'm not taking no for an answer. I want to hear about your General Marion. He's already become a legend. Did he really send handbills offering a reward for Cornwallis?" He was delighted when Connor grinned.

Ten minutes later they were on their way to the Demerest plantation.

Connor had always liked Dennis Demerest. Although Denney was several years younger, they had met in Charleston and had served together at Sullivan's Island in 1776. Denney reminded Connor of Brendan: outgoing, friendly, always ready to laugh. Now his company helped dull some of his feelings of loss. At Denney's urging, Connor told him about Marion's skill and a few of his commander's more outrageous exploits. Denney listened enthralled but flinched at Connor's tales of life in the swamps.

"I think I'll stay with Morgan," he said. "I like my comforts, as borrowed as they are."

Connor laughed for the first time in days. "Tell me, do you have relatives all over the Carolinas?"

"Near about," Denney answered cheerfully. "There are more Demerests than foxes. And I've taken advantage of every one."

"How did your uncle's plantation escape harm?"

Denney's face sobered. "He has arthritis and can't fight. He has no sons, and while my uncle has made no secret of Whig sympathies, neither has he been actively involved. Everyone has always liked him and he's always helped neighbors in need, Tory or Whig. He's pretty well left alone." His eyes twinkled. "He also has a very pretty daughter that no one wants to see in distress."

"Your cousin?"

"My cousin," affirmed Denney. "Much to my regret."

Connor turned to his friend, hearing a serious undertone to the reply. "Cousins often marry," he said.

"Not in my family," Denney answered shortly, and abruptly changed the subject.

Arriving at the Demerest plantation, Connor and Denney dismounted, handing their reins to a servant, and climbed the stairs, two at a time. Without waiting to knock, Denney threw the door open, yelling for his uncle.

The room was suddenly full of servants and the loud booming voice of Brett Demerest bidding them welcome. Within minutes of Denney's introduction and description of Connor's last several days, Connor was lodged in a large comfortable room with a copper bathtub filled with pails of steaming water. Connor gratefully slid into the tub, slowly relaxing his tired and sore muscles. Then, more than half-asleep, he crawled between two impossibly clean and soft linen sheets and drifted off.

When Denney woke him hours later, he could already hear music downstairs. His friend was wearing the dress uniform of a Continental captain and had laid out dress clothes for Connor: light gray breeches, a darker gray coat and white linen shirt and cravat. Connor was surprised, thinking the attire somber and unlikely for Denney, but it was much to his own liking. He nodded his thanks and slowly dressed, not at all eager to join the festivities downstairs. Although sleep had restored him physically, mentally he was depressed and at this moment wished he had not agreed to come.

As if facing a firing squad, he followed Denney downstairs to a ballroom in motion with dozens of dancing, laughing couples.

Denney dragged him from group to group until he found Colonel Henry Lee, a handsome florid dandy in striking blue breeches and coat. He and his legion of three hundred had already won acclaim for their bravery and speed, earning him the name of Lighthorse Henry Lee. Looking at him now, Connor questioned whether this clotheshorse could adapt to Marion's swamps and unorthodox tactics.

He was reserved in his greeting, though Henry Lee was effusive and wanted to know everything there was to know about Francis Marion. His enthusiasm and unabashed admiration for Marion were so sincere that he soon won Connor over, and the two found a place in the Demerest library and talked for more than an hour.

As they left the library, Connor couldn't help noticing a pretty young girl, whose eyes were fixed directly on him. As he returned the measuring look, she flushed and turned back to the covey of young men surrounding her. Now alone, Connor leaned against a wall, his legs crossed lazily as he studied the occupants of the room. On the surface, it was like every other ball, but somehow there was a frantic urgency to the flirting and laughter. Parting had become commonplace, as had death, and everyone seemed determined to exact as much pleasure from these hours as possible. He wished he could capture even a little of the gaiety but it was as if he had ceased to feel. Feeling hurt too much.

Caroline Demerest was fascinated with the stranger her cousin had brought to her home. He stood against the wall, making no effort to join the others. His eyes roamed over the crowd as an onlooker, not a participant. He was very handsome, and the gray clothes emphasized the dark stormy gray of his eyes. His face was bronze from constant exposure to the sun and contrasted sharply with the undisciplined ash-blond hair that seemed destined to escape the ribbon at the back of his neck.

Excusing herself from one of the young men with a smile, she floated through the crowd, searching for Denney, her eyes lighting when she discovered him.

"Denney..." Her voice was soft and melodical, and it caught at Denney's heart. His hand grasped hers and squeezed.

"What can I do for you, little cousin?" he said fondly, wishing again that she were not kin.

"Your friend . . . introduce me."

"Haven't you captured quite enough hearts tonight without adding his?" Denney's tease hid the ache he suddenly felt as he looked down at her. Caroline was beautiful by any standards. She was tall and slender; her light brown hair sparkled with strands of burnished gold, and her large brown eyes expressed her every thought. Now they were unexpectedly serious. "He looks so sad."

"I think he is, Caro," Denney replied gently. "He has much reason. His brother was killed last year, his father several months ago. His plantation was burned and confiscated. He himself was imprisoned on the hulks for much of the year."

Denney watched, touched as her eyes filled with tears.

"If I'm going to introduce you, you better rid yourself of those tears," he said more sharply than he intended. "I don't think Connor would appreciate them."

She flinched at his harsh tone but quickly did as he said, blinking back the tears and dabbing the wetness with his proffered handkerchief. Confident they were gone, she straightened her back and started for Connor, knowing Denney was behind her.

Connor was lost in thought, wondering how it would feel to have Sam in his arms in the brightly lighted room. Hell, he didn't even know if she danced. There were so many things he didn't know about her. He was startled by Denney's amused voice.

"Connor?"

His eyes slowly focused on Denney and the girl beside him. "I beg your pardon," he said immediately. "I'm afraid the music put my mind to wandering."

Denney smiled. It was one of the few times he had seen a man's attention not on Caro when she was near.

"I would like to present my cousin, Caroline. Caro, this is Major Connor O'Neill."

"Major," Caroline said softly in response, "you are very welcome in our home."

Connor smiled at last. "Your family has been very kind to a tired stranger."

"Have you had something to eat?" she asked, pleased at his smile.

His look told her no.

"Then come with me. We will have no hungry guests," she commanded.

"Watch out, Connor," Denney said quietly. "She makes a habit of breaking hearts."

Caroline smiled at her cousin, and there was something more than family affection in the look. She offered Connor her arm and led him to the banquet table. She allowed him to fix two plates and pour each of them a glass of wine, then led him out onto the wide porch.

It was cold, and they were the only ones outside. Connor felt relief. Away from the music and noise he slowly relaxed. He looked at his companion and thought how pretty she was. She was the type of woman who had always attracted him in the past: tall, fair haired, with a decidedly female body. So why then did Sam's dark hair and small thin form stand between them?

"You are a million miles away, major." Caroline's voice was quiet and kind.

"I'm sorry, Miss Caroline." Connor's voice was heavy, his eyes masked.

"You don't have to be. Denney told me about your family. I imagine you miss them very much right now. And please, it's Caro."

He attempted a smile and Caroline felt his deep sorrow. She touched him lightly. "If you want to go back in, to your room, don't be afraid you'll be thought rude."

Connor was astounded at the comment. It was exactly what he wished to do but he hadn't wanted to hurt his friend. She was exceptional, this Caroline Demerest. No wonder Denney talked about her with such wistfulness.

"Denney," he said suddenly. "Tell me how he's been?"

Delighted that the black mood seemed lifted, Caroline smiled. "He's my best friend...."

"Nothing more?"

There was a pause. "He's my cousin."

"I know," Connor said patiently, obviously waiting for her to go on.

"He asked for my hand, and my father refused. He said the relationship is too close. There was a marriage of cousins in our family before and it turned out badly."

Connor knew he was interfering where he should not, but there was something between Denney and Caroline, and his own pain with Sam made him want to help the young couple. They were obviously in love, though both tried to hide it.

"My grandparents were cousins," he said slowly, "and they were very much in love."

She shivered, and he took off his coat, placing it over her shoulders. Her face was sad when she looked up at him. "My father's brother married a cousin. They had two children. Neither was quite right and they died early. My aunt killed herself. My father won't even discuss a marriage with Denney."

Connor took her in his arms and held her comfortingly for a moment, understanding now as he never could before Sam.

They were interrupted by one of Morgan's officers, a Captain Willard Lewis. "Oops," the man exclaimed. "So sorry." He turned, embarrassed, and left rapidly.

There was a small sigh of distress from Caroline. "He's the biggest gossip in the command," she said.

Connor took his coat. "We should be going in anyway." He offered his arm, and Caroline, her chin high, accompanied him back into the crowded room.

Connor spent Christmas dinner with the Demerest family along with several other invited officers. It took some of the edge from his loneliness and he found he liked the family very much, particularly Denney and Caro, who teased and laughed their way through the dinner. That evening he was asked by Brett Demerest to remain for the rest of his stay and he accepted.

He half suspected that the invitation was made partly to keep Caroline occupied with someone other than Denney. Caroline's parents would not deny Denney their home, but they were obviously very pleased to have another eligible young man available.

During the next week, the three of them were together often and it wasn't long before the rumors grew and the officers were taking bets on a possible engagement.

Connor and Caro did little to squelch the talk. They liked each other immensely, and Caro became the sister that Connor had always wanted. More important, it allowed Caro and Denney more frequent access to each other. Prior to Connor's presence, they had been watched and discouraged from being in each other's company.

Connor observed the two of them with quiet amusement and concern. They were obviously in love and seemed well suited. He felt uncomfortable taking their side against that of his host, but his own recent experience made him sympathetic.

He and Denney were kept busy during the days, training the recruits. Connor often grew exasperated at the independent soldiers who knew little and seemed to care less about the most rudimental orders and tactics. He despaired of ever making a coherent unit from these Marylanders, Carolinians and Delaware men, all of whom had their own way of doing things.

Between long days on the field and evenings at the Demerests', Connor had little time to think, or worry, about Sam, though she haunted him nightly.

During the first week of 1781, Morgan's men struck the Post of Ninety-Six, one of Cornwallis's main supply areas. A total of one hundred and fifty loyalists were killed and another forty taken prisoner.

Morgan sat back and waited for Cornwallis to retaliate. The move came quickly. True to General Greene's hopes, Cornwallis divided his forces into three groups and sent one of them after Morgan, under the command of Ban Tarleton.

Connor was relieved of training and reassigned as a scout. He promptly found Tarleton's camp and followed as the man dogged Morgan to the Cowpens, a rolling plain famous for cattle roundups. With the Broad River cutting off an American retreat and with open woods permitting easy entry for Tarleton's horsemen, the Cowpens looked like King George's terrain.

Arriving back in camp after a day's scouting, Connor reported on Tarleton's strength and expected strategy. He watched as Morgan posted his militia and riflemen on two low hills, one behind the other.

The night of January 16 was a long one. Connor stayed with Morgan, who spent the night among the volunteers, joking with them about their sweethearts and encouraging them to keep in good spirits. They listened raptly as Morgan told each man only two shots were expected of him, then he could retreat in good order.

The next morning, Connor joined the Delaware men on the first hill and watched Tarleton's green-clad dragoons approach, their helmet plumes tossing in the wind. Fire crackled out from the militia, and the dragoons fell back. Then the fields were suddenly thick with British and Tory infantry and the dragoons formed up on each flank.

The militia fired, then fired again and fell back in seeming disarray. Connor, who had fired and reloaded, saw the exultant looks on the British faces as they watched an American

rout, and he allowed a grim smile. He joined the disorderly retreat, watching as Tarleton, confident of victory, swept his
whole line forward. There were British everywhere, their once
exact ranks now confused and scattered. As the British reached
the top of the hill, they ran smack into an unbreakable line of
Delaware troops. The trap was closed by a troop of American
horsemen that smashed into Tarleton's flank and rear, and the
Tories and British, surrounded on all sides, threw down their
weapons. Connor, who had entered the fray with his bayonet,
downed two Tories before seeing Tarleton wheel his horse and
make for a break in the American line. Connor was up on his
own horse and after him, but Tarleton had too much of a lead
and Connor finally lost him in the woods.

Morgan's six hundred men had defeated a British force of
more than thirteen hundred.

That evening Connor learned that twelve Americans had
died, and more than nine hundred British had been killed,
wounded or captured. Tarleton had escaped.

He and Denney took Caroline to a victory party. Giant bon-
fires spread their flames against a dark blue velvet sky, and
Connor watched his friend and Caro quietly hold hands in the
night. He wondered what Sam was doing and wished with all
his soul that she were beside him, savoring American triumph.

He could think of little else but her pixie face and dancing
blue eyes. It was time to make some decisions. Tomorrow,
Morgan would retreat northward, before Cornwallis could
catch him, and meet up with Greene's main force. Connor had
been given the option of returning to Marion's base or continuing as scout for Morgan. Watching Denney and Caro together, he remembered Sam's tight face as she refused him. The
pain was still too raw. He told Morgan that he wanted to go
with him to meet Greene.

Chapter Seventeen

Samantha brushed Sundance with her good right hand. The horse shivered with pleasure at the attention. Every stroke took five seconds, twelve strokes a minute, and every minute seemed an eternity.

It had been twenty-nine days since Connor left. It seemed like twenty-nine years. Sundance turned suddenly and gave her an affectionate nip as if aware that her attention was not wholly on the task at hand. Rubbing the horse's nose in apology, she abandoned her brushing. Sundance was burnished to a fare-thee-well. What to do now? She had already seen to the other horses and to the care of the new prisoner.

Her arm was nearly healed and her restlessness was evident to everyone. When Marion had brought in British Brigadier General Sir Brian O'Mara two days ago, he had asked Sam to see to the man's food and water.

Despite her growing anger against the British, Samantha felt a certain sympathy with the man, who was obviously humiliated by his capture. O'Mara had been lodged in the barn, and in retaliation for the treatment and chaining of American prisoners held by the British, his hands and feet were kept tied even at mealtime. She had to feed him and bring water to his lips, each time seeing the anguish in his eyes at his own helplessness. Nevertheless, the officer had been unfailingly courteous and even grateful for her quietly efficient care, which had none of the hostility of those who had brought him here.

Even her extra chores did little to hurry the hours. Samantha looked down at her new boots, the present from Connor, which she had finally opened late Christmas day. They were of a soft supple leather and fit perfectly. She wondered when Connor had purchased them, before or after he had discovered her gender. She finally decided it had to be before, for he had little opportunity after their departure from Georgetown. Whatever the case, she treasured them more than anything she had ever owned and left them on even at night, feeling they brought her closer to Connor.

As she left the corral she heard a rider coming in and hurried to Marion's hut. It was a stranger. She moved within earshot and started when she heard Connor's name.

"Major O'Neill sent these dispatches, sir," the man was saying. "There was a great victory at Cowpens. We completely wiped out Tarleton's command. More than nine hundred killed or taken."

"And our losses?" Marion's question was soft.

"Only twelve. It was the damnedest thing I ever saw, sir. Morgan trapped them easier than a hunting dog trees a coon. You should have seen old Tarleton skedaddle."

"And Major O'Neill?"

"He's fine, sir, pays his respects but said Morgan needs him."

Samantha gulped, trying to stifle a cry of protest. How Connor must hate her to stay away from his friend for so long. She stumbled away, not wanting to hear more. She must find something to keep busy. In desperation, she looked toward the barn. At least someone needed her . . . if only an enemy.

General O'Mara had few doubts about his prospects after this episode. An officer spirited from the barracks at Charleston, right under the nose of Cornwallis, could be sure of losing his post.

Francis Marion had been quick to explain in detail what was expected of him. Cornwallis had sent South Carolina Vice Governor Christopher Gadsden to a prison in Saint Augustine. The citizens of Charleston had protested so strongly that six additional civilians, including one of Marion's own family, had also been sent. General O'Mara would write Cornwallis and tell him to release the civilians immediately or O'Mara would be executed and the life of every British officer would be in jeopardy. Marion's expression and curt words had told him that he meant exactly what he said. O'Mara had written the letter, realizing with every word that his career was ending.

He had been held prisoner for three days now, and he honestly wondered whether Cornwallis would accept Marion's terms. He could almost feel the rope around his neck.

The barn door creaked open, and he watched the young rebel who fed him approach, a bucket and ladle in his right hand. O'Mara's throat was suddenly dry with anticipation and he struggled to sit upright against the barn wall.

"Thank you," he said, as he took a long swallow of the proffered water. There was something about the boy that fascinated him. Perhaps it was the face, not yet hardened like the others in camp but still vulnerable. Or perhaps it was his eyes, which seemed at the moment unusually bright.

Samantha's eyes rested on the prisoner's bound wrists, watching the small rivulets of blood running from where the rope had rubbed the skin raw. She thought of Connor and the scar on his ankle.

She looked carefully at the British general. She guessed he was of middle age, but his face was drawn and tired and his auburn hair untidy. He wriggled uncomfortably, his back aching from the cramped positions and the hard dirt floor. She felt a sudden compassion for him and dislike for what was being done, though she knew Marion thought it necessary.

She gave him another drink and left, going straight to General Marion's tent to plead his case.

"At least," she begged, "loosen the ropes and let me bandage his wrists."

Marion smiled slightly. "You will take responsibility?"

Samantha straightened. "Yes sir."

Marion called one of his sergeants and told him to accompany Sam to the barn and allow him to bandage the prisoner's wrists and remove the ankle ropes. Marion liked Sam's concern; the basic humanity the boy continued to show was something he did not wish to destroy.

Minutes later, O'Mara was far more comfortable. His wrists were now coated with ointment and swathed in white, and although firmly rebound, the rope was not cruelly tight as before, and he could stand and walk. As Samantha started to leave behind the sergeant, O'Mara stopped her with his voice.

"Sam."

She turned around, surprised.

"This was your doing, wasn't it?"

"'Twas by the general's order," she replied.

"Thank you," O'Mara said softly. "I'm indebted to you."

"It was the general," Sam insisted again, not wanting the man's gratitude or to feel closer to him.

"Why?" O'Mara said, as if he hadn't heard.

She looked down at the ground, then squarely at O'Mara. "The British held a friend of mine prisoner and he will wear the scars from your chains as long as he lives. No one should have to do that!"

O'Mara looked puzzled at the change in the boy's speech; this was no ignorant lad.

Samantha had consciously dropped her rough speech. Marion's men were all outside, and O'Mara had never met Samantha Chatham. It was a relief, for a moment, to drop the pretense and speak normally.

"Where's your family?" O'Mara said finally.

"Dead," she replied flatly.

O'Mara paced carefully, working out the cramps in his legs. "The war?"

"Partly," she replied cautiously.

O'Mara stopped moving and looked at her. "Would your Colonel Marion really hang me if General Cornwallis doesn't comply?"

She met his stare. "Yes," she said softly. "He wouldn't like it, but yes, he would."

O'Mara gave her a small bitter smile. "That's very comforting. To know he wouldn't like it."

"You asked," she said frankly.

O'Mara sat down and stared at the floor. "I have twin sons I have never seen," he said.

Samantha tried to explain, as much for her own benefit as his. "Your army," she said slowly, "has hanged our people, burned our homes, imprisoned our civilians. General Marion believes that retaliation, the sure knowledge that such behavior will be duplicated, is the only thing that will deter it.'' She looked at O'Mara. "I'm sorry."

O'Mara looked up, and his eyes cleared. "You've been kind. I hope I have a chance to repay you someday."

She smiled. "General Marion is convinced that Cornwallis will agree to his demands."

Samantha continued to care for O'Mara over the next several days, changing his wrist bandages and serving him food and fresh water. He would often ask her to stay and talk, and she would comply, sensing a loneliness that matched her own. It was nearly a week before Cornwallis consented to the terms and O'Mara was found tied and gagged outside the main Charleston entry post. Marion had won again, and General O'Mara felt a certain debt to a youthful rebel.

Chapter Eighteen

Five more days passed slowly, each one longer than the last. Even Sundance couldn't lighten Samantha's heavy mood, and she spent more and more time by herself. On the fifth day she was alone by the creek when noise suddenly echoed through the woods as hundreds of riders and horses invaded Marion's camp. Compelled by curiosity, she left her retreat and found herself surrounded by handsomely uniformed figures and tired horses.

"Look at them dandies," one of Marion's troopers said derisively.

Samantha looked askance. "Who are they?"

"Henry Lee and his men," the man answered, spitting in disgust. "We was doin' jest fine without 'em."

Her eyes traveled from man to man, wondering if it were possible Connor was among them.

"Major O'Neill," she asked anxiously. "Did he come with them?"

"Ain't seen 'im," the man answered. "Cain't 'magine what he would be doin' with them tin soldiers."

Without bothering to listen to any more, she hurried over to Marion's hut and watched him greet a young, well-tailored officer.

Marion saw her pinched face and gestured her over. "This is one of our youngest and bravest men," he told Lee, pride evident in his voice. "And this, Sam, is Colonel Henry Lee...he's going to be with us for a while."

Marion saw Lee's quizzical look as he studied the young boy.

"He's an excellent horse thief as well as marksman," Marion said, amusement in his voice. "You said you saw Major O'Neill at Cowpens. Well, he was there because of this young man and a shot of a hundred yards."

The doubt in Lee's eyes changed to admiration as he gave the boy a second look. He saw the brilliant blue eyes and the delicate lines of the face, but it was the determined jut of the boy's jaw and his complete lack of awe at higher authority that caught his interest.

Henry Lee laughed, a booming sound that attracted Samantha, who looked at him as curiously as he had studied her. "By God," Colonel Lee said, "I knew explosives came in small packages, but not this small. I'm glad to know you, Sam. I met Major O'Neill a few days back, and he told me a great deal about Francis Marion but he neglected to warn me about you." There was no condescension in his voice, and she decided she liked him, despite his natty attire.

Her question came hesitantly. "And 'ow was Major O'Neill?"

"In love" came Lee's deep voice, his eyes missing the sudden strain in hers. "He apparently has fallen under the spell of a certain young lady in western Carolina. 'Tis said they're already engaged."

"Connor?" Marion interjected. "I had expected him here by now. I can't believe a lady is holding him back."

"I don't think that's the entire reason he hasn't returned," Lee replied. "Morgan asked him to stay until they meet up with Greene. Cornwallis is hot on their heels."

"Damn it," Marion said. "I'll not permit it. I want him back and I'll dispatch orders to that effect." Then, bemused, he asked about Connor's lady. "Who is she?"

"Her name is Caroline Demerest," Lee said, a chuckle in his voice, "and she would distract the best of men. A real beauty, and a fine lady, as well. They were nearly inseparable until Morgan moved to join Greene."

Neither noted the growing distress on Samantha's face as she murmured something about "seein' to the 'orses" and escaped.

"A real lady," she repeated to herself. Everything apparently she no longer was. An ache started in the region of her heart and spread slowly to encompass all of her. She tried to breathe but couldn't, and she walked with jerky little steps away from watching eyes. When finally alone, she sank deep in a ridge in the ground, trying to get hold of herself, but the misery was too deep and she broke into muffled sobs.

When all the tears were spent, she felt only a total emptiness. Everything was gone. She had no home, no family, no place to go, no one to love. There was only Sundance and that, she knew, was no longer enough. Slowly, her grief evolved into anger. Connor had told her he loved her, and now, just weeks later, he blatantly displayed his love for another. How deep a love was that? Damn him. Her anger turned into resolve. She would show him. She may no longer be a lady, but she was a damned good soldier. Her hands twisted together. She had promised she would stay safely in camp. But he had left her and chosen another. The promise was no longer valid.

She had regained full use of her arm and she would go on the next operation, regardless of where it was. She had Marion's promise and at least she could depend on his loyalty.

Lee's three hundred men more than doubled the size of Marion's force. Technically, as part of the Continental Army, Lee had command over Marion's militia, but despite their startling differences, the two men immediately became friends and shared the leadership amicably.

Samantha thought how strange they looked together. Henry Lee was in his mid-twenties and impeccably dressed in a tailored green-and-white uniform that never seemed to get mussed. Francis Marion was close to fifty and dressed in bits and pieces of worn uniforms with a rusted scabbard and a ragged cap. But there was no denying the instant respect and friendship that developed between the two.

This affectionate bonding did not extend to the men under their respective commands. Marion's woodsmen scorned Lee's well-tailored legion and there were constant fights between the two groups. Even Samantha was drawn into one after being repeatedly teased about her size.

She was aware her mood was already feisty and she was hurt and angry and bound to prove her worth. The Lord protect anyone who got in her way. It did not sit well at all when one impeccably dressed soldier, his bright plume waving obnoxiously in the air, started making aspersions about her size, her clothing and her abilities.

"I always heard Marion had men, not nits," he said in a loud voice, followed by general laughter among his comrades.

"He ain't even big enough to sit a horse," the man continued.

Samantha's rage started to grow. It had needed little stoking. From the corner of her eye, she knew her own friends were silent, waiting.

"I'm big enough to tell a horse from an ass. That's more than yer friends can do."

The man's face reddened. "I'll teach you to respect yer betters. . . ." He grabbed for her but she was too quick, and she punched him squarely in the eye as she whirled out of reach.

With that, Marion's men waded into Lee's and it was a free-for-all until Lee and Marion arrived to break it up. Samantha had held her own as she scratched and bit a legionnaire nearly twice her size, much to the amusement of her companions. When it was finally over, no one admitted to starting it, and Marion and Lee could merely glower.

The whole episode gave her new stature she could just as well have done without. For someone who did not want to draw attention to herself, Samantha admitted that she had not acted wisely, but at least the teasing stopped.

The newcomers kept her busy, however, and for this she was thankful. She would often serve meals to Marion and Lee and their officers. She was there when they agreed on final plans to attack Georgetown and she decided to approach Marion the morning before decampment.

Face-to-face, she hesitated. She didn't know if she was quite ready to kill again and that could well be demanded of her. But neither could she remain behind. The emptiness inside had increased her restlessness. Now, seeing Marion's searching black eyes, she straightened, her mouth compressed in a tight grim line.

"I want ta go wi' ya this time," she said, holding Marion's gaze levelly.

Marion's face reflected his surprise. For months the youth had seemed content overseeing the care of the horses. Although they had never discussed it, he sensed the boy's dislike of killing.

"Connor thought it best you stay in camp," Marion said slowly, wondering at Sam's change of heart and uncomfortable with the conflict presented by the request.

"He ain't 'ere," Sam said bluntly. "An' he was jest worried 'bout my arm. It's good as ever now."

Marion studied the determined face.

"Ya promised I could do as I pleased," she reminded him. "After that salt raid."

"So I did," Marion reluctantly agreed. A promise was a promise, although he now regretted it. Connor, if he ever returned, was not going to like this at all.

"Besides," Sam persisted, "I was in Georgetown jest a month ago. I know all there is to know," she added airily.

Marion smiled fondly at the boy's arrogance. He had indeed promised Sam long before the promise to Connor.

"All right, Sam," he said. "You can go. But be careful, or Major O'Neill will have my scalp."

Samantha nodded, the elation of her success fading as she thought that Connor O'Neill no longer cared what she did.

Samantha swung easily into the saddle with a feeling of recklessness that was new to her. Every risk she had taken up until now had been out of necessity. She had never tempted danger just for the excitement of it, but now she needed it to feel alive again. To awaken her from the stupor that had dulled her since Christmas. She could feel the anticipation of the more than five hundred men saddling their horses beside her in the deepening dusk.

She had decided against taking Sundance. She had had too many losses to risk one more. Billy grinned at her as she guided her bay up next to him, pleased to have her company on the long trip. She squared her shoulders and settled deep into the saddle, prepared for the long march to Georgetown. She had spent nearly an hour that morning with General Marion and Colonel Lee, explaining the exact whereabouts of the guard posts, the patrols and the sleeping quarters of the various British units.

Erasing all thoughts from her head, she concentrated on the upcoming battle. Two hundred of Lee's men would row to a heavily wooded island just off the business section of Georgetown. A second group, composed of both continentals and militia would attack from the woods behind Georgetown. Samantha was to be a part of this group.

More than once during the long ride, she questioned her presence there. She knew she might well be called upon to shoot another human being, but she needed desperately to feel a part of something, to chase away the sense that nothing could ever be right again.

There was also, she knew, the compulsion to prove something to Connor, although she admitted to herself she wasn't exactly sure what. That she didn't need him. That she didn't care if he courted another. But she did, desperately. It was an act of defiance. Nothing more. And it didn't help her spirits to realize it.

Her backside ached and she stretched uncomfortably in the saddle, taking satisfaction that others were doing the same. The only sound was the irregular rhythm of hundreds of hoofbeats in the night. The noise of so many men had cleared the woods of other creatures.

Samantha was almost asleep in the saddle when her horse slowed. She could hear the sound of men dismounting and of rifles being drawn from their holders. She slid down gratefully, happy to feel the hard earth beneath her feet.

She stretched, watching others do the same. Except for the wheezing of the horses there was silence, and Samantha could feel the tension. It was not yet dawn, and the night was uncommonly still and black, unlit by even one star. She shivered under her thin jacket, knowing it was as much from fear as from the cold wind rustling through the trees. She was grateful for Billy's presence next to her and for the warm pressure on her arm as he pressed it reassuringly.

"It's always like this," he whispered. "The waiting is the worst part."

Samantha nodded, relieved to know others might feel as she did. Still stiff from the long ride, she reluctantly remounted as the order whispered from man to man.

Several minutes later they heard the first distant sounds of rifle and musket fire, and the stillness turned to chaos. She heard the sharp order to advance and was instantly caught in the confusion of hundreds of horses being spurred toward the lightly guarded entrances to the town. As she touched her knees to the bay's side, she realized her fear was gone, replaced by a heady exhilaration, and she couldn't restrain herself from joining the others in a brief yell.

Finally clearing the woods, she raced the horse with Marion's undisciplined cavalry, vaguely aware of Lee's legion approaching neatly, riding four abreast in straight lines. No such tin soldier tactics for Marion's brigade as they thundered through the quiet dirt-packed streets of Georgetown. There were occasional shots, and the thud of a horse or body falling, but there were also the exultant cries of townspeople tumbling from their homes. Samantha caught up with Marion, who was riding in the front with Lee, and kept up with their pace as they made their way to the British stronghold near the town's center.

The British bastion was a small log fort with twin towers. It was amply manned at the moment and as they approached, Sam could hear the intense fire between the fort's defenders and the two hundred men of Lee's legion who had arrived from the water. Among the smoke and deafening noise, she saw a number of red-coated British, caught outside the fort, being led off by Lee's tight-lipped men. As her eyes followed their progress, she heard a bullet pass an inch from her leg. Without further musing, she guided her horse out of the line of fire and dismounted, taking her rifle with her.

Marion and Lee had split, each guiding their men toward one of the two towers. The gunfire from the fort's walls was deadly accurate and Sam saw men on both sides of her fall. She quickly found protection and aimed her rifle. No longer did she hesitate. The British on the fort's walls were wounding and killing her friends. She aimed carefully at a figure reloading a musket and shot, watching him fall from sight. Then she heard a tremendous explosion behind her and felt an intense pain in her side. She closed her eyes and concentrated, trying to drive it away. Almost automatically, she reloaded her rifle and fired again, this time failing to see her target fall. She sank down on the ground and poured another measure of powder, her movements slow and jerky. She was about to aim again when orders came to withdraw.

The pain had lessened to a steady throb and Sam could feel a wet stickiness on her shirt. She tried to cover it with her jacket and moved to where Marion and Lee were conferring with several of the officers.

"We'll never take it this way," Marion said. "Not without losing half our force."

Sam heard Lee's soft agreement. "But I'm not going to give Georgetown back to the British."

There was a new voice, one Sam hadn't heard before. "We've some bows with us" came the harsh sound. "Maybe we can fire the fort."

Within seconds, Marion had men stripping ornamental gum trees, wrapping the inner bark around arrows and setting them on fire. A steady stream of burning arrows, each trailing a path of red-gold color, pierced the gray dawn, finding their way to the dry wooden structure. Within minutes, the Union Jack was hauled down from its standard, and red-and-green-coated figures came rushing from the gates, only to be quickly disarmed and made prisoner.

Sam watched at a distance; she was tired, weak, drained of the savagery that was there minutes earlier. She could now see the results: dead bodies, burning buildings; twisting figures on the ground. The red glow and rancid smell of burning made her think of hell. Slowly, painfully, she raised herself with the help of her rifle and turned her back on the scene. She needed some aid, but she couldn't risk seeing the doctor who rode with them. This time she couldn't avoid a more personal inspection of her body.

Annabelle's house was not far. She would go there.

Sam found her horse and painfully mounted, wondering where Billy was at this moment, hoping he was not one of those writhing bodies on the ground. But she could do him no good now...it would be all she could do to get to Annabelle's. She turned the horse slowly, barely conscious of the activity around her, and made her way to Cherry Street.

Annabelle and her girls were on the porch, watching the vivid red glow of fire mixing with the muted colors of a cloudy morn. Only an hour earlier the house had been in confusion as gunshots signaled trouble, and clients came tumbling out of rooms, pulling on trousers and boots, cursing and asking questions that had no immediate answers.

The house had been vacated of all but its permanent residents quicker than Annabelle thought possible. That there had been more speed than efficiency was demonstrated by the bits and pieces of clothing, money and equipment left in the rooms, on the stairs and the porch. Always practical, the girls had gathered the money; they suspected that few would be back to claim it.

Annabelle needed only one look at the wild riders thundering through the streets to guess that Marion had arrived. She sent a manservant in the direction of the fire. There was a sense of elation, especially since they realized their own contribution might have been of some help. They were laughing and joking when a single horse with its rider sitting unnaturally stiff wearily approached the railing.

Annabelle was down the steps in seconds, taking the bridle in her hands and guiding the horse to the porch. She looked up and saw the blackened face of Samantha.

Wasting no time, she turned toward the girls. "Evie, Becky, come help me." Together they caught Samantha's body as she slid down from the horse and half carried her inside.

"My room," Annabelle said curtly, and led the way while the two girls helped Samantha up the two flights of stairs. It was not ideal, Annabelle knew, but she wanted the girl well out of sight if Marion withdrew. Once inside the room, Annabelle helped them place her gently on the bed. She chased both of them out, asking them to remain outside the door. As Samantha fought to stay conscious, Annabelle removed her jacket and inspected the long red slice along her left side. The wound was still bleeding slightly, but it did not seem serious. Annabelle suspected that Samantha's weakness came mostly from exhaustion and pain.

"It needs some stitches," she said in answer to Sam's unspoken question, "but it should heal fast. I'll send for a doctor."

Samantha shook her head. "They'll all be busy, and I don't want General Marion to know."

Annabelle looked at her for a long hard minute. "Is Connor with you?"

She wasn't prepared for the dark cloud in her young guest's eyes. "No...he's...with Greene...can't I just stay here a few days?"

"Won't someone be looking for you?"

"Confusion...there's too much confusion...no one can find anyone. I won't be missed."

Annabelle studied the girl's determined face. "I've done some stitching before...fights that needed to be kept secret. I'll try it if that's what you really want."

"You won't tell anyone?"

"Connor?"

"Anyone!"

Annabelle shook her head. "You can't keep this up forever. Has Connor discovered who you are yet?"

"He knows I'm not a boy."

"But not Samantha Chatham?" Annabelle guessed with a sigh. "I won't ask you about it, not now," she added, seeing the misery in Samantha's face. "I'll get some fresh water and soap...and I'll have to wash that wound with alcohol." Samantha merely nodded and closed her eyes.

The pain was rejuvenated and magnified several times over as Annabelle washed the wound first with soap and then with alcohol. Annabelle had hoped her young charge would lose consciousness, but she didn't, and Annabelle clenched her own teeth against the waves of sympathy as she darted a needle and thread through the ragged edges of the wound. Sam bit on a piece of cloth to keep from crying out, and her hands clutched the bedposts. Annabelle thought she had never seen anyone with more courage and determination, and she felt herself even more drawn to the young girl. When she finally finished, she gently washed the soot and black powder from Samantha's face and tucked her in the big bed.

"Sleep, little one," she said finally. "You will be safe here." She then quietly left the room to discover what else had happened this surprising evening.

Francis Marion did not miss young Sam until late in the evening. After the British surrender, there had been hundreds of prisoners to send north in order to exchange them for their own. The British fort was completely demolished; what had not burned had been torn down. British stores and arms throughout the city were located and stripped. Lee and Marion did not intend to stay in Georgetown and await the British reaction, and orders had already been given to prepare for withdrawal.

It was Billy James who first noticed Sam's disappearance. After the firing of the fort and the quick surrender, he had hunted among the wounded for his friend and tent mate, then among the survivors. But the longer he looked, the less he found. This man and that had seen Sam firing, but the noise and confusion were such that no one had seen him leave. Billy's concern turned into real worry and he found the courage to approach a busy Francis Marion. He stood there, at the side, cap in hand, until Marion noticed him.

The general's eyes softened. He liked these young lads who had so much courage...who had lost their childhood in war but who, nonetheless, were among the least complaining of all his troops.

"Billy, lad, you want to talk to me?"

"It's Sam, sir. I can't find him anywhere."

Marion's face tightened. He had promised both Connor and himself to take care of Sam. "The wounded...the dead?" He said the last word with dread.

"He's not among them, sir."

"That's one mercy," Marion replied. He thought for a moment, remembering Sam in the midst of the shooting, not far from himself. There had been a cannonade in that vicinity.

Perhaps Sam *was* wounded and had sought help in one of the nearby homes. Marion called a sergeant and told him to take several men and search the area. Damn. He would never forgive himself, nor would Connor, if anything happened to that boy.

There was a long line of officers and men awaiting instructions, and with a feeling of disquiet he turned his thoughts in those directions.

Billy and five others kept searching through the night and into the morning. There was no trace of Sam Taylor. It was as if he'd disappeared off the face of the earth.

The sheen of the overwhelming victory lost some of its luster as Marion and Lee prepared to leave. They were leaving a number of good men behind—both dead and too seriously injured to travel—as well as a young boy who had disappeared. They led their men out of Georgetown, trailing wagons of powder and weapons and medical supples and blankets. For the first time since they'd come together, Lee's Continentals and Marion's militia mixed congenially. They had seen one another in battle and gained a healthy mutual respect. And they both mourned those left behind.

Chapter Nineteen

Connor lounged in the saddle with an easy tired looseness and stared at the long lines of cavalry and infantry that stretched wearily for miles. They had been marching for days on the narrow dirt path ironically called a road, keeping just barely ahead of Cornwallis. They were all tired, hungry and sore. At least, Connor thought wryly, the infantry, during the altogether too-short rest periods, could avoid aggravating their sore feet. The cavalry men could just stand so long before putting their backside, blisters and all, to ground.

But it was coming to an end. There were signs Cornwallis had grown tired of the race and his neatly clad armies were falling further and further behind.

Connor crumbled the piece of paper in his hand. He had little excuse now to stay with Greene. The danger was over, at least for the moment. The paper contained orders from Marion. He was to return. Immediately.

He sighed, knowing he had little choice in the matter. The militia was a loose affair with its members coming and going almost at will, depending on crops, trouble at home or just plain whim. That tolerance, however, did not extend to officers. Nor should it. Fran had to know he had officers he could depend upon, and Connor realized he had taken advantage of their friendship. It was not a comfortable feeling, nor did he enjoy the knowledge that he was running away from a problem. His fingers forced the crumpled paper into a ball. He had always faced things head-on. What was it about Sam that had changed that?

He knew, somewhere deep in his soul, that if he forced Sam he would lose her. And yet he couldn't keep himself from prying. It hurt, more than anything in his life, that she trusted him so little that she chose to remain a stranger. Now, with the sun high in the heaven and the sky a near-blinding blue with winter brilliance, he knew a want and desire that had evaded him most of his life. He was never without her; her smile and laughter seasoned every thought, every dream. Why her, he did not know. He had puzzled through it so many times. But the answer was always beyond reach.

Suddenly, his hesitancy was gone. He was going home to Sam. Nothing this compelling could be wrong. They could work out any problem. She loved him, he knew she did. He was unaware of the emotions that had flickered across his face, of the tender smile that had replaced confusion.

"You look a man in love . . . I thought I was the only one so afflicted."

Connor looked up at Denney Demerest, half annoyed at the interruption, half amused at Denney's own confession.

"Go after her, Denney. If you love Caroline, fight for her," he said, surprising himself. He hadn't meant to interfere in Denney's problem but it was suddenly important that he do so. His advice, he knew, was also meant for himself.

"You're a damned idiot if you don't," he said slowly, pronouncing every syllable, "because you may never have another chance."

Denney studied his friend with consternation. "You sound like you're speaking from experience."

"Maybe I am," Connor said. "And I plan to do something about it. I'll be leaving in the morning, returning to Marion."

"You have someone there?"

Connor's face gentled. "Yes," he said simply. "And I'm not going to let her go . . . and you're a fool if you let Caro go."

"Our families . . ."

"It is you who matter," Connor replied slowly, carefully. "You and Caro. Your lives. To hell with everyone else. Denney, don't deny yourself for other people's prejudices."

Denney looked at his friend with wonder. Connor had kept his own counsel the past several weeks. He had been helpful in allowing him and Caro to be together but had carefully restrained from expressing an opinion. Denney had tried to draw Connor out several times but always met with a kind but noncommittal response.

"I thought you halfway disapproved," he said now.

"I never disapproved," Connor said briskly. "But I thought you needed to be certain...you and Caro. If you are, you won't let anything stand in your way. If you're not..." His voice trailed off, and he realized he was speaking of himself as much as Denney.

Denney's face was almost glorious in its joy. "By God, I'll ask her...we'll elope. And we'll name the first boy Connor."

Connor's expression was wry. "You'd better ask her first, Denney." He leaned over and offered his hand. "I wish you the best."

"And I you, my friend. You won't tell me about your lady?"

"Only that she has the bluest eyes in the universe...and the bravest heart. And I'm going to be sure it's mine." Connor gave Denney a quick smile and was gone, his horse racing under his impatient knees. To hell with the damned blisters.

Soothed with a heavy dose of laudanum, Samantha had slept around the clock and more. When she awoke, the sun was well into the room, filling it with a warm golden light. She stretched out, enjoying the comfort of the bed, before a sharp pain reminded her of why she was there. How long had she been here? Was it just this morning when she had been hit?

Her head was dull from sleep and the laudanum, and her throat was still parched and sore from the smoke. Each time she moved, she felt as if someone had hit her in the side with a large stick. She had neither the energy nor will to move, and that surprised her more than anything.

Just then, the door opened and Annabelle glided in. "You're finally awake. Good." She went to the side of the bed and poured a glass of water from a pitcher on the table. "Here. Drink this. I'll send for some soup."

"General Marion?"

Annabelle's face clouded. "They left this morning. I wanted to send someone to tell him you were here, but you exacted a promise from me. An unwise one, I think. The British will be back shortly.''

Samantha closed her eyes. She knew Marion well enough by now to realize he would be more than a little concerned about her absence. He had always been protective of the younger members of his band, and they had formed a special relationship. And Connor? Would he also care? But then he was a hundred miles away or more. And he had another woman. The pain of that realization was much greater than the physical one in her side, and it showed brightly in her eyes.

Annabelle noted the sudden distress and sighed. Everything, apparently, was not well between Samantha and Connor. She rang the servant's bell and requested a bowl of soup. Then she sat down next to her patient.

''Tell me everything,'' she demanded. ''Tell me what Connor knows and what he doesn't know...and what's making you so unhappy.''

Samantha looked up at her, her eyes glazed with tears. ''Connor's engaged,'' she said simply.

''Engaged?'' Annabelle repeated, shock in her voice. ''To whom?''

''A girl named Caroline Demerest. Do you know of her?''

''Demerest. I know a lot of Demerests. They're all over the state. But I'm afraid I know mostly men. I quite understand why they are so prolific.''

She noticed that Samantha did not react to her tiny effort at humor. The smile quickly left her eyes. ''You said Connor knew you weren't a boy. What happened?''

''It was when we left Georgetown,'' Samantha said slowly, her words drawn out. ''I fell and he caught me, and...well...''

''Well?'' Annabelle asked impatiently. ''Well what?''

''He made love to me.''

''And what did you do?''

A small whimsical smile settled on the girl's face, making the glistening tears all the more heartbreaking. ''I made love back. It was wonderful. I didn't know anything could be so wonderful.'' Annabelle's soul ached for the girl...for herself. How she wished she had had that innocence when she had fallen in love.

''And . . . ?'' she asked softly.

"Connor got very angry, but then I broke my arm, and he fixed it and we made love again and it was more glorious than before." The words came tumbling out so quickly that Annabelle was finding it difficult to keep pace with them. "But he wanted to marry me, and I can't...you know, I can't, not with my name...he would hate me and I couldn't bear that, but he hates me anyway because he thinks I don't want him, and I do. I do, so desperately." As the words came faster and faster so did the tears until they made a stream down her face.

"Oh, Annabelle," she cried. "He left Marion because of me...because he couldn't stand being near me, and now he's engaged...and I don't think I can bear it."

"Slower, little one. Slower," Annabelle said soothingly. "How do you know he's engaged?"

"One of General Greene's men brought dispatches to General Marion. He said it's common knowledge."

"Common knowledge is probably only common rumor," Annabelle said quietly. "Did Connor say he loved you?"

Sam looked at Annabelle, complete misery in her face, and nodded slowly.

"Then," Annabelle said confidently, "I shouldn't worry, were I you. Connor's not the type of man who tells one woman he loves her and proposes to another a month later."

"But if he's hurt..."

"Not even then. Connor has always known what he wants...and he's never been satisfied with less."

For some reason, the words didn't make Samantha feel any better, and a whole new deluge fell from her eyes. She disliked her weakness and had vowed to herself that there would be no more tears, but Annabelle's quiet sympathy had broken the barrier she had erected against them.

Annabelle shook her head, mystified at what to do or say next. Everything seemed to make things worse. She was amazingly grateful when the soup finally arrived. She helped Samantha sit up, threatening her with mayhem if she failed to eat every last spoonful.

When the young woman had finally finished, Annabelle closed the draperies and urged her to get some more rest. It was the only way, she warned, that she could quickly rejoin Marion. With that admonition, Samantha obediently closed her eyes, exhausted from the emotional upheaval. But images and words reverberated through her consciousness until one dominated all else: Connor and a pretty stranger whirling around a dance floor, his eyes warm and laughing and his mouth curved into a loving smile.

Connor rode into Snow Island, tired and aching but with a lilt in his heart. He would soon see Sam.

He had been wrong to push her, he realized, and he had decided on the long ride back that he would give her as much time as she needed. He would lead her into trust...and marriage would follow. In the meantime, he would have the joy and comfort of her company. He just needed time. He knew now that he would never feel this way again and he wasn't about to lose it.

As he neared Marion's stronghold he picked up the various signals, but the woods seemed emptier than usual, and he knew Lee should have joined Marion by now.

He urged his tired mount faster and guided the horse into the clearing that was the Goddard plantation. There was a minimum guard...no more. He looked anxiously for a small slight figure but could find none. He couldn't help a surge of disappointment...he had been so ready to see her, to throw his arms around her, despite the stares, and feel the warmth of her body.

Struggling against his disappointment, he dismounted and strode over to a lone sergeant.

The man unhurriedly looked up. "Major O'Neill...the gen'l's been looking for you."

"Where is he?"

"He and Lee went to Georgetown three days ago...he left only me and thirty others here." He made it obvious that he was unhappy about that decision.

"Sam Taylor...where is he? He didn't go."

"I guess he did, major. I ain't seen him since the gen'l left."

"Damn," Connor whispered under his breath, more angry than he had been for a long time. He had asked Marion to keep Sam in camp, and Sam had promised to do so if he kept his silence. "Damn," he said again with even more vehemence.

The sergeant looked at him curiously. It was rare that Major O'Neill was anything but calm and deliberate. "They should be back 'most anytime," he said helpfully.

Connor's hand rubbed his stubby cheek. He had not even had time to shave in the past several days, and his body was weary beyond response. He knew he could ask little more of it.

He subdued his first instinct to get another horse and ride out...toward Marion. He would probably miss him if he didn't drop from exhaustion first. Besides, he knew Marion would keep a watchful eye on Sam.

"I'm going to get some sleep," he told the sergeant abruptly. "Wake me as soon as there's word." Connor found himself a blanket and a place beneath a tree and was asleep in seconds.

Despite his deep weariness, the unease in him responded immediately to the first birdcalls signaling Marion's return. He shook his head, clearing it of sleep, and stood against a tree, one foot propped against it. He was trying to control the fear and apprehension that were bubbling up inside him. He saw Marion first and knew Marion had seen him just as quickly. The flicker of emotion in his friend's face told him his fears were justified. He looked anyway, watched every face, studied every form. There was no one remotely close to Sam. His eyes returned to Marion.

Marion slowly dismounted, his face controlled. He walked over to Connor and took his arm, leading him away from the others. They walked silently into the woods, Connor barely hearing the trill of birds. He wanted to ask but couldn't form the question. Finally it came.

"Sam?"

"I don't know," Marion said softly. "He just disappeared."

"In Georgetown?"

Marion nodded. "He was seen while we were attacking the fort . . . then he vanished. We looked all night. He's not among the dead or wounded. I'm sorry, Connor. I shouldn't have taken him, but he was insistent and I had promised him earlier that he could make his own choices."

Connor was silent, beyond recriminations. He felt himself hopeless, drained of every emotion.

"He can take care of himself," Marion said. "He's shown that time and time again."

"Not he," Connor said without emotion. "She. Sam is a she, and she can't take care of herself although she takes great pride in thinking she can."

Marion's face went white. "What are you saying?"

"That Sam Taylor is really Samara Taylor...that she is very much alone and vulnerable and God help her if the British discover who and what she is."

"How long have you known?" Marion's voice was filled with anger.

Connor's lips tightened; a muscle throbbed in his cheek. "Since we went to Georgetown."

"And you feel a little more than brotherly concern?"

"Yes," Connor said belligerently, a most untypical attitude that would have amused Marion if he hadn't been so concerned and angry.

"And she returns these . . . this interest?"

"I thought so," Connor admitted honestly.

"Damn you, Connor," Marion exploded. "This is no place for games. You know my rules. You know I have to trust my officers. You have made one hell of a mess."

Connor's hostility vanished. "I know," he said, and there was such sadness and loss in his voice that Marion's own anger vanished. "I thought she would be safe here...she had no place to go. She said she would stay in camp."

Marion suddenly understood a lot more than he wanted. "She did," he said, "until she heard you were betrothed."

Connor's face furrowed in confusion. "Betrothed?"

"Colonel Lee . . . he said you probably would stay north because you were betrothed to a Miss Demerest."

"Oh, my God," Connor said. "That's Denney Demerest's girl . . . his cousin. You remember him . . . he was at Sullivans Island. I was just accompanying them because there was some trouble with the family."

"Unfortunately," Marion said, "that's not the impression Sam had. So that's why she was so unhappy." He looked at Connor. "What do you know about her?"

"Not much more than you," Connor admitted wryly. "Except she's much better educated than she first led us to believe. She won't say anything about her family other than her father's dead. She said she had no place to go, and that's why she begged me not to tell you."

"If she was hurt, where would she go?"

Connor's eyes reflected his bafflement. "I don't know. If she was wounded, she wouldn't want to be seen by your doctors, that's for certain." His eyes suddenly cleared. "Annabelle. That's it. It has to be."

"Annabelle . . . your Annabelle?"

Connor had the grace to flush. "We stayed there in December . . . before I knew Sam wasn't all he seemed."

Despite the nagging worry, Marion smiled. "That must have been interesting."

A small smile lighted Connor's haggard face. "It was. And somehow I think Annabelle and Sam became friends. Sam never said so, but Annabelle had to have found out and she sure as hell didn't say anything to me about it." The more Connor thought about it, the more he believed Sam must have gone to Annabelle's.

"I'm going there," he said abruptly.

"No," Marion said. "Georgetown will be swarming with British now, and you're too well known. I'll send someone else."

"I'm going," Connor repeated, "with or without your permission."

"I could put you under arrest," Marion said, anger flickering in his eyes.

"You could," Connor answered, his voice just as determined as Marion's. "But you couldn't hold me long." His voice became pleading. "Fran, I know Georgetown like the back of my hand . . . and I'll go disguised. She's my responsibility . . . I'm the reason she went with you. I have to find her."

Marion knew anything he said or did would be futile.

"Will you take someone with you?" Marion finally asked, admitting his surrender.

"I'll take Pat O'Leary."

Marion nodded his consent. O'Leary was sixty years old and looked seventy. But no one, not even the men in their twenties, seemed to have the man's stamina. And O'Leary had a talent for blending into the background and appearing senile. He was often sent by Marion into British-held towns for information.

"You're not to go until dusk," Marion warned. "The roads will be heavy with soldiers hunting us."

Connor chafed at the request but finally agreed. He knew he had pushed Marion as far as he could.

Chapter Twenty

In the three days Samantha spent with Annabelle, she grew to like the older woman immensely. There was a no-nonsense acceptance of life about Annabelle and a humor that refused to kneel to the foibles of a past that Samantha knew would have defeated most. They had something else in common, something they both avoided discussing, a mutual love for Connor O'Neill.

It had been obvious to Samantha since the first visit in December that Annabelle was herself in love with Connor. That her friend had the generosity and compassion to help a rival humbled her. It was a kind of love and sacrifice that she could not imagine. She wanted, more than anything in the world, to bodily attack Caroline Demerest, whoever and wherever she was. The hateful name was stamped in her mind and seldom left it.

Samantha slept and ate and slept and ate some more. She had never felt such hunger. Her appetite seemed to grow daily. It was a good thing, she mused privately, that she would leave Annabelle's tomorrow, for indeed, if she did not, she would grow greater than a cow.

But in between eating and sleeping she and Annabelle talked. She told Annabelle about her father... about wanting his love and never having it... about Connor's stewardship when she and Bren were children... about the carefree joy she and Bren shared and the day he died... about the week following her earlier visit to Georgetown... about Connor's care and love and anger.

She admitted that she had almost told Connor about her identity, as Annabelle had advised, but that Connor had chosen that time to tell her about his brother, the prison ship and his father, and the role the Chathams had played. "He thought," she said brokenly, "that I had seduced Bren and then told my father it had been Bren's fault. He said I as much as killed him with my own hand." She met Annabelle's sympathetic gaze. "I couldn't tell him then...I couldn't watch his love turn to hate. It's better he find someone else...." Her voice trailed off, misery in every difficult word.

Annabelle was a superb listener, never forcing, never judging, rarely commenting. She had privately become even more convinced that in some mysterious way Connor and Samantha were destined for each other.

Only once did Annabelle become disconcerted, and that when Samantha fastened her large blue eyes on her face and asked the question that hovered between them. "Why are you helping me...you love him, too, don't you?"

It was an honest question deserving an honest answer, and Annabelle respected her forthrightness in approaching it.

Nonetheless, she chose her words carefully. "You told me about your childhood. I'll tell you about mine. I didn't know my mother and I guess she didn't know who my father was. My earliest memories are of hunger and being alone. I grew up in an orphanage and I hated every minute of it. Beatings were punishment for the merest infraction and—" Annabelle smiled slightly "—I was never one to conform. A couple came to pick a child, and they chose me. I was so happy. I was ten and wanted desperately to belong to someone."

Her voice turned bitter. "*She* didn't want a child, *he* did. He used me until I was thirteen and I started fighting back. Then he beat me. I finally ran away and came here. I didn't know anything else." Annabelle's eyes wandered to another time, and Samantha could have wept at the infinite sadness in them.

"I was nineteen when I first met Connor. I had tried to listen to and imitate the gentry. I had learned to read and write and cipher. Connor was only fifteen. Even then he was extremely attractive and much older than his years. Serious...considerate...but with that quiet sense of humor that is always unexpected. He noticed a book one day and we started talking. He then started to bring me other books and we would discuss them. He became sort of a teacher, I suppose. He was…is…the only person who ever treated me like that…with respect for me as an individual. He helped me buy this place and trusted me with his funds. He made me feel I was worth something. There is nothing I wouldn't do for him."

This time it was Samantha who gave comfort. She leaned over and pressed Annabelle's hand. "*I* think you're the nicest person I've ever met."

Annabelle smiled at that. "Still and all," she said, "for all Connor's trust and friendship, he never really loved me. And I don't think I could have ever really loved him…in the way you do. I have experienced too much, been used too much. He needs your brightness and laughter and optimism."

She hushed the young girl's protest. "You may not believe that at this very instant, but it is very much a part of you, and I think that's one reason Connor is so attracted to you. He is, in so many ways, a very gentle man. He can be extremely dangerous when fighting for what he believes is right, but he longs for peace and belonging. And I think you can provide that."

Samantha closed her eyes. "How can you say that? He thinks I killed his brother…."

"He thinks that because no one has ever told him differently."

"But Caroline Demerest…"

"Horsefeathers!" Annabelle retorted. "I don't believe that any more than I believe Tarleton has sprouted a halo and wings. If you care for him, fight for him, because if you don't, you are both going to regret it forever."

Samantha looked at Annabelle and smiled. "I hope you will always be my friend…no matter what happens."

As Annabelle left the room, her words hung in the air like heavy storm clouds.

Samantha ate another good dinner and later Annabelle checked her wound. It was healing nicely. They had both decided it had been caused by a piece of wood splintered and sent flying by a cannonball. There was no sight of infection, and

Samantha was ready to leave in the morning, just after curfew lifted. Marion would be wondering what happened to her.

She would have preferred leaving at night, but the British, who arrived in great numbers after Marion's retreat, were compulsive about locking the barn after the horse was stolen. No civilians were allowed in or out of the town from sunset to sunrise. Even those who braved the sentries during the day were questioned extensively.

Annabelle had been reluctant to agree to her departure but understood her restlessness. And dressed as a boy, Samantha certainly looked inoffensive enough. Annabelle sighed; perhaps it was just as well. She was almost beginning to feel like a mother.

Samantha crawled out of bed just before dawn and ate a large breakfast. She pulled on some boy's clothes Annabelle had found; her own had been torn and covered with powder stains. Definitely not the thing to wear before suspicious and angry British soldiers. Annabelle thought of everything.

She regarded herself in front of a mirror. Her hair was longer and curly, but she couldn't bear to cut it again. Instead, she pulled it back and tied it with a leather thong. A battered farmer's cap and a few dirt smudges completed the picture.

Annabelle slipped in the room and wished her "Godspeed" before ushering her down the steps and through the back door. Instead of her own lovely chestnut, there stood a sorrowful-looking plow horse without a saddle. Samantha reluctantly mounted. With a small wave to Annabelle, she finally persuaded her transportation to plod slowly down the dirt street.

As Samantha rode down the dirt lane in back of the house, Connor O'Neill and Pat O'Leary were coming down Cherry Street. They had arrived outside Georgetown in the early-morning hours and discovered the town closed. They had tried to catch some sleep in the woods, but Connor's anxiety had kept him awake. He couldn't stop thinking about Sam. Dear God, let her be at Annabelle's. Let her be safe.

He angrily begrudged the night every one of its seconds. O'Leary, looking every bit a man near death, had approached the night guard and been told of the curfew. There had been nothing to do but wait. Connor stared at the stars, ignoring their beauty, willing them to fade into dawn.

When they finally did, he and O'Leary joined a large crowd waiting admittance into town. It was a blessing, for the tired and harried British sentries gave little attention to a crippled, one-eyed man traveling with an aged father to get some salt.

As they drew up before Annabelle's, O'Leary stayed on horseback while Connor forced himself to drag a leg up the steps. 'Twould not do to get careless now, he warned himself. If accosted, he could always claim he was looking for an errant daughter. If he hadn't been so worried, he would have smiled. More like an errant, disobedient young lad.

He didn't stop to knock but entered loudly, as an angry father would. It was, as he had hoped, empty. The patrons had disappeared with the night. But even then, he was cautious and resisted the temptation to yell for Annabelle. Instead he climbed the two flights of stairs to Annabelle's room and knocked impatiently. There was a rustling inside, an impatient "go away."

"Annabelle," he said with a quiet but quite distinct rage.

The door opened, and Annabelle faced him with no little shock.

He pushed by her and looked around. "Has Sam been here?"

One look at his eyes and Annabelle knew it was no time to lie. She nodded, noting every aspect of his ravaged face. She felt a strange contentment at his obvious distress.

"Where is she?"

"You shouldn't be here, Connor," she said at last. "Tarleton's here and I've never seen him so angry. Marion's taking Georgetown was a personal insult to him."

"Where is she, Annabelle?"

She could no longer evade his cold, angry gray eyes. "She left a little while ago... she's going back to Marion."

"Why was she here?" The question was curt, not at all like the Connor she knew.

"She was wounded the night Marion took Georgetown. She didn't want Marion or the doctors to know."

"Where... how badly?"

"A flesh wound in her side...she lost some blood. But I think she was mainly exhausted."

Connor's head went back in combined relief and frustration. He whispered a tiny prayer of thanksgiving for Sam's survival.

Annabelle's voice broke through his thoughts. "I thought you were with Greene. Sam said you were betrothed."

Anger flickered in his eyes and a muscle throbbed in his cheek. "Is that why she pulled this damned fool stunt?"

Annabelle shrugged. "Is it true?"

"No!" he thundered, and Annabelle was suddenly comforted. "Why, then," she asked logically, "don't you go find her and tell her so?"

Connor stared at her, then swung around, taking the steps two at a time, his lameness all but forgotten. Sam would be going out the main gate...the one they had entered thirty minutes earlier. Reaching the front door, he halted long enough to mold his features back into the hopelessness of a battered soldier, but even then there was a spring to his uneven stride and O'Leary didn't miss it.

"He there?" O'Leary had not yet been informed of Sam's sex.

"Not thirty minutes ago...he should be reaching the main gate...let's go and meet him outside."

O'Leary couldn't help but catch Connor's excitement, although he wondered a bit about it. He, too, liked young Sam Taylor, but Connor's actions seemed a little extreme. He shook his head in bafflement but spurred his horse to catch up with his major.

Samantha tried her best to look unobtrusive. Why was it that every eye seemed upon her? She hunched her shoulders together, trying to look even smaller.

Her horse plodded on through the main street, noisy with British troops. She knew fear now as she had never known it before. She was more alone than she had ever been. There was no one else to depend on, only her wits, and she felt very much bereft of them at the moment.

She was keeping her eyes toward the ground. If she didn't see anyone, perhaps no one would ·see her. But then her horse stopped, and she looked up. Her eyes slowly climbed from the ground upward, to a fine bay stallion and red-clad legs to a stiff back and up to a face that looked all too familiar.

"Sam, isn't it?" came the slightly amused, slightly warning voice.

She gulped as her eyes met General O'Mara's. His were quizzical, his face stern.

Her eyes went quickly downward again. There was absolutely nothing she could say. She was caught as surely as a treed coon.

"Your business in Georgetown?" Did she detect a note of sympathy?

"Gittin' some medicine for my pore ol' pa," she answered in a low voice, thinking maybe, just maybe, he would let her go. Perhaps if she played along...

"He wouldn't be living in a swamp now, would he?" O'Mara's voice was harsh now, the amusement gone. He was to return next week to England. His career was in ruins.

Samantha just looked up at him miserably and shrugged, not knowing what else to do.

O'Mara looked down at his wrists. There were still marks there. He remembered how Sam had intervened for him...and his kindness. Damn these rebels anyway. He knew with a sudden sure instinct that Britain would lose this war. It couldn't win when fourteen-year-old boys took up rifles, and men gave up families and everything they owned to live in the woods on potatoes. He hated the rebels who had taken him, but he had admired them, too. He realized he was glad to be leaving.

He moved his horse out of her way. "You better be getting home, boy," he said. Then he smiled, a gentle sad smile. "I will be seeing my boys soon...I hope they'll never have to go so far to get medicine." He moved away, thinking she was safe, not noticing another British officer who watched them closely with dawning recognition.

William Foxworth was completely frustrated. His career had stalled, and Samantha Chatham had completely disappeared.

He believed now that even her father didn't know where she was. His hopes for the Chatham fortune had died a slow agonizing death.

The whole affair had angered him to the point of madness. It galled him beyond belief that a woman might have fled not only his attentions but his hand in marriage. That damned bitch. And under it all had been that funny nagging feeling about the boy on the golden horse. It couldn't be...no woman would go to war and live in a camp with Marion's ruffians...not one of Samantha's obvious breeding.

He had heard whispers, of course, about her affair with the young O'Neill boy. It was said that he had bedded her, but Samantha's father had assured him the rumors were not true. It had not mattered to him overly much. He wanted the fortune, and, yes, he wanted Samantha with her dark hair and taunting blue eyes. He wanted to tame her, to show her who was master. Just thinking about her now sent his blood burning and his manhood swelling.

Uttering a curse, he started for the main gate of Georgetown. Tarleton had been in a rage since they had arrived yesterday, only to find the town abandoned and stripped of everything of any practical use. Stores of guns, powder, bullets, blankets and foodstuffs had been systematically looted. The fort had been completely destroyed; the barracks burned. Tarleton, whose command had been so badly decimated at Cowpens, had been given new inexperienced troops and it had taken them longer than expected to travel from Charleston to Georgetown. The only signs of the enemy remaining were the satisfied smirks and grins of Georgetown's citizenry. Tarleton planned to wipe them away quickly. Anyone known to have helped the rebels was to be imprisoned. Homes were to be searched for wounded rebels and anyone harboring them arrested.

Foxworth had been sent to check the guard posts, a duty he considered far below his status, but there was no arguing with his commander at this time. His thoughts of Samantha did not lighten his mood.

As he moved into the main street, he watched O'Mara stop a boy on a plow horse. O'Mara, he knew, was in total disgrace

and was to be sent home. He had obviously seen many of
Marion's men during his captivity and could be of some use in
recognizing them. Foxworth saw parallels in his own career.
None of the British officers in the Carolinas had distinguished
themselves or helped their careers. He could see himself mired
here forever. If he could only take Marion; that would be an
accomplishment no one would ignore, and, of course, there was
the reward.

Some instinct made him look again at O'Mara and the boy.
There was a strange expression on the general's face. Foxworth took a closer look at the boy, and his whole body jerked
to attention. There was a certain grace in the slumped figure,
and the head was held high. Even from here, he could see the
flash of startling blue eyes under the low cap. He started forward, then decided to wait and watch. If O'Mara knew the boy,
then he was protecting him; if not, then Foxworth wanted the
boy for himself. He waited for O'Mara to pass out of sight and
then he followed the boy to the main guard post leading out of
town. He sauntered up, listening to the exchange between the
sentries and his prey.

The boy's attention was focused on the sentry as he told, in
rough speech, a long rambling story about a sick father and
medicine. Then the boy's eyes reached Foxworth and involuntarily widened, the voice stilled for a moment. In that instant, Foxworth knew all his suspicions and instincts had been
correct.

His eyes were icy and his mouth set in a tight cruel line as he
turned to the sentry. "I'll take care of this."

He then faced Samantha. "Get down." As she hesitated,
Foxworth's hands went to her arms and pulled her down,
dropping her like a sack at the side of the horse. Then one iron
hand clasped her arm and pulled her up, thrusting her away
from the guard post and safety. She could only stumble behind him as Foxworth dragged her across the square and down
the street to his quarters.

Connor and O'Leary arrived just in time to see Foxworth
dragging Samantha away. Connor immediately recognized the
officer from the salt raid and thought that Foxworth had seen

the boy who had shot so well that day. He clamped his lips together. What damned bad luck. The man could also possibly recognize him, even through his heavy disguise. Foxworth had been very close to him and had studied him intently after learning his name. Connor had wondered about that particular interest, and now he cursed it. He turned to O'Leary and met his questioning gaze.

"What do we do now, major?" the man asked.

"We follow. We follow and wait."

Foxworth took Samantha to his quarters, a room in a home formerly owned by outspoken Whigs. It was crawling with red-and-green-clad British regulars and dragoons. Without words and disregarding the stares of his housemates, he dragged her up the flight of stairs to a large room. Once inside, he quickly bolted the door and turned his attention to the frightened and sullen girl in front of him.

He smiled but there was no amusement in it, only mockery as his eyes traveled over every feature. He took off her cap, and his hand fondled a lock of her short hair.

"Such a shame, Samantha. You shouldn't have done that."

"I doan ken yer meanin'," she blustered, fear weakening her legs. She wondered how long she could stand on them.

It didn't help when his hands started unbuttoning her jacket, then her shirt. His eyes rested on the linen cloth binding her breasts. "You don't ken, huh," he taunted. "Perhaps you can ken this." His hands undid the binding and reached for the suddenly outstretched breasts.

She jerked away, but he caught her, and his lips settled wet and moist on her own. She pretended to give way, opening her mouth to him, but as his tongue eagerly sought hers, her teeth bit down on it and she could taste the quick flow of blood.

"Damn you," he spit as he jerked away from her. His hand came up and slapped her; the force of it sent her across the room and she could feel her own blood trickling from a cut on her mouth.

"You will regret that, you little hellion," he said, digging for a handkerchief.

Samantha looked at him with hate and contempt in her eyes.

Despite the smudges of dirt and dye...the rough clothes...the short colorless hair, Foxworth felt a surge of admiration and desire. God, she was striking, even like this.

She couldn't miss the desire in his eyes and she backed even farther away. "It's too bad you couldn't do something with those eyes," he continued. "I would know them anyplace...even that day at the Garrison plantation. Where did you learn to shoot like that?" The question was almost conversational, but Samantha didn't miss the menace behind it. He had been badly humiliated that day and someone was going to pay for it. She had a lot to pay for, starting with making him look like a fool.

He approached her, taking pleasure in the fear that leaped into her eyes. His hand stroked her face but there was no gentleness in it. She flinched from his touch, and anger glittered in his eyes.

"Do you enjoy those backwoods ruffians...do you prefer their bed to mine?"

Samantha regained her courage. "Aye," she said. "By much...why do you think I left?"

The second blow was even stronger than the first and sent her spinning down to the floor, but her battered face looked back at him with defiance.

Foxworth tried to control his rage. She was besting him. He had never hit a woman before and now he had done it twice. Instead of fear or hatred or surrender, he found only icy contempt in her steady gaze.

He turned away, trying to gather his thoughts. He had meant to offer again for her hand, but there was no question of that now. She had admitted sleeping with Marion's woodsmen...and she made no secret of her dislike for him. He thought, briefly, about turning her over to the provost, but probably very little would be done to her. She was, after all, still the daughter, however wayward, of one of the strongest and most loyal Tories in the Carolinas. He couldn't bear to see her go unpunished...or think of the derision and shame confronting him when his fellow officers learned of his runaway fiancée.

He turned around and studied her. She was trying to pull her shirt back together but her eyes had never left her tormentor. His mind went back again to the Garrison place and that unique shot. It had, unquestionably, saved that rebel major's life. He wondered exactly what else she had done for him, not realizing the thought turned his face red with anger. There was nothing handsome about him now. His florid features were twisted with hate and his eyes gleamed with sudden greed.

Perhaps she would be worth something to him, after all. The reward for Connor O'Neill was almost as great as that for Marion. And, with luck, he could trap them both. She was a tempting piece of bait. They couldn't deny him his promotion if he were the one to capture the Swamp Fox. But he would have to do it on his own, with men loyal only to him.

Samantha didn't like the expression on Foxworth's face one bit. It had gone from hot to cold rage and then to a blank thoughtfulness before becoming a mask of malicious satisfaction. She backed up against a wall as he approached again and watched warily as he stopped at the bed and tore a sheet into strips. He started toward her again, jerking her to her feet and twisting her arms behind her. He tied them thoroughly, then thrust a piece of cloth in her mouth, binding it there with yet another strip. Foxworth picked up her cap and set it atop her head, then reached inside her shirt, rebinding the breasts despite her struggles. He didn't want anyone to know who she was...not until they were well out of Georgetown, and he didn't want to take a chance she might tell the sentries or send them for O'Mara. O'Mara. That was another puzzle he would unravel when he had her alone.

With one hand on her arm, he unlocked the door and pushed her out and down the steps. Meeting some officers who looked quizzically at the gag, he merely yawned wearily and sighed. "One of Marion's leftovers with a treasonous mouth...I grew tired of listening."

They grinned. "These rebels grow them young, don't they?" one said, his interest gone.

Once downstairs, Foxworth ordered an enlisted man to find his sergeant and five other men he named, and to see that eight horses were saddled. He waited impatiently as the men appeared, one by one, and he gave them orders. Then Foxworth lifted Samantha onto one of the saddled horses and, taking her reins, mounted one of his own. The small group of heavily armed soldiers moved down the main street and out of Georgetown.

Connor and Patrick watched their departure from across the street. Hidden behind his horse, Connor caught only a brief glimpse of Sam, but it was enough to spur his rage. She stumbled as if hurt, and he could see traces of blood on her face. His hands knotted into tight fists. He felt completely helpless, even more helpless than when he had been taken a year earlier. British troops were numerous throughout the city and even if they weren't he was terrified she would be hurt in any battle. She was closely circled by the troops, and Connor believed it was no accident.

What did they want? Why, if they'd found her out, didn't they turn her over to British authorities?

He looked over at Patrick and saw the same questions in his face. He simply shrugged, indicating his own confusion.

The two men watched as the eight riders passed the sentry post and quickened their pace on the road west. Connor tightened his cinch for the eighth time in an hour and mounted, O'Leary behind him. The two men carefully arranged their faces into numb dullness, and they, too, passed through the sentries and became part of the endless parade out of town.

Connor blessed the fact that the road was a busy one. It was easy to keep sight of the eight riders without being noticed. He shifted in his saddle and thought of how uncomfortable Sam must be, struggling for balance with her hands tied behind her.

He wondered again what Foxworth was up to. It was passing strange that he would interest himself with such a small fish, even if he had discovered Sam was a girl. Perhaps that was it, he thought, bile rising in him. Perhaps he wanted to take advantage of her. But if that were the case, why take so many soldiers with him? The questions kept hammering at him, and he could find no answers. He would never forgive himself if anything happened to her.

It was O'Leary who finally suggested their destination. Traffic had fallen off, and the two had lagged further and further behind to keep from being seen. O'Leary's sharp eyes saw a flicker of red disappearing behind some trees. When Connor and his companion reached the spot in the road, they saw a nearly invisible path leading through what seemed to be impenetrable woods.

"The Beakers," O'Leary said, distaste evident in his words. "They're going to Beakers' Island."

Connor groaned, realizing O'Leary was right. The Beakers had been thieves and outlaws before the war, terrorizing the area and retreating to a small island surrounded by water and bog. They had been left to their nefarious pursuits by lawmen who feared them more than they respected their duty. But the war had made them respectable. As Tories, they claimed British protection as they burned and looted and murdered.

Few uninvited guests ever emerged from the Beakers' territory. The greatest problem was that quicksand protected almost the entire area and only the Beakers knew the one safe path to the island.

O'Leary looked at Connor. "At least we know where they're going with the wee lad."

"But not why," Connor replied thoughtfully. The only answer that had occurred to him was a trap. But a trap for whom? Surely no one would think a boy would demand much of a ransom or bargaining power.

Just then they heard hoofbeats and quietly moved their mounts into the woods out of sight. They watched as a red-coated figure emerged from the woods and galloped away from them.

O'Leary looked at Connor. "That means only six of them."

"But we don't know about the Beakers or how many of their kin they have with them." He didn't waste much time on thought. "Go after him, Pat, and take him. See what you can find out. Then go to Marion. Tell him what's happening."

The old Irishman studied Connor's face. "Hell of a lot of trouble for a wee laddie they'll probably let go anyway."

"Not a laddie, Pat," Connor said slowly. "A lassie . . . and I don't like her there with the Beakers at all."

O'Leary stared at him, his face growing red with anger. "Well, damn me," he spit. "Can't say I do, either. That lobster's as good as taken." Without another word, he spurred his horse and was off in a whirl of dust.

Connor permitted himself a small smile. All the stubborn Irishman needed was a nudge to his gallantry. Old as he was, he was still twenty in his heart. He had an unequaled love for all members of the fairer and gentler sex, as he called them. Connor knew O'Leary would waste no time in accomplishing his mission.

He urged his horse through the dense woods until he was completely blocked by its thickness. He dismounted, making a tiny natural corral for his horse. He took off his rough jacket and with a knife cut tiny slivers of cloth. As he wormed his way through the overgrowth, he left a tiny trail of them. The brown melted into the earth and someone not searching for such a sign would surely overlook it.

After several hours, he knew he had gone less than half a mile. But he had reached the water, and now he rested in a small ditch. When he had caught his breath and his heart had reached a more normal rhythm, he carefully raised his head. A wide ribbon of river separated him from the island. It looked calm and clean enough, but appearances were deceptive. It was as treacherous a piece of water as any around Snow Island.

Connor could see movement on the island and supposed sentries were being strategically placed. There were none across from him; the river was its own sentry. It was the widest section, and the water was freezing cold. The bottomless quicksand would keep any horses from making it across.

Helpless at the moment, Connor lay back and waited. Marion should be here by dusk. Meanwhile, a plan formed in his mind.

Chapter Twenty-One

Every part of Samantha hurt. She felt as if the ride would never end. Her mouth was still gagged, and her nose had filled with dust from the road. Every breath was a struggle, and she was slowly suffocating. But the pain didn't end there. Her wrists, still bound tightly behind her, were almost numb with agony. And her legs. The stirrups had not been adjusted for her small size, and she had to use her thighs and knees to keep her balance. Adding to the symphony of hurts was the recent wound to her side, jarred as it was by Foxworth's rough handling.

Her thoughts did not help. She could not fathom why Foxworth had taken her from Georgetown instead of handing her over to either the British authorities or her father. It bode little good for her future.

She tried to keep her mind on better times as Connor told her he had in prison. She concentrated all her efforts on him now, recalling his smile and rare but full laughter. She loved him more than she thought it possible to love another human being. She wondered if others loved with this much passion and longing and pain. They didn't, of course, or the world would come to a stop. Perhaps that would not be such a bad thing...if everyone were frozen as they were this minute, like Lot's wife in the Bible. No more war. No more pain. No more longing.

She shook the traitorous thoughts from her head. She would never give up...no matter what they did. Someway... somehow...she would best Foxworth and escape.

Their pace slowed. New torments came to her as the briars and branches hit her unprotected face and body. She would duck one, only to be caught by another. They finally rode out of the woods and she saw a wide band of water. Foxworth had stopped and now he waited. The minutes seemed endless. Samantha watched carefully as a dirty ragged stranger came out of the woods on the opposite bank and pointed to a section of the river. He then disappeared and several minutes later reappeared on horseback. He made his way carefully across the area he'd previously indicated, the water never more than three feet deep.

When he reached Foxworth, he was curt. "I don't 'member any invite."

Foxworth eyed him with distaste. He didn't like dealing with these vermin but at this point he had no choice. They had something he shared—an equal hatred for the Swamp Fox.

"You want Marion, don't you? And O'Neill?"

The man's eyes glittered with hatred. Marion's militia, under O'Neill, had killed his brother two months earlier. "Go on," he said.

"I'm thinking O'Neill will come after this one." He nodded at Samantha. "And maybe Marion, too."

"After that brat," the man replied, contempt spreading over his face. "You're crazy."

Foxworth started to tell who she was but stopped. That was something he wasn't ready to share yet . . . it could be useful in the future.

"That brat," he said, "saved O'Neill's life. I saw it. And I've heard enough about O'Neill to know he won't let him hang."

The woodsman studied her with new interest. "Maybe you're right."

"If O'Neill comes, Marion might come, also," Foxworth continued. "How many Tories can you get before morning?"

"Enough," the man replied.

"Good," Foxworth said. "I've already sent a message to Marion, offering to exchange this boy for O'Neill. I set the time for morning, a mile north of here. I told him that if anyone other than Marion or O'Neill came, the boy would die."

The stranger's face suffused with anger. "Without asking me or mine?"

"I knew you wouldn't want to disappoint the king," Foxworth said smoothly, "or your own vengeance. Remember your pardon depends on your continued loyalty."

The man controlled his anger with visible effort. He hated these arrogant English almost as much as he hated Marion. But for now, he would use them . . . just as they thought they were using him.

"Come," he said sharply, "and beware of wandering off that bank. There's quicksand on both sides."

Foxworth nodded and turned to Samantha, a smirk on his face. He knew she had heard the entire conversation and her eyes were almost black with hate.

"Be careful, my love," he said in a voice too low to carry. "I would hate to see you slowly sink before I hang your rebel friends." With a jerk he took the reins to her horse from the trooper who had been leading her, almost causing her to lose her balance.

She held what breath she had as they slowly traversed the river to the other bank, releasing it only when across. Only one thought kept her going. Foxworth didn't know the name Sam Taylor. He evidently thought Marion and O'Neill knew who she was. At that moment, she didn't know whether to laugh or cry...if, in fact, she could do either. Little did Foxworth know that no one, particularly Connor, would lift a finger for Samantha Chatham. He would probably applaud her demise. One less Chatham in his world. And even were that not true, she knew Connor was hundreds of miles away, courting another girl. Poor Foxworth. Poor inept Foxworth. She wanted to giggle at the arrogant colonel who was soon to be so disappointed, but the gag made it impossible.

When they finally arrived at a rough cabin, Foxworth pulled her down from the horse, watching with amusement as her weakened and stiff legs folded under her. His hand jerked her upright again and forced her inside.

The cabin was as filthy as any she had ever seen. The smell made her nauseous and she struggled once more to breathe. Foxworth pushed her down on a dirty cot and went to the door, talking again to the man who had helped them cross the river. She could only hear snatches of words but she could understand that Foxworth was urging the other to round up more Tories. When he was through, he closed the door and came over to her, deliberately withdrawing a knife from its leather holder on his belt. She shrank back against the wall, and she heard his taunting laughter.

"I'm not going to do anything to you...not yet. But if your new friends aren't here in the morning, I'm going to give you to the Beakers. They'll demand something for their efforts. After I have my turn, of course." He saw the revulsion in her eyes and knew anger again that she preferred Marion's rabble to himself. "If you're harlot to them, you can be harlot to the Beakers."

He used the knife to cut the gag from her mouth and she took a long breath. Her mouth was hot and dry and she longed for a drink of water.

"Thirsty, Samantha?" Foxworth said as he watched her tongue wipe her lips. "If you beg, I might give you some."

Her chin lifted, but her thirst suddenly overcame everything else. She would sell her soul for a drink. It was the hardest thing she ever did, but the word finally came out. "Please..."

"Not quite sincere enough, Miss Samantha. I think I require a kiss, as well. A willing one."

Her mouth snapped shut. "Never." Maybe she wouldn't sell her soul, after all.

He laughed, enjoying her humiliation. "You will before long, Samantha. I promise you that." He left the cabin, leaving her tied, thirsty beyond reason and hurting everywhere.

With Connor's added incentive, it didn't take O'Leary long to overtake the British soldier and even less time to subdue him. To the hapless private, sent on an errand that terrified him, O'Leary looked like the vengeance of God with his wild beard and sword waving in the air. He surrendered quickly, happy he would be unable to make the trip to Snow Island and confront the terrible Swamp Fox.

His relief didn't last long when O'Leary searched his saddlebags and found a folded note with lettering on it.

O'Leary cursed his inability to read. "What say this?" he demanded.

"It's for the Swamp Fox," his prisoner mumbled.

"What's that? Say louder or I'll be done with ye now." He swung the sword for emphasis, seeing the terror in his victim's eyes.

"It's for the Swamp Fox," the man said louder. "I don't know what it says."

"Well, then, we'll just take it to him, won't we," O'Leary said jovially, watching the man pale. He took the man's reins and set out at a gallop.

When O'Leary reached the Pee Dee, he blindfolded the man and led him through the tangled trails to Marion's camp. He quickly found his commander.

Fran Marion watched O'Leary and the redcoat approach. "Connor?" he asked.

"Beakers' Island. They caught Sam Taylor and we followed 'em there...this fancy-dressed gent was comin' to find ye. Says he has a message."

Marion took the now wrinkled paper, but before he could read it, O'Leary, distress in his voice, couldn't halt a question of his own. "Connor says Sam Taylor ain't a boy...could that be?"

Marion looked at him squarely. "I'm afraid so, Pat."

"We got to go after 'em. Them Beakers are as mean as snakes...and that redcoat officer's even worse. She had blood all over 'er...poor little lassie."

Marion's face hardened, and his eyes glittered with anger. He looked down at the note.

To the Swamp Fox...

We've taken a traitor, Samantha Chatham, and will hang her tomorrow unless we receive a traitor of equal or greater importance. The only two acceptable exchanges are the self-styled General Francis Marion or Major Connor O'Neill.

Unless one of these two rebels presents himself—alone—at the spot on the map by dawn tomorrow, Samantha Chatham will die. Any attempt to rescue her will meet with her immediate death.

It was signed by a Colonel William Foxworth.

That was Colonel Foxworth's second mistake, Marion pledged to himself. Signing the letter. His first had been taking the girl.

He knew it must be an independent action on Foxworth's part. The British command would never countenance the hanging of a woman, regardless of the provocation. It would incite the countryside to a fever pitch.

Marion fingered the note, again looking at the name. Samantha Chatham. So Sam Taylor, alias Samara Taylor, was really the daughter of Connor's arch enemy. That explained much, particularly Sam's unhappiness. What a web she and Connor had woven for themselves.

He ordered the British private locked in the barn and told fifty of his men to mount.

"You can find Connor?" he asked O'Leary, who simply nodded.

Almost as an afterthought, Marion threw the note in a cooking fire. Within minutes he and his woodsmen were moving rapidly through the forest.

Connor had used the afternoon to good advantage. After searching for more than an hour, he found exactly what he was looking for: a downed tree, an apparent victim of lightning. The lower trunk was large and not yet beset by rot. He sat down beside it and took out his knife. Connor started carving.

It was approaching dusk before he felt he had made an impact. His arms and hands were aching from his efforts when he heard the first soft footsteps and found himself surrounded. How quiet Marion had been, he mused. Even his well-trained ears had heard nothing until they were upon him.

He and Marion conferred while others replaced him at the side of the log and chipped away at Connor's rough dugout. Marion described the note, leaving out the fact of Samantha Chatham's identity. Connor, in turn, explained to Marion that he thought he could make a ferry out of ropes and the log and take approximately ten men across. They could take the Beakers' cabin and rescue Sam while the others ambushed those awaiting either Marion or Connor. The remainder of their opponents would then be trapped between the two.

Marion agreed and they asked for volunteers to cross the river. Every man demanded to go, now understanding from O'Leary that Sam was a she and in very great danger. Connor finally selected those who said they could swim—those he believed, anyway, because all of them claimed such skills, though Connor knew otherwise.

By midnight the dugout was ready and carried to the river. A system of ropes was tied around the log with makeshift pulleys. The trick, Connor explained, was to allow the passenger to lie within the log so it resembled a drifting piece of debris. They could not risk paddling.

When Connor was finally satisfied, he solicited clothes from those who had extras with them and placed them in the log. He then stepped into the icy water, holding on to the log, and swam, pushing his would-be ferry in front of him.

He had never been so cold. The swim took every ounce of effort and strength he had, and even then he thought he might not make it. He was too cold and tired to rejoice when the log hit the other bank. He slowly crawled out, shivering so greatly that it took several minutes before his body did what it was told.

He changed to the dry clothes, then rigged up ropes on his side, tying them low so they could not be seen from a distance. He gave a soft hoot and felt the tug on the rope. The log returned to the other side. Within an hour, his ten were safely on Beakers' Island. They would attack the cabin just before dawn while, he hoped, the majority of British and Tories, thinking the island impenetrable, would be awaiting their prey more than a mile away.

Dawn came slowly. The stars disappeared from the dark night sky, which lightened imperceptibly, a small degree at a time. Connor's men had neared the cabin but stayed well out of sight. Two men stood guard outside; Connor wondered if anyone was inside with Sam but doubted it. Foxworth would think his danger lay outside the island.

He signaled two of his men to take one guard, and he approached the second. The sentry never heard the steps behind him and felt the danger only when a knife touched his throat.

Connor pressed the knife deeper against the man's neck, then whispered to his captive. "Who's inside?"

The voice croaked in fear. "Just the prisoner."

"If you lie, you'll never leave this island," Connor warned.

The man trembled. "I swear... there's no one else."

Connor finally believed. He hit the man with his pistol, and the guard went down, unconscious. He opened the door to the cabin.

His heart constricted. Sam was sitting on a filthy cot, her eyes almost closed from the effects of the blows and weariness and bites. Her cheek was bruised and cut, her mouth swollen. Her clothes were covered with dried blood. But when she saw him, her mouth twisted into the sweetest smile he had ever seen.

He quickly cut the ropes binding her hands, and his arms went around her.

"Thank God," he whispered. "Thank God, you're alive."

Samantha thought she must be dreaming. Connor was hundreds of miles away. She was delirious. She must be.

"Connor?"

His finger tenderly lifted her chin. "Yes, love... it's me."

All of a sudden, reason came back to her. It was a trap. A trap to catch Connor.

"Connor... you must go... it's a trap."

"Hush, little one," he said. "We know. But Foxworth is the one who will be caught." His voice hardened. "And I'm going to kill him. By God, if Marion doesn't, I will."

"General Marion?"

"Aye," Connor said. "He should be ambushing them right now." He turned his attention back to her. "Did he touch you?"

"No... he said he didn't want to be sullied by Marion's leavings. But he was going to give me to the Beakers." She shuddered.

She felt his lips touch her forehead with such tenderness that her heart almost stopped. She tipped her head, and her lips met his in a soft sweet joining.

Hope touched her. She knew the note to Marion mentioned Samantha Chatham. Did Connor know? Was he accepting her? She didn't want to ask. She didn't want to break this spell. Instead, she snuggled deeper in his arms and felt utter contentment.

She rested there, silent, soaking in his nearness, reveling in his protectiveness. Nothing else mattered at the moment, not her identity, not his rumored betrothal. They were, again, as one.

Connor let her snuggle, feeling her need. His hand gently ruffled her dusty hair and caressed her arms, reassuring her. She was a mass of bruises and sores. He held her there as several of his men came in, then retreated swiftly in embarrassment. Finally a sergeant came in, his face covered with a wide smile.

"All secure, major," he said. "The prisoners are tied, and I've placed pickets at the crossing point." His attention turned to Sam. "We're sure glad to see you, Miss..."

Samantha managed a small smile. "Sam," she said. "It's still Sam. And I think I'm much happier to see *you*."

The sergeant ducked his head. He had been comfortable with Sam; he wasn't so sure about the girl he had turned out to be. He slipped out the door.

Connor turned his head to look down into her face. "Why in the hell did you go to Georgetown? I thought you had promised me..."

His abrupt question suddenly brought her back down to earth. He had not mentioned Samantha Chatham. Was it possible he still didn't know? "And I thought," she started defensively, "that you weren't coming back... that you didn't care what I did, that you were..."

"Betrothed," he finished her statement wearily. "I wasn't... not then, not now, not ever."

"But..."

"It was a good friend of mine," he answered the unspoken question. "He was in love with his cousin. The family disapproved. I just helped bring them together."

"You're not engaged?" The voice was small and unbelieving. So much agony for nothing.

"How could I," he answered gently, "when I love you?"

"No matter what?" she asked cautiously.

"Even when you run off and get yourself in so much trouble," he answered tenderly. "Even then."

Even, Sam thought to herself, afraid to voice her fears, if I am a Chatham?

Instead, she asked, "Did you see the note Colonel Foxworth sent?"

"No," he said. "I followed you from Georgetown. I went there looking for you when you didn't come back with Fran. I just missed you at Annabelle's, and then I saw Foxworth take you."

She sighed with disappointment. So he didn't know. So he hadn't forgiven her or accepted her. Nothing had really changed. Nothing except her need for him . . . which had increased to overpowering extremes. She tucked her head against his chest and was silent while Connor waited, knowing his men would alert him if anyone approached the island crossing.

It was an hour later when one of his men came running. "Riders, sir," he said. "We think it's the general."

Connor gently placed Sam back on the cot and hurried out, only vaguely aware that she was behind him. He mounted quickly and galloped to the crossing.

One of his men was high in a tree. "It's General Marion, sir," he affirmed.

Connor went to the edge of the woods and waited. He was probably the only one who knew the safe crossing and he guided Marion across.

"Foxworth?" Connor said tightly.

"Dead," Marion replied tersely. "So are the Beakers. We took several of the redcoats prisoner. Sam?"

"She's badly bruised and hurting but nothing permanent," Connor replied. "Foxworth had promised her to the Beakers if anything went wrong today."

"No one is going to miss them," Marion said. "Or that redcoat colonel, either. I'll be bound he did this all on his own. I just wonder why. Has Sam said anything?"

Connor shook his head. "She's said very little."

A dark look crossed Marion's face but it went as quickly as it came, giving Connor little time to wonder about it.

"Can she ride?"

Samantha suddenly appeared next to Connor. She nodded her head, then looked intensely at Marion. "Thank you," she said softly, and Marion knew it wasn't just for her rescue.

"We'll talk later at Snow Island," he said, and she couldn't miss the warning in his voice.

Chapter Twenty-Two

Samantha had never felt so pampered in her life. She had been given Marion's cabin and thoroughly examined and treated by a doctor. And then there was a steady stream of visitors, many of whom brought tiny gifts.

The men in Marion's brigade had developed both respect and liking for Young Sam, but he had done little more than that expected of anyone joining the brigade. For a woman, however, to do what he had done, was extraordinary in their mind, and their admiration and curiosity knew no limits. They brought flowers and little trinkets and called her "miss" or "mistress" or "ma'am" or "lassie" until she became immensely uncomfortable.

"Just Sam," she kept telling them. "It's still just Sam."

Billy James sidled in one day, his face a mixture of embarrassment and pride. Sam was his friend, and that created the pride. But he had also shared a tent with her, and now that caused him no little discomfort. He had been teased unmercifully about not knowing the difference between men and women.

He gave her a small smile. "I was worried about you," he said simply, and she knew he meant it.

"I wasn't very smart," Sam admitted wryly. "I shouldn't have gone in the beginning, and then I shouldn't have left you in Georgetown. I should have let you take care of me." Her voice was suddenly gentle.

His face split in a wide grin. "You'll still be my friend?"

She smiled back. "Always."

"I've been taking care of your horse for you," Billy said.

"I know," she answered. "Major O'Neill told me. He said you were doing it very well, too. Thank you."

Billy's face grew serious. "She knows me now, but she misses you . . . she keeps looking for you."

"I'm going to try to go see her today," Samantha replied.

"No, you're not," came a voice from the door, and both looked up, surprised.

It was Francis Marion, and Billy rose respectfully.

"You're going to stay right where you are," General Marion said, "until the doctor says differently."

Sam felt a shiver of fear. She had been here two days, and this was Marion's first visit. It was the time of reckoning, she suspected, and she did not welcome it.

Her instinct was right. Marion turned to Billy. "I want a word alone with young Sam," he said, and Billy quickly backed out the door, closing it behind him.

"You're Samantha Chatham," he said, and it was not a question. Yet he waited for a reply.

She nodded forlornly.

"You knew Foxworth?"

"Yes," she said, her voice low. "My father wanted me to marry him. That's why I ran away."

"But why here? Why come here? Why not go to friends somewhere else?" Marion asked, his tone unreadable.

"I had none," she murmured. "There was no place to go. Not after Brendan died. His friends blamed me. My father's action destroyed my own reputation. There was simply no place. And—" her voice hardened "—I hated my father for what he did, not only to Bren but to all the O'Neills and our other neighbors. I wanted to do something about it. I knew Hector was helping you, and I helped him, giving him information. That's why everyone thought I would marry Foxworth...I was trying to get information from him and the other British officers Father entertained. But when Father insisted I marry him, I had to leave. I hated him."

She said it with such vehemence that Marion winced. He was understanding more and more, and his sympathy was growing.

"Does anyone know who you are, or where you are?"

"Just Hector...and Foxworth, but I don't think he told anyone. He wanted to use me for his own purposes. It was part of his revenge."

"I guessed as much," Marion said. "But what now? You can't keep it a secret forever."

Samantha's face was full of despair. "I know," she said, so softly Marion had to lean closer to hear her. "I never meant this to happen with Connor. I just wanted a place to go. But I found him in the cave, and then I fell in love with him. I tried not to. I tried to stay away, but I couldn't." Her eyes begged him to understand, and he felt an ache in his own heart.

"He loves you, too," Marion said. "That's very obvious. Don't you think you can tell him now?"

"I've tried to," she answered hopelessly. "But each time, something's come up to remind him of Robert Chatham and his hate surfaces. I keep hoping that time will weaken it."

"I think you underestimate him," Marion replied. "I think you do him an injustice by not telling him. If he knew everything..."

"No," she said, this time her tone firm. "I can stand anything but his hate. Maybe time..."

Marion sighed. This was one problem not easily solved. He sympathized with both Connor and Sam. His liking for Sam had grown steadily during their conversation. He had never met a woman so determined, so willing to sacrifice.

"You won't tell him...you'll let me do it when the time is right?" Her voice was pleading.

"I don't know," Marion said honestly. "Connor is my friend. He has a right to know before things go any further."

"A month," she said. "Give me a month. Please. Then I'll find a way."

He looked at her eyes and couldn't refuse. She and Connor were both loyal, intelligent, courageous. There was no doubting their love. They would make a good match. If only they could conquer this seemingly impossible barrier.

"All right," he said finally. "One month."

"Can I stay here?" she asked in a small voice.

He smiled. "I don't like breaking my own rules but in your case I think I might. It's pretty late to say you wouldn't fit in. But, mind you, you'll carry your own share. In camp. You've seen your last raid. Is that understood?"

Samantha nodded eagerly. She was to remain.

The next few weeks were the happiest Samantha had ever known, and the most heartbreaking.

Lee's legion had left, rejoining Greene, and Marion's camp reverted back to the easygoing pace of December. Spring was early, and the sun gently kissed the earth again, bringing forth a bright green vibrancy to the forest. The birds seemed to sing with more joy. Rebirth was evident everywhere.

There was also optimism about the war, the first in several years. Marion and his men had great faith in Nathaniel Greene, something they lacked in his predecessor, General Gates. The Battle of Cowpens and the inglorious defeat of Tarleton's dragoons delighted them. There was new spirit in Carolina's communities. Volunteers were flocking to join up with Marion, and civilians were growing increasingly bold.

Good news kept coming. Great Britain had declared war on the Dutch. England was already at war with the French; and the Spanish were now sending money to the young fledgling American nation. General Washington had survived the winter and was getting ready to move again.

She knew all this and was heartened by it, but her real joy came from her time with Connor.

He had remembered his pledge not to push Sam, and her narrow escape had made him realize even more how much he loved her. There was no other woman like her, no one with her courage or spunk or delight of life or humor or compassion. He loved them all and he was aware of her growing beauty.

Now, three weeks after her capture and rescue, Sam looked very little like the lad who had wanted to "ride wi' Marion" five months ago. Her hair was growing out and framed her enchanting elfin face. She smiled often. Only an occasional stubbornly determined scowl reminded Connor of the boy of months earlier.

In the past several weeks of care and attention, she had gained weight. Her dark blue eyes seemed to shine with hundreds of tiny bright lights, and her cheeks flushed becomingly with a mixture of sun and happiness. She was more alive than anyone he had ever met, and she made him feel alive. For the first time in his life, he laughed without cause and took deep pleasure in every minute. He had never understood Bren, had never experienced his brother's intoxication with life... until now.

As Sam's body healed, they took long walks together, their hands slightly touching, or sat and talked for hours. They had lost what little privacy they had had now that everyone knew Sam's sex. Both were determined not to abuse Marion's decision to allow her to stay. They knew the general's strong sense of morality although he never forced it on others. It had been one of the reasons he had never allowed women in camp.

How agonizing it was, Sam thought. Her body burned at Connor's touch. It never failed to ignite a deep burning inside that never quite went away. She looked at him now as he leaned lazily against a tree, one foot propped against it.

She loved his long, hard, lean body. There was a subtle, almost unconscious violence in it, placed there by years of war. But she had also tasted its quiet gentleness, and the combination of the two were irresistible. Her eyes moved up to his face, that handsome countenance, with eyes that warmed a room or froze it as suddenly as any winter storm. His hair ruffled in the breeze, and he impatiently brushed it aside, looking much like a small boy as he stole a look at her.

They were sitting near the river, and he had moved away when he felt the heat growing between them. In another moment, he would have taken her, to hell with everyone else. The tree was a poor substitute for Sam's body but a much safer one.

He wanted to marry her, to take her someplace safe until the war was over. But she had given no indication her answer had changed, and he feared pressing the issue. He had done that before and almost lost her. He would wait. He smiled at the thought of living with her. It would be a constant adventure. Sam would always be a surprise.

Samantha looked at his face and saw him smile. It was so wistful she wanted to cry. But all her tears were gone. She had one more week to tell him. That was all General Marion had given her, and she had to make a decision. To tell and risk all. Or not to tell and give up all. It was a damned poor choice.

And now there was something else to consider. Her body felt strange, as if something inside had forever changed. Her flow had stopped months ago, but at first it had not worried her, nor had she really noticed it. It had been irregular since Bren's death, when she had almost starved herself.

But now she knew she was much overdue, and she also realized she had not eaten enough to justify the swell in her stomach. The thought of a baby, of Connor's baby, both terrified and gladdened her. At the very least, she would have something of the O'Neills, a tiny version of Connor whom she could love without fear. If Connor rejected her, she didn't quite know what she would do. She did realize she could never go home again. But she was strong and well-educated and she would find a way. No one would take her baby, she thought fiercely.

Connor watched the emotions cross her face. Some he recognized; some he did not. The recurring sadness and secrecy he knew and hated. But then there was something else. A fierceness. He wished he knew what she was thinking. Suddenly, he reached out his hand, and almost unconsciously she took it.

She knew from his eyes what he wanted, understood that his defenses were gone. Hers had gone weeks earlier. Now they would be together again, in the truest sense of the word, she thought, every nerve in her body tingling.

They stumbled and tripped in their eagerness as he pulled her along the bank, finally half carrying her. He knew every sentry post, every blind spot, but he wanted to be far from camp, far from any restless wanderer or hunter. He finally found what he wanted, a nearly invisible pool hidden from sight by moss-covered oaks and thick brush. He cleared a place near the pool where the season's first water flowers were reaching for the sun.

Their joining was unlike any other. In the past month, both thought they had lost each other forever. The knowledge filled them both with a sense of wonder that they were, now, together, and their gentleness was beyond any either had known. Their hands were tender as they touched each other, entranced by the mere closeness of the other.

Connor's hand traced the still angry-looking scar on Sam's side, flinching at the pain he knew it had caused. Then his hand moved to her face and his touch was as light as a breeze, although she could feel his restrained need.

They finally joined, and the coupling was as gentle as the foreplay. It was dominated by their need for closeness. They both wanted to show the other a very special kind of love, and every touch became more sensual, more moving, more enchanting than either thought possible.

When he finally moved from her, they lay together, overwhelmed by the pure sweetness of their union. Neither wanted to break the spell.

Connor didn't know whether it was minutes or hours before they moved. He sat up and looked at her, his eyes drinking in every beloved feature . . . every curve of her body. They finally rested on her stomach, and his hand touched it, exploring its new roundness. His face held a question, but it went unanswered, and his mind dismissed it. It could not be or she would have said something. It was merely her health returning; he was just used to the slender, lanky form.

They dressed slowly, reluctantly, then sat again, both afraid to express their thoughts and spoil the contentment they momentarily shared.

Samantha's voice finally broke the silence. There was something she had to know, and she could wait no longer.

"After the war," she said haltingly, "can we ever go back to living together . . . the Tories and Whigs, I mean?"

"Francis thinks so," Connor answered.

"But do you? Can you forget everything that's happened?"

Connor looked at her, and his face became a hard mask. There was nothing left of the gentle man who had lain with her.

"With some, I suppose," he said. "With others, no. I won't rest until Chatham's paid for what he's done to my family. I made that vow to my father. He and his will not escape justice." There was iron in his voice, and she didn't doubt him . . . not for one second.

She had her answer. She realized now he would never give up his rage toward her father…and her, and she could not tell him what must be said if she stayed. There was only one option: she must leave, and she must do it quietly. She looked at Connor's now contented face, and her heart contracted. He would not understand when she left; he would be hurt and puzzled, but he would survive, and he would be better served than if he knew who she really was.

With great strength of will, she kept her thoughts from her face and her voice light, though her heart was breaking.

"We will be missed," she said, "and we might soon be surrounded by a bevy of mother hens." Both she and Connor had been amused at the mothering Sam was receiving from nearly every one of Marion's hardened militia.

"I don't ever want to leave," Connor said lazily as he slowly, deliberately straightened up from his sitting position. He took her hand, his larger one making patterns on it before lifting it to his mouth and allowing his lips to play with it. "I love you, Sam. I want to spend the rest of my life with you."

She met his look squarely. "I love you, too, Connor. More than you will ever know." Her hand touched his face for what she knew could be the last time.

Connor heard only what he wanted to hear, that she loved him. He missed the nuance of sadness in her voice. His eyes caressed her, and his mouth melted into a pleased happy smile. She was his.

Samantha knew she could do nothing until there was a raid and the camp emptied. Both Marion and Connor were watching her. But the hours and days were speeding by, and the need to escape was growing more critical. One more day and the time Marion had given her would be up. Her determination now outweighed her anguish, and her mind worked at feverish pitch on the problem of how to accomplish her objective.

She had no money, yet she had to flee the area. Between her father's acquaintances and Marion's brigade, she was far too well known to live quietly and anonymously in this part of the Carolinas. The only solution was to travel north, perhaps as far as Boston, where she could lose herself. There she could claim widow status and take work as a governess or teacher. But first she had to have traveling money and there was, she knew, only one possible way of getting it. She would have to sell Sundance.

Just the thought was painful, but her heart was already shattered in so many pieces she knew she could withstand almost anything. The important thing was to make sure that Sundance would never be used by the British as a war-horse. Through the process of elimination, she finally came once more to Annabelle. Annabelle, who had saved her several other times. Sam would never accept money from her but she could sell her the horse without telling her exactly why.

Samantha formulated her plans and needed only an opportunity to carry them out. In the meantime, she curried and fed the horses, finding ways to avoid Connor, who was kept equally busy by General Marion. In her few spare hours, she would ride Sundance through the forest, allowing the sentries to become accustomed to her comings and goings. Every ride was painful, knowing as she did it was one of the few remaining. Her mother, Bren, Connor. Everything she loved she lost. But now there would be the baby, a little person all her own whom she could love. A tiny version of Connor without the legacy of hate.

She never quite decided whether the gods were with her or against her, when Marion announced an expedition that night.

Greene had met Cornwallis in North Carolina at a place called Guilford Court House and there had been a major engagement. Although technically a British victory, it was a tactical defeat. Cornwallis had lost a fourth of his army while Greene's army, Cornwallis's main objective, escaped with little damage.

The main British army had then headed for Virginia, while Greene, instead of pursuing them, decided to head south. It was time to free the Carolinas. The news was met with elation by Marion's brigade, which had long felt deserted by the southern Continental Army. Lighthouse Henry Lee was to be reattached to them, and Marion, along with the militia troops of Pickens and Sumter to the south and west, were to intensify their disruption of British communications and supplies.

The British hold on South Carolina was based on a chain of strong points, stamped on the land like an inverted T. If the traffic along this T could be broken, the British would be forced to withdraw back to Charleston. Greene knew he lacked the strength to crush any major post by himself but he was counting on nullifying the British military might by having Marion, Pickens and Sumter deliver swift hit-and-run blows at various strong points, thus choking off reinforcements destined for the larger targets at which he himself wished to strike.

Marion knew it to be sound strategy and he planned to begin his part of it immediately. Tonight they would raid a major enemy supply depot near Monck's Corners. He planned to take nearly every man in camp.

Samantha was unusually quiet as Connor said goodbye. He attributed it to the fact that she probably wanted to go, but General Marion had absolutely barred her from any additional activities outside camp. He had been delighted that Marion had laid down the law.

He leaned over and kissed her, oblivious to the amused and envious stares around him. "I'll be back by noon tomorrow," he said. "Then I think we ought to talk." He had been trying to do so for the past two days, but she had always managed to slip away. Now he received no answer, just an intense look from her brilliant blue eyes. There was no smile on her face, and he felt a sudden cold premonition of disaster. His hand lingered on her face as his eyes searched hers, but he could find nothing. It must be his imagination....

"Major O'Neill!"

Marion's voice was unmistakable, and Connor reluctantly turned from her, still feeling that all was not right. "Tomorrow," he said, and was gone, never hearing the whispered words trailing him.

"I love you, Connor."

Only a handful of Marion's brigade remained in camp. Billy had gone with Marion, a fact for which Samantha was grateful; he, too, had continued to feel a responsibility for her and often hovered nearby.

She fussed with the horses for a while, then ate a dinner of stew. A full moon rode the sky, and she saw it as a good omen. It would guide her through the swamp. She knew it well by now and had no fear. Getting by the sentries was the only problem, but they were used to her rides and also knew her competence.

She saddled Sundance slowly, taking one last look at the camp where she had known joy and pain and comradery. Where she had known the feeling, for the first time in many years, of belonging. She mounted Sundance and, for the last time, bid a silent farewell to Snow Island.

Chapter Twenty-Three

By now Samantha could practically ride the road between Snow Island and Georgetown with her eyes closed. This was her third trip in four months, and the hardest of them all. This was the final parting with those things she had come to love and value, and she questioned the steps she was about to take. She dreaded going back into Georgetown, remembering as she did her too-recent encounter with Foxworth. But he was dead now, and so were most of those with him, and the others had been sent to a prison camp.

She didn't really like the idea of approaching Annabelle again and straining their newly forged friendship. But she had to have money, and she had to be sure Sundance would be safe. There was no way she could ride Sundance north, not without money and without papers. No one would believe a boy could own such a fine animal, nor would a woman be safe alone on horseback. She would not take a chance with her child.

She also knew Connor would come looking for her and probably stop first at Annabelle's. It meant she had to be on a coach well before he could reach the town. And she had to continue to hide her pregnancy, which she knew would not be easy. Her stomach was already straining against the boy's britches, and only a heavy loose-fitting coat swallowed the female curves.

As she neared Georgetown, she stopped and reassessed everything. Her hair was now too long, but she scooped it up and pinned it underneath a floppy hat. The coat made her completely sexless. In one of its pockets was a note she had written earlier. Signed by Robert Chatham, it told the British authorities that the boy was to deliver the horse to a new owner. It was a calculated gamble, but Samantha knew her father was held in high esteem by the British; she doubted they would question such a paper.

Finally satisfied all was in order, she joined the heavy traffic on the road into Georgetown. She and her paper received only cursory examination, and she was impatiently shrugged on her way. Now came the hardest part, convincing Annabelle to help her. Strange how she had come to rely on someone she would have shunned just months before. Her life was so topsy-turvy she wondered if it would ever be normal again. She had become an accomplished liar; in fact she sometimes wondered if it had not become an integral part of her. Every time she opened her mouth, another lie popped out, one breeding another in an endless succession of falsehoods. It was not a quality she admired.

Annabelle's house was, from the exterior, as serene as always. Samantha rode Sundance to the stables in the back and asked the stable hand to keep her there. Recognizing her as one of Annabelle's frequent surreptitious visitors, he quickly agreed, and she slipped in Annabelle's back door.

The large house was almost beginning to feel like home, and at that disquieting notion, she allowed the first smile of the day to touch her mouth.

Then Annabelle, alerted by a maid, was there, astonishment in her face. Her eyes swept the kitchen. "Samantha?" she finally said, a question in her tone. "Are you alone?"

She nodded, her face bleak.

"What is it? Has something happened to Connor?"

"No," she said in a low voice. "And I won't stay long. I have a horse I thought you might like to buy."

"A horse?" Annabelle now was completely confused. She had heard through one of Marion's spies of Sam's capture and rescue and thought Georgetown was the last place the girl should be.

Samantha ignored the censure in Annabelle's voice. "Sundance," she said. "She's the finest mare you'll ever find."

The crack in her voice broke Annabelle's reserve. "Why?"

"I can't tell you why," she said, her voice strong again. "I just need the money, and Sundance is well worth the price. Will you look at her?"

"Whatever you need..."

"No," she said, and Annabelle knew instantly she would not change her mind. "If you don't want her, I will find someone who does. I came here first because I know she will be well treated, but I am going to sell her...." Her voice was hard and implacable.

"All right," Annabelle said. "I'll look at her. Stay here and eat something. And for Lord's sake, take off that damned coat."

One look at Sundance, and Annabelle wanted her. She had never seen such a fine mare, nor one, she admitted, that had been so well cared for. Her coat fairly sparkled with grooming and her eyes were bright and intelligent. Even after what must have been a long ride, the mare showed no sign of exhaustion. The stable boy stood there and watched the close examination. "That's one fine horse, Miss Annabelle," he said.

Annabelle nodded and returned to the kitchen, looking in disgust at Samantha, who still had not shed the stifling shapeless jacket. "Come to my study," she ordered, leading the way then waiting for her to sit. "Will you tell me what this is all about?"

"I'm tired of living in the woods," Samantha said. "I'm tired of dressing this way and spending my time with soldiers. I have some friends in New York, and I'm going to visit them."

"What about Connor?"

Samantha looked down. "He can never forget what happened to Brendan. It's better for both of us now that it's over."

"He knows about this then...that you're leaving."

"Of course," she lied.

Annabelle didn't believe it, not for a second, although the girl's face was innocence itself. Something had indeed happened, and she wished she knew what it was.

She opened her safe and counted out a large number of coins and gave them to Samantha. "Will that be sufficient?"

Sam's eyes widened at the sum. She started to protest at its magnificence but quickly reconsidered. She nodded.

"You will have breakfast with me?"

She started to decline, but her hunger changed her mind. She knew the Boston coach didn't leave until late in the day and she didn't particularly want to loiter in the crowded streets. She nodded.

"I'll be back in a minute," Annabelle said, and returned to the stable. "Zack," she said, "get that young friend of yours...John, is it...tell him I have a job for him. I want him to follow the boy who brought the horse and tell me where he goes. If he buys a ticket for anyplace, I want to know where. As quickly as possible. Do you understand?"

The boy nodded.

"I can keep him here about an hour...no longer. Can you get him that fast?"

"Yes, ma'am."

Annabelle turned and went back inside. She had never fully appreciated how peaceful things were until she'd met Sam. She was still stubbornly wearing that damned coat and Annabelle decided it wasn't worth fighting over. If Samantha wanted to perish from heat exhaustion, let her. Annabelle ordered a meal and sat down.

"Are you going to New York like that?" she finally asked with gentle humor.

Samantha colored. She knew only too well how she looked. Awful. "I thought," she said stiffly, "I would buy a dress in Georgetown and change someplace after we leave. I'll say it's for my sister."

Annabelle shook her head. There was no end to Sam's ingenuity. "Connor still doesn't know who you are, does he?"

"No," she answered honestly. "But I asked him several days ago about after the war...whether he could forget...and he said no...never where the Chathams are concerned. And he won't. It's better if I leave now."

Annabelle was silent. She wasn't quite sure that she didn't agree with her. As well as she knew Connor, she had always recognized his one raging blind spot. Robert Chatham.

She shook her head. There was no ready solution. At least she would know where Samantha was going, and that was the best she could do other than tying the girl down and keeping her prisoner.

Annabelle kept her talking as long as she could, then reluctantly let her go, quietly satisfied when she saw a shadow slip from the stable and follow the unsuspecting girl down the back street. If she had watched a moment longer, she would have seen two additional figures join what was fast becoming a procession.

Samantha's first destination was the coach office, where she purchased a ticket to Boston. The coach, she was informed, was due to leave at five, but she was also warned that the time meant little. It was often late, what with frequent inspections and searches by both sides. Her second stop was the dress shop.

Her arrival created little enthusiasm. One look at the smudged raggedy lad and the proprietors were ready to send him flying out the door. But Samantha pulled out her purse, and their disdain quickly turned to a rather snide form of obsequiousness; there was not a lot of commerce in Georgetown at the moment. She finally found a plain cotton frock that would probably fit . . . more or less . . . and purchased it. It was growing late, and she was hungry again. She purchased some cakes from a tea shop and returned to the coach station to wait.

Two of Samantha's three shadows had been close enough behind her to hear her destination. One had sped off to Annabelle's. The other conferred with his fellow, then took the road out of Georgetown. The third continued to follow his quarry.

Connor O'Neill was angry. It showed in the tight fist that uncharacteristically clutched his reins, in the thin line of his mouth and in the frosty gaze of his uncovered eye. He was, in fact, furious.

He had arrived back at Snow Island earlier than expected, spurred by the need to see Sam and get things settled between them, and had been greeted with news of her defection. She had ridden past the sentries. Since they had no orders to stop her but feared for her safety, the sergeant had sent a man out after her. He had not yet returned. She was headed toward Georgetown.

Connor had quickly donned his farmer's clothes, rubbed his hair with a smelly substance that turned it white and found his eye patch. His lower face was already covered with stubble. He changed horses and, staying only long enough to leave a curt note for Marion, wearily mounted once more. Damn her. Damn this whole puzzle. She was like quicksilver. Here one moment, gone the next. The more he tried to hold her, the greater her need seemed to be for flight. He searched for a reason and, as always, one eluded him. But one idea kept haunting him; that brief moment days ago when he suspected a babe. Her body had changed radically in the past few months, and he wondered again if food could be the only cause.

He spurred his horse to a faster pace.

He was several miles from Georgetown, carefully skirting the road, when a horse suddenly darted out at him. The movement was so abrupt his horse reared and it took a moment to calm him. Even so, his one eye quickly identified one of Marion's sentries, the one who had followed Sam. As his hand soothed his horse, Connor's questions were sharp.

"You followed her?"

"Yep...she went by Miss Annabelle's, then to the coach office. She bought a ticket to Boston."

"You left her there!" There was an angry accusation in Connor's voice.

The man sighed. He had done quite the best he could. "Major," he said slowly, "my brother lives in Georgetown and he's with her. I met him in Georgetown and he promised to keep an eye on her while I came back for you or the general."

Connor knew he should apologize, but he couldn't force himself to. "What time is she leaving?"

"They say five...but it's always late. He'll stay till the coach leaves..." His words trailed off as Connor turned his horse and galloped toward Georgetown.

Samantha paced impatiently. Every minute was dangerous. Redcoats strolled past the station, frequently eyeing the waiting passengers. One had asked for papers, but her apparent youth had saved her. She ducked her head and told her questioner that she had delivered a horse to Miss Annabelle's and was traveling home. The name of Annabelle abruptly ended the questions. The sergeant didn't want to know who or why.

She asked once more about departure and received only a careless shrug in response. She dropped in a chair, the packaged dress beside her, her chin drooping disconsolately on the collar of her increasingly uncomfortable coat.

Which was the way Connor found her.

Her eyes were closed but she felt his presence. They opened slowly, following his long legs upward to his extremely angry face and regarding him much as one would a coiled snake.

She had no time to think. His hand fairly flew for her right wrist, and she found herself pulled quite roughly to her feet. She could do nothing but scamper after him, her wrist imprisoned by his tight fist. His fast pace slowed suddenly as they both heard a quick shout.

"Hold there!"

Samantha felt the shudders echo through her as Connor stopped suddenly. She heard his voice, but it was unlike the one she knew so well. It was high and whining and oh so obsequious. "Sir," he whined, "many pardons, sir..."

The coolly accented voice interrupted him. "What are you doing with this boy?"

"A runaway bond servant, sir...just barely caught him, I did. And I paid good coin for him."

She darted a look up. A British officer stood there, his eyes flashing with contempt. "Is that right, boy?" he said.

Samantha ducked her head and nodded slowly.

"Get on with you, then," the officer said, and she felt her body jerked forward again. She had to run to keep up with Connor's long strides, and he made no effort to modify them. He wanted both of them off the street as quickly as possible.

They finally arrived at a row house. Sam had no idea where she was but meekly followed Connor up the stairs and waited wordlessly as he rang the bell. When a black servant answered, Connor gave him a note and both she and Connor were ushered in. Only then did Connor release her wrist. She glanced around warily. Her brief interlude ended quickly. Connor said a few words to the man and took her shoulders, leading her into a parlor, where he forced her into a chair.

When she refused to look at him, he took her chin in his hand and forced her to. He was furious and he took no pains to hide it.

"Boston," he said finally. "Why Boston?"

"How did you . . . ?" She stopped.

"Did you really think Fran would let you go, knowing everything you know, without finding out why and where?"

Her mouth clenched tight. That was the one thing she hadn't considered.

"I wouldn't betray him," she said quietly.

"But you would me?" His voice was bitter.

"No," she cried. "Never you."

"Just what, then, did you think you were doing? Disappearing without a word, without a note?" His voice was cold and his left eye colder. The eye patch still covered the right one and gave him a menacing look.

Samantha merely folded her hands and looked down, infuriating him even more.

"Take off that damned coat," he said quietly, but there was a threat in his voice.

She obediently did what was asked, knowing she had no choice. He pulled off the patch and his eyes examined every inch of her, finally settling on the thickening waist.

"Are you with child?" The voice had lowered, gentled.

She looked at him and he needed no additional answer. Her eyes were full of despair, and he was suddenly drained of his anger. He took her hands and wondered at the icy feel of them despite the day's warmth.

"Why couldn't you tell me? Don't you know how pleased I am, how much I want to marry you?"

She couldn't stand the gleam in his eye, the slow pleased smile. "The time is wrong," she cried out. "It's all wrong."

He put a finger to her lip to silence her. "No," he said, "it's not wrong at all, and we will get married in the morning. He—" Connor grinned "—or she must have a name, you know."

Samantha looked at Connor, tired of fighting, tired of fleeing. She answered in a voice that was almost toneless, "If that's what you want."

Elated at her answer, Connor again missed the note of sad surrender in her voice. He leaned down and, taking the floppy hat from her head, kissed her tenderly, running his fingers through her hair to free it. At last, he thought, she will be mine. A sense of euphoria bubbled within him and he laughed from pure joy. Suddenly life looked very grand. "We'll have a fine supper tonight," he said suddenly, "and—" he laughed again "—we both need baths."

Then he was gone, and she could hear him shouting orders in a loud happy voice. She shivered, knowing she was caught in her own trap. He would not let her go, not unless she told him she was Samantha Chatham. And she wasn't, she admitted, yet capable of doing that. A few more memories, she bargained with herself. Just a few more days. The marriage would not be legal if she didn't use her rightful name. That way he would be free and not tied to a Chatham for life. But they would be happy tonight, tomorrow and perhaps a bit longer. The thought of lying in Connor's arms was suddenly irresistible. She would take what she could today.

When Connor returned, her mood almost matched his. He snatched her up and whirled her around, then carried her upstairs, where a bath was already being readied. He set her down on a huge bed, and she took a quick peek at the room. It was masculine looking, darkly paneled and starkly decorated. Yet she liked its unpretentious comfort.

"It belongs to a friend of mine," Connor said. "Denney Demerest . . . he told me to use it whenever I'm in Georgetown. He keeps servants here for protection."

"But the British . . ."

"The house is in a cousin's name . . . an inoffensive cousin," he said. "Denney has many, many cousins," Connor added, a twinkle in his eye, "including one named Caroline, with whom he is very much in love."

"Your Caroline?" Samantha asked teasingly.

"It was," Connor said with a laugh, "the world's shortest courtship . . . mostly wishful thinking on the part of her parents. They don't want her to marry Denney."

"But why . . . if they love each other?"

"They are cousins, my love, and while I do not believe that a problem, their families do. They have had cousins marry before . . . with unfortunate results."

Samantha didn't understand. She had known many cousins who had married. In the limited society of the Carolinas it was a frequent occurrence. Her chin lifted stubbornly. "I think if they're in love, they should marry."

Connor cocked an eyebrow and regarded her with bemusement. "I was beginning to think you had something against marriage . . . I have certainly been trying long enough." It was a half question, but she ignored it and he decided not to press her. Things were fragile enough already.

Samantha was grateful when they were interrupted by the two servants, a black man and his wife, both carrying huge pails of steaming water. She watched with delight as they filled the copper tub.

"Dinner will be ready in an hour, sir." The man smiled. "Sure is nice to have someone here again. Gets mighty lonesome without Mr. Denney."

Connor quickly introduced them to Sam and watched her warm acknowledgement with growing pleasure. He loved her open heart, which seemed to embrace everyone, regardless of station or position. He had been more than a little startled at her immediate friendship with Annabelle, which had taken place behind his back. Such a friendship was almost beyond ken, but then Sam was unlike any woman he had ever met before. Overwhelmed, suddenly, by his emotions, he touched her with wonder, letting his fingers caress her face, barely aware that the servants had departed.

"A bath," she reminded him gently, and his hands went down to her shirt. Slowly, sensually, he undressed her, his eyes devouring her, his hands lingering as they gently pulled and tugged the clothes from her body, then gaining momentum as her lovely body emerged from its ugly cocoon. His hands touched and moved and loved until she was on fire, and the bath was forgotten. It was her turn now, and she reached for his clothes with hands frantic with need. Buttons tore and cloth ripped, and then he was gloriously free, and they fell on the bed, laughing, groaning, whispering, giving until they were both swept away into currents too deep to fathom. Nothing mattered but their intense need for each other and the wild ecstasy of their joining....

Later they played like children in the lukewarm bath. Connor got in first, then Sam sat on top of him as he washed her back. His arms wound around her, and he washed her breasts before his hands moved down to her stomach. He explored it possessively, searching for some sign of the young life inside. When she sighed with contentment, he chuckled and nibbled her neck until her head darted around and she nipped his lip in reprisal, setting off a laughing howl of protest. She splashed him with the soapy water and he retaliated, and before long there was more water outside the tub than in, and the two of them were doubled over with laughter.

A hesitant knock brought them back to reality, and Samantha grinned at him. "I haven't even had time to wash you yet," she said with an evil glint in her eye.

A look of absolute horror came over his face as he remembered the last time she had undertaken such an activity. He fairly leaped from the tub.

The tentative knock came again, and this time Connor answered. "Yes?"

"Dinner, sir," Cecil said.

"We'll be down in several minutes," Connor replied, winking at her. "Miss Taylor is quite slow in grooming. Of course there was a lot to do...." He ducked as a bar of soap came flying at him.

The nonsense stopped and they quickly dressed, both feeling inordinately hungry after such a long day. Samantha had had breakfast and some cakes at noon; Connor had had nothing since the night before, and he was famished. She put her dress on almost shyly, knowing it was the first time he had seen her clothed in any but the roughest garments. He watched, fascinated, as the rather plain blue cotton dress hugged her full breasts and still small waist and flared gracefully over her hips. The blue seemed to darken her eyes to the dark velvet shade of a summer sky at dusk. She brushed her hair, still brown in color from dye but now curling attractively around her face, until it shone. She needed no words from Connor when she turned to face him; it was all in his eyes.

He borrowed some of Denney's clothes but did nothing to the stubble on his face or his hair. He would need them again tomorrow. He had too much at stake to risk carelessness.

Samantha thought the dinner wonderful. The servants had managed to find a fresh chicken and there were plates of dumplings and biscuits and hot gravy and, finally, a newly baked apple pie. They ate every scrap, enjoying both the food and the fact it was the first time they had sat together, alone, to a civilized meal at a table. After they had sated their hunger, they feasted on each other's faces as candlelight flickered and danced, and their hands played with the crystal glasses filled with wine. Finally, without words, Connor rose and went to her chair and took her hand. Together they walked up the stairs to the bedroom and, this time, took their time undressing each other, enjoying the simple intimacy of the act. Samantha snuggled her body into his hard curves, and with his arms wrapped possessively around her, they both went to sleep.

When they woke the next morning, they made love again...slowly, almost lazily. Then Connor sat up and with a tone that allowed no discussion told Sam they would be married that day.

"But the banns..." she protested. When she had agreed yesterday she thought it impossible so quickly.

He kissed her into silence. "I know someone," he said. "He's been very helpful to us and I've given him money for families who need assistance. He'll understand and waive them."

"But..."

"No," he said. "No buts. And then you can stay here, in this house. I'll contact Denney." He quieted her protest with his fingers. "You're safer here with the baby. There are doctors here...and Mary and Cecil. And Annabelle if you need her. I'll leave you enough money for everything, and if you have any more needs, you can contact Annabelle."

"I want..."

Connor smiled. "I know what you want. But Snow Island and long rides and an occasional doctor are not what I want for you." His smile disappeared. "If you don't think of yourself, think of the baby," he said. "I know it will be hard . . . being cooped up here, but I'll come as often as I can."

"I want to be with you!"

"You are the most contradictory person I've ever met," he exclaimed with a crooked smile. "Yesterday you were running away from me."

"That was yesterday," she said smugly, as if that answered all his questions.

But he would have none of it. "I want your promise, Sam. I want your promise that you will stay here and that you won't take any chances. That you'll let Cecil do the shopping, and if you need company, send for Annabelle. Your promise, Sam."

"It will be like jail," she protested.

"I don't think it will be long. We will take Georgetown shortly. In the meantime, I want you safe."

Samantha was silent, neither agreeing nor disagreeing, and Connor finally took her lack of protest as consent. He could tell he wasn't going to get much more. Why was she so damned frustrating?

Connor asked her to put on her dress . . . he would be back shortly with a minister.

"What about you?" she said. "I'm not entirely sure I want to marry an old one-eyed, stiff-legged unshaved tyrant."

"This is a hell of a poor time to point out my deficiencies," he said, laughing. "I wish I could do better for you, but it's either this or quite possibly a hangman's rope."

Samantha was suddenly silent, realizing all the risks he had taken for her. She touched the rough bristles on his cheek. "At least when the minister asks whether I'll take you for better or for worse, I'll know exactly what the 'worse' is," she said finally, not able to resist teasing him.

"Ah, Sam," he said. "You're a constant delight . . . a comfort. You know how to make a man feel admired." He kissed her, letting the stiff whiskers scrape along her cheek. "I'll be back soon," he warned. "Be ready." Her giggles warmed him as he carefully went out the door, dragging a leg behind him.

True to his word and contrary to her expectations, Connor was back quickly with a Reverend Thomas Smith and his wife, Molly, who would be a witness.

Samantha liked them both immediately. Rev. Smith was of medium height with mild but compassionate blue eyes. His hair was thinning, and he wore glasses, which gave him an owl-like appearance, but his face was gentle, and he wore a broad smile. He obviously liked weddings. His wife looked much like him, a plump merry-looking person with twinkling eyes and a mothering manner that made Samantha instantly at ease. Molly clucked around her and took charge immediately, sending a disapproving look at Connor's appearance. Her husband had explained that he was a militia officer whose life was in danger, but still ...

The ceremony was short and Samantha remembered little of it. She did not want to remember it. It was certainly not the ceremony she had once dreamed of...and the knowledge of the charade with unsuspecting Connor did little to improve her spirit. While Connor's voice was strong and sure, she could merely mumble her vows, wishing desperately it would all go away. Her happiness of the morning was gone, lost in the conviction that she was doing something utterly despicable to the one person in the world she loved. When it came time to sign the register, she reluctantly scrawled Samara Taylor, recognizing that with that one act she had completed the sham. Her lips were ice cold when Connor leaned down and kissed her lightly. She ignored the questioning look in his eyes.

They shared a glass of congratulatory wine with the Smiths, who then, quite diplomatically, took their departure, leaving a spate of good wishes in their wake.

Samantha and Connor ate a silent luncheon. He had told her he had to leave that afternoon. Henry Lee was due to arrive at Snow Island immediately and Marion was planning a major campaign. "He's been amazingly tolerant of me already," Connor said. "I can't stretch it any further."

She nodded, wanting him to stay yet needing to be alone. Her guilt was overwhelming, and every time she looked at him, it struck anew. Every moment with him was agony; every moment away from him was worse.

Connor couldn't help but notice her change of mood, but he attributed it to his departure. After lunch he took her once more in his arms. "It won't be long, Sam. I promise."

She kissed him with a desperate intensity that completely shook him. It seemed more than goodbye and he wished once again that he knew more about her. Whatever was haunting her he knew with certainty was still there. And its elusive shadows had started to haunt him, too.

But he could tarry no longer, and he gently pulled her back, studying her face. He kissed her quickly once more and was gone.

Chapter Twenty-Four

As Connor rode into Snow Island, Lee's bright green uniforms were everywhere, contrasting starkly with the leather and homespun of Marion's troop. Connor was quickly directed to the main plantation building, and he quietly entered what apparently was an officers' meeting. Both Marion's and Lee's top aides were gathered around a table where a map was displayed.

Marion looked up. "It's kind of you to join us, Major O'Neill," he said wryly. "I would appreciate it if you stay after the meeting." His eyes returned to the map, but Connor knew he was in trouble.

Connor barely heard the rest of the discussion. They were to attack Fort Watson and then Fort Motte, a major relay station for the British. It was part of Greene's plan to split the British T and their hold on South Carolina.

As the other officers departed, Connor lingered until only he and Marion remained. Marion showed his displeasure by making Connor wait while he carefully and very deliberately rolled up the map. He finally looked up.

"Are you planning to stay with us this time?" he asked, an unusual edge in his quiet voice.

Connor stood there awkwardly, realizing he was in the wrong. He had ridden off to Georgetown without seeking permission or even notifying Fran. Connor knew only too well that the general couldn't be effective if his officers disappeared at will.

"I'm sorry," he said finally. "It won't happen again."

Marion's expression relaxed. That promise was exactly what he had wanted, and he knew Connor would keep it. He needed Connor's easy leadership now more than ever. O'Neill had an instinct for danger, and more important, of all his senior officers, O'Neill had the strongest rapport with Marion's independent warriors. He was, ironically, a born peacemaker and could solve bitter disputes with several soft words.

"I take it you found Sam," Marion said finally.

Connor smiled for the first time. "We were married this morning," he said. "She's staying in Georgetown at the Demerest house."

Marion's expression changed from surprise to dismay as he realized, from Connor's voice, that his friend still did not know Sam's true identity. A streak of disappointment ran through him. He had expected more from the girl.

"No congratulations?" Connor's voice was puzzled. He knew that Fran liked and respected Sam.

"This is not exactly the best of times," Fran replied. "Did she tell you why she left?"

Connor's smile wavered. "No," he said. "Not exactly." He was not ready to tell Fran about the child.

Fran was silent for a moment, then held out his hand and Connor took it firmly. "I wish you both luck and happiness," Fran said finally. Connor completely missed the fact that Marion had avoided offering his congratulations.

"Snow Island has been taken," Annabelle told Samantha.

They were sitting in the tiny parlor of the Demerest house. The flamboyant madam was now chastely dressed in dark brown with a great covering cloak and a hat that hid her very distinguishing hair.

The girl's eyes sparkled with alarm, but Annabelle quickly reassured her. "No one was there, just some sentries and they escaped. But Marion lost all his supplies. I think he considers it an insult more than anything else. They were off raiding a British depot. Tit for tat, I would say."

"Where did they...?"

"Someplace in those terrible swamps of his, I imagine," Annabelle said. "I understand he has tens of places, but you would know more about that than I."

Just the thought depressed her. She wished she were back there. She was lonely and she missed Connor with every fiber of her being. She hated the idea of him being shot at and in danger while she stayed here, safe, restless and bored. Except for the servants and Annabelle's visits, she was alone with only a small, and not very interesting, library for entertainment. But her pregnancy was more obvious now and she feared venturing into the streets. The town was crawling with Tories and many had known the Chathams well.

She sighed. It had been six weeks since Connor had left. It seemed like six years. The heat didn't help. It was only mid-May, but Georgetown was already suffering from unusually high temperatures and the normal stifling humidity. She felt hot and sticky and fat.

Annabelle regarded her with tolerant eyes. She had been angry when first told of their marriage. Connor had stopped by and asked Annabelle to keep an eye on his new wife. He had been exultant and Annabelle hadn't the heart to question him. She merely agreed and wished him safe journey. But she had immediately visited Samantha, and she found not a happy bride but a sobbing one.

After substantial prying, Samantha had told her about the baby and the fake marriage.

"Just how long do you think you can go on with this?" she prodded.

"I don't know," Samantha said desperately. "But I love him so much...and every time I try to tell him the truth, something happens, and I'm terrified of losing him."

"Every day makes it worse," Annabelle said. "You are making it harder and harder for him to understand."

"I know," she said miserably.

"And this marriage..." Annabelle's eyes went skyward.

"It's not a real marriage...."

"Do you really think that's going to make him feel better?" Annabelle asked, shaking her head at Samantha's reasoning.

"What other news?" her young friend prodded. "Anything about Connor?"

Annabelle smiled and reached into a pocket, pulling out a paper sealed with wax. "I thought you would like to read it alone," she said, "and I wanted a few minutes of your undivided attention."

Samantha didn't even notice Annabelle's quick steps to her waiting buggy but clutched the letter and flew up the stairs to the bedroom, where she felt Connor's presence so strongly. She stood for a moment, holding the letter, knowing that Connor's hands had touched it not many hours ago.

It was in a fine, bold, confident hand.

My love...
When you read this you will probably already know that the British found our camp on Snow Island. Our only losses were supplies and I am grateful for that. We are moving rapidly, anyway, and it seems our fortunes are, at last, changing for the better.

We took Fort Watson, although it was a bitter prolonged siege. The victory was due to a very clever friend who designed a tower from which our best marksmen could shoot directly into the fort. The commanding officer, a British lieutenant, surrendered almost immediately when he lost his protective walls. It was a major loss for the British and helped our spirits tremendously.

I believe I will see you soon...F is impatient and we are traveling your way.

Take care...both you and the babe. I love you and think of you both constantly.

C.

Sam read it until it was wrinkled and she had memorized each word. She then lighted a match and put the paper to the flame, watching it brown and curl and disappear into ashes.

Samara...Samara...Samara. Connor tasted the sound on his lips, but as often as he tried the name, it never completely rang true. It was Sam he loved. Just plain Sam. But Sam was anything but plain. Puzzling. Exasperating. Enchanting. She was all that ... and more.

A bullet whizzed by and landed with a solid thump inches from where he was lying. He moved back quickly, out of range of the increasingly accurate British marksmen. They had improved considerably in the three days since Marion and Lee laid siege to Fort Motte.

Damn, he had to stop thinking about Sam. She was ruining his concentration.

His practiced eye swept over the scene in front of him. Marion, on impulse, had generously handed his command over to Colonel Lee, who had decided to take the fort by storm. They had been digging trenches for days now, creeping closer to the heavily fortified British stronghold, and every day more men fell to British bullets.

Fort Motte had been erected around the spacious mansion of Mrs. Rebecca Motte. British engineers had added fosse, earthwork and strong palisades, and the fort/home had proved unexpectedly resistant. The British commander, Lieutenant Donald McPherson, had only one hundred and forty British regulars and Hessians to Marion and Lee's four hundred. But numbers meant little when the British had protection and the Americans had none.

It had proved to be increasingly frustrating to Connor. He knew Marion was chafing to attack Georgetown; his commander had a sister there and had spent much of his childhood in the town. Marion desperately wanted to be its liberator. For other reasons, Connor was just as eager. Only Fort Motte stood in the way.

Another bullet spit earth nearby. "Damn," he exploded again and moved even farther. They would never take the fort at this pace, and the stubborn McPherson was taking his toll of Americans. In sudden anger, he rose and made his way to Marion's side.

Marion's face was glum. His scouts had discovered a large British force just two days away. He knew now why McPherson had been holding so tenaciously; he expected reinforcements.

Marion and Lee conferred while Connor listened. If they didn't take the fort immediately, they would have to retreat. Both commanders remembered Georgetown and the fire arrows that led to surrender. But this was a private home, and Mrs. Motte, the owner, was a loyal patriot. She had suffered the indignity of being removed from her home to a rough log cabin, where she now lived. Neither Marion nor Lee wanted to destroy her home.

Finally Mrs. Motte was consulted, and all three officers stood in admiring amazement as the widow calmly berated them for not doing it earlier.

"If it were a palace," she said with determination, "it should go."

With misgivings, Marion ordered the fire arrows readied, but first he warned McPherson and gave him another chance to surrender. McPherson declined and within minutes the housetop was blazing. British soldiers who tried to reach the fire were picked off by Marion's sharpshooters, one by one. Within minutes, McPherson surrendered, and both American and British were fighting the fire, a common cause at last.

Connor was one of the first to reach the roof, and he, together with a British private, reached for buckets and splashed their contents onto the flame. They worked easily in tandem, ignoring the heat, intent on preventing further destruction. Gradually the flames were beaten down and crushed under hundreds of hands and feet as endless buckets of water traveled the line of mixed uniforms.

When it was over, the house still stood, its proud perfection marred by bullet holes and a gaping hole in the roof. But it stood, and soon men of both armies were repairing the hole while Mrs. Motte looked on with tears in her eyes.

As Marion and Lee saw to the separation and disarming of prisoners, Mrs. Motte approached them. "With your permission," she said, "I would like to invite all the officers to dinner."

General Marion smiled. "We would like that, ma'am," he said. "We've been on salt beef for weeks."

"All of the officers, General Marion," she replied. "The British, too."

Marion turned to Lee with a twinkle in his eye. "What do you think, colonel?"

"I think Mrs. Motte is the most gracious lady I have ever had the pleasure to meet," Lee replied grandly. "You may invite them, madam."

Marion's brigade and Lee's legion left Fort Motte the next day after taking, or destroying, the extensive British supplies. They would move toward Georgetown after attacking several minor British depots. Marion had already written Greene, asking his permission to take the city. He was only awaiting final approval.

Francis Marion entered Georgetown on the twenty-seventh of May and it fell easily before him. Lord Rawdon had moved on, leaving only a small garrison. At the approach of Marion, the remaining British slipped on board ships and Marion took possession of the town two days later.

As Marion rode in, huge crowds gathered in celebration, Samantha among them. Bells were ringing throughout the town, and militia and townspeople exchanged shouts and greetings. Marion rode directly to the home of his sister, Henriette.

Connor, sitting tall and straight on a bay stallion, scanned the noisy crowd. He knew that Sam would not stay meekly at home during such a momentous time. He finally found her, her face wreathed in a smile and eyes shining brightly as they regarded him with a mixture of emotions, one he wished wasn't quite so public. He carefully made his way through the cheerfully cooperative mob until he reached her, and he continued to sit on his horse while his eyes raked over her in pleasure.

"You are getting quite fat, madam," he finally said, satisfaction and pride evident in his teasing words.

"'Tis all your doing," she retorted quickly.

He leaned down and kissed her, heedless of anyone watching.

"I can tell I'll have to make reparations," he said, a chuckle in his voice and a decided gleam of lust in his eyes.

"They will be high," she answered, staring at him with identical want. How handsome he looked in the saddle, his face bronze with the sun and his gray eyes crinkling with warmth and laughter. She could stand it no longer. "If you don't take me home this minute," she said, "I might well embarrass you...."

He threw back his head and laughed, his light hair catching the sun. He looks like a god, Sam mused, growing warmer by the moment.

Connor saw the flush in her cheeks and caught the same urgency. He leaned down and carefully lifted her into the saddle in front of him. He had to move back further than usual.

The laughter was still in his voice when he whispered, "We can't go on doing this much longer, madam. The horse can take two, but three...." One arm tightened around her, just above the babe, while the other took firm control of the horse and guided him easily through the streets to Denney's house. He lifted her down and hand in hand they chastely entered the house, only to fling themselves hungrily into each other's arms as the door closed behind him.

"I've missed you," she whispered, "every minute you've been gone." She stood on tiptoe and nibbled his lips, preventing a reply.

Instead, he laid his cheek on her head and fitted her neatly inside his arms, holding her as he would a priceless piece of crystal, knowing a sense of completeness he had never had before. How he loved her! How he loved her laughter and teasing and unabashed passion, which aroused him so completely.

Samantha melted as deeply into his body as the baby would permit. For the first time, she had a feeling of safety and security. In the past weeks she had pushed her own problem aside in worry for his safety. Now she knew everything would be all right. Once the baby was born, she would tell him everything. He would understand. But for these few moments, they were the only two people in the world.

Later, upstairs, she put his hands on her stomach, and he felt the baby kick and move. The baby became real to him, and his face creased in wonder and delight. A depth of tenderness he hadn't known existed flooded him. My child, he thought, my wife. Such happiness was new to him and he couldn't quite comprehend it. His hands touched Sam with reverence, but she would have none of it. With a low sensuous growl she demanded something quite different, and they laughed and played and loved until they fell asleep, wrapped in each other's arms.

Francis Marion's brigade rested in Georgetown for several weeks. They were all exhausted from the past months of constant fighting. It was time to relax and gather strength for what everyone expected would be a long and bitter summer. Although the British had retreated when their supply lines were destroyed, they were still strong in numbers between Charleston and Orangeburg. They were, by no means, defeated.

For Sam and Connor, it was a time of unprecedented happiness. Every day was a new adventure, eagerly started and gently ended. Connor still had some duties and would disappear for a portion of each day, but each arrival was an event of celebration.

It was well into the third week when Connor announced he would be leaving in two days. Francis was planning a new campaign and would leave only a small guard in the city. The British were clinging to Charleston and Orangeburg, making forays into the countryside for food and supplies. Marion was to stop these raids until Greene could replenish his army and attack the two cities.

They were having a late supper, knowing their time together would be soon over, when they heard a buggy in front and, seconds later, a commotion at the door.

Connor was up immediately and nearly to the door as it was flung open.

"Connor," came the loud booming voice as an impeccably uniformed Continental officer entered the room, a pretty girl at his side.

Connor stared for a moment, then grinned. "I see you finally took my advice." He gave Denney Demerest a bear hug of congratulations.

The girl smiled, her eyes glowing. "And I thank you for it." She stood on tiptoe and kissed him.

Then they both turned and saw Samantha, an uncertain smile on her face. She had followed Connor to the door.

Connor swept her up in one arm. "This," he said proudly, "is Sam."

Denney raised an eyebrow. "She doesn't look like any Sam I ever saw."

Connor laughed. "Believe me, she's not *like* any Sam you have ever met, or anyone else, for that matter. Sam, this is Denney Demerest, whose house we've so enjoyed, and Caroline."

Denney clicked his heels together and gave a small bow. "My pleasure, Mrs. O'Neill. When I heard Connor had married I knew it must be someone special. I see that it is."

Samantha flushed with pleasure. She liked Denney immediately. And her curiosity was raised by Caroline whom she had hated fiercely for a while.

Now she smiled. "You are newly married?"

"Three weeks now," Denney answered happily. "But I have to get back to Greene, and I thought . . . hoped that Caroline could stay here."

"Of course," Connor answered. "We'll look for a house tomorrow."

"No," Denney said, distressed that he had been misunderstood. "I'll be gone a lot and Caroline's all alone. Her family is still very angry about the marriage. So is mine, for that matter. I was hoping she could stay here with you and Sam. They would be company for each other when we're gone."

Samantha thought it was a splendid idea. She had been lonelier than she had let on. She now went to Caroline and took both her hands. "I think it's a wonderful idea. I have longed to have someone to talk to while Connor's gone. Please say you will."

The liking between the two women was almost instantaneous. They both recognized a warmth in the other, and they were both very much in love. There would be no jealousy here.

"It's settled then," Denney said, as he roared out, "Cecil." In seconds, there was more noise and confusion as Cecil and Mary crowded around Denney, meeting his new wife and happily carrying in bags.

The four ate supper together, and it was a merry meal. Samantha confessed she had heartily disliked the unknown Caroline earlier that year, and Caroline smiled. "If it weren't for this great oaf, Denney, I might have tried to give you reason, although I doubt I would have much success. I think we both have excellent taste in husbands."

The laughter disappeared as Denney and Connor talked of the war. Neither saw a quick end, though the tide was finally turning. It was on this somber note that they retired to bed, Sam and Connor retaining the master bedroom and Denney and Caroline taking the guest bedroom.

Samantha was quiet, subdued by the talk of war and the knowledge that Connor would soon be back in the middle of it while she stayed here.

"I like them," she said finally. "It will be fine to have a friend."

Connor suddenly realized how lonely she must have been. His hand fingered a curl of her hair, and he leaned down to kiss her gently. She reached for him, and he lowered himself next to her. There was passion now, as there always had been, but there was also a stronger need to feel the other's nearness.

Both men left two days later, and Samantha and Caroline settled into a pattern of waiting. Their friendship grew deeper day by day, but Caroline sensed that all was not quite as it should be and wondered about the girl's reluctance to talk of family or friends. But it was none of her business and she settled for giving Samantha her unquestioning support. They sewed little garments for the baby, read, talked and waited.

Chapter Twenty-Five

A cold chill had settled permanently in Robert Chatham. He had lost.

Throughout the spring and summer, one British fort had fallen after another, and now the British were pushed back all the way to Charleston. Nearly all the Williamsburg area was thoroughly in control of the South Carolina militia. It was only a matter of time before everything would be gone. He had no doubt that his plantation would be taken, as well as those he had claimed from rebels.

Some hardened Tories refused to accept what Chatham considered the inevitable. They pointed to a still strong army under Cornwallis in Virginia and Henry Clinton's stubborn presence in New York.

But Chatham knew it was over. A French army was even now marching to Virginia and a large French fleet was under sail to join Washington. Britain was under attack throughout the world, and it had neither the resources nor finances to further strengthen its armies in America.

Seeing the handwriting on the wall, Chatham had called a meeting of Williamsburg's foremost Tories.

It was loud and bitter and divisive. Some still clung to the belief that Britain would never let itself be defeated by such an upstart nation. Others, like Chatham, knew the end was nearing. Among the latter, there were even more divisions. One group planned to move to Canada or the British-owned islands in the Caribbean. A larger group had decided quietly to accept

American terms and try to remain. A third, of which Chatham was a member, would fight to the end.

The meeting broke up amid bitter accusations and recriminations. Only five men remained; all had sworn to continue the fight.

Chatham now paced the floor of his study. The men who remained with him had little to lose by continuing the battle. All were badly wanted by Marion's militia; they had killed and burned and robbed for the past three years; they would not be left in peace after the war. Nor did they want to be. Hate and destruction had become a way of life.

Chatham knew he particularly would have no future in the Carolinas. Francis Marion and Greene were currently busy trying to bottle up the British at Charleston, but once free, they would turn their attention to the Tories of Williamsburg. And Connor O'Neill would be among them.

Even the thought of O'Neill enraged him. He would never forget his humiliation at his hands the day he went to Glen Woods after the death of his wife, or that the O'Neills caused Elizabeth's death. And he knew that Brendan's death was the reason behind Samantha's disappearance. He laid no blame on his own door for that. His daughter had been seduced and tricked by the O'Neills. And now everything was gone. Everything. And all because of the O'Neills.

Chatham did not want to live with the rabble that would take over this country, and he did not have the strength or desire to start over again. He would die here in the Carolinas...he would die for the king, and he would die joyously if he could take Connor O'Neill with him.

He sat down at his desk and slowly unveiled his plan to the others in the room....

Francis Marion had urged South Carolina Governor Rutledge to issue a proclamation granting clemency to Tories. Bitter fighting was continuing in the countryside and neither Greene nor Marion had the resources to stop it. Rutledge, looking ahead to the end of the war and the need for domestic peace, realized something must be done to neutralize the Tories.

The proclamation declared that all Tories, except those who had signed congratulatory addresses to Clinton or Cornwallis or who held commissions from the British government, could have "a free pardon" if they appeared at American headquarters or before a brigade or the colonel of any regiment and agreed to serve the state faithfully as a militiaman for six months. A number of Tories who wished to stay in the Carolinas had already done so.

It was this proclamation that Chatham intended to use as bait for his trap.

Connor was hot, depressed and aching with weariness. He had not seen Sam since late July and it was now mid-August. But Marion had kept him moving as liaison between himself, Greene and General Sumter, an independent partisan leader much like Marion but without Marion's strict code of ethics. Connor had again been designated peacemaker as squabbling continued between the partisan bands, particularly between Marion and Sumter, who was growing increasingly bitter about Marion's higher authority. It had all exploded during the Battle of Quinby when Sumter, in Marion's absence, ordered Peter Horry into an exposed position while he and his men remained safely behind. Horry's troop was decimated, and he bitterly blamed Sumter. Marion, through Connor, was desperately trying to hold everything together to keep the militia from leaving and returning home. The British at Charleston remained a serious threat.

Connor had just reported to Marion's camp near Monck's Corners when a message caught up with him. Marion had left to meet with General Greene, and Major John James silently handed Connor a letter and watched him with curiosity. It had Robert Chatham's seal.

Connor's face was unreadable as he scanned the short text. Wordlessly he handed it to James.

James studied it. "Do you believe him?"

"Hell, no," Connor said. "Chatham surrendering? Surrendering to me particularly? All in the name of ending 'this fruitless feud.' He has to be mad."

"But if," James said, "he means it, it would do much to quiet the Tory activity in Williamsburg. He's their principal leader."

"Robert Chatham would never agree to that proclamation," Connor said, and there was something in his face that James had never seen before. A look of terrible intent.

"He wants me," Connor said, "and he wants me alone. And that's exactly what he is going to get."

John looked at his friend. Connor's face was harder than he had ever seen it. His eyes were cold and steady and his mouth tight with determination.

"It could be a trap, Connor," John said. "Wait until Fran gets back or take some men with you."

"No," Connor said flatly. "I've waited too long. This is between Chatham and me."

John regarded him hopelessly. "Fran isn't going to like this."

Connor laughed but it wasn't a pleasant sound. "It doesn't make any difference," he said. "No one can stop me. Tell Fran I'll be back as soon as I can."

Connor quickly saddled a fresh horse and within minutes was riding out of camp, leaving John James clutching Chatham's note.

James was pacing worriedly when Fran returned less than an hour later. The militia major quickly explained, and Marion ordered fresh horses saddled, asking six men to accompany him. His face was even more dour than usual, and he berated himself under his breath. It was almost certainly a trap; if not, it could well be a tragedy for Sam and Connor. He damned himself for not telling Connor earlier who Sam was. He set off at a gallop.

For two days, Chatham had been waiting. Four of his friends had taken posts in various parts of the house and stable. A fifth was watching the road.

Chatham had grown more and more impatient. He knew O'Neill would come if he received the message. With some freak piece of luck, Marion might be with him. Either way he would eliminate a major enemy of the crown.

He didn't know what he would do then. Probably wait until others came to avenge their friends. He wouldn't care. Not if he got O'Neill first.

Chatham wandered from room to room, once more admiring their classic elegance. He had built the house thirty years ago, and it was lovelier today than it had been then. The fine paneling had darkened to a richer hue; the chandeliers he had imported from England sparkled in the sun.

But it was empty. His mouth grimaced with the pain of remembering. Elizabeth. Elizabeth, who had been brighter and more beautiful than any sunbeam.

And Samantha. He had been surprised at how much he had missed her. He had never paid any attention to her, resenting her resemblance to Elizabeth and the constant painful reminder it inspired. But when her smile and laughter were gone, he realized his loss. "Where are you, Samantha?" he whispered.

He closed his eyes in pain, seeing his barren life for what it had been. No. He would not be sorry to end it. Especially if O'Neill went with him. That hate had kept him alive these years; he would have been lost without it.

He went back to the porch. It was there he finally saw his sentry come riding in, his horse lathered. Minutes later, everyone was positioned. One man was in the loft of the barn, two others were in upstairs bedrooms, the fourth and fifth hidden among the trees.

Chatham went inside and took a dueling pistol from its case. It was the same pistol that had killed Brendan O'Neill as well as others. He was an excellent shot.

He put the pistol in his belt and walked out on the porch just as O'Neill approached the house. The militia officer was alone.

Connor moved cautiously. He had little reason to respect Chatham's honor. His eyes quickly inspected the entire area and didn't miss the flutter of curtains in the second floor. A sixth sense warned him there were others around. He had been a fool to come alone. But this was a meeting too long delayed. At least, he thought, I'll take Chatham. He dismounted, taking a rifle. A pistol was tucked in his belt.

"I understand you want a pardon, Chatham," he said coldly.

Chatham laughed. "Did you really think so?"

"No," Connor said quietly. "But *I* want *you*."

His quick darting eyes saw a face in another window and he mocked the older man. "You need help when you aren't facing a boy?"

Chatham's mouth grew tighter but he refused to be baited. As good a shot as he might be, he suspected Connor was better. He wasn't going to lose his chance to wipe out the O'Neills.

His smile was almost pleasant. "I just want to make sure I end the task I started two years ago. I really thought the prison ship would do it for me. How was it, Connor?" he goaded. He had given orders to his men to shoot when Connor raised his gun. "Did you think of me there? Did you think of me when your father died?"

"You bastard," Connor replied, and his rifle came up. Chatham had still not drawn his pistol, and Connor suddenly knew the greatest danger came from above. His rifle spit flame, and a figure came toppling from a window. Connor dived to the ground, throwing his rifle away and reaching for the pistol as another gun sent dirt spraying around him. Then he saw another figure crumple in the hayloft of the barn and heard more gunfire. Finally it seemed that only he and Chatham remained, and he watched as Chatham, hate contorting his face, grabbed for his pistol, and he did the same. Just as Chatham aimed, the Tory jerked back, red spraying from his chest as he slowly twisted to the ground.

Connor's gun remained unfired, and he turned around, fury darkening his face. Chatham had been his. Damn it.

Fran rode up, his rifle still smoking, and behind him were five men. Two bodies were on the ground. Fran pointed to them. "That was a stupid thing to do, Connor, coming alone."

But Connor merely glared at him. "He was mine. You knew that. I had the right to kill him."

"And I would have lost a major. I'm sorry, Connor. I didn't think your pride worth the cost."

But Connor was beyond thinking reasonably. "You had no right to interfere."

Fran dismounted and went over to Connor. It was time Connor knew. Not knowing had almost killed him.

Slowly, carefully, he looked into Connor's eyes. "You would have killed your child's grandfather, or Chatham his grandchild's father. I wonder if either of you could have lived with that."

Connor stared at him blankly as the words gradually penetrated. He stepped back. "No," he whispered. "No."

"Connor..."

"No," Connor said again, and this time it was a shout. Marion merely looked at him, and Connor saw the truth in his face. Connor's face crumpled. "Not Sam...." But the minute he heard the name, he realized what he was saying.

"She loves you, Connor. She gave up everything for you," Marion said, trying to make his friend understand.

But Connor's face had turned to stone. He walked slowly to his horse and mounted. He looked once more at the dead body of Chatham and suddenly whipped his horse into a gallop.

A sergeant looked at Marion. "Do you think one of us should go with him?"

Marion shook his head. "I think he needs to be alone. Let's get back."

Chapter Twenty-Six

Samantha was in the parlor reading when she heard the hoof-beats through the open windows. Denney was with Greene's army and Caroline was upstairs resting. The August heat had drained both of them, but Samantha knew lying down would not help her. It was much better, she mused, to get lost in a book.

She rose awkwardly, feeling every ounce of the baby's weight as he kicked and turned inside her. She smiled. Everyone had told her she would hate this last month when she grew more grotesque and heavy and clumsy. But she didn't. She savored every minute of it; it reminded her constantly of the healthy little boy she knew was there. She loved him with an intensity born of a lonely childhood and a heart whose love had been too often rejected. Here, at last, was a being, a tiny being, that she could love without fear or qualification.

She heard the sound of boots on the porch and knew instantly they were Connor's. No one else moved with quite the same impatience and confidence. A delighted smile started on her face as the door opened and he faced her. But it slowly faded as her eyes eagerly searched his face.

It was whiter than she had ever seen it, and his eyes were like thousands of pieces of broken glass, glistening empty shards.

She took one step toward him. "Connor..."

"Samantha, I believe," he said in a tone so quiet she barely heard it.

In that second, her world fell apart. The emptiness in his face, the unnatural quiet, were more frightening than any rage.

She took a step backward, her hand reaching to a table for support.

"So it is true," he said in the same soft tone. "I had hoped Francis was wrong, but then he never is, is he?" His tone was conversational, almost polite. "Sam...Samara...Samantha...tell me, do you ever tell the truth? What a fool you must think me. And you would be right. The world's greatest fool."

Her eyes were mesmerized, like a butterfly whose wings are being pinned to a board. She couldn't move them from his face, couldn't see his hands ball up in tight fists as he struggled for control.

In the same reasonable tone, he continued, each word a whiplash to her soul. "What's the matter, Samantha? Wasn't Brendan enough? Or did you want to destroy two O'Neills with that lovely smile and childlike innocence? Did you think I would end up like Brendan, Samantha? Did you?"

As she started to back up, his hand reached out and clasped her wrist. "Oh, no, Samantha. You're not running away. Not this time. Not until you tell me why. Why you lied and lied and lied."

But she had no words. She could only stare at him as horror filled her. She could have dealt with anger or hurt or even rage. But not this cold distant contempt, not this cruel stranger whose words were carefully selected to do the worst damage.

"No explanations, Samantha? You were never shy of them before. You were very good at them, in fact."

He regarded her critically. "You do not look very well, Samantha," he observed, making the very mention of her name more and more obscene. "Perhaps you should sit down." A flick of his wrist forced her back down into the chair in which she had been sitting a few minutes earlier, or was it a thousand years?

"I think," he said slowly, "you should be sitting down when you hear the news. Your father is dead, Samantha. It was him, not me. Not exactly what you planned, is it?"

Connor did not feel the satisfaction he thought he would. Her eyes closed briefly but then opened, and he was bewildered by the strength in them, the sad acceptance of something she had already sensed.

"You?" she said finally.

"No, though I tried. Fran took that pleasure from me." The words were intentionally cruel, but she was numb now. The pain had become so great, it was devouring itself. There was only a yawning emptiness.

The baby, perhaps sensing the distress, gave an unexpectedly hard kick, and Samantha's arms went protectively around her stomach, trying to protect it from her own despair.

Connor misunderstood the gesture and his words hurt her more than any blow. "I won't hit you," he said. "I don't ever want to touch you again. Or see you. Or it." His eyes went to her bulky stomach.

He turned to leave. "I will see to your financial needs but I want no part of a Chatham...you or the child. If you need anything, contact Annabelle."

At the door he turned once more, and for the first time his voice lost its iron control. "Was anything not a lie?"

But Samantha was so steeped in misery she could not speak immediately, and he was gone before she was finally able to whisper, "That I love you, that I will always love you."

Outside, Connor threw his head back in agony. He wanted to howl like an animal in pain. He wanted to fight, to hurt, to attack, to do anything to keep from seeing those clear dark blue eyes that he knew would haunt him the rest of his life.

His rage, needing a focus, centered on Francis. He had known. He had known and said nothing. He was Connor's friend, and he had betrayed that friendship. And Connor was going to find out why.

Caroline, hearing the door slam downstairs, aroused herself from a restless half slumber. Hoping it might be Denney, she quickly dressed and went down.

Sam was sitting in a chair, her form as stiff as a board, her face and eyes completely blank. She didn't acknowledge Caroline's presence or make any movement. It was as if she had turned to stone.

"Sam?" Caroline's voice was sharp, worried.

There was no response, absolutely none at all.

Caroline tried again. "Sam...who was here? Was it Connor?"

At the sound of the name, Sam's eyes flickered, but she still didn't move. Something inside her had frozen, and she knew if she moved it would shatter. Better not to feel. Better not to think. Better not to move.

"Mary...Cecil," Caroline called. When the two servants appeared, she questioned them.

"No, ma'am," Mary said. "I was out getting food...just got back as you called." Cecil, too, had been out of the house, feeding the horses.

Caroline knelt next to Sam, looking up at her. "What is it? Did something happen to Connor?"

But Sam just continued to sit there. It can't hurt this much. Nothing can hurt this much. It was as if her heart had been ripped out. There was only a shadow left, an empty form with an empty soul.

Caroline was frantic now. "Cecil, get the doctor," she ordered. "Mary, help me take her upstairs."

Caroline took Sam's hand, urging her to stand, and was surprised when she obediently did so. There was no resistance, but she felt as though she were leading a sleepy child rather than a woman. She and Mary began to undress her. Sam didn't help, but she didn't fight them, either.

Mary stood there, shaking her head. "That's not Mrs. O'Neill. It just ain't."

"I know," Caroline said quietly. "I just wish I knew what had happened...perhaps the doctor can tell us something."

But the doctor could not. Mrs. O'Neill had been one of his favorite patients. He had enjoyed her complete delight with the approaching baby and her obvious love for her husband. He was as deeply puzzled as the others. "She's had a shock, that much is obvious, but I've never seen anything like this. It's as if she's willing herself out of existence."

Caroline approached the young woman. "Sam...the baby...think about the baby."

Only then did Samantha show any sign of emotion, and the doctor knew he had never seen such agony.

He leaned down. "Mrs. O'Neill...you must take care of the baby. No matter what has happened, you must protect the child."

Slowly, she nodded, accepting the words, but her face had settled back into nothingness.

The doctor motioned Caroline outside. "Try to find out what happened...get in touch with her husband. And try to get her to eat. She's only a week or so from delivery, and she needs her strength." Caroline nodded, and the doctor continued, "Call me if you need me, anytime. I'll drop in tomorrow."

Caroline sent a message to the last place she knew Marion had camped, but Marion had moved, and the messenger, rather than pursuing the elusive Swamp Fox, returned to Georgetown. Caroline promptly dispatched several more.

In the meantime, she looked after Sam as she would a child. Sam continued to lie there, responding to very little. She would eat when Caroline reminded her of the baby, but she ate as she had two years earlier when Bren died: in tiny little pieces, which she chewed and chewed. Caroline would think of the whirlwind Sam had once been and wanted to cry. She had never felt so helpless in her life.

On the fourth day, Caroline approached Sam's closed door and was delighted to hear movement inside. She knocked, then entered. Sam was up, moving around listlessly, her face still locked in the same expressionless mask. She was packing, but her movements were abnormally slow, as if each took stupendous effort.

"Sam," Caroline cried. "What are you doing?"

Sam looked up and when she answered her voice was as empty as her face. "Away. Connor wants me away."

"No," Caroline cried. "He loves you...he loves you more than any man I have ever seen."

Sam smiled, and it was the saddest smile Caroline had ever seen. "No," she said simply, repeating in the same toneless voice. "I have to go before he gets back."

"But where? And the baby...it's almost time."

"I'll take care of the baby," Samantha said. "He's all I have left." She went on packing.

Caroline stared at her friend in horror. She knew from Sam's tone and demeanor she couldn't be stopped. She searched for words, but she couldn't find any. If only she knew what had happened . . . or where Connor was. . . .

Suddenly she thought of Annabelle. Caroline had never met the notorious woman, but Sam had told her of the woman's friendship. They had giggled together when Sam told Caroline of her first visit to Cherry Street and Connor's good intentions. At first Caroline had been horrified, but Sam had quickly dispelled that. She told of Annabelle's kindness and generosity, and Caroline had become fascinated.

Now she wrote a note to Annabelle, asking her to come. It was a measure of Cecil's concern that he agreed to deliver it.

Annabelle was there within the hour, her body once more swathed in anonymous brown clothing. She listened to Caroline, then quickly went upstairs to Sam's room.

Sam was still moving around, and Annabelle was shocked at her appearance. All the vitality was gone; Sam appeared in a daze. She hadn't even heard, or cared, that someone had entered.

"Sam," Annabelle said softly, and she turned.

Nothing had prepared Annabelle for the look of utter emptiness on Sam's face. Annabelle swallowed, a hard lump in her throat. She went over to her, putting her arm around her. "What happened? Was it Connor? Did he find out?"

Samantha just looked at her with blank eyes. "I'm leaving, you know. He never wants to see me again."

The calmness with which she spoke frightened Annabelle. "Where will you go?"

"I don't know. It doesn't matter. Somewhere."

Oh God in heaven, Annabelle thought. What had Connor said? It was worse than she had ever imagined. She had always believed that Connor's good sense and innate fairness would make everything all right. It was why she had kept her silence.

"Tell me exactly what he said," Annabelle instructed, leading Sam to the bed where they both sat. Sam turned to her, her chin slightly tilted, and she looked impossibly young and vulnerable. Like a child who had been beaten . . . not complaining because she had expected it and took it as due but still not quite prepared for the immense pain it had caused.

"He said that he wanted no part of a Chatham . . . me or the child. He never wants to touch me again or see me. He called our baby 'it.' Like a distasteful object." Her eyes, wider than ever before, looked at Annabelle with such puzzlement that Annabelle wanted to weep.

"Oh, Sam," Annabelle said. She took the girl in her arms and held her there. "Cry, Sam," she demanded, instinctively knowing the girl needed that release.

"I can't, Annabelle," Sam said simply. "It hurts too much. Tears are for little things. Besides, I don't have time. I have to go."

"You aren't going anyplace in that condition," Annabelle said. "When is the baby due . . . one week, two? If you don't care about yourself, then think of the child."

"I can't be here when Connor comes back," Sam said adamantly. "I can't bear to see him again."

Annabelle abruptly made up her mind. Samantha needed her. Connor was being a damned fool. She felt something less than respect for her longtime friend.

"You will come with me," Annabelle said decisively. "We won't tell anyone where . . . we'll say I'm taking you to the coach station. Then you'll stay with me where we can look after you. After the child is born, I will help you go wherever you want. If that's still what you want."

"But Connor . . . he stays with you. . . ."

"Don't worry about that," Annabelle said. "I'll take care of it." And Sam knew from her tone, she would indeed.

"Thank you," she said slowly, and Annabelle was delighted to recognize a small bit of life back in her face. "I'll tell your friend that I couldn't prevent you from leaving," Annabelle said. As she started out the door, she added, "Don't you think you should write a note in case Connor comes back?"

Samantha nodded. She had to make Connor understand that she had never meant all of this to happen. That she really did love him. That they weren't really married and he wouldn't be tied to her.

Several minutes later they were on their way to Cherry Street, leaving behind a tearful Caroline and one rather wrinkled note.

Connor was, at the moment, enmeshed in one of the most desperate battles of the war in South Carolina.

After leaving Sam, he had ridden for Marion's camp but found the general was on the move to join Greene. Greene had surprised and captured one hundred British foragers at a place called Eutaw Springs on the road to Charleston. The action had brought out the main British force, and it appeared a major battle was forming.

As angry as he was, Connor knew this was no time for personal problems. He took command of his militiamen and placed them quickly beside Greene's regulars.

On a hot and muggy day in September, two thousand of the king's soldiers, many of them loyalists, met the Americans' force of twenty-four hundred.

Connor, in the midst of stifling dust and smoke, fought to keep his militia intact as they attacked and attacked again. At one point he almost lost them when a number of Continentals broke into the British camp and turned their attention to rum and plunder rather than battle. Only Connor's soft persuasion kept his men together.

But Connor saw they had lost their momentum and their chance. After three hours of desperate close fighting, Greene retreated. Connor had escaped without a scratch although he had courted death throughout the day.

Later that evening, he learned that although the Americans had tactically lost the battle they had probably destroyed what was left of the British army in the Carolinas. The British had lost nearly half their army in casualties and prisoners taken. They were creeping slowly back to Charleston.

It was nearly two days later before Connor had a chance to meet with Marion. Time had done nothing to reduce his anger and, in fact, had merely served to fuel it.

Marion, who saw Connor coming, excused himself from a group of men and drew his angry major off into the woods.

Before Connor could say anything, Marion's eyes silenced him. "Sam?" It was a question.

Connor disregarded it. "Damn it, Fran, why didn't you tell me? You've obviously known...how long? Why?"

"How is Sam?" Marion asked again, disregarding Connor's explosion.

"I don't know," Connor said bitterly. "I don't want to know."

"You're a complete ass, Connor, if you've done anything to hurt that girl. I've never seen anyone love as completely as she does you."

Connor stared at him, completely off balance from the attack. "You're supposed to be my friend...."

"Aye," Francis replied. "I hope I am. But that doesn't make you any less a fool in this case."

"You should have told me!"

"You're right. I should have. It was a poor decision on my part. But I didn't find out until Sam's capture, and she said she would tell you. Then she disappeared and you showed up married. She kept trying to tell you, Connor, but each time you would say some damn fool thing about Chatham."

"She was responsible for Brendan's death," Connor insisted stubbornly. He wasn't ready to give up his long-standing conviction of Samantha Chatham's culpability in Bren's death. It was his only justification for what he had done.

"Horsefeathers. Did you ask her?"

"Her father told..."

"And you believe everything Robert Chatham said."

Connor had no answer for that. His anger was slowly being replaced by confusion.

"Did you know Sam spied for us long before she found you in the cave? Did you know she and your brother planned to elope the day he was killed?"

At that, Connor's eyes flew wide open. "Elope? Bren and Sam? But Bren said nothing."

"I expect," Marion said dryly, "that's why people do elope. To keep it secret. But somehow Chatham heard. That was the reason for the duel. Connor, I heard Sam talk about Brendan. There's no doubt that she loved him. Just like there's no doubt she loves you. She's given up everything for you. She has lived in terror that you would turn from her if you knew who she was. I should have insisted. I know that now. But she was so sure time would solve everything...."

Softly, quietly, he continued. "Can you forget she saved your life twice...that she's been as courageous and true as anyone I've ever met? Connor, don't let your pride or anger destroy you both. I only wish that I had found someone with that much love and light. You are incredibly lucky."

Connor stood there as the words hammered at him. His mind, now drained of anger, finally looked at things logically. His face went white as he remembered his last words to Sam...and her face. He would never forget that expression on her face. He buried his face in his hands as he tortured himself with every word he had uttered.

Marion, watching him, saw the despair spread over his face. "Go after her, Connor," he said softly.

"I can't," he groaned. "She can never forgive me...not after what I said."

Marion didn't even want to think about what Connor had said. "She loves you," he said simply, "though at the moment I don't understand why. Just go."

Connor lifted his head and there was a glimmer of hope in his face. He nodded and with new determination ran to find a fresh horse.

It took him half a day to reach Georgetown, and it was dusk when he finally arrived at the Demerest home. He stopped to knock, thinking to give warning. He had thought about how he could approach Sam since he had left Marion. He didn't think bursting in on her was the way.

Caroline opened the door, and Connor's spirits, which had alternated between up and down, plunged. She looked at him with absolute hostility.

"Where's Sam?" Connor managed.

"Gone," Caroline said coldly. "I don't know where." She disappeared and returned in a moment, holding a note. "She left this for you."

"May I come in?"

"If you wish," she said, holding the door open but keeping her distance. "I don't know what you did or what you said, but you practically killed that girl." She slammed the door and disappeared, leaving Connor alone with the note. He fingered it, afraid to open it. His hands finally straightened the paper and he stared at it.

Connor...
I am sorry for everything, for the hurt I've caused you, for the lies and deception. I know you can never forgive them, but please know also that it was because I loved you. You were my life, and I couldn't bear to lose you. That is my only excuse.

The one thing I can leave you is your freedom. We are not legally married because I didn't use my real name. I sincerely hope you can find someone who will make you a good wife. I want you to be happy.

You needn't worry that I will ever claim any funds from you. I will not. I have sufficient for my needs.

I know you don't want to see me again. You have your wish. I am leaving Georgetown and will not return.

I hope someday you will forgive and think kindly of me. I shall love you always.

                                                          Sam

Connor crumpled the note in his hand. Every sentence was a condemnation of what he had done. The stiffness of the writing, so unlike her, told him only too well of her anguish. He had to find her. He had to make things right.

"Caroline?"

Denney's wife appeared in the doorway. "What?"

"Don't you have any idea where she went? She must have said something."

"No," Caroline said, "and if she had I don't think I would tell you. If she wanted you to know where she was going she would have included that in the note." There was ice in her voice.

"Caroline?" Connor's voice was pleading.

"I don't know. I really don't."

Connor nodded, defeated, and turned to go. There were other places to look...perhaps she had gone home to Chatham

Oaks. She would have possessions there . . . perhaps funds. He tucked the note in his boot and mounted again.

For the next two days, Connor hunted ceaselessly. Chatham Oaks was empty. Many of the slaves had run off or been stolen by one side or another. The stables were empty, having suffered the same fate. He went from there to the cave and spent several minutes remembering.

"'Ave a way with 'orses, I do." Her voice seemed to echo in the empty confines. There was still the bucket with which she had washed him so furiously. A slight smile creased his hard face. Sam. Sam. I miss you. Oh, how I miss you.

He rode to Snow Island, knowing she would never have gone there, not now with the child so near. But he felt a compulsion to return. Her presence would be close there, and he needed that. He needed it to keep from going mad.

But there were only ruins. The British had burned everything. Even his memories were only bitter ashes.

He slowly turned back to Georgetown, thinking now of that first trip they took together . . . when they went to Annabelle's. *Annabelle.* Suddenly he knew. Sam was with Annabelle. He kicked his tired horse into a gallop.

Chapter Twenty-Seven

Connor went up the stairs at Annabelle's two and three steps at a time, hope and fear waging an impatient battle within him. As he started to turn the knob, he found the door locked and uttered an unconscious oath of surprise. It was never locked. As long as he had been visiting Cherry Street he had never encountered a locked door. He pounded on it now, his fists slamming against it in a furious tattoo.

It opened so suddenly he nearly fell against it, and he saw Annabelle. He flinched at her expression. There was disappointment in it, even a little disgust, and certainly no welcome. It was the first time in his memory she had not greeted him with a smile and enthusiasm. Now there was only an unfamiliar censure.

"Sam? Is she here?" Annabelle's face lost some of its disapproval at the frantic note in his voice. He, too, was suffering.

Her face relaxed into a half smile. "It took you long enough," she finally said.

"*Is* she here?" he insisted once more. "Damn it, Annabelle, I've looked everyplace."

"I thought you never wanted to see her again," Annabelle reminded him heartlessly.

Connor closed his eyes against the condemnation, both hers and his own. "Annabelle..." His voice was pleading now. "Where is she?"

"Upstairs, just about to have your child," Annabelle answered, finally relenting.

"My room?"

"Where else?" But she knew the answer went unheard as he bolted up the steps, leaving her with a small satisfied smile on her face.

When he reached his door, it was half-open and he heard the sounds of people moving within. He took a deep breath, realizing his entire life depended on the next few seconds. He wouldn't blame Sam at all if she ordered him away. Let her understand, he prayed to whoever might be listening. Let her forgive. He finally pushed open the door.

Sam was in bed, half-propped against a mountain of pillows. Her face seemed even smaller than usual, and her eyes were enormous in her pale face. As they turned toward the noise at the door, he saw them wince and the expression wounded him more than any words. Unlike Annabelle, there was no censure or judgement, just enormous hurt and the obvious fear it was to be compounded. He had never hated himself as much as he did at this moment, and he was unaware of the wetness forming in his eyes. Even if he had, he would not have recognized it. He had never before shed tears.

He looked at Darlene and another girl. "Please leave us," he said quietly, and flinched once more as they hesitated, then looked at Sam for direction. They obviously thought him capable of hurting her once more, and there was no question they had switched their allegiance from him to her.

Samantha nodded, and the two girls left quickly, aware that Connor and Sam no longer even knew they existed. Their eyes fixed on each other, both consumed by fear and uncertainty. They dwelt for several minutes in a world that excluded everything but themselves. Then Connor saw a flicker of pain cross her face and her body tremble, and he was at her side, his hand brushing her face with a wondering touch, unaware of the tears falling from his eyes. And then he was on his knees next to her bed, his face in torment.

"Sam . . . Samantha . . . Oh God, I love you. Can you ever forgive me?"

But at that moment an almost unbearable pain came, and she couldn't comprehend his words. She just saw the tears. Her hand reached up and brushed one away. He mustn't cry...not Connor. Not strong confident proud Connor.

He misunderstood her silence. "Francis told me everything...about you and Bren...how you spied for him...how you tried to tell me...."

"I loved Bren, you know," she said, her voice low, miserable. "I really loved him. I wanted to die when he did. But I couldn't." Her eyes, meeting his, were swimming in tears. "If I could have died in his place, I would have...."

"I know," he soothed, his heart hurting. He closed his eyes, remembering all the times he had unknowingly accused her of killing his brother, of voicing his hatred. And then, worst of all, was that day when he told her of her father's death. Something inside him was being ripped apart and he could barely breathe.

"And then I found you in the cave, and something happened." She was talking in the same low but now almost detached voice. "I didn't want to love you...I knew you would hate me. But I couldn't stop it. I loved you so much."

Loved. That word rang discordantly in his mind. Please, God, don't let it be too late. The knife in his stomach twisted until he was ready to scream in agony.

"I'm sorry," she said then. "I'm sorry I caused you so much pain."

Connor could stand no more. Of all her words, nothing pierced him with the excruciating impact of the last ones. She was apologizing to him. His face was anguished, and again they misunderstood each other.

"I'm going," she whispered. "You won't have to be reminded. We will be fine...."

"Is that what you want?" he said finally in a voice that belied the turmoil inside him. He couldn't stop her, he didn't have the right to even try.

Another pain came, and she flinched. Connor took her hand and she held it tight, and when she looked at him he knew he could never let her go.

"Oh, Sam," he said, his gray eyes piercing hers, "don't go. Please don't go. I love you. I love you so much. And I've been such a fool. Please forgive me."

This time she understood, and a glimmer of hope lighted her face. "You want me?" she said in a voice so timid he almost laughed.

"Want you?" He took both her hands. "I want you very much indeed. I want you now, tomorrow, forever. "And I want *him* or *her*...." He looked down at the bulge under the sheet. "I want you both more than anything in the world."

"Really...?" She still couldn't comprehend it. "But I..."

"Not you, my love," he said. "Me. I've been the world's greatest fool and if you don't believe it, ask all my friends. They certainly think so."

"But..."

"I love you, Samantha. I don't care what your name is. The question is, can you forgive me? Can you love me after all I've done?"

He knew he had never seen anything so lovely as her face at that moment. Her eyes became heaven to a thousand stars and her mouth curved into a bewitching smile, twitching with a familiar mixture of contentment and fervor.

"Don't you know, Connor? I'll always love you. Always."

He took her hands and pressed them together, opening the palms and kissing them. Then he moved upward, his mouth barely touching her eyes, then her mouth. Unwilling to relinquish his contact, he moved his hand to her cheek, touching it lightly as he looked deep into her eyes, finding a shining hope and love that matched his own. He was suddenly filled with such a rush of joy that he threw his head back and laughed with unrestrained happiness. It was so contagious, so unexpectedly wonderful, Sam's face split into a grin and she, too, started laughing until both were nearly hysterical.

Outside, where Annabelle and several of her girls were hovering anxiously, the unfamiliar sound alarmed them and they rushed in, stopping suddenly at the sight of Sam and Connor. The two were still laughing, their hands clutched tightly together. As one would try to stop, the other would be off, infecting the other all over again.

Annabelle shook her head in seeming disgust, but laughter danced in her eyes, and she motioned the others back out of the room. Once outside, they, too, started giggling and Annabelle began wondering about the sanity of all of them.

Inside, reason started to prevail when Connor saw another flutter of pain in Sam's face, and he became instantly contrite. "Soon?" he worried out loud.

Sam shook her head, but she was unable to stop one last giggle. "Annabelle says he's just like you...stubborn. He's taking his time. She says it's not time yet to call the doctor."

"He?" He asked the question with a smile.

"Definitely he." She grinned. "He kicks much too grandly to be anything else."

Instantly, Connor remembered the note still in his boot. The words echoed painfully in his mind. He squeezed her hand.

"Samantha Chatham...will you marry me?"

Happiness welled up and overflowed as she heard her name on his lips...spoken softly, tenderly, lovingly. In those words, he told her everything she wanted to know, everything she would ever need to know.

"Yes," she whispered. "Oh, yes."

He grinned, a happy unhaunted grin. "Now? Right now?"

She nodded, caught up in his excitement. "But how..."

But he was gone, the door shaking from the slam it had taken against the wall in his haste. She had barely time for a smile as another pain attacked her. Her son was catching his father's impatience.

"Annabelle," she called to the woman who was still staring after the tornado that just whirled down her steps, "I think it's time to call the doctor."

Connor practically ran the two blocks to Rev. Smith's church. The bells were ringing, as they always did at noon, and Connor followed his ears to the bell tower, where he found Rev. Thomas Smith, his ears muffled, contentedly pulling the long bell rope.

"Reverend," Connor shouted impatiently, receiving only a blank stare for his efforts. "Reverend," he tried again as the bells clanged in his ears, echoing in the small narrow tower until his whole body seemed to reverberate with the sound. Finally, frantically, he whipped the mufflers from the reverend's ears, at last gaining his attention as the mild blue eyes regarded him in surprise.

"I need you," Connor said as the echoes reduced in intensity. "I must get married."

Rev. Smith stared at him, dumbfounded. "Major O'Neill . . . again?"

"You must come with me now," Connor demanded, taking the man's arm and almost pushing him from the tower.

"But . . . but you're already married," the puzzled minister said, remembering the attractive young lady of several months earlier. He looked at Connor as if he had lost his wits.

"No," Connor said, too impatient to continue. "I can't explain now . . . no time . . . but it's extremely important."

The minister's face creased in concern as he struggled to understand. "Your wife died . . . that pretty young thing?"

"She's the one I want to marry," Connor said, growing exasperated with the minister's denseness.

"But don't you remember . . . ?" Rev. Smith tried again.

Completely frustrated, Connor started dragging Rev. Smith through the church. "She used the wrong name . . . it wasn't legal," he said, muttering an oath under his breath. He was still not making a great deal of sense to the minister, who, nonetheless, was growing more and more intrigued by the moment. It was beginning to sound like a fine adventure to tell Mrs. Smith. His steps started to match Connor's.

Rev. Smith was on the church steps before he fully understood what Major O'Neill was telling him, and his pace sped up considerably as he finally realized a child's legitimacy might well depend on him.

"Where are we going?" Rev. Smith asked when Connor stopped just long enough to catch his breath.

Connor hesitated, wondering how wise it was to reveal his destination. "Just a little way," he finally said evasively. "Not far now at all."

And it wasn't. A few more steps and they were at Number Two Cherry Street. As Connor started up the steps, he realized Rev. Smith was no longer with him. Looking back, he saw the black-clad minister regarding the house with shocked reluctance.

But Connor was not to be thwarted now. He went back down the steps and gently but quite implacably took Rev. Smith's arm and forcibly led him up the steps, adamantly disregarding the string of protests. Up they went, or down, as the minister halfway suspected, and through the door, which was held open by Annabelle herself.

Annabelle's face was anxious as she looked at both of them, then she turned to Connor. "The doctor just arrived ... you don't have much time." She gave the minister a brief but harried smile.

Rev. Smith offered a brief prayer asking for both strength and forgiveness as he entered the foyer and politely but quite distantly nodded to Annabelle. He had received money from Annabelle for his charitable pursuits, particularly for Whig families who had been burned or turned out by the British, and despite protests, he had allowed several of her girls to worship in his church. He strongly believed a house of God belonged to everyone and that no one should be denied its comforts. But never had he ventured a foot in her establishment, which he considered contrary to God's laws. But Major O'Neill was giving him no choice unless he wished to make a scene. He shuddered at the idea of being seen in the midst of an altercation at the entrance of Georgetown's most notorious establishment. Ministers had been dismissed for much less. So he allowed himself to be led inside, closing his eyes as if to shield himself. As his foot met a step, he opened one eye, suddenly realizing that Mrs. Smith would never forgive him if she knew he had been inside Miss Annabelle's and couldn't tell her every detail. His wife had an avid curiosity, even about those things she shouldn't, Rev. Smith thought wryly. But Connor gave him precious little time to glance around; he was being urged up first one flight of stairs, then a second.

He heard a small involuntary cry as they came to a door, and Annabelle pushed through them and entered the room, bidding them to wait. Then she returned, a small smile on her face. "You'd better be quick about it, Rev. Smith. The doctor says the babe will be here any minute."

The room was full and became fuller as Annabelle's girls learned of the impending wedding. Most had never been to one, and they all wanted to be guests at this one. The doctor just sighed and raised his eyebrows at poor Rev. Smith, who was fumbling with his Bible, holding on to it for dear life. His eyes scanned the scantily clad witnesses and he suppressed a slight shudder until his sense of humor righted things. A twinkle unexpectedly lighted his usually solemn eyes as he started, "Dearly beloved..."

When Annabelle glanced around, there were misty eyes and tears everywhere, including her own. Annabelle was surprised; she believed she was immune to such things. Connor and Samantha, however, had no such tears. They exchanged their vows in strong clear voices and regarded each other with naked adoration.

"For those whom God has joined, let no man put asunder," Rev. Smith was finishing, when Sam's whole body arched.

"For God's sake, man," the doctor cried, "get on with it."

Almost frantically, Rev. Smith finished, "I now pronounce you man and wife." As he was hurried out of the room with the guests, he had one last instruction, "You can kiss the bride," which Connor quickly did before he, too, was ushered out, a mixture of pride and worry battling for control on his face.

Once outside, Annabelle led them down to the parlor, where bottles of champagne were being opened.

"Rev. Smith," she asked cautiously, "will you have a glass with us?"

He started, almost automatically, to refuse, then reconsidered. He was thoroughly bemused by all that had taken place and his own role in it. He couldn't deny the compulsion to stay and hear of the child. What a tale for Mrs. Smith! In any event, he had gone this far; just a few more moments wouldn't do any harm. A crooked self-conscious smile settled on his face and he relaxed. "Why, yes," he said finally, "thank you."

Remembering the reverend's reluctance to even enter the house, Connor choked on his champagne. By now, Reverend Smith was thoroughly intrigued by the drama despite himself. He glanced around with a slightly beatific expression.

Annabelle returned upstairs to see if she could help the doctor. Connor spent several minutes with Rev. Smith then followed Annabelle upstairs, where he paced outside the door. Minutes seemed like hours before he heard a long strong wail and Annabelle appeared at the door. "You have a son, Connor. A fine, strong, healthy son." In answer to his unspoken question, she added quickly, "Samantha's fine, she's just fine. And I think you owe her a nice long wedding kiss."

Annabelle leaned up and kissed him, a light brief touch. "You're a very lucky man, Connor, and if you ever mistreat her again you'll have me to contend with."

Connor's face creased into an affectionate smile. "You never have to worry about that, and I owe you more than I can ever repay... both Sam and I."

"You already have... just by being my friends," she said softly. "Now go on in there and meet your son." She turned away so he couldn't see the tear in her eye. Damn. She was getting soft. Now to see about the minister. A chuckle escaped her. This would be a day to remember. It would indeed.

Downstairs, Rev. Smith was sitting, a slightly addled look on his face as he shared the gaudy parlor with a bevy of Annabelle's girls. He stood as Annabelle entered.

"It's a boy, Rev. Smith," Annabelle reported, "a fine loud replica of Major O'Neill." She smiled. "It was good of you to come today and to wait for the news. Will you toast the baby with us?"

Rev. Smith, who in his nervousness had already consumed several glasses, did not refuse. Together he and Annabelle and her girls raised their glasses to the tiny life upstairs. After he had drained his cup, he turned to Annabelle and cleared his throat.

"Miss Annabelle, may I ask you something?"

She nodded, waiting for some moral condemnation. Well, he deserved any lectures he wished to deliver after his work today.

He swallowed, then asked with embarrassment, "Do you have a back door?"

Annabelle laughed, and he was shocked to discover he liked the sound.

"Yes, indeed," she said. "Just follow me." They went through the kitchen and she led him to the back door used mainly by Connor. As he started to open it, Annabelle pressed a pouch of coins in his hand. At his protest, she shook her head and smiled. "For the poor...in the child's name."

He smiled and nodded. Slipping out the door and weaving only slightly, he made his way home. He had decided not to tell Mrs. Smith. He would never hear the end of it.

Connor entered the room slowly, passing the doctor, who was just on his way out. "I think double congratulations are in order," the elderly physician said with amusement in his voice. He thought he had seen everything, but today...maybe he wouldn't retire after all.

Connor approached Samantha, her face intent on the baby. He had often thought her beautiful but now she was glorious. Her mouth curved in a tender smile and her eyes glowed with exquisite joy. As her eyes met his, he thought he had never seen so much love expressed so openly.

"Come see your son," she said softly, and he knelt beside her and studied the little squirming figure with delight. He was larger than Connor had imagined and the child's hair looked as if it had been woven by a sunbeam. Just then, the baby stretched and regarded his father with deep blue eyes, and Connor would have sworn he saw a familiar mischievous smile. But then it was gone, and the eyes closed, and the baby snuggled deep in his mother's arms. Sam looked up at Connor, watching the slow lazy smile she loved so much. "What should we name him?"

"Not Sam," Connor said teasingly. "One Sam is enough. Ornery...cantankerous...prickly...and very, very disobedient. All in all a very trying lad."

Samantha's smile faded slightly. "What about Brendan?"

"My brother would be very proud," Connor said slowly, steadily, and there was a wealth of emotion in his voice. "And so would I."

And Samantha Chatham O'Neill knew that all the ghosts had finally been laid to rest.

Author's Note

The battle at Eutaw Springs was the last major conflict in the Carolinas.

In the north, George Washington defeated Cornwallis one month later at Yorktown and the war, for all practical purposes, was over. Yorktown was the last real battle, although there were additional small skirmishes, and the British continued to fight the French and Spanish. Charleston was one of the last British garrisons to surrender and did not fall until early 1782.

Francis Marion, a bachelor, returned to his burned-out plantation and married a distant cousin, Esther Videau.

Most accounts of Francis Marion are fragmentary and contradictory. All agree, however, that he was both shy and resourceful, hard-bitten and sentimental, clever and pious.

His band did include boys as young as fourteen and he was known to be extraordinarily kind to them. In one account, he made a ceremony out of presenting a horse to a boy who had killed the horse's British rider.

But though he was a master at war, he despised it and would dismiss any man found committing atrocities against Tory families or soldiers, regardless of the provocation.

Many of the adventures in *Swampfire* actually happened. These include the capture of General O'Mara, the burning of the Motte home, the raid on Georgetown and others. Similarly, Peter Horry and Billy James were Marion's real-life companions.

I have tried to remain true to the essential character of General Marion and the time.

* * * * *

Look for SAMARA, the story of Samantha and Connor's children coming next summer!

COMING NEXT MONTH

VIXEN—Marianne Willman

Frustrated in her attempt to convince stubborn Josh Deveril to help her reclaim her birthright, Vivienne Rocque stowed away on his keelboat. But by the time the rugged Deveril discovered the young beauty, it was too late—for the enchanting vixen had already stolen his heart.

SHARED PASSIONS—Lucy Elliot

Two years in Boston playing the perfect Victorian lady had made Sydney Spencer yearn for the carefree adventures of her country childhood. Then an impulsive moonlit ride to celebrate her homecoming threw her into the maelstrom of danger surrounding the Underground Railroad...and into the arms of the mysterious Virginian, John Randall.

AVAILABLE NOW:

PASSION IN THE WIND
Cassie Edwards

SWAMPFIRE
Patricia Potter

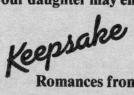

**There was no hope in that time and place
But there would be another lifetime...**

The warrior died at her feet, his blood running out of the cave entrance and mingling with the waterfall. With his last breath he cursed the woman. Told her that her spirit would remain chained in the cave forever until a child was created and born there.

So goes the ancient legend of the Chained Lady and the curse that bound her throughout the ages—until destiny brought Diana Prentice and Colby Savagar together under the influence of forces beyond their understanding. Suddenly each was haunted by dreams that linked past and present, while their waking hours were fraught with danger. Only when Colby, Diana's modern-day warrior, learned to love could those dark forces be vanquished. Only then could Diana set the Chained Lady free....

Next month, Harlequin Temptation and the intrepid Jayne Ann Krentz bring you Harlequin's first true sequel—

DREAMS, Parts 1 and 2

Look for this two-part epic tale, the

Temptation

"Editors' Choice."

Harlequin Temptation dares to be different!

Once in a while, we Temptation editors spot a romance that's truly innovative. To make sure *you* don't miss any one of these outstanding selections, we'll mark them for you.

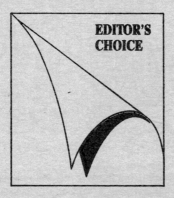

EDITOR'S CHOICE

When the "Editors' Choice" fold-back appears on a Temptation cover, you'll know we've found that extra-special page-turner!

THE *Temptation* EDITORS

HARLEQUIN SIGNATURE EDITION

Editorial secretary Debra Hartway travels to the Salvador family's rugged Cornish island home to work on Jack Salvador's latest book. Disturbing questions hang in the troubled air over Lovelis Island. What or who had caused the tragic death of Jack's young wife? Why did Jack stay away from the home and, more especially, the baby son he loved so well? And—why should Rodare, Jack's brother, who had proved himself a man of the highest integrity, constantly invade Debra's thoughts with such passionate, dark desires . . .?

Violet Winspear, who has written more than 65 romance novels translated worldwide into 18 languages, is one of Harlequin's best-loved and bestselling authors. HOUSE OF STORMS, her second title in the Harlequin Signature Edition program, is a full-length novel rich in romantic tradition and intriguingly spiced with an atmosphere of danger and mystery.

Watch for HOUSE OF STORMS—coming in October!

HOFS-1